Dedicated to Tom, Dörte, Markus,
Ben and Erin,
and in memory of Harry,
beloved sons and daughters of my heart

ACKNOWLEDGMENTS

The process of creating a book is a dedicated team effort. I'd like to acknowledge the following people (and one hound) for their significant contributions to *Bindings of Peril*:

My beta readers:

Will Julius, Liz Smillie, and Neil Bantleman, all of whom dedicated countless hours to reading and thoughtfully responding to the manuscript.

My editors:

Betsy Mitchell, who brought to bear her professional experience from 35 years in the New York publishing world on the work, including pointing out opportunities I'd missed to enrich and enliven the story. www.betsymitchelleditorial.com

David Gatewood, aka "editor to the stars of indie publishing," whose sharply observant criticism and unerring eye significantly improved the book and far exceeded the mandate of copy/line editing. A talented writer himself, David offered many well-crafted and insightful suggestions to keep the storyline both tight and credible. www.lonetrout.com

I feel very fortunate Betsy and David have continued this shared journey to see *The Drinnglennin Chronicles* to its closing line. A huge "thank you" to both of them for their considerable contributions, and for generally cheering me on.

My artists, designers, and more:

Gwen Shackleton, talented artist and lovely friend, whose stunning design graces the cover of this book.

Kevin Sheehan, the amazing cartographer who translated my scrawled vision of Drinnglennin and the Known World into the marvelous maps found within. www.manuscriptmaps. com

Martina Walther, my website designer, who guided me through the trickier technology and helped me create an attractive, easy-to-navigate site for my readers. martina@mw-onsite.com

Kevin Summers, for his detailed, exquisite formatting, and for his patient support. www.literaryoutlaw.com

Bear, my constant companion and daemon/dog-familiar, who gets me out in nature to stir the creative flow.

And as always, my loving gratitude goes out to Uwe, my best friend and partner in life, who makes every day one worth celebrating.

THE MAIN CHARACTERS

The Royal House

Roth Nelvor—High King of Drinnglennin

Queen Grindasa—Roth's mother

Members of the Nelvor Court

Lady Hadley—Roth's cousin

Lady Maitane—Roth's cousin

Lord Vetch—High Commander of the Royal Forces

Lord Lawton—King Roth's Master-of-the-Chamber and distant cousin

Thameth Wynnfort—Lord Chancellor

The House of Konigur

Princess Asmara—cloistered sister of Urlion & Storn (both deceased)

Maura—bastard daughter of Storn

Drinnkastel denizens

Heulwin—Maura's maid

Llwella—Asmara's maid

Gilly—proprietor of The Tilted Kilt, a tavern in Drinnkastel

The Tribus

Selka—a sorceress from Langmerdor

Audric—a wizard, and Morgan's former mentor

Celaidra—an elven princess of Mithralyn, cousin to the elven king Elvinor

The Northerners

Leif—grandson of Avis and the late Pren Landril, son of Lira Landril (deceased), former apprentice to Master Morgan

Morgan—discredited wizard and former Tribus member

Sir Heptorious du Bois—Earl of Windend

Borne Braxton—mercenary soldier serving in Gral, Heptorious's former ward

Maisie—mistress of Port Taygh

Horace—Maisie's husband, master of Port Taygh

The Midlanders

Lady Inis of Lorendale—widow of Lord Valen, sister of Rhea, cousin of Urlion

Halla—eldest child and only daughter of the late Lord Valen and Lady Inis

Nolan—Lord of Lorendale, son of Lady Inis and Lord Valen

Gray—second son of Lord Valen and Lady Inis

Pearce—youngest son of Lord Valen and Lady Inis

Lady Rhea—Lord Jaxe's widow, sister of Inis, cousin of Urlion

Whit—Lord of Cardenstowe, only child of Lord Jaxe and Lady Rhea

Cortenus—Whit's tutor from Karan-Rhad

Wren—*Lord of Elthing and one of Whit's vassals*

Mistress Ella—*chatelaine of Trillyon, a hunting lodge of Cardenstowe*

The Southerners

Sir Glinter—*mercenary leader of Drinnglennian company serving in Gral*

Lord Grenville Fitz-Pole of Bodiaer Castle, Langmerdor

Lady Guin—*Lord Grenville's wife*

The Gralians

Crenel Etiene Fralour Du Regis —*King of Gral*

Latour—*Marechal of Gral*

Comte Rapett—*King Crenel's cousin*

Du Mulay—*powerful rogue knight*

Comte Balfou—*leader of the Gralian mission to Olquaria*

D'Avencote—*aide to King Crenel's herald in Olquaria*

The Albrenians

King Jorgev—*ruler of Albrenia*

Seor Palan de Grathiz—*High Commander of the Albrenian forces*

The Helgrins

Fynn Aetheorsen—*son of Aetheor Yarl and Jana, his Drinnglennian mistress*

Jered Aetheorsen—*elder son of Aetheor Yarl and Wylda Olviddotter, his lawful wife*

Aksel Styrsen—*nephew of the yarl, Fynn's cousin*

The å Livåri

Grinner—Fynn's cellmate

Bria—Halla's childhood friend

Florian—Bria's brother

Nicu—leader of rebels in Albrenia

Chik—follower of Nicu

'o—follower of Nicu

'av—friend and informant of Master Morgan

Lehr—Barav's cousin, leader of his clan

The Olquarians

Zlatan—Basileus of Olquaria

Mir—bastard son of Zlatan and a Drinnglennian member of the hareem

Kurash Al-Gir—hazar of the Khardeshe, the Seven Thousand Companions

The Elves of Mithralyn

Elvinor Celvarin—the Elven king

Egydd—an elven mage

Tarna Mrenhines—the Faerie Queen

The Dragons

Ilyria—bronze, bound to Maura

Rhiandra—blue, bound to Leif

Isolde—silver

Gryffyn—gray

Emlyn—forest green
Aed—red
Syrene—gold
Una—sea green
Menlo—indigo
Ciann—white
Zal—black

Other
Lazdac—wizard, last of the infamous Strigori brothers

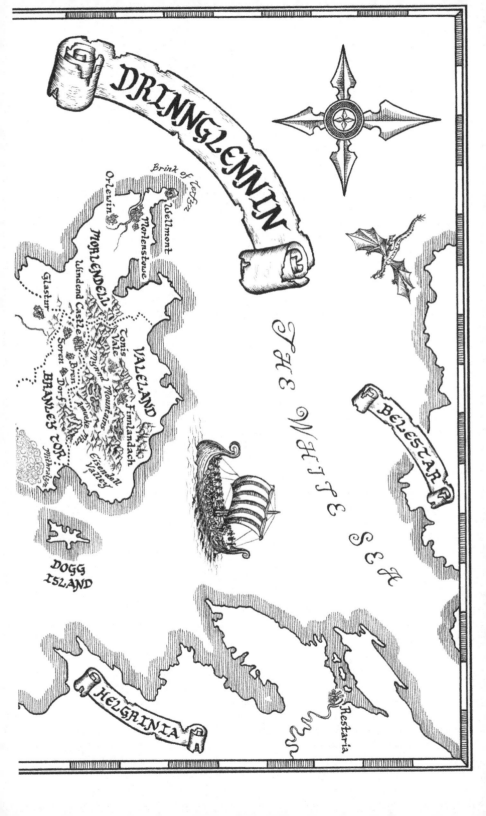

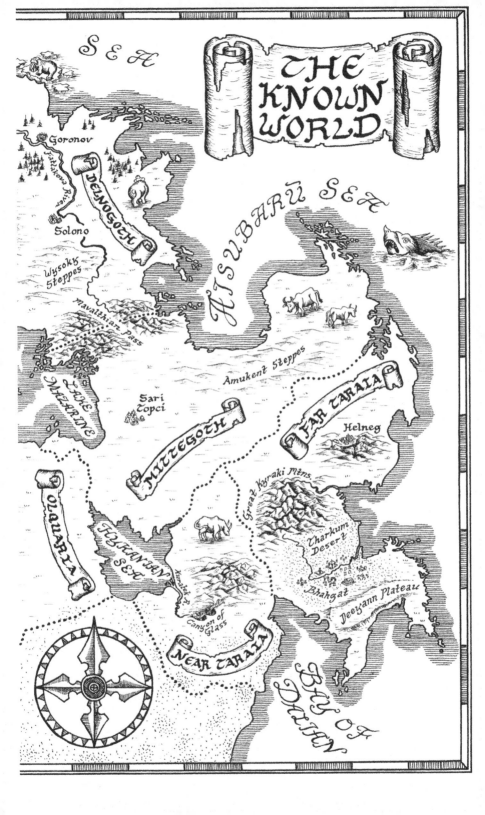

PROLOGUE

The drakmøøt had ended at last. Zal and Menlo were the first to lift into the sky and wheel away, then one by one, the other dragons went off to sleep or feed.

Except for Emlyn. Fear, not hunger, stirred in her gut. Since the very moment Zal had proposed to seek Ilyria and Rhiandra in Mithralyn, she had been suspicious of his motives. Those misgivings drove her now.

She lingered until Syrene, the last of them, took flight. Then with swiftly beating wings, Emlyn went after the two drakes who had pledged to bring their bound sisters back to Belestar. Only when they returned—if they returned—would the *drakmøøt* reconvene, and the dragons determine once and for all whether the unbound dragons must seek bindlings.

This debate had been ongoing for centuries, and with good reason. Passions ran deep on both sides of the argument, and a unanimous decision was inconceivable. If the vote went in favor of binding, as Emlyn believed it would, the drakes opposed would be furious. And their outrage might lead to the unthinkable: an irreparable rift within their weyr, pitting dragon against dragon. It would mean the doom of their kind, and dragons would pass from the Known World.

Although it had been centuries since Emlyn made the journey south, the way to Drinnglennin was mapped in her mind, for she had dwelt in the mountains of Valeland in the days of Before and had often soared over Fairendell's broad meadows to hunt. Her heart lifted as she winged across the wide sky. Confined for so long to Belestar's boundaries, she'd forgotten the joy of unrestricted free flight.

Her brothers' earlier departure had given them a significant lead, and despite her haste, when Emlyn reached the string of small islands pebbling the White Sea halfway between Belestar and the north coast of Drinnglennin, she still had not sighted them. She wondered if they had stopped on the scattered isles to feed. Regardless, she decided she herself must eat, for the drakmøøt had gone on for days.

Hunting by the light of the moon peeking through high drifting clouds, she swiftly made a kill, a young hrossval, its flesh tender and sweet. She was preparing to launch herself once more into the air when she heard the rushing sound of dragonflight. Zal and Menlo were somewhere above her.

Emyln waited for them to appear below the clouds, until she realized the drakes were climbing at great speed. The greenwing scanned her surroundings to determine if there was some reason to flee, but saw nothing in the sky. She felt a creeping unease as the rushing noise shifted to a whine. The drakes were now descending so swiftly she feared that they were injured.

Or that one of them was.

Her blood ran cold at the thought.

Fearing treachery, she hunkered down at the water's edge so that her shining scales might be taken as luminescence on the sea, and held herself very still.

An instant later, the two drakes plummeted through the clouds. Zal's talons were embedded in Menlo's back, and his lethal teeth were sunk deep into the indigo's neck. Before Emlyn could rise to her brother's aid, the black drake wrenched Menlo's head back, snapping his spine like kindling.

As Menlo's broken body plunged into the dark sea, fiery fury coiled in Emlyn's chest, but she held her breath. Only when Zal was out of sight did she give vent to her rage and sorrow, sending a roaring blast of fire to the heavens.

Then she took flight, the image of Menlo tumbling out of the sky tearing at her heart as she raced southward, the wind of terror driving her to reach Mithralyn before her murderous brother.

CHAPTER 1
Morgan

At Rhiandra's insistence, Morgan had endured the long, cold flight to Restaria bound and gagged. The dragons' mistrust of wizards ran deep—with good reason—and so Morgan had accepted the conditions of travel, for there was no faster way to cross the Erolin Sea, and time was of the essence. He hoped that in Helgrinia he would fulfill the dying wish of Urlion, the last High King of the Konigur line, and find Urlion's lost wife, Georgiana, and their child, believed to be held captive in this northern realm.

When at last they slid off the bluewing's back, Morgan offered his bound wrists to Leif. As the lad bent over to free them, the wizard noted how much he'd grown in recent months. Elvinor's son had crossed into manhood.

So swiftly do the years of innocence fly.

The dragon departed silently, and Morgan lifted his eyes to watch as she spiraled down to the sea to feed.

Leif followed his gaze. "I can whistle if we have need of her, master."

Morgan raised an amused eyebrow. "Your magnificent lady comes to a whistle?"

Leif shrugged. "She didn't say no when I suggested it."

In the gloom of the cold dawn, they started down the trail ringing the settlement, and Leif's mood was bright. But when the ruins of the longhouses came into sight, the youth stopped in his tracks, for there was little left but ash and a few timbers.

"What happened here, master?" Leif's voice was hushed and somber.

"I'm not certain, but I'd venture to guess this is the work of Lord Vetch and the Nelvor armada."

Leif drew a sharp breath. "Drinnglennians did this? On the High King's orders?"

"Maybe. Urlion must still have been alive when the fleet set sail for Helgrinia. He mentioned to me he wouldn't mind if Princess Grindasa committed her ships and soldiers to an invasion. As a result, it's likely we're too late for whom we seek, but there's only one way to be sure. Stay close to me."

As they continued on, it became clear that few dwellings had been spared the torch. The remnants of daily life—kitchen pots, shattered dishes, shredded bedding, and soiled linens—lay scattered in the street. Even the dogs had run off, leaving the rubbish heaps to scuttling rats.

There were no signs of survivors. The dead had clearly been burned, for the tang of their passing to their afterworld still singed the air. Whoever had built the pyres were either well-hidden or had fled south. The latter was more likely, for winter was fast approaching in this unforgiving land, but for the sake of caution, Morgan and Leif moved stealthily through the deserted streets.

"Only death resides here now," Morgan muttered under his breath, then seeing Leif's pallor, he added, "Let us head for the river. We can refresh ourselves and have a bite to eat while Rhiandra feeds."

It was lucky they did, for when they reached the bridge, Leif's sharp eyes caught movement within the trees. "There's someone ahead," he whispered, "on the opposite bank."

In mute accord, they crossed over the stone archway. A wide allée, spanned by majestic oaks kissed with the fires of autumn, led to a grove that Morgan recognized at once as a sacred place. And within it sat perhaps the only surviving resident of this forsaken settlement.

An old man rested on a stone bench, clutching a twisted staff in his gnarled hands. His hair and beard were long and grizzled, his tattered robes covered with soot. He looked right at them, but didn't speak. He merely waited, taking slow, deep breaths, as if each might be his last.

"We mean you no harm," Morgan called softly in the Old Tongue.

Leif's eyes lit up. "They speak runic?" He'd gained a firm grip on the ancient language over the months he'd spent in Mithralyn.

"A form of runic," the wizard confirmed.

The old man gave no sign he'd heard them, and Morgan, considering the possibility that the fellow's senses were impaired, approached the bench slowly so as not to startle him.

"I'm nae full blind yet, and I still have my hearing," the man announced suddenly. "And my ears tell me you're not Helgrin. So who are you?"

"Seekers, master," said Morgan.

"Seekers? Well, unless you're looking for me, you're wasting your time." The old man's voice was rusty with disuse. "There's no one else here."

"I see. Is there anything we can do to help you?"

The man shook his head. "That's most kind of you, but the end of my story is fast approaching."

The mention of a story brought Leif closer. "I would hear your story, master," he said politely.

"Ah." The trace of a smile curved the man's thin, cracked lips. "Do you have a name, young seeker?"

"Leif."

"Leif? That's a fine name. I've been known, for many years now, as Old Snorri. Once I told the stories of the gods and sang of the glory of our warriors in the battles of yore. Now... there's no one left to listen."

"We will listen." Morgan lowered himself onto the bench beside Old Snorri. "What can you tell us of this last battle?"

The smile vanished from Old Snorri's lips. "What happened here was no battle. It was a massacre. Babes and old women brutally cut down—" His cloudy eyes glistened with sudden tears. "I will make no song of this horror."

"Was it…" Leif cleared his throat. "Were the attackers Drinnglennians?"

"Aye, although there were those among them who spoke Albrenian. While they were at their butchery, I escaped here to the grove, hoping to die beneath the great Wurl."

Morgan followed the lift of the old man's chin to the magnificent oak rising above the grove.

"But they never came for me." Old Snorri shook his head ruefully. "All gone now, those children who used to sit at my feet, just as you do now. Ragnarr, Jered, Ingrid, Gunnvora… of course, they'd grown too old for my tales. Those who were at sea when the raiders came were spared to do deeds another will praise. As for the rest…"

The old man fell silent, his gaze somewhere far away.

Morgan waited a respectful moment before asking the question that was foremost on his mind. "Master Snorri, were there ever any Drinnglennian children among your listeners?"

The old man's brows lifted in surprise. "There were many thralls in Restaria who came from the Isle, and some of them quite young, but they had no time to spare from their chores for my stories, except on fest days."

"Do you recollect a thrall called Georgiana?"

Old Snorri tilted back his head and studied the rustling leaves. "Georgiana? No, I never heard that name here."

"She would have arrived over a decade ago. She was fifteen when she was taken, and quite a beauty."

"Young, pretty girls are always the first taken in a raid. She would have been one of many."

Morgan nodded. "Yes, of course. We won't disturb you any longer. Thank you, master, for your time." He caught Leif's eye, then rose.

"We wish you well, Old Snorri," Leif said. He lowered his forehead respectfully to touch it to the tale-weaver's proffered hand, clearly reluctant to leave the old man alone.

"Thank you, my boy. I regret I have no tale for you to take with you. I spun my last for Einar and Fynn." The faint smile returned. "*There* was a fine lad, young Fynn. You remind me of him, a bit. 'Twas a shame he and Jana were shunned."

Jana, the wizard thought. Was it possible this was a shortened name?

He had turned to leave, but now swung back toward Old Snorri. "Jana, did you say? Why was she shunned?"

"She was taken by Aetheor himself in a raid on the Isle." The old man's laugh was warm with memory. "He thought *he'd* stolen *her*, but it was Jana who captured our yarl's heart. It was said that from the moment he laid eyes on her, he was smitten. He set her up in a house of her own and made her his mistress. The yarla was wild with jealousy, and made life difficult for Jana and the boy whenever Aetheor was at sea. But once he returned home, he always went straight up the hill to them. Who could blame him for loving such a one as beautiful as Jana? Even I, at my age, confess to having fallen under her spell."

Morgan felt his heart quicken. "What became of them— Jana and her son Fynn?"

Old Snorri planted his staff and heaved himself to his feet with a grimace. "Come. I will show you."

* * *

The house was surprisingly in order, despite having been plundered. Morgan suspected this was Old Snorri's doing. The wizard noted the costly gowns hanging in the wardrobes, the quality of the furnishings that hadn't been carted off, the ornate carvings on the lintels and mantels. Whoever had raised and furnished this home had spared no cost.

The old man led them through the kitchen and into the yard at the back of the manor. "I found her here," he said, a quaver in his voice.

Leif drifted over to the bright cornflowers that circled a memory stone laid at the edge of the woods. The men joined him, and together they silently read the runes on the stone.

"Did she follow your gods?" Leif asked quietly.

"I don't honestly know," Old Snorri admitted, "but I'd like to think so. Then, when I travel to Cloud Mountain, I shall see her again, and perhaps the boy as well."

Morgan hadn't failed to note there was only the one stone. "What happened to her son? Did he perish here as well?"

The tale-weaver gave a slow shake of his head. "I found no trace of him. I'd say it's likely he died in the fires in town, except that he wasn't welcome in anyone's home. Perhaps someone with a good heart took him in all the same, before the end." He gazed down at the stone and sighed. "I miss her. Others saw Jana's outward beauty, but it was the beauty of her spirit that shone brightest for me."

"And Fynn?" Morgan asked. "What was he like?"

"Fynn?" Old Snorri looked up with a smile. "Lively of mind and body. High-spirited. He worshipped his father and half-brother—followed them around like a besotted pup when they weren't at sea. A regular boy, Fynn was, with the occasional lapse in judgment, but no real penchant for mischief. He was a *good* lad at heart." He reached down to pluck a wilted blossom, then cast it aside. "If Aetheor Yarl and Jered have made the Leap as well, perhaps they're all together in the Sky Hall."

"If? You mean you're not sure?"

"Our yarl and his older son were at sea when Restaria was attacked. His fleet has never returned. The same raiders who wreaked havoc here must have waylaid Aetheor on his home-

ward journey—otherwise he would have been back by now."
The tale-weaver looked between them. "You never said what it is you're seeking here."

The wizard met the man's questioning gaze for a long moment. "That which was lost," he said at last, "and shall remain so."

* * *

They left Old Snorri by the grave of Jana—the woman Morgan now felt certain had been born Georgiana Fitz-Pole of Bodiaer Castle—and climbed back up to the bluff. The buffeting wind tugged at their cloaks while Morgan pondered the circumstances that would have compelled a young girl, newly with child, to flee her ardent royal husband and go to Meregate, a place his enemies were raiding.

Leif, beside him, stared down at the white peaks spreading over the waves below like a flotilla of miniature sails. The lad hadn't spoken a word since they'd left the old man. Morgan was not insensitive to the fact that the demolished settlement was the lad's first glimpse of the reality of war. Morgan's own initiation into the gruesome destruction men leave in the wake of battle had occurred long ago, yet it was forever emblazoned on his mind. At the time, he'd been in the service of Anarwyd, the first king to sit the Einhorn Throne after the bloody forging of Drinnglennin's realms into one nation. He could still see the wide eyes of the fallen, many in the flower of manhood, with hacked limbs and pinioned chests, their arms flung across their enemies in still, cold embrace. Most men become inured to war's carnage, either out of necessity or because it fuels the bloodlust roaring in their veins in the heat of the fray. But none escape the deep scars it leaves on memory.

"Now I know what dark doings are," Leif said when at last he spoke. His expression was clouded. "It's beginning, isn't it, master?"

"I fear it is."

"Where will we go from here?"

"Back to Mithralyn, once night falls. After that, I'm afraid I must go south alone. While I was at Port Taygh, I received new information regarding the disappearance of the å Livåri, which I need to follow up on." He rested a reassuring hand on Leif's shoulder. "At least our journey here has revealed the fates of Urlion's wife and heir. And although Georgiana has made the Leap, her long-grieving parents will finally learn what became of her."

He raised his hand and pointed to a dark crescent in the sky. "I didn't hear you whistle, but I believe that's your dragon."

Leif followed his gaze, but it was clear his thoughts were still on the devastation they'd just witnessed. "What will you say, master, to Georgiana's parents?"

Morgan's heavy heart lifted as the dragon skimmed toward them, and he gave Leif a small smile. "Something that should bring them comfort in their last years. I shall tell them that their daughter chose a different path, and in doing so, she found love."

CHAPTER 2
Whit

Whit sat up with a jolt, his heart thundering in his ears. The scent of brimstone was heavy in the air, which could only mean one thing.

Dragons.

Vividly recalling Leif's and Maura's horrifying descriptions of the piercing talons that had marked them as dragon-fast, he scrambled out of the pavilion where he'd fallen asleep and scoured the sky.

Sweat streamed down his neck as he braced himself for an unseen onslaught. Instead, there was a crackling in the bracken, and the dragon he'd expected to barrel out of the clouds came from the woods instead. Whit retreated several quick steps before he recognized Ilyria, who was already bound to Maura. He hadn't seen the bronze dragoness in many months, for Maura had been away in Drinnkastel since springtide, and according to Leif her dragon had gone into seclusion deep in Mithralyn's forest.

From which she had apparently just emerged.

After a brief meeting of the eyes, Whit forced his gaze away, willing the dragon to pass.

The dragon loomed over him. "You've been scrying?" she asked. This close, her contralto voice reverberated in Whit's very bones.

He gave a weak smile of acknowledgment. "I've been trying, but only once have I received a true vision through the stone."

11

"Yet you dream." Ilyria's emerald eyes, flecked with gold, bored into his, raising the hairs on the back of his neck.

"How—how do you know that?"

A puff of blue smoke emerged from the dragon's curved nostrils. "I too have prophetic dreams."

Whit's pulse quickened. "Does that mean you… you can see into my mind?"

The dragon's snort startled him. "Even if I could," she replied imperiously, "I would have no desire to do so. Your aura is too vibrant, which is what led me to distrust you in the first place." She narrowed her jeweled eyes. "A wizard who is also a seer is known to be most dangerous to our kind."

Whit felt a stab of fear. The memory of his encounter with Encertesa, the only seer he'd ever met, still made his skin crawl. The sorceress of Altipa had almost succeeded in blood-binding him to her will, and he would bear the scar of her attempt on his wrist until the end of his days.

An uncomfortable silence ensued as the dragon continued to regard him with her luminescent eyes. He wondered what the grey streams of smoke wafting from her nostrils signaled. When at last she opened her mouth, he couldn't help but imagine a stream of fiery breath shooting out and incinerating him.

"He is coming."

"Who?" Whit anxiously scanned the sky.

"The other wizard. Along with my sister and her bindling."

At last, Whit thought, with a flood of relief. Leif and Master Morgan had been absent from Mithralyn when he'd returned from his unsuccessful mission to bring Halla home from Albrenia, and he'd been awaiting their return with impatience. Egydd, the elven mage, had returned to his woodland home, and hadn't invited Whit along with him. And while Elvinor's library was stocked with rare texts on the magical arts, Whit craved instruction from a master wizard who could answer his inevitable questions.

Not that he could depend on Master Morgan to stay long. Over the months Whit had been in Mithralyn, he could count on his fingers the number of days the old man had lingered there. He felt a familiar stab of frustration at the thought. This time, Whit intended to see the wizard only long enough to take his own leave. There was no longer a need for him to stay—any possible threat to him as an eligible candidate for the Einhorn Throne had ended when Roth of Nelvorboth was proclaimed Urlion's heir by the Tribus—and he was long overdue at home. By now his mother would be beside herself with worry. It was time to take up his responsibilities as Lord of Cardenstowe.

At least, some of them, anyway. He intended for Horst, his late father's reeve, to carry on with the actual day-to-day management of Cardenstowe, leaving Whit free to devote himself to achieving that which only a handful of wizards throughout time had accomplished: mastery of the imperative spells.

The Three Pillars.

Shade-shifting and shadow-casting, its higher evolution, was the power to harness shadows to one's will, then move like the wind within them. Illusing was a form of glamour that made others see what one wished them to see, rather than what is. And the greatest challenge of all was to raise the Shield of Taran, the ultimate wall of defense through which not even the most powerful spells could pass.

Mastering these spells would require all his time, energy, and skill.

Whit suddenly realized he'd been staring into Ilyria's eyes all the while these thoughts had flitted through his mind. He cleared his throat nervously. "Was there something else you wanted from me?"

Ilyria snorted. "You?" Her slender tongue flicked rapidly from between her jaws, eloquently communicating her scorn. "I only came to inform you about the wizard, lest you were feeling abandoned."

13

Whit stiffened, for that was exactly how he'd been feeling. "Well then... er... thank you." He half-turned, then froze as Ilyria's eyes narrowed. Belatedly, he recalled Maura explaining it was always up to a dragon to conclude the discussion. "Do you know how long it will be before they arrive?" he added hastily.

"I'm in possession of the Sight," the dragoness said with a sniff. "I'm not an hourglass."

She raised her snout dismissively, and Whit quickly bowed. As she glided back into the brush, he considered that Ilyria, too, might be feeling forsaken.

In any event, the exchange with the dragoness had produced one good result: Whit wouldn't have to tangle again with Gywna's Fire this day, for Master Morgan had been the one he'd been seeking in the scrying stone. Very soon, he'd have his final say with the wizard in person, and then be on his way.

As he headed back to the elven palace, Whit wondered if Elvinor might bestow upon him a few of his precious spell-craft tomes as a parting gift. Brightening at the thought, he took himself off to the library to compile a selection—just in case.

All thoughts of books fled, however, as Leif came bounding toward him across the bower.

"Hallo!" the elf-boy called, and might have thrown his arms around him if Whit hadn't taken a discouraging step back. Instead Leif gripped his arms and shot a volley of questions at him. "When did you get back from the continent? Where's Halla? Did someone tell you we're to go to my father? Master Morgan is already with him."

Whit realized Elvinor would at this moment be telling Master Morgan how Whit had failed to bring Halla back from Albrenia. Not that this was in any way Whit's fault. He had found her, as he had intended—but his incorrigible cousin had chosen to stay with a band of renegade Lurkers.

His spirits plummeted. "Where have you been?" he countered.

Leif's reply caught him by surprise. "In Helgrinia!" The lad's bright expression darkened. "The settlement we visited had been put to the torch—by Drinnglennians. It was horrible."

"Helgrinia? What were you doing *there*?"

"Master Morgan was seeking someone, but she died in the attack." Leif shook his head. "It was horrible," he repeated.

Whit had no idea what to say. This disheartened Leif was as difficult to respond to as the overly ebullient Leif from moments before.

"Well," said Leif, brushing his hair off his brow. "We shouldn't keep them waiting."

Whit found he had no desire to face Master Morgan just yet.

"You go on ahead," he muttered, then brushed past Leif and hurried to his chambers.

Only to find the wizard awaiting him outside his door.

Attempting to gain the higher ground, Whit spoke first. "Have you come to tell me you're leaving again?"

Master Morgan ignored his deliberate rudeness. "Hello, Whit." He stepped aside to allow Whit to enter his chamber, then followed. The wizard cast a glance at the rucksack and neatly folded tunics on the bed. "It looks as though you're the one who's preparing to travel."

The old man's composure brought Whit's blood to a sudden boil. He grabbed a handful of shirts and stuffed them into his bag. "I'm going home to Cardenstowe."

"I see. With Cortenus? Or is he staying on?"

Whit had assumed wherever he went, his tutor would accompany him. Cortenus was, after all, in his employ. On the other hand, in the past months he'd seen little of the man, for he'd tapped the limits of his tutor's knowledge of spellcraft long ago.

"I haven't asked him," he replied, "but I'm going all the same."

Master Morgan leaned against the doorframe, his arms folded across his chest. "Are you angry with me, Whit?"

Whit spun around. "Am I angry with you? *Yes*, I am. And why shouldn't I be?" He cast aside the belt in his hand. "You tricked me into coming here with the promise of learning powerful magic from you, Master Morgan, the greatest living wizard of our age!" He laughed bitterly. "Master Morgan, whom I've only seen cast the simple spells of a hedge witch—kindling fires and laying protective boundaries and the like. Why *is* that? Wasn't it you who told me I have to 'employ my gifts'? To use my magical arts to help others? How are *you* helping anyone, if you won't use yours? I'd say the accolades heaped on you are undeserved!"

Whit braced himself for a furious response, but the old man's expression didn't alter. "You're right," Master Morgan said quietly. "I am no longer the wizard I once was. Nor will I ever be again."

His agreement took the storm from Whit's sails. He released a shaky breath and sank down on his bed. "What do you mean? What happened to you?"

Master Morgan inclined his head to the place beside Whit. "May I?"

Whit nodded.

The wizard settled on the coverlet and rested his gnarled hands on his knees. "You are overdue an explanation, which I have neglected to give you for the selfish reason that it stirs up unhappy memories. I know that's no excuse." He raised his gaze to the wild gardens beyond the window. "I believe it was Sir Gablyn, one of your vassals, who mentioned I was removed from the Tribus. It's true. My former mentor, Master Audric, was installed in my place, for I was no longer worthy to serve on that august body. With one terrible, rash act, I cast away not only the right to the position, but the right to practice magic."

In the stillness that followed, Whit felt the tension in his shoulders shift to his chest.

"I served three Konigur High Kings in my days on the Tribus," Master Morgan continued at last. "Gregor was the first, and after him, his son Owain. I rode with both in the Helgrin Wars. And then came Urlion. He was a boy king at the time I was dismissed from the Tribus—and though I didn't deserve it, I kept his trust and friendship until his death."

"What did you… why did you lose your place on the Tribus?"

Morgan met Whit's gaze solemnly. "Some will tell you it was because I set fire to the Alithineum. I didn't, but the real reason is no better. The truth is that I lost my powers because of a duel—a duel I fought with Lazdac Strigori."

"*Lazdac*? He was the most powerful wizard to ever live— no one could hope to defeat *him*! But you fought Bedjel, his brother. I read about that famous duel in Xander's *Wizard Wars*."

Master Morgan shook his head. "Xander was a fool. He wrote what had been rumored, and no one contradicted him because there were no witnesses to report what really happened. The truth would have been recorded in the *Drinnglennin Chronicles*, but by that time it was lost to the world. Only Lazdac and I know what really transpired that night.

"Xander was half right, though. Lazdac did not come alone for our contest. He brought his brother Bedjel, and they ambushed me before I reached the agreed-upon place. I was forced to fight them both. My arrogance, Whit, was my undoing, and the repercussions of my foolhardiness are still coming to light."

Whit could hardly believe what he was hearing. "You're saying you *lost*? But Bedjel is dead, and Lazdac hasn't been a presence in the Known World for decades. You must have defeated him... otherwise, he wouldn't have let you survive."

Master Morgan's smile held more than a hint of irony. "Lazdac was also grievously injured in our battle, otherwise he might indeed have finished me off. I believe he could have killed me and chose not to. I think he savored the pain it would cause me to live the life he'd left me with."

"But if you didn't defeat him, then where has he been? I thought he was believed to have perished."

"For a time, I believed that as well. But now he's resurfaced, apparently fully recovered, and in an arena that won't long satisfy his hunger for domination."

Whit stared at him with wide eyes. "You'll have to fight him again."

Master Morgan's soft laugh was mirthless. "I'm afraid that's impossible. I was not only stripped of my pride. The conditions of the duel required the loser to give up all but the simplest of magic, on pain of death."

Whit felt the blood drain from his face. "Surely you didn't—"

"I'm afraid I did," said the wizard. "You see, I believed Lazdac had something that I very badly wanted. When he offered to fight me for it, I accepted, and we took a binding oath beforehand. Perhaps things would have turned out differently had Lazdac and I met alone, face to face. But when both Strigori attacked me from behind... I managed to slay Bedjel, but the effort took its toll on me. And Lazdac claimed victory."

"But he cheated!" Whit found himself on his feet. "You never agreed to duel them both."

"Life is not fair, Whit. A wiser wizard would have exercised prudence in dealing with the Strigori. I was defeated by my own vanity."

Whit couldn't begin to imagine what giving up his power must have cost the great wizard. "I don't know if I'd want to go on living." He was horrified to realize he'd spoken aloud.

But Master Morgan merely nodded his agreement. "For many years, I didn't. Wounded in body and spirit, I fled to the continent, traveling all the way to Far Taraia. For a time, I thought I might sail with the last of the Gothian dwarves across the Temonin Sea to the World Unknown, but… something held me back. So I traveled to Olquaria, a land I'd always wished to see, and there I served Radan Basileus, whose son Zlatan now sits on the throne. I fought Radan's enemies at the side of the Basileus's commander, Al-Gahzi. He became one of my dearest friends, and for a time his family took the place of the one I'd left behind in Drinnglennin."

Whit had never contemplated the idea of Master Morgan having kin, but of course he must have. "Where is your real family now?" he asked, returning to sit by the wizard's side.

"Dead and buried, every one. The last of them, my sister's grandson, made the Leap nearly twenty years ago."

Whit knew a wizard's life might span four times as many years as that of a normal man, but it was the first time he'd considered that outliving his own family was to be his fate as well.

As if reading his thoughts, Master Morgan gave his knee a kindly pat. "Your magical gift will not be without sacrifice, Whit. It can be a lonely life. You will see those you love grow old and make the Leap while you go on. You will experience more loss than anyone can prepare you for. That's why it's so important to find worth in your craft, and to dedicate your rare talents to the greater good. If you don't seek to serve, there's always the danger your otherness will make you bitter, and that is when your power can corrupt and alter you, as happened to the Strigori."

If that was meant to comfort Whit, it had the opposite effect. The idea of being corrupted by the dark sent a shiver down his spine.

"What... what *did* happen to the Strigori?" he asked.

The wizard frowned. "That is a long tale. Suffice it to say the name Strigori was not always synonymous with evil. Since the dawn of time, the Strigori were respected wizards of great skill. It wasn't until Rendyl Strigori grossly abused his powers when, as a member of the Tribus, he murdered his king, the ill-fated Lindic the Younger, then enslaved the dragon Chaos and used her to terrorize the Isle, that their family fell to dishonor. The scorn Rendyl brought upon this once noble house drove the last of the Strigori—Lazdac and Bedjel—to seek glory through the dark arts. And that power stirred within them a terrible appetite, one that could only be sated by committing wanton acts of violence.

"It wasn't long before they took a more calculated approach to their terror, manipulating men and women in positions of power to their own destructive ends, and fomenting fear of magic as a means of enlisting these leaders to aid them in eradicating any who opposed the aims of the Strigori."

Morgan suddenly grasped Whit's arm, and his voice was stern. "You must be ever guarded against the temptation to stray to the other side, Whit. The line between good and evil is more difficult to discern than you might think."

Whit was taken aback by this declaration, as it seemed Morgan had meant him to be.

The wizard's expression softened. "To be sure, there are consolations to be had as a result of your gifts. If you're fortunate, young wizards will seek to learn from you, and you might take pleasure in teaching them. Although I could train Leif only in rune raveling, I quite enjoyed it. Of course, now he no longer has need of me." He levered himself up with his staff. "Nor, I imagine, do you, now that you know the truth."

Whit stood with him. "There must be a way to free you from this terrible oath. You say Lazdac bound you to it, but how? With what dark magic?"

In answer, Master Morgan pulled back the sleeve of his robe and extended his left arm. The sun slipped below the trees, casting the room in shadow so that Whit had to lean forward to see the crude scar marking the wizard's wrist.

Whit felt his heart turn to ice. He had a scar just like it, carved into his flesh by Encertesa's cruel blade.

"By blood, Whit," said the wizard, his voice starkly hollow. "My blood, mingled with Lazdac's."

CHAPTER 3
Borne

The rogue knights' attack on Latour's camp came just before dawn. The sentries, their horns blaring, roused Borne from his bedroll, and he sprang up, sword in hand. Emerging from his tent, he immediately threw himself to one side, warned by the hiss of the blade falling toward him. He felt its bite nevertheless. He dropped and rolled, then thrust out his legs, sending his attacker slamming to the ground.

Borne clambered to his feet as his opponent, a giant of a man, lurched up, a great sword clutched in his huge hands. Borne parried the next strike, then returned one of his own, sidestepping as he brought his blade down. He leapt forward and brought the heel of his boot down hard on his attacker's knee. The man groaned, his leg buckling under him, and reeled back clumsily to avoid Borne's following slash.

Borne felt the sticky warmth of his own blood running down his arm. He'd apparently received more than a nick, which meant he'd have to finish the rebel off quickly. Feinting, he tossed his sword high in the air, and as his startled foe flicked his eyes upward to follow its arc, Borne pulled out his dagger and sent it spinning toward the man's heart. With a soft whistle of air, the giant pitched to the ground.

Borne caught his falling sword and selected his next target, stealing a swift glance around at the swarms of his comrades-at-arms rushing to meet the invading horsemen. The renegade knights were disorganized and appeared to have underestimated the size of the royal Gralian force. He judged the fighting would soon be over.

The knight bearing down on him must have come to the same conclusion, for as Borne ran at him, the man wheeled his horse and galloped off, shouting to his fellows to retreat. A party of Latour's soldiers gave chase, and Borne was looking around for a horse to join them when Sir Glinter hailed him.

"There's enough men after the bastards," Glinter said. "The ones taken alive can count themselves lucky. They'll be given the option of swearing renewed allegiance to King Crenel, and since a refusal means immediate execution, they'll gladly take the pledge."

"Why even give them the choice?" Borne asked. "They're traitors, and could easily turn their coats again."

"It may seem they're getting off lightly, but if the country's to avoid falling under Helgrin control—or falling into anarchy—King Crenel needs every man he can get. Offering amnesty is one way to find them."

Borne saw the sense in that. Gral needed men not only to fight, but to administer their estates, so that the famine of past years could be averted. And educated men were needed as well, to serve as justices and to regulate the guilds. That said, if Borne were in the king's shoes, he would have serious reservations about making judges out of these renegades. These unruly knights had been the primary cause of the appalling state of decline in this ravaged land. If not for the army led by the king's marechal, Latour, who knows how bad things would have become. Latour had not defeated the rogues, but he'd met with significant success in bringing many of them to heel and back under the rule of law.

It was under the marechal that Borne had begun his military career in earnest, and he'd taken to it like a fledgling to the sky. He'd seen plenty of fighting, which was exactly what he'd come for. And not only during battle. In the brief lulls between skirmishes, the men got up to all manner of rough, dangerous entertainment, and as Borne was often singled out as a representative for the Drinnglennin contingent, he suffered more than his share of blows at the hands of the hardened Gralians—which he took in stride. When he finally succeeded in disarming Du Charney, a renowned knight from the province of Santones, in a mock hand-to-hand skirmish, Sir Glinter glowed with pride, and henceforth treated him as his prodigy.

Borne spent the bulk of his free time learning whatever he could, mostly by listening to the more experienced soldiers and storing away their recounts of tactical errors and strategic brilliance for future reference. It helped that he spoke the language, having mastered it under his tutors at Windend, and that his wit was as sharp as his sword.

Now, as Borne wiped his blade on his soiled tunic, Sir Glinter remarked, "You're a born fighter, just as I told the marechal." The old knight tapped the side of his nose. "Your dispatch of that great hulking brute caught Latour's attention, too. He's asked to see you, so you'd best get out of that filthy gear."

When Borne reported to Latour, he found the marechal stripped to the waist outside his tent.

"You play chatraj," the Gralian said, without preamble. The hard-bodied, angular soldier with the sharp nose and piercing eyes of a hawk didn't stand on ceremony. He treated his men as equals, yet commanded supreme respect.

"I do, Marechal," Borne replied, realizing then it was not his prowess with a weapon that had earned him this audience.

"Lethally, D'Orses informs me." Latour gave him a shrewd look. "He says you've won thirty ecru off him in the past three days."

"I apologize if this is an affront, Marechal. I'm still learning the customs of Gral."

Latour bent over a barrel and scooped water onto his face. "An affront?" He wiped the water from his eyes. "You mistake me. I would test your prowess against mine." Raising the tent flap, he directed Borne to a board already laid out on a low table.

When they were seated, Latour made the opening move—archer to serf. "Tell me about yourself," he said.

"There isn't much to tell," Borne replied. "I come from the north of Drinnglennin. My people were coilhorn herders. I would be a shepherd still if our earl hadn't made me his ward. It's because of him that I received an education and training at arms."

"Serf to knight," Latour noted, studying Borne's move. "Interesting." He sat back and lifted his gaze from the board. "And why then, given these advantages, did you leave your homeland to fight here in Gral? Is there something else I should know?"

"No, sir."

Latour seemed to be waiting for more, and Borne fell back on a Gralian shrug. For a breath he recalled Maura, standing by her window, a letter clasped to her heart.

"There was no future there for me," he said at last, "and I like fighting."

Latour laughed. "Well, you're very good at it. And the gods know, opportunities for combat abound in our land." He slid his falcon forward to face Borne's leaper. "Let's see if you're equally adept at play."

It took half an hour for the marechal to win the first game, and twice that for him to claim Borne's king in the second. As they were setting up for the third contest, Latour sat back and crossed his arms. "Tell me—do you think I am someone who thrives on conceit?"

Startled, Borne looked up into his opponent's predatory gaze. "Not in the least, Marechal. I believe you to be a selfless and most honorable man."

Latour inclined his head. "Then why did you not deploy your monter when I moved mine?"

25

Borne returned to placing his pieces on the board. "I was attempting another gambit. It failed."

"I saw how you rallied the men at La Morcher, when we were in danger of being routed. Glinter tells me it was your idea to split the company. It saved the day for us." He gestured to the board. "I don't think a natural strategist such as yourself would sacrifice a commander to capture a foot soldier."

Borne met the hawk-like eyes and gave a slight nod, conceding the marechal's point.

"Come then, shepherd," Latour demanded, reaching for a flagon and two goblets. "You will give me a game worthy of us both. Otherwise, I will make you very, very drunk."

* * *

By the time Borne left the marechal, they were both drunk. He staggered back to his tent, and found Glinter waiting inside.

"Who won?" the commander growled.

Borne sank heavily onto his bed and grinned as Magnus thrust his great muzzle into his hands, his tail fanning the air. "It was thrust and parry. But in the end, I claimed victory." He took hold of the hound's ears and tugged them gently. "I was lucky. He's a master player."

"Did you leave the marechal as mortal guttert as yourself?" Glinter asked, then frowned as Borne tried and failed to remove a boot. "Here, let me do that, you muzzy fool!"

"The marechal has retired," said Borne thickly. He fell back and obligingly lifted his foot. "I helped him to his bed myself, although I left it to his woman to see to his footwear."

"He hasn't got a woman." Glinter wrested off one boot and tossed it into the corner. "And don't go getting any funny ideas about me." He tugged the other free, then dusted his hands. "You're lucky it was the marechal you were drinking with, otherwise I'd take a few strips off your back. Now sleep it off, then report to me once you're sober and presentable."

It was after dark when Borne, sore of head, went to seek his company commander. He found Glinter playing *ventre*, a Gralian variation of the game known as Guts in Drinnglennin.

"About time," the bald man growled, tossing his cards aside. "Your drinking partner was up long before you. You made a right bloody impression on the marechal, Braxton. I'm to release you from the company."

Borne couldn't believe he'd heard correctly. "What? But—"

"Latour was quite clear. He wants to see you. *Now.*" Glinter dismissed him with a flick of his hand.

Cursing himself for a fool, Borne headed to the marechal's tent, Magnus padding at his side. He should have followed his instincts and let Latour win at chatraj. As a result of his cockiness, he'd gotten himself ousted from his unit. What was he going to do for employment now? He could never return to Bergsehn; his presence there would only serve as an offensive reminder to Lord Heptorious of Cole's death. He supposed he'd have to contact Master Waman, who managed Bergsehn in his absence, to arrange for some income until he figured out how he was going to support himself.

Caught up in these depressing thoughts, he nearly collided with a man standing in his path.

"I hope I look better than you do," said Latour. "I've been unpleasantly reminded of why I seldom partake of strong drink during the day."

"Marechal." Borne placed his fist respectfully over his heart. "I've just come from Sir Glinter. Is it possible—"

Latour held up a forestalling hand. "If you've come to ask me if you can remain with your company, the answer is no. I've made up my mind, and there'll be no dissuading me."

Borne's heart sank, but he straightened his shoulders and saluted once more.

"There's no need for all that," said Latour, his gaze coolly assessing Borne's condition. "You'd best return to bed, else you'll be of no use tomorrow. Report to Du Cervole at dawn. He'll see you're outfitted with the regiment colors and arms. I'm told you'll need a horse as well, unless you can ride that massive dog."

"Marechal?" Borne shook his throbbing head in an attempt to clear it.

Latour had already started past him. "I've commandeered you, shepherd," he called back over his shoulder. "From now on, you ride with me."

* * *

Borne soon discovered there was much to be learned from the Gralian commander. The marechal was, quite simply, the most brilliant man Borne had ever met. In the long hours spent around the commander's desk, Borne was privy to the breadth of Latour's strategic knowledge, and he gleaned more about tactics from one night's debates than he'd gotten from any military account he'd ever read. And in the field, the marechal was a soldier above all, wielding his sword with deadly accuracy as he harried the lawless knights who continued to wreak havoc across Gral. Riding with him, Borne saw what a true warrior could achieve in the field of battle.

The two men also found that they had other interests in common besides military maneuvers and chatraj. Latour was on impressive terms with the classics, which he had studied at the prestigious Universitat Imperial, along with history, rhetoric, and philosophy. He was also a fierce patriot, and Borne had heard it said that without Latour, King Crenel would have been forced to abdicate or go into exile long ago.

One night, after his other officers had retired, Latour confessed to Borne that he feared their efforts to rein in the rebels would not be enough to ensure his king retained his throne.

"His Majesty must raise a greater army to oppose the Helgrins seizing our northern coastal towns. We lack men, even with hired mercenaries like yourself, and the cost of obtaining more is draining the royal coffers. In the meantime, the noble houses who've survived these years of unbridled rampage—and the wealthy merchants who supply them—are paying the renegade knights to skirt their estates and guildhalls." His expression darkened at this blatant disloyalty to the Gralian king. "Our own people are keeping these bastards in food and arms."

And in the meantime, King Crenel sits in pampered comfort on his throne at Lugeneux, thought Borne.

On watch the following day, Borne was approached by Versel, a Gralian with a foxy face and a sly nature to boot. "You're wanted by the marechal," Versel said tersely before pushing past Borne on his way toward the nearest lean-to. Versel had long since made clear his resentment of a foreigner holding a position of trust with their commander.

Nevertheless, Borne thanked him, then whistled for Magnus, who was curled under a ledge out of the rain. He pulled the hood of his cloak closer as he made his way to Latour's tent, the hound on his heels.

He found the marechal with Du Charney and Balmon, both of whom had served with Latour for years.

The marechal waved Borne in out of the rain. "You can bring your beast as well."

On Borne's command, Magnus shook himself before entering the relative dry of the marechal's quarters.

Latour tapped a map spread on the table before them. "We've been discussing our options."

The company had been following an elusive band of renegades for over a week, and Latour explained that scouts had ridden in this morning at dawn to report that the outlaws had made an unexpected about-face. Instead of heading for Viscay, a fortified town not far from the Albrenian border under the rule of Comte Rapett, cousin to the king, the rebels were now riding toward L'Asdies.

"Our success against the rogue knights has encouraged them to band together under Du Mulay, one of the worst of them," Latour continued. "He's estimated to have a force roughly twice that of ours, and he has the advantage of knowing the countryside around here well."

"Can we count on Viscay for additional men and supplies?" asked Balmon, a burly man with a mass of black curls and a full beard.

"Comte Rapett's new comtessa has provided him with the means to vastly improve the fortifications at Beauaguil," said Du Charney. "I wouldn't count on his willingness to have his knights swell our ranks. The lord of Viscay has been vocal in his criticism of the king's lack of protection for law-abiding citizens—and not without cause, it must be said. No, Rapett won't be inclined to risk his men against the renegades, not unless he's certain of victory."

"Even when the rogues set fire to his villagers' crofts outside the city?" asked Borne, for this was ever the pillagers' response when denied bribes or booty.

Du Charney shook his head. "The peasants will all be lodged within the castle walls by now. Their crops have been harvested, and anything that might sustain the raiders will have been burned. That's sure to put Du Mulay and his rabble in a murderous mood."

"Before we engage with Du Mulay," said Latour, "I intend to remind Rapett of his duty to his king." He turned to Borne, a speculative gleam in his eyes. "What do you say, shepherd, to a little sojourn?"

Borne grinned. "I am yours to command, Marechal."

CHAPTER 4

Avoiding the main road to Viscay, Latour's small company set out across rough terrain. The further east they traveled, the wilder the land grew, and brambled bushes soon crowded the trail, offering concealment to any who desired it, which forced the travelers to be ever more cautious. A few peasants might still remain here, surviving by hunting the forests and fishing the rivers of their former lords' abandoned estates, and it was anyone's guess as to where their loyalties lay.

Nevertheless, Borne's spirits were high. He set his horse at a canter, Magnus running at the roan's side, and found himself looking forward to seeing the marechal in parley with Rapett. Hopefully Latour would succeed in convincing the comte to send reinforcements from Beauaguil back to L'Asedies. There should be time to organize the defenses there before Du Mulay launched his inevitable attack; the renegade troops would need to stop and rest after they made their advance, for only a fool would ride directly into battle with cold, weary men.

When they arrived at Viscay, the wind was on the rise, and the same grey skies they'd left behind in L'Asedies hovered overhead. The only visible sun was on the royal standard Balmon unfurled, its golden flames bright on a crimson field.

The gate into the city was drawn open in a clatter of chains. They passed through, then were instructed to await an escort, which eventually arrived in the form of two cowled men sitting astride burros. Their silver habits identified them as Tertulite monks, devoted to the worship of Priscinae, the Mother Goddess of Gral. Borne recalled from his studies that the members of this order had been the most ruthless persecutors of wizards and magical folk over the centuries, and had played a zealous part in driving the continent's indigenous å Livåri across the sea to Drinnglennin.

One of the monks drew back his cowl, exposing a balding pate sparsely encircled by thin, straw-colored hair. He looked as though he'd just eaten a lemon.

"I am Fra Hugon," the monk said dolorously, "and this is Fra Tumas."

Fra Tumas's long legs hung close to the ground, his face obscured under his hood.

"Fra Tumas is under a vow of silence, as was I until I was summoned by my lord's seneschal to greet you. It is the fasting month." The monk's accusatory tone indicated he held the newcomers culpable for his broken vow. "I'm to escort you to the palais, but I can't promise you an audience with the comte. My lord Rapett has been much occupied, what with the rogue knights ranging so near."

"It is about these knight that we've come," Latour replied. "I'm certain Comte Rapett will be happy to receive an envoy from his sovereign, King Crenel, to whom he owes his first allegiance." He fixed the monk with his fierce gaze. "We will see him at once, and then I must return to my army."

The monk was clearly taken aback by the marechal's boldness. "I will inform my lord," he muttered, with a stiff nod of acquiescence, then kicked his burro to lead them up the winding street toward the hilltop castle.

Borne caught his breath when Beauaguil's towers and cupolas came into view, rising gracefully above the town. He trotted up beside Fra Hugon. "A magnificent castle! It was designed by Jules L'Odrey, was it not?"

The monk nodded. "Half a millennium ago, at the dawn of the After Age. Since then, Beauaguil has withstood fire and siege, and with the recent improvements, it shall still be standing five hundred years hence." As he warmed to his subject, pride replaced his dour expression. "It took Ser L'Odrey and his artisans seventy-four years to build the palais, then over a decade more before the water gardens were completed. It was his life's work."

By the time Borne dismounted, he'd learned that the palace boasted an astounding 444 chambers, warmed by 262 fireplaces and connected by 87 staircases. When it came to the history of Beauaguil, Fra Hugon was a fount of information. Or perhaps he was just making up for all the words he had failed to speak during his self-imposed silence.

Leaving Latour and his party waiting outside the palace's tall gilded doors, the two monks plodded slowly into the palace, without any promise as to when they might return. Borne, seeing a look of impatience cross the marechal's face, decided he was glad he wasn't Rapett.

Fortunately, they weren't kept cooling their heels for long. When the doors reopened, a stream of heralds emerged and blew a fanfare, then ushered the visitors through a long, vaulted hall hung with chandeliers and lined with tall mirrors that reflected the light in glowing pools. Borne counted thirty pilasters crowned with gold that served as buttresses, and the expansive arched ceiling was adorned with paintings depicting Gral's glory days.

They were escorted into a smaller but equally opulent chamber at the hall's end, where Comte Rapett received them in what appeared to be his dressing gown, a silver robe edged with squirrel and loosely tied with a golden cord. Although no longer in the bloom of youth, Rapett had the look of a soldier about him, which Borne took as an encouraging sign. His steel-shot hair was tied back from the long planes of his face, and he moved forward to greet them with athletic grace.

Once his guests were seated, the comte invited them to partake of a fine Calhora wine, accompanied by delicate crescents of freshly baked bread and buttery cheese. But though some of the marechal's men gladly partook of both food and drink, Latour himself ignored the refreshments and got straight to the point.

"We need a force of men from Viscay to return with us at once to L'Asedies. Du Mulay is our last real obstacle to peace, and with these reinforcements, I believe we can at last put an end to the stranglehold the renegade knights have on Gral."

The comte's smile was one of regret. "I appreciate the great work you and your men are doing, Marechal, and hope you succeed in defeated Du Mulay. But here at Viscay, we've managed until now to avoid any encounters with these scoundrels, and it is my intention that we shall remain neutral in this affair. You will understand that, before all else, I must think of my people. Who will succor them should this action of yours fail and the knights under Du Mulay prove the victors? If I give you men, he will surely seek revenge upon us."

"Which could just as easily be the outcome should you refuse us," Latour countered. "Should we fail, there is nothing to prevent Du Mulay from laying siege to Viscay."

Rapett laced his elegant fingers together. "We have succeeded in discouraging him from this course of action in the past."

Which meant, Borne felt certain, that Du Mulay's knights had been paid off.

Latour was not easily rebuffed. "That was when Du Mulay knew that we were on his trail. He couldn't discount the possibility that you would send out a force against him while we closed in on his rearguard." The marechal's mouth formed a grim line, and though his voice remained quiet, he was every inch the fearsome commander. "We have a clear indication that he intends to engage with King Crenel's forces now encamped at L'Asedies. You yourself are well aware of the size of the army Du Mulay has amassed. Your king has need of you now, Comte Rapett, and will reward you handsomely for this service to Gral."

The comte laughed, the lift of his shoulders implying doubt. "Do you really think so, Marechal? I don't share the same level of confidence in my cousin. It's my understanding that Crenel has drained the royal coffers in his thwarted attempts to drive the Helgrins from our shores. Now he reaps the repercussions."

Latour's eyes narrowed. "You should guard your tongue, Comte Rapett. No one shall speak ill of our sovereign in my presence."

The two men eyed each other across the table, the air between them dense with tension.

Rapett was the first to look away. "I see that you are determined to involve me," he said. "If so, then of course I must abide by the wishes of my king." He lifted his goblet, a rueful smile on his face. "Let us drink, gentlemen, to a swift victory... else Priscinae have mercy on our souls."

* * *

"I don't trust him," Balmon said, when the adjunct and Borne reconvened in private with the marechal. While Borne and Balmon had snatched a few hours' sleep, the marechal had been debating strategy with Ser Valeik, commander of Viscay's force. From Valeik, Latour had received the welcome news that Du Mulay's horde had diverted inland to scavenge, which meant they were not yet en route to L'Asedies.

"Rapett has given his word to serve Gral's best interests," Latour replied.

Privately, Borne shared Balmon's misgivings. The comte was clearly hesitant to commit his men, and it wasn't ties of kinship or fealty to his king that had prodded him into agreeing to Latour's demands. Rapett knew, as did they all, that if he failed to send the force the marechal required, and if Latour nevertheless defeated Du Mulay decisively, the comte would lose everything, including his life. Refusing to obey the mandate of the king's marechal was an act of treason. This threat alone had extracted from Comte Rapett the promise of two hundred horsemen and four hundred foot.

As Balmon and Latour discussed this turn of events, Borne gazed down from the narrow window at a flurry of activity in the courtyard below. Horses were being led out, and squires trundled after them bent under the weight of their lords' arms. A number of silver-cloaked monks milled among them.

"Marechal," Borne said slowly, "I've just had an idea. One that may increase the odds of our success against the renegades."

Latour turned a speculative gaze on Borne. "I'm listening, shepherd."

* * *

After Latour and his men had departed Viscay, Borne, who had lingered behind, set off in search of the monk with the dangling legs. Eventually he located Fra Tumas in the deserted stables. Borne greeted him cordially, then delivered a powerful fist to the monk's temple that knocked him out cold before the man could make use of his rested vocal cords. Borne relieved the monk of his silver habit, left him trussed in a haystack, and slipped into the bustling courtyard, cloaked in his purloined disguise.

So it was that when Rapett's force got underway, Borne was with them, his silver cowl pulled low as he bounced along on his burro. The monks led the ceremonial exit through the city gates, and he was the last in a line of his brethren, riding just ahead of the Viscay soldiers. Naturally he observed the silence to which Fra Tumas had been sworn, but he kept his ears attuned to the fervent conversation between Ser Valeik and his second, who was riding at the commander's side.

"We're to stand off," Ser Valeik seethed, his frustration clear. "We're not to engage until it's clear that Latour's force will triumph. And if it goes badly for the marechal, we're to abandon him and ride hard for Viscay. For certain I'll have my hands full just keeping the men back—they're burning for a fight. Their lands have been scourged by that lawless pack of curs."

"I know it's a bitter draught to swallow, my lord," said his adjunct, "but don't forget that Rapett's pleas to the king for support have come to naught. In these lawless times, it seems every man must be responsible for his own survival."

"I happen to think our survival may reside in the hands of Latour," retorted Ser Valeik. "Let's hope he emerges the victor."

* * *

As the comte's men approached the outskirts of L'Asedies, a distant blare of trumpets signaled the armies had already met. Calling a halt, Ser Valeik sent three scouts west to higher ground to covertly assess the opposing side's ranks. Borne boldly struck out after them, half expecting to feel an arrow between his shoulders at any moment. But none came, and no one called him back. Indeed, after exchanging a surprised glance, the scouts seemed to find the silent monk's presence reassuring.

They rode parallel to the tumult of the fighting. When they came to a ridge, they left their mounts and crept forward to take the lay of the land. From this vantage point, they could see the outlawed knights and the king's host facing off, Latour's red-plumed helmet visible to all. The renegades had the advantage, for although their backs were to the river, the terrain dipped before them, which would force the loyalists into an uphill charge. Du Mulay had also gathered a vanguard of infantry. Borne remembered that this was the land of Du Mulay's birth—most likely he had recruited the foot soldiers from his own fief.

An exchange of crossbow fire had already begun, but was having minimal effect due to an insufficient number of archers and too much distance between the opposing forces.

And then came the signal to charge.

Du Mulay's men streamed down over the rutted field and were met by the shield wall of Latour's infantry. The loyalist archers were having more success now, but so were those of the renegades advancing behind the men on foot.

As Borne and the scouts watched from the hillside, it appeared at first that the loyalists' wall would hold firm. But then a shower of spears from the enemy arched over their shields, finding fatal marks in the men of the third and fourth ranks.

Du Mulay's force, seizing the advantage, rushed forward behind their own combined shields to drive the loyalist army back over their dead. The two walls clashed with a reverberation that drowned out all other sounds of battle.

It was Latour's shield wall that cracked first. Du Mulay's knights poured through the resulting fissure, hacking away at the king's men behind the broken barricade. A bloody melee ensued, and the loyalist troops slowly but surely gave ground toward their reserve shield wall at their backs.

For once, it seemed Latour had underestimated the size of the opposing army. His men were fighting hard, but as the swords, pikes, and halberds rose and fell, the majority of the vanquished wore red and gold, and Du Mulay's men continued to gain ground.

The marechal was headed for defeat.

Valeik's scouts, no doubt having come to the same conclusion, began to inch back from the ridge. Borne knew he would have to act swiftly.

"Give me your horn," he ordered one of the bigger men, who dutifully surrendered it. "You two," Borne continued, as he slipped the horn's cord over his head, "will stay to observe the course of the battle." Ignoring their startled expressions, he turned toward the third knight. "You shall ride with me to inform Ser Valeik that it appears the marechal will be defeated. I'll sound the horn to call you both back once this is confirmed. I speak the will of the Mother," he added before any of them could argue, "for whom I am a humble conduit."

For a moment, Borne wondered if they'd refuse, and was greatly relieved when the third knight started down toward the horses and, after a moment's hesitation, the other two edged back up the rise.

Now Borne had only one of the scouts to deal with. They remounted and headed back toward Valeik and his waiting army. But as soon as they were out of sight of the ridge, Borne called for a halt.

Frowning, the knight reined in. "What is it, Fra…?"

"Fra Tumas." Borne slid from his burro. "I need to relieve myself. You can water our animals at the stream just there." He pointed vaguely to a small stand of trees.

As he pretended to fumble with his robes, Borne heard his companion drop to the ground. Borne wheeled toward him, sidestepping just in time as the knight lunged past, flailing his sword.

The man spun around and angled the tip of his sword at Borne's face. "I know Fra Tumas," he growled.

Borne, who had no weapon of his own, retreated a step.

"Before I kill you," the Gralian said sternly, "you will tell me for whom you are spying, although I think I can guess. You're Du Mulay's man. Do you deny it?"

Out of the corner of his eye, Borne saw that the knight's courser had ambled off to graze. His own burro remained close at hand. He lunged toward it, then dropped into a crouch as the *swish* of the blade passed over his head.

He scrapped up two fistfuls of dirt, sprang up, and flung them in his attacker's face. While the man coughed and clawed at his eyes, Borne threw himself onto the burro's back and kicked it toward the courser. He made a snatch for the horse's reins, but the warhorse shied away as he surged past.

Cursing, he urged the burro to a gallop, determined to get to Ser Valeik as swiftly as possible and tell him Latour was winning. If Viscay's men joined the fray and attacked Du Mulay's flanks, there was still time to turn the tide of the battle. Neither side's cavalry had made a charge, and victory was still possible. Latour's men just had to hold firm a little longer.

Borne looked over his shoulder to see the knight he'd just evaded riding hard after him. The little burro was no match for the man's destrier, and within the space of three ragged breaths, Valeik's scout had nearly closed the gap. Before Borne could decide how best to handle this, he was knocked from his saddle and hurled to the ground, the air slammed from his lungs.

A cry behind him was followed by a silencing thud.

Struggling for breath, Borne heard the burro and the horse trotting on. With a groan, he rolled painfully to his side. The knight lay in the grass, his neck bent at a sharp, unforgiving angle. Then Borne saw the taut rope, strung at rider height, that had felled them both.

He pushed himself onto his hands and knees, and looked up to find a large company of armed men on horseback closing on him. Their dark, bearded faces and plain garments indicated they were not Viscay men. They carried makeshift weapons, many of which were directed at him.

Borne raised his hands above his head as he rose carefully to his feet.

"It wasn't our intention to kill your friend." The man who spoke had the proud air of a prince. Gralian was not his native tongue.

There was no time to observe the proprieties. "Do you serve Du Mulay?" Borne demanded.

The man spat on the ground. "No." He gave Borne a measured look, taking in his religious attire. "Do you?"

Borne's ears were still ringing from his fall, but there was something about the voice that was familiar. "I serve under Marechal Latour, who is King Crenel's man," he said. "As we speak, our company is about to be overwhelmed by Du Mulay. I was on my way to urge the men of Viscay to come to our aid."

"I see," said the mounted man. "Then I regret to inform you that we saw the Viscay force riding east, away from this conflict."

Borne uttered an extremely un-monklike oath. Valeik's other two scouts must have gotten past him and delivered their own report after all.

His interlocuter raised his dark brows. "You swear in Drinn, yet you serve the king of Gral." Before Borne could respond, he demanded, "How many men in Du Mulay's army?"

"Half again Latour's numbers. But we could have easily defeated them with Rapett's reinforcements." Borne didn't attempt to disguise his bitter frustration.

A gleam lit the bearded man's dark eyes. "Ah," he replied, "do you tell me now? Perhaps we can be of assistance—for a price."

CHAPTER 5
Halla

The life of a soldier suited Halla in every way. No one cared if she combed her unruly hair. No one wished she'd act more "like a lady." Her simple tunics and trousers didn't hamper her every movement like the skirts she'd been forced to wear at home, and she could train without anyone interrupting to insist she attend to her embroidery.

Nevertheless, in her early days with Nicu's company, she still found herself on the outside looking in. Not because of her gender, but because of her lack of å Livåri blood. More than once Nicu's wary men asked her to explain her reasons for adopting their cause. But with each raid in which she risked her life alongside them, she earned more of their trust, until now she felt they were, at last, beginning to accept her as one of their own.

Initially she'd chafed at playing the role Nicu expected of her on their forays into towns. But she couldn't deny that posing as an Albrenian noblewoman traveling with slaves had met with success—so much so that the å Livåri had been able to rescue scores of their stolen women. The company's bold exploits had even drawn the attention of Palan, the Albrenian commander of the king's army, who'd set a high price on their heads.

Halla wondered what Palan would think if he knew that his escaped "property" was among the emancipators.

To avoid Palan's long reach, the å Livåri had established their headquarters over the border in Gral. The camp wasn't far from the coast, as Nicu needed to hire ships to get the freed women back to the relative safety of Drinnglennin. To Halla's relief, he hadn't again mentioned sending her with them. Still, she maintained a distance from the å Livåri females. As much as she missed having a friend like Bria, she feared too much association with the women might cost her her hard-earned place among the men. So instead she kept company with Mihail and Baldo, the two men who had rescued her in the street in Segavia and who had since become her fast friends. When they weren't all out on a raid, she foraged and trained with them—and in the evenings she passed the time laughing at their rough jokes and their boasts of prowess, both on the field and between the sheets.

It wasn't only Halla who avoided spending too much time with the å Livåri females—the men did as well. Of course every man in camp was well aware of the presence of these young, attractive women; Halla noted with much amusement the increased frequency of bathing and beard-trimming among her comrades. But the men were sensitive to what the women had endured at the hands of their captors. The rescued women didn't speak of their captivity—nor did they mention their separation from husbands, brothers, fathers, and children—but their silence spoke volumes. As such, the men made none of the bold overtures Halla had often witnessed from the males of Bria's clan. Occasionally a man and woman would pair off, but these were quiet arrangements, seemingly as much for solace as for sex.

One evening, Halla was drinking with Baldo when she saw Guaril approaching her with a disturbing gleam in his eye. Baldo must have discerned it too, for he rose and uttered a single, unfamiliar word that stopped Guaril in his tracks.

As Guaril veered off toward his tent, Halla turned to Baldo. "What was that you said to him?"

"Nothing."

She shoved him with her shoulder. "Tell me. What did you say?"

"Off limits." His grin looked suspiciously sly. "Nicu's orders."

"Nicu's orders?" Halla felt a strange flutter in her chest. "Why?"

Baldo shrugged. "Perhaps he feels protective of you because you're a *gago*," he suggested, using the term for all those who were not å Livåri. "Or maybe…"

But he seemed to think better of whatever he had been about to say, and instead lifted his flask to his lips.

Halla reached over and took the bottle from him. "Or maybe what?"

Baldo shifted, avoiding her eyes. "Nothing."

Halla laughed. "You're a singularly unconvincing liar. Tell me. Nicu doesn't think I'm able to fend off unwanted advances without his help? Has he not been watching me best all of you in sparring?"

Baldo made a noncommittal grunt, then looked pointedly at the bottle in her hand. "Are you going to drink or not?"

Halla shook the flask enticingly. "You were saying?"

"Only what others have said before me," he growled. "We've all seen the way his eyes follow you when he thinks you're not looking."

Halla felt the curious flutter again. "What… exactly do you mean?"

"I mean that our Nicu," said Baldo, tugging the bottle from her relaxed grip, "fancies you for himself."

"That's—that's ridiculous," Halla sputtered. "I can count on one hand the number of times he's spoken to me. He barely knows I'm alive!"

Baldo choked on the wine he had tipped into his mouth. Wiping his chin, he replied, "You may wield a sword like a man, Åthinoi, but that doesn't change the fact that you look very much like a woman. Believe me, he knows you're alive."

Halla rose, letting her hair fall forward so that Baldo wouldn't see the blush that colored her cheeks. "What rubbish." She gave him a cuff in passing. "You're stewed to the gills. I'm going to bed."

Baldo grunted something she chose to ignore. But once she was in the shelter of her tent, she wished she'd hit him harder, for the tumult he'd provoked in her mind.

* * *

The next morning Halla forced herself to cross paths with Nicu, joining him when he went to check their snares. And now that she was attuned to his possible interest, she *did* feel his eyes on her from time to time. She pretended not to notice, keeping her face averted when he looked her way, and was relieved he couldn't sense the unsteady beating of her heart.

As they rode back toward camp with a sack filled with hares and a brace of peasants, Halla found herself stealing glances at Nicu as well. The man was absurdly handsome, with his bronze skin, his chiseled features, and his smoldering eyes fringed with long, full lashes. She noticed for the first time the elegant tapering of his fingers, the shell-curl of his ears below his shining black curls, and how when he spoke, the tenor of his voice somehow resonated deep within her own breast. His passion when he spoke of their cause made her pulse quicken, and she knew that she, like the others, would follow him anywhere.

Yet she also understood it would be unwise to confuse Nicu the warrior with Nicu the man—whom she still knew so little about.

And then, as she looked upon him, her gaze lingering a fraction too long, their eyes met—and Halla felt her breath catch. At Casa Calida, she had been trained to recognize the signs of a man's yearning. There was no mistaking the light she saw reflected in those smoky eyes. He wanted her.

Now it was left to Halla to decide what *she* wanted.

* * *

The next day, scouts rode into camp to report that two large forces—one loyalist, one renegade—were preparing to engage in battle less than a mile from their secluded encampment. In addition, a large Gralian force was heading their way from the east. Nicu ordered the men to take the necessary precautions, then led a small group of his men, and Halla, out to investigate. They hadn't gotten far when they heard hoofbeats approaching, followed by a single shout. Apparently the ropes strung around the borders of the camp as a safeguard had taken the oncoming riders down.

Nicu signaled for silence, then led the way to where two men lay sprawled on the ground, a horse and a burro milling around them. Halla saw that one of the fallen would not be rising again. The other, dressed in monk's robes, got carefully to his feet, his hands held high in surrender.

Halla was as surprised as the rest when, after a brief exchange with Nicu in Gralian, the monk switched to Drinn. Apparently, the man rode with Latour, the marechal of Gral. The monk quickly explained that the comte of Viscay had sent a company of soldiers over to support Latour against a rebel force led by a knight named Du Mulay. Viscay's men had not yet engaged with the rogues, and having determined that Du Mulay would carry the day, were now reneging on their part of the bargain.

A swift round of negotiations ensued, resulting in Nicu agreeing to come to the aid of the Gralian loyalists in exchange for arms and training in their use.

Halla could hardly believe she'd heard correctly. It was true they could use better weaponry; their current arsenal had been taken piecemeal from fallen enemies, and much of it was of poor quality. But for the å Livåri to involve themselves in internal warfare would be beyond foolish. So far, the Gralian authorities had turned a blind eye to their presence, but that situation would change in a hurry if the å Livåri took action that could make them appear to be outside aggressors.

Besides, Halla didn't trust the monk's motives. Why was the man not with his company on the battlefield? When she saw him riding at Nicu's side, she couldn't resist spurring her horse forward to join them.

"Ah, Halla, you'd never guess," Nicu said, "but Borne here is from Drinnglennin, and as it happens, we've met before." A shadow crossed his face, and he turned back to the monk. "Did you ever find out who did it?"

The man's cowl had fallen back to reveal bright, fair hair and a ruggedly handsome face. "I'm afraid not," Borne replied, his Drinn pegging him for a northerner.

"Did what?" asked Halla.

The monk's eyes widened when she spoke, but he didn't respond. Instead, he raised a hand and signaled for silence as if he, and not Nicu, were in command. They reined in, and Halla was about to voice her disapproval when she heard the sounds of conflict ringing from beyond the ridge to their left. Nicu and the monk were already dismounting, and she did the same. The three of them climbed to the top of the ridge, then edged forward on their bellies.

A battle was in full pitch below, and judging by the number of bodies strewn across the muddy ground, it had been going on for some time. Even to Halla's less experienced eyes, it was clear the Gralian outlaws were on the brink of victory. She spotted their leader—this Du Mulay—waiting on an incline with supporting cavalry, poised to issue the command to sweep down into a final, crushing clash with the outnumbered royal horse.

Borne spoke quietly with Nicu, then the two men started back down toward the others. As Halla followed them, her suspicions grew. Why would a Drinnglennian dressed as a monk claim to serve the Gralian marechal? And why had he been riding *away* from this battle when they'd come across him, rather than earning his wages?

Nicu called softly to one of his men. "Shandor, give this man my spare blade. He's come up with a brilliant strategy, and if it works, it will be to our advantage as well."

The monk, two deep dimples punctuating his cheeks, accepted the proffered sword, then swung easily onto his burro's back and tugged the cowl back up to cover his golden hair. "You'll have your reward," he promised Nicu, then took up the horn hanging round his neck. "I'll wait until you're in position, but you must be quick about it. We haven't much time to turn the tide."

Nicu hoisted himself into his own saddle. "We'll raise a glass together when the battle's won."

The company circled to the far left of the battlefield and entered the woodlands bordering it. Here they were shielded by the trees, but were still able to see the fighting. The renegades under Du Mulay had gained ground, and their second shield wall was now advancing. As the low roll of drums accelerated, the formation shifted from a straight line to a wedge, primed to break through the last resistance of the royalist force.

Nicu signaled for a halt and outlined the plan of attack.

"Once the wall moves to strike, the rebels will run hard toward Latour's last line of defense between his cavalry and their own. Wait for my command."

Du Mulay's men were already trotting forward, keeping their formation tight, shields overlapping, the tips of their spears glinting in the rays of light breaking through the low clouds. The taunts of the loyalists, aligned behind their own rigid wall, died away, no doubt replaced by prayers. The only reason they were still alive was because Du Mulay's cavalry still hadn't charged. Halla suspected Du Mulay was wary of Latour's counterthrust if they went too early. But it was only a matter of time now. There was no way Latour's force could hope to withstand this attack, and it would be suicide for Nicu to lead them into a lost battle.

Halla was about to say as much when, from the far side of the field, a lone rider, garbed in a monk's silver robes, careened into the fray, a trumpet raised to his lips. The blare of the horn resounding across the corpse-strewn meadow clearly startled the drummers, for their beating faltered, and men on both sides of the fighting craned their necks to identify the army they assumed was at the rider's back. Only it was very soon apparent that there *was* no army.

"The man's stark raving mad," Halla said to no one in particular. She suspected it was only the sanctity of the monk's order that prevented someone from striking him down.

As the frenzied troubadour wheeled his burro in a tight circle, the strident horn still to his lips, two of Du Mulay's knights detached themselves from their fellows and rode to apprehend him. Although Borne must have seen them coming, he continued to belabor the horn, and the cacophony— or perhaps it was merely the mad spectacle of it all—continued to rivet both armies in place.

Nicu's sudden order to charge took Halla by surprise. But she didn't hesitate to dig her heels into her rouncey, her companions on either side streaming along with her out of the woods.

Du Mulay's men—still staring, bemused, at the lone horsemen—didn't turn to meet this new threat until the first contingent of á Livári was driving straight into their cavalry, carving its way through with thrusting swords and cleaving axes. Halla's blood sang as she hacked off the arm of the first knight to challenge her. Beside her, Nicu brandished his sword just as lethally, driving the point of his blade into an oncoming renegade's throat.

After dispatching several more men, Halla became aware that Borne had ceased his trumpeting. His distraction had served its purpose. Du Mulay's infantry had lost their measured rhythm, and in the space of that hesitation, a second wave of à Livâri had already surged against Du Mulay's left flank, behind their shield wall, felling the foot soldiers and hindering those trying to scramble forward to take their places.

Latour wasted no time in making the most of fortune's sudden swing in his favor. His wall swiftly advanced, and his archers, now able to find their marks, sent a steady barrage of arrows streaming into the melee. What had looked to be a certain victory for Du Mulay had turned into a bloodbath for his men. Thanks to the arrival of the à Livâri, Latour had been able to split his troops so that the outlaws faced attack on three fronts. The loyalist cavalry, unleashed at last, corralled their opponents between their mounts and those of the à Livâri.

Halla plowed further into the fray, burning with battle lust as she lent her voice to the cries of her comrades. One after another, her opposition fell under her broadsword, and the groans of the dying men pleading with their strange, dark goddess, rose around her. At her side, Nicu was clearing a path for his following men. The monk appeared on her other side, flashed her a disarming grin, then moved forward, wielding his sword with deadly accuracy, dispatching men left and right.

The à Livâri had now gained the center of the field, and Du Mulay's cavalry was spiraling into chaos. Its once-orderly ranks had now dissolved into a rabble of men desperate to escape with their lives. A high clarion sounded, and those Gralian outlaws who could still fall back did so, abandoning the remnants of their shield wall to its fate. Du Mulay's foot soldiers, aware that their lives were now forfeit, began throwing down their weapons and pleading for mercy.

Halla felt a rush of frustration; it had been over too fast, and her blood was still hot. Turning away from the surrendering soldiers, she rode hard after a pair of fleeing renegades. Already Latour's foot soldiers were passing among the wounded, dispatching those whose injuries were mortal, and signaling for litter-bearers when encountering those still clinging stubbornly to a thread of life.

Baldo loomed up alongside her on a massive destrier he'd obviously taken as a prize. "Turn back—Nicu's orders. We're not to pursue them."

With reluctance, Halla reined in, leaving the pursuit of the retreating renegades to Latour's cavalry. She understood the order—the laden sacks swinging from the defeated army's saddles were the loyalists' rightful booty—but she still resented being pulled from the battle. She only hoped that this Borne would make good on his pledge to Nicu. The truth was, she doubted he possessed the authority to grant such a reward, seeing as he was as much a foreigner in this land as they were.

The promise of rain scented the air, and the louring sky darkened. Soon the stains of the violence done this day would be cleansed from the dank earth. Halla wheeled her horse. She wanted to be close at hand when Nicu learned whether he'd been right to trust the monk.

* * *

Halla had just rejoined Nicu when the monk approached, accompanied by two men garbed in the red-and-gold uniforms of Gral. One of them wore a sash of command. Borne glanced once in Halla's direction, then chose to ignore her.

He turned to the lean, hawk-faced Gralian with the sash and said something in the Gralian tongue. Halla knew little of the language, but he addressed the commander as "Marechal," and finished with "Master Nicu of Drinnglennin." Making introductions, then.

Nicu had picked up on this as well. "Nicu will suffice," he said.

Halla was struck by a similarity between the two men. Although Nicu's black curls and dark coloring were in sharp contrast to the pale Gralian commander's hollow cheeks and straight, bound hair, they both had something in their bearing that commanded respect.

Her gaze shifted to the marechal's attendant. The man was scowling at Nicu, his thin lips curled with distaste. Halla bristled at the contempt in which too many continental folk held the å Livåri.

Borne translated smoothly as the marechal, seemingly unaware of his glowering adjutant, spoke in his own tongue. "I'd be pleased if you would call me Latour. I would style you *co-marade*—friend of Gral—for without your dramatic entrance into the battle today, it would have ended badly for us."

Halla relaxed her grip on the hilt of her sword. It seemed the marechal was prepared to offer Nicu the respect he was due.

Nicu shrugged. "We didn't need to do much. The blackguards allowed your clowning monk here to divert them, then they lost their nerve."

A dimple indented one of Borne's cheeks as he relayed this to the marechal.

Latour laughed softly and spoke again.

Borne's smile widened. "The marechal says my performance was compelling, if incredibly foolhardy."

"Du Mulay, the entertainment came at a steep price," Nicu observed dryly. "It served its purpose well."

"The burro deserves the bulk of credit," said Borne. In the face of his humility, Halla found herself slightly warming to the man.

Borne sobered as Latour addressed Nicu, and this time she understood the marechal was confirming Nicu's requested payment for his services. She noted the lack of a title, religious or otherwise, in Latour's reference to the monk. Yet Borne clearly spoke flawless Gralian, which was only taught to children of nobility in Drinnglennin. *Who is he?* she wondered.

"Barring an army," said Nicu, "we need weapons, and training in their use. If you could provide these, we would feel ourselves well compensated."

When this was translated, the marechal's adjunct stepped forward, waving his arms in apparent protest. Halla didn't care at all for the way he was gesturing at Nicu.

"What's he saying?" she demanded, forgetting for a moment that it wasn't her place to speak.

Borne's mouth formed a grim line. "That their own peasants are forbidden to carry weapons, and these—"

He drew a sharp breath and in rapid Gralian cut off the adjunct's argument.

Latour was also frowning at his aide, and with a stern word from him, the man fell silent.

Borne inclined his head graciously as the marechal turned back to speak to him, then translated Latour's words. "The marechal requests a short time in which to confer with his officers, then he shall see what can be done. In the meantime, he invites us to partake in a victory feast. With today's joined action, we've dealt a crippling blow to the strongest of the renegade bands. He says we have cause to celebrate."

Halla silently willed Nicu to refuse the invitation. There were sure to be other Gralians who shared the adjunct's clear disdain of å Livåri. To sit down with them at a meal could only result in trouble.

But to her dismay, Nicu gave a nod of acquiescence.

"*Excellente!*" said Latour. He clapped the shoulders of both Nicu and Borne, then led them off.

Before Halla returned to her å Livåri comrades, she took a moment to enjoy the sight of the marechal's disgruntled second trailing sullenly in their wake.

* * *

It was well past midnight when the victory feast concluded and the å Livåri returned to their own camp. Thankfully, the night had passed without incident, though Halla wasn't happy when Borne—whom she'd now confirmed was no monk—accompanied Nicu back to their fire. As the tall man sank down across from her at the fireside, she made no attempt to hide her disapproval.

Nicu remained standing to address those of his men who had not already succumbed to weariness and drink. "We have a decision to make," he declared, then proceeded to detail what their engagement had earned them this day. Halla listened without comment until the false monk's name was mentioned.

"You can't be serious!" she cried, leaping to her feet. "*He's* to lead us as a force fighting for the *Gralians?*"

"If you have an objection to voice, Åthinoi," said Nicu, in the quiet tone she'd learned to be wary of, "we will hear it after I have finished."

Halla sank back down and glowered at Borne, whose mild gaze remained fixed on the fire.

After a censorious silence, Nicu continued. "We're to receive a range of arms—crossbows, swords, pikes, and axes—and training in their use. In exchange, some of us will serve as a paid unit of the Gralian loyalist army for a term of no less than three months and no more than six, depending on how long it takes to root out the last of the renegades. After this, we're free to take our weapons and return to our mission."

"What about our people held in slavery in Albrenia?" Baldo demanded. "What of those who disappeared to places unknown? They may not have that much time."

"As I said, only a small number of us will remain with Latour's forces," Nicu replied evenly. "And I will be one of these. Mihail, I would ask you to assume command of the rest and carry on with the rescues." He let his eyes travel over his men, and pitched his next words so none could fail to hear him. "The reality is that at present, we're poorly equipped, which limits us to small-scale raids. Latour is offering us the chance to become professional soldiers, under this man's tutelage." He pointed at Borne. "He's not å Livåri, but I judge him an honorable man. Indeed, I made his acquaintance back on the Isle, so I've known him longer than I have some of you. Because we share a common language, he's an obvious choice to lead us for this period, should we agree to the terms. None of you who saw him on the field of battle today can deny his ability as a warrior, and his strategic expertise receives high praise from the Gralian marechal."

Borne looked as if he would make a joke, but caught himself when he saw, as did Halla, that the men were hanging on Nicu's words.

"Once we've acquired the skills and weapons, we will use them to protect ourselves from any who seek to oppress us, and fight for our right to exist in the Known World as a respected people! *Noi stunte* å Livåri!"

A shout of accord broke out amongst the ranks, and Nicu let it resonate a moment before raising his hands for quiet. "If we are agreed, I will ask you to choose who will follow Mihail. I need thirty men to stay with me and the Gralians."

The men, recognizing their leader had had his say, began to talk among themselves.

As Nicu made to walk past Halla, she rose to her feet. "And what about a woman?"

Nicu stopped and turned his well-deep gaze upon her. "A woman who knows her worth will choose her rightful place."

* * *

There was still a light shining from within the small tent. Halla lifted the flap, stepped inside, and let it fall behind her.

Nicu looked up from his maps and drew a sharp breath, but spoke no word as she crossed to the table and extinguished the single candle.

He smelled of horse and sweat, but when their lips met, she tasted sweet mint. He held her carefully when she slipped into his arms, as if she might still choose to break away, and he left it to her to lead them in a slow spiral down on to his bedroll.

Only when they lay face to face in the dark did she speak.

"A woman," she said, her lips softly brushing his ear, "has chosen."

CHAPTER 6
Fynn

Fynn would survive the cold, for he was Helgrin-born and had known far bitterer autumns than this one. He could endure the rats, the foul, cesspool stench that permeated his cell, and the same thin gruel twice a day. What threatened to break him—what preyed on his thoughts through the long, tedious hours, what brought him daily to the brink of despair—was simply this: he had lost his family.

He would never again see his father or Jered, if indeed they still lived. He would never again feel his mother's loving arms, for she did not. And because he had failed to honor the oath he'd made before Wurl, the sacred oak, to become the greatest hero of the Helgrins, he was barred from Cloud Mountain in the afterlife. When all those he loved were reunited there, they would not mourn his absence. Nor should they; he had proved unworthy of his father's name and his mother's love.

He would die in this stinking gaol and descend to Nagror, the murky underworld where those who don't warrant entry to Cloud Mountain dwell in misery. Poisonous serpents would gnaw away his decaying flesh and bones, then feast on his hapless soul as he screamed in torment for all eternity. It was a harsh fate to accept.

He'd stopped counting the days since he'd been separated from Teca at the port. He had no idea if she too was imprisoned. She'd fought to stay with Fynn when they bound and gagged him, and the last time he'd seen her, she was lying on the ground, struck down by Vetch. Perhaps she was dead.

The thought evoked no tears, for he had shed enough.

It was likely that Lord Vetch, the enemy commander who had burned and plundered Restaria, had discovered that Teca was not his mother, nor he her son by a Drinnglennian father. It made Fynn feel ill that he'd gone along with the improbable tale in the first place. It had been a cowardly betrayal.

His fingers sought the chain around his neck, from which hung the strange pendant his dying mother had given him. He suspected it carried ill fortune, and he would have cast it down the pisshole if safeguarding it had not been his last promise to her. It was a wonder he still had it in his possession, but Lord Vetch had ordered his men not to search Fynn, and to instruct Fynn's gaolers to keep their hands off him as well, on pain of death. As a result, Fynn still had both the pendant and the small pouch he wore under his tunic. He patted the comforting bulge of the dried bloodteeth against his thin chest—a final escape, should he choose to use it.

As he lay listening to the rats rooting in the rushes, the heavy cell door grated over the stone floor. Fynn scrambled up, shielding his eyes from the blazing torchlight as something thudded against the back wall of the cell and slumped to the floor.

The door scraped closed again. Fynn held his breath for ten counts in the ringing silence; he sensed a new presence. Cautiously, he groped behind his back for the spoon he'd found in the bottom of his bowl one day, where it must have slipped when the cook wasn't looking. He'd sharpened it to a fine point against the rough stone and kept it hidden in the filthy rushes. It wasn't much, but it could poke out an eye or pierce a throat. Clutching the spoon, he waited. He'd wait as long as he had to. Let the other make the first move. If he proved to be a foe, Fynn would be ready.

When the whimpering began, he ignored it, suspecting the fellow might be feigning injury. It wasn't until the man began to moan that Fynn decided he must be ill—then amended that to mad as the stranger started raving and crying out reedy, unintelligible pleas.

Fynn propped himself against the wall, holding the spoon tight in his grip.

Despite the noise, he eventually slept. He jerked awake to weak daylight and snatched up the spoon that had fallen to his lap.

His cellmate was huddled against the opposite wall, his body twitching and shuddering. He was wrapped in a filthy cloak, and the side of his face was badly bruised.

When their breakfast arrived, Fynn drew in the two bowls through the roughly cut hole at the base of the door, then nudged one of them toward the quivering man.

"This is yours."

The only response he got was the clacking of teeth.

"Don't you want it?"

With a shrug, Fynn lifted his own bowl and drank its contents in small sips, making it last as long as he could. When he finished, he eyed the second bowl.

"Are you going to eat that?"

The stranger raised his head, and Fynn saw that the blue on his face wasn't a bruise, but a mottled tattoo. The man retched up a string of spittle onto the rushes, and Fynn took that to be as good an answer as he was likely to get. He reached for the other bowl and drained it.

Feeling full for the first time in weeks, Fynn curled on his side and slept again. He dreamt he was staggering across a grey field strewn with the gory aftermath of battle, gripping his belly where a sword had pierced it. Trying not to tread on the fallen, he cried out for his mother.

One of the corpses in his path lifted its cracked skull, embedded with the axe that had split it. "Stop yer snivelin', ya lily-livered cuss!" the man growled.

Fynn reeled away, doubled over from the stabbing pain in his groin. Looking down, he saw his guts spilling out through a bloody gash. When he tried to push them back inside, they writhed into snakes and began to tear at themselves in a frenzy.

His eyes flew open, and he lay panting on the floor of the dingy cell until the terror of the dream receded. His hair was damp with sweat and his stomach burned and churned, the pain pinning him on his back. When he tried to call out to the guards, he could only manage a weak croak.

The rustle of the rushes sent a jolt of fear through him. He'd forgotten he was no longer alone. *He'll make me pay now,* Fynn thought, *for eating his gruel.*

The thought of food sent sour bile surging up into his throat, and he began to retch and shiver uncontrollably, waiting for the blows to fall.

*   *   *

Someone was bathing his face again. His head pounded as it was lifted, and he felt the press of a ladle against his cracked lips. "Drink," said a now-familiar voice, and he managed a little sip before his belly clenched. He felt hot and cold at the same time, but willed himself to look up at the monster with the blue face bending over him.

"I'll not harm ye," the man growled. As if to belie the words, his mouth twisted. A tremor shook his body and he let out a low groan.

Fynn remembered then that his cellmate had vomited too. Perhaps they'd both been poisoned by the guards.

As if on cue, the heavy door opened and the two gaolers thrust their heads in, one pale as straw, the other flaming red.

"Cor, what's that stench?" said Strawman. He pressed a filthy rag against his bulbous nose.

"The Lurker has the jits, and the young 'un's taken ill," said the one Fynn had mentally dubbed the Owl because of his wide-spaced eyes.

"Wit' any luck, it'll finish 'em off," muttered Strawman. "You there! What're you doin' to 'im?"

"Tendin' to 'im is all," his cellmate retorted.

"Well, don't," said the Owl. "You just keep t' yerself and let nature take its course."

So it's true, thought Fynn. *I'm dying.* Now he'd never have the chance to redeem himself, in this life or the next.

The door closed with a thud, and his head was lifted again.

"Drink," said his tormentor.

* * *

It was two more days before Fynn could keep down more than a few sips of water and a mouthful of gruel. He owed his life to Grinner, as the blue-faced man was called, despite the fact that Fynn had turned away from Grinner when the man himself had been in need.

Once Fynn could sit up, he forced himself to meet his cellmate's eyes. "Why did you bother with me?" he whispered weakly. "I mean, when you were sick, I didn't help you."

Grinner shrugged. "Someone done me a kindness once." He let out a sharp bark of laughter. "And gettin' thrown inta this stinkhole were another, in a way. I tried and tried b'fore to get clean, but I were ne'er able to get past the jits. Locked in 'ere, I've had no choice; the crennin's out o' me now."

"Crennin?" said Fynn. "My mother uses… used that in her healing. What are the jits?"

"What ye get when ye don't have crennin. Once yer hooked, crennin don't let ye loose."

"Is crennin what made me sick?"

"D' ye mean, did I slip some inta the soup ye nicked from me?" Grinner snorted. "Not hardly likely. I reckon ye just got a bad batch o' gruel, or might be yer belly couldn't handle the double rations."

Fynn hung his head. "I'm sorry I took your food."

"*I* weren't goin' ta eat it! Jus' don' go tryin' that again. Since I'm o'er the jits, I'm hungry now." He gave another barking laugh. "And here I be, where the food's free!"

"And so appetizing," said Fynn, pulling a face.

Despite his aching stomach, his heart felt lighter. Grinner was strange and coarse, but it was good to have someone to talk to, even if the fellow's Drinn was different from that which Fynn had spoken with his mother and Teca.

Over the following days, they began to become acquainted, each sharing the bits of their pasts they were willing to reveal. Grinner thought he was about twenty years old, but he wasn't sure. He came from a people called the å Livåri, but he hadn't grown up among them.

Fynn didn't ask why; doing so might lead their conversation to a place where he was asked about his own losses, and he wasn't ready to talk about them. He told Grinner only that his mother's people came from Langmerdor, and Grinner didn't press him for more information.

But in the second week of their shared captivity, Fynn unintentionally let something slip. He'd been explaining to Grinner about sailing, and encouraged by the wonder in his new friend's eyes, he became careless. "My father reads the waves to gauge the speed of the wind. He can tell from the way the breakers roll where dangerous shoals lurk under the water. His men call him the Sea Whisperer."

A look of incomprehension crossed Grinner's face. Too late, Fynn realized he'd used the Helgric word. "I mean… I…"

"I knowed from the start ye ain't from these parts," said Grinner. "That weren't the first time ye spake tha' strange tongue. When ye was in the grip o' the fever, ye was mostly spoutin' gibberish."

Fynn felt the blood drain from his face.

"Dinna fash," Grinner said. "Ye kept yer clap shut when the guards was about. No one heard ye, save me."

Fynn saw no reason not to tell Grinner the truth now. "I'm Helgrin," he said, feeling a curious lightness of heart upon making the confession. It was like claiming a piece of home. "I was taken a few month ago in a Drinnglennian raid on our settlement, Restaria. Perhaps you heard about it?"

Grinner shook his head. "The likes o' me don't hear much more than market gossip." He sat back and eyed Fynn curiously. "So why're ye rottin' in this stinkin' hole here in Toldarin? Are ye worth somethin' in ransom?"

"I've no idea," said Fynn, which was true. All he knew was it had been a terrible mistake to honor his mother's dying wish to come to this land. To change the subject, he said, "What happened to your face?"

Grinner rubbed the blue patch. "Tattoo gone wrong. Tha' lyin' bastard Ferka said 'e knowed what 'e were doin'. I told 'im, I says, I want me a alphyn t' honor the good King Gregor o' yore, what saved our people from the Purge. 'Course that were before they got at it 'ere in Drinnglennin."

"Got at what?"

Grinner scowled. "Blamin' the å Livåri fer whate'er vexes 'em. Making us all out t' be thieves, murderers, and worse. Nowadays it seems we'll be chased off again, only there's no place left fer us t' run. Drinnglennin were our last refuge."

"I thought you just said the High King saved you from the Purge."

"That were in King Gregor's day. We swore allegiance to 'im and 'is son Owain after 'im. To the grandson as well, but Urlion, well, 'e didn't pay us much heed. Now the last o' the Konigurs' made the Leap..." He shook his head. "It'll be the same 'ol story. Folks're findin' any reason t' make our lives a torment, takin' offense that we hold to different gods, or that we live a free life, widout lords and such. It don't bode well fer the å Livåri on the Isle."

"Is that why you're in here?" Fynn asked.

Grinner shrugged. "I've no idear what they nabbed me fer, but I s'pose if they were thinkin' t' hang me, they'd 've done it by now. I were in Dveld, the dream place, when I were taken, an' afore that I were jus' passin' through the city, mindin' me own business. When yer a rusher, not even yer own kind have much t' do wit' ye. Come t' think o' it, though, I don't recall seein' any å Livåri about. Like as not, they'd already headed south t' Glornadoor fer the winter."

Even with Grinner's company, time passed slowly in the dismal cell. To combat boredom, Fynn asked him to teach him Livårian in exchange for lessons in Helgric. When he discovered Grinner could neither read nor write, Fynn set out to teach him runic, which Grinner proved quick to learn.

It was also Fynn's idea that they practice wrestling, for he could feel his muscles growing weak from disuse. Grinner had little stamina at first; his body was still recovering from the damage his long addiction had inflicted on it. But he was game to grapple with Fynn as best he could in the cramped cell. They were always careful to listen for approaching footsteps, for if the guards thought they were fighting, they might be separated. Neither of the two cellmates wanted that, for gradually, a bond of friendship had grown between them.

Food proved to be another distraction, though not a very good one, given the quality of their gruel. In an effort to make their porridge more appealing, they imagined they were consuming more enticing dishes.

"I've got eels simmered in beer, with sage and bay leaves," said Fynn, his mouth watering at the thought.

"Cherry tarts," Grinner sighed, "hot from the oven."

"Meatballs with dumplings and cabbage, swimming in thick gravy," countered Fynn. They both took a moment to savor this in their minds.

Closing his eyes, Grinner smacked his lips. "Milk rice wit' a great knob o' butter an' a dollop o' honey!"

Fynn frowned. "You already said that at breakfast."

"I can't think o' nothin' better," admitted Grinner, then peered dolefully at the watery contents of his bowl before tipping it into his mouth.

In the evenings, they traded stories. Grinner knew only a few Livårian folk tales, but Fynn, having sat at Old Snorri's feet on many an occasion, was able to recount dozens of the old man's sagas. To his surprise, Grinner hung on every word.

"Tell the one 'bout the serpent and the owl goddess again," he'd demand, then hoot and gasp with a touching innocence as he listened with wide eyes, as though hearing the story for the first time.

One such evening, Fynn told him a memory instead, recounting the last time he'd run the wheel at the Midsommer celebrations. Afterward, his heart ached with longing for the life he'd never know again.

"We have a Gatherin' at midsummer," Grinner said cheerily, as if he'd guessed Fynn's homesickness. "Most times I was off me head, as it were always a time I could pick up a few chinkers t' pay fer crennin. But when I were still a laddie, I recollect me pa buyin' me a milk rice from a vendor in Palmador." His eyes lit up at the memory. "'Twere at the end o' the day, and I'd been bawlin'—most like I had the wearies. Me people were mummers, y'see, puttin' on all manner o' plays 'til late in the night. I passed the hat fer the coppers after."

Then his face hardened, like a door slammed shut. "'Twas in Palmador me sister and me was taken."

For a moment, Fynn thought Grinner would roll over and go to sleep, as he did sometimes when he got that angry look. But this time he kept talking, his flat, cold tone making goose bumps rise on Fynn's skin.

"Petra were four years older than me, and charged wit' mindin' me while our parents was on the stage. We was sittin' by our wagon when a woman come o'er t' us, holdin' out a little poppet wit' yellow plaits, makin' it dance about. Petra wanted tha' poppet somethin' fierce, and went t' the woman, me traipsin' along at 'er heels. Snatched us then, the bitch Margred did," Grinner growled, "an' that were the last we seen o' our kin."

"That's terrible!" Fynn cried. "What did the woman want with you?"

"Needed servants, did Margred, and she figgered we'd do. Worked us like mules from tha' day on, keepin' us locked in a cage at night so's we couldn't run. 'Twere bad fer me, but fer Petra…" Sudden tears pooled in Grinner's eyes, and he swiped at them angrily with the back of his fist.

"You… you don't have to tell me if you don't want to."

But Grinner seemed not to have heard; his eyes had gone flat as well. "The bitch used Petra t' earn the chinkers fer 'er crennin. After the first time Margred sent her t' the barn, me sister quit talkin'. Just went somewheres inside 'erself, I reckon, somewheres where she could pretend she were safe. Didn't worry Margred none that Petra went dumb." He shook his head, his expression bitter. "No, the sow were pleased, said she'd had enough of me sister's snivelin'.

"After a time, I come t' understand what were happenin' t' 'er in the barn. Night after night, tha' bitch'd come fer Petra, and when Margred pushed 'er back in the cage agin later, me sister had the stink o' men on 'er.

"Then Margred started fergettin' t' feed us some days, lest I howled at her. She were thin as a reed, an' I s'pected she were veerin' toward the Leap. I knowed if she died whiles we was in the cage, we was done fer too."

Grinner's lips curled in a cunning smile.

"So one day, I tells Petra, I says, 'Don't ye go out when Margred comes fer ye. Ye just lay still 'til I gives a cough. Then ye spring out, d' ye hear? I'll see t' the bitch.' When Margred opened the cage tha' night, I edged aside, an' me sister did as I'd tol 'er an' curled up agin' the back o' the cage. It riled Margred, as I knowed it would, an' she came inside ragin' and grabbed Petra by the foot t' drag 'er out. She tugged an' pulled, an' I could see she were in a bad way, not far from the jits.

"Quick as a minnow, I slid out o' the cage an' snatched the key from the lock. Then I give a cough, an' Petra come over Margred's head faster 'n a snake at the strike, an' give her a good kick in the face, too, as she passed." A look of satisfaction spread over the å Livåri's face. "I'll ne'er ferget the ol' shrew's shrieks when I slammed the cage door and turned the key in the lock."

Fynn swallowed hard. "So you and Petra got away then?"

Grinner's eyes took on a hollow look. "We left Margred and 'er filthy hut, but we took 'er curse wit' us. I knowed where she kept 'er crennin, see, an' I stole it. Might be I'd a mind t' sell it, but after a few hungry nights on the run wit' Petra, I recollected Margred sayin' crennin were the best food she ever et, so we chewed a few leaves, Petra and me, hopin' t' sate our hunger. That were the first time we went t' Dveld."

He looked down at his bony hands, which he'd clenched into fists. "'Twere the wrong turn we took."

Then Grinner turned abruptly away. Fynn was relieved to hear no more of his tragic tale. He had sorrows of his own haunting his dreams—he didn't need to take on Grinner's as well.

CHAPTER 7
Maura

The weeks following the announcement of the High King's betrothal were a blur of celebrations. Lavish feasts were held at the castle, with glasses repeatedly raised in salute of the soon-to-be bride and groom. Much to the citizenry's delight, Drinnkastel's guilds expressed their approval of the joining of the Konigur and Nelvor houses with a dazzling display of fireworks, and largesse was liberally distributed.

The king even organized a small tourney, curating the knights who would compete, many of whom came from Nelvorboth. He himself had taken the prize in the lists, emerging the shining hero before his new and glamorous court.

"It's because I carried your token," Roth told Maura gallantly, and she was touched to think he still had the hair ribbon she'd given him on the day they'd first met.

All around the city, new banners were replacing the gold-edged pennants of Urlion Konigur. For his royal sigil, Roth had decided to exchange the Nelvorboth black panther for a red one, poised to strike on a silver field. When Maura ventured to suggest it might lead some of his subjects to think he favored his birth kingdom over the realm, Roth laughed off her concerns. "It's no secret my mother was married to Lord Nandor, and Urlion was my father. My choice is an acknowledgment of both."

Life was gay these days in Drinnkastel, with a lively young court filling the grand hall each evening. Still, Maura missed several familiar faces at the boards, among them Lord Oscar, the elderly Earl of Brezen, who had been one of her uncle's regular dinner companions. Lord Oscar's place was now occupied by Sir Lawton, Roth's closest friend and a distant cousin. The sharp-faced Nelvorbothian was polite enough when sober, but after a few drinks, his narrow gaze would often linger on Maura's breasts.

Queen Grindasa was placed in Maura's former seat at the right of the king. Roth assured Maura that once they were married, she could reclaim it, but Maura secretly preferred her present placement with Lady Hadley and Lady Maitane. Although their conversation centered almost exclusively on gowns and the eligible men at court, it was preferable to the rough banter of Roth's gentlemen of the chamber.

What Maura really desired was more time alone with Roth. She still hadn't kept the promise she'd made to herself to tell him about her Lurker blood. But between the whirlwind of festivities and the seemingly endless preparations for the royal wedding, Maura's life was now a blur of constant activity. She rose early to go out riding with Hadley or one of the other cousins, broke her fast with Roth and assorted members of his family, and then spent the rest of her day compiling guest lists, organizing accommodations and menus for the banquets and other entertainments. She often felt like she spent more time with Master Quaney, the bluff chief steward of Drinnkastel, than she did with anyone else.

And yet, there was an energy to it all that she savored. It was true that at times she found herself longing for the solitude of Elvinor's gardens and the time she'd had to read there—but it was hard not to be caught up in the daily rush of excitement.

So it was with a pang of regret when Roth suddenly suggested that their wedding be postponed until the following spring. He broached the topic during a rare solitary walk with her in the winter garden.

"I hope you aren't too disappointed," he said, studying her face. "You see, Mother's set her heart on having all our relatives from Albrenia at the wedding, in particular her brother Palan. I squired for him in Albrenia, and I'd quite like to have him here as well. But he can't get away at present, as he's on campaign fighting rebels near the Gralian border." He lifted Maura's hand tenderly to his lips. "You don't terribly mind waiting, do you, my dear?"

Maura assured him she didn't, though this wasn't entirely true.

Compounding her disappointment was the fact that a postponement meant she would be in black for several more months. Convention no longer required her to wear the somber gowns Princess Asmara had sent her, but Grindasa, recently returned from Nelvorboth, had strongly suggested she continue to dress in mourning clothes until the week before the ceremony. "It will remind the people of your close connection with your dear late uncle, which is important for the transition, as I'm sure you understand. Then once you put aside your dreary attire, think how joyful Roth's subjects will be, seeing you entering a happier stage in your life." Maura wasn't sure she followed this logic, but it was easier to agree than to come into conflict with her future mother-in-law.

It later occurred to Maura that continuing to wear weeds also meant that she wouldn't be able to dance at the fete marking the end of the forty-day mourning period. When she mentioned this to Roth at breakfast the next day, he frowned.

"I shan't dance either then."

"But you must!" Maura insisted. "I don't mind, really."

"Maura is right, *muiero*," Grindasa agreed, setting down her buttered toast. "When the lords of the lesser realms come to court, you must bestow honor on them by dancing with their ladies. It is one of your duties."

Roth's expression darkened, and Maura thought he might object. She'd never witnessed a disagreement between her betrothed and his mother, and she hoped she wasn't about to, especially seeing as it involved her.

"It's settled then," she said brightly. "It will please me to watch you enjoying yourself."

Roth raised an eyebrow. "If you've seen Lady Elburga of Glornadoor, you'd not refer to partnering her as pleasure. It's a test of muscle to move her around the floor."

Maura laughed, for Roth seldom attempted humor, but she felt a bit guilty doing so. Lord Ien's wife, Elburga, was a genial woman whose plump figure could be attributed to the eleven children she'd brought into the world. Sir Simm, the eldest of these, was one of the few gentlemen of Roth's chamber whom Maura really liked. Unlike Sir Lawton or Sir Herst, who rarely acknowledged her, Sir Simm was always gracious.

As the days passed, Maura found herself in Roth's company less and less. "It will be different once we're married," he promised, when he had to forgo yet another ride with her to meet with the Tribus instead. Maura didn't see how being married would lessen the demands on his time, but then she remembered they would have their nights together. She felt an odd anxiety at the thought.

For she couldn't deny that occasional doubts had begun to cross her mind about the future she'd agreed to. For a brief time after she became dragonfast, she'd felt empowered, as if she could do anything she set her mind to, and being Roth's queen hadn't been the slightest consideration. The thought of a life with him didn't fill the hollow place in her heart that had been there since she'd learned the truth about how Dal died. And her yearning for Ilyria, who had been so constantly in her thoughts when she'd first come to the capital, was fading, as if her time with the dragoness and the elves had been naught but a wondrous dream.

She told herself it would be different once they were reunited, as Maura was determined they would be soon. And she would see Leif then too. Her heart ached when she remembered how angry and hurt he'd been when they last parted.

We'll see each other soon, she promised herself. *Once Roth knows about Ilyria, I'll return to the elven realm, and perhaps Roth will even come with me.* On their wedding day, she would reveal the oath she'd sworn before they'd even met—*by all the gods, to aid and succor the next true heir to the Einhorn Throne, to serve the realm of Drinnglennin, in peace and in war, for all the days of my life.*

Thinking of this, she felt her troubled heart lift.

* * *

When Maura saw the breakfast tray by her bed, she knew she'd overslept. Throwing off the covers, she dressed quickly, for the last time she hadn't appeared at the morning meal, Grindasa, recently returned from Nelvorboth, had come to see her—ostensibly to express her concern, but with the effect of making Maura feel unaccountably guilty.

The day was dreary. Rain pelted the windows and the wind whined mournfully around the turrets, ruling out a ride with Hadley. Roth had told her he would be engaged elsewhere for most of the day, so after nibbling a bit of a bread roll, Maura decided it was perfect weather to curl up with a good book. Before her uncle had made the Leap, she'd been working her way through the classics in his library, and had also discovered some historical and philosophical texts that sparked her interest. She'd even begun to refresh her Gralian from an old primer she'd found among the stacks.

As she headed for the library, she didn't meet a soul. That wasn't out of the ordinary; besides the reclusive Asmara, Maura was the only one housed in the west wing. But when she came to the central hall, it, too, was empty. Usually courtiers passed through here at all hours, and lately Grindasa's Albrenian mercenaries had been patrolling the corridors as well.

Yet the only sound of activity now was the pounding of hammers from within the royal suite. Grindasa, recently returned from Nelvorboth, had decided it required refurbishing. "It has the lingering stink of the sickroom," the queen had complained. Maura had taken offense at the callous remark, and when she replied that it had been unfortunate that her uncle had suffered from illness for so long, Grindasa's eyes widened. She swept Maura into her perfumed embrace and proclaimed, "We do miss him so, don't we, *muiera?*"

Maura knew better. From the lingering looks she'd seen passing between her future mother-in-law and Vetch, the royal lord commander, it was clear the queen was not much concerned with Maura's departed uncle.

It's none of my business, Maura reminded herself as she entered the library.

As always, her heart lifted at its whimsical beauty. Elaborate moldings of leafy tendrils encircled a magnificent painting of a sunlit forest that dominated the central wall. It transported her back to Mithralyn and the summer days she'd spent with Ilyria and her dear Leif.

She knew this library was but a shadow of the Alithineum that had once been housed here at Drinnkastel. Thousands of precious manuscripts were said to have burned in the fire that destroyed the east wing fifty years ago, most notably the *Drinnglennin Chronicles,* the magical book in which the true history of the realm was recorded. But to Maura, any library was a wondrous place, and she would ever be grateful to Urlion for having given her the key to its doors.

As she wandered slowly along the glass-encased shelves, her slippers making no sound on the dark polished floors, a slender volume with gold lettering caught her eye. It was by Guiliard de Courty, her favorite poet. Her heart gave a strange jolt as she recalled how Borne, overcome by loss, had grieved himself to sleep in her rooms. In his tortured dreams, he'd mumbled the same line of poetry several times over. How had it gone? Something about shivered trees and golden tears.

She slid the book off its shelf, her mind lingering on the image of Borne asleep on her bed, his tousled golden hair on the pillow. His face had looked so vulnerable in the candle's glow, and she'd glimpsed the boy he'd only recently left behind—the boy from her own childhood, racing with sheer abandon in the Gathering contests, wrestling and laughing and joking with the circle of other boys who always surrounded him. She remembered the times he stood behind interested breeders at her parents' lapin stalls and stared at her, while she determinedly avoided meeting his insistent gaze. He never seemed put off though; on the rare occasions she did venture to look up, she always caught the flash of his dimpled smile before she could look away.

And now he'd left Drinnglennin, and if Roth, who had shared this news, was right, he might never return.

"Lawton heard it from one of the barmaids down at the Tilted Kilt," Roth had confided. "I'm sure you knew Borne was quite the ladies' man. Left a string of broken hearts in his wake when he joined up with Glinter's mercenaries and sailed off against the express orders of Lord Vetch. It's a shame," he added ruefully, "that he's chosen a path such as this."

"Such as what?" Maura asked.

Roth released a sigh. "Well, fighting for money is hardly the most honorable of professions, is it? And Glinter broke the law by taking his ship out of Toldarin. Unfortunately, all aboard the *Bailerin* are subject to penalties upon their return." He lifted her hand and stroked her fingers. "You were rather fond of Borne, though, weren't you?"

Maura's cheeks grew warm at the suggestion. "I barely knew the man," she replied. When Roth looked as if he would say something more on the topic, she pulled her hand free and changed the subject.

Now she slid the book of poetry firmly back into its place and moved to the long windows facing the rain-washed courtyard below. *Admit it,* she thought, gazing out at the rain. *You were fond of Borne.*

She only now realized how dearly she wished he hadn't left court, for he was the only one who'd known her as a girl from Branley Tor.

Well, that girl is no more, she reminded herself.

She returned her attention to the shelves and pulled out another book at random. It was a tale by Piers Wolff, entitled *A Song of Seasons.* No doubt a silly saga of courtly love, but it would pass the time. She lifted the cover and began to read as she slowly retraced her steps back to her chambers.

The sound of voices jolted her out of Master Wolff's world of troubadours and maidens fair, and she looked up to discover she'd made a wrong turn. She vaguely recognized where she was—recalling she'd been in this corridor once before with Leif. They'd taken this route to the tourney grounds during the Twyrn.

The speakers were coming her way, and although she couldn't discern their words, they sounded angry. She debated whether she could make it to the end of the corridor before they crossed her path, for she had no desire to witness an unpleasant scene.

"Why did you not tell me as soon as you knew of this?"

Maura's heart lurched. The voice was Roth's.

"I thought the child might prove useful in some way," his mother replied soothingly.

Maura felt a further twinge of dismay, knowing she would soon be accosted by Grindasa about missing breakfast. When she spied the door to the storeroom Leif had wanted to investigate, she dragged it open and slipped inside, offering a prayer of thanks to any gods listening that it remained unlocked.

She was pulling the door shut when she heard Roth say, "He's a dangerous obstacle. He should have disappeared the moment Vetch came across him in Restaria."

Maura froze then, the door still slightly ajar. Who were they talking about, and what did Roth mean by "disappeared"?

"The boy speaks Drinn, and his mother, too," said Grindasa. "I imagine Vetch felt it prudent to bring them home."

"His *mother*? This is worse than I imagined." Roth uttered a crude oath. "Who is she? *Where* is she?"

"Calm yourself, my son. Together, we will see this matter dealt with, but it must be handled delicately."

Maura would later wish that she'd pulled the door closed, so that she had never have heard her fiancé's callous reply.

"Why?" Roth demanded. "Doesn't his throat slit like any other?"

CHAPTER 8
Leif

"It's out of the question!" Master Morgan paced furiously back and forth between Leif and Elvinor, his long cloak swinging behind him. "It would be beyond foolhardy to trespass in the dragons' secret refuge. They would never let you leave!"

Leif ignored the thrill of alarm the wizard's ferocity evoked. "Rhiandra would be with me. She says she must go—that it's a matter of life and death. Surely as one of them, she can bring her dragonfast with her to Belestar."

"It will mean your own death should you accompany her!" Master Morgan spun toward Elvinor. "I beg you, sir, dissuade your son from this reckless course of action, or better yet, forbid him to pursue it!"

Elvinor's response surprised them both. "It's true there is great risk in this venture, but I trust Leif to make his own choices. He is dragonfast, Mortimer, which means his first loyalty lies with Rhiandra before all others, including you. If he truly believes he must make this journey, I cannot find it in my heart to discourage him." The elven king folded his elegant hands before him. "As a matter of fact, Leif discussed this venture with me before the two of you flew to Helgrinia, and I already gave him my blessing. The dragons *must* be convinced of the elves' good intentions toward them, which is why I am offering them safe haven in Mithralyn. Without it, they may well depart over the Vast Sea. There is little enough magic and mystery left in the world. And with the rise of Lazdac, the dragons may be all that stands between us and chaos."

The wizards, seeing he would have no support from Elvinor, turned to Leif and tried another tack. "What of your oath, Leif? To the one true king?"

Leif forced himself to meet Master Morgan's stern gaze. "I will honor it when and if I am called on to do so. But since that time has not yet come, I want to help Rhiandra."

In his heart, Leif hoped the call from Drinnkastel would never come. He had no cause to feel antipathy toward King Roth, invested only days before. It wasn't the new king's fault that Maura had chosen to stay with the Nelvorbothian in Drinnkastel rather than return with Leif to Mithralyn. That had been her decision—and it still rankled, as did the fact that she'd sent no word to him since they'd parted nearly a month ago. Yet he still hoped that once the formal mourning period for Urlion Konigur came to a close, she would come back to the elven kingdom. If not for him, then for Ilyria.

He suspected the bronze dragon was as unhappy with Maura's absence as he was, but he couldn't say for certain: Ilyria had been in deep seclusion for months, and Rhiandra said she would only reappear when they flew north to Belestar.

Master Morgan stood with his back to Leif, looking out over the coloring forests of the elven realm. When he turned at last, the wizard appeared to have recovered his usual calm. "It seems you are determined on this course of action. If I thought the dragons would allow it, I'd go with you." He released a resigned sigh. "Promise me you'll be on your guard at all times, and never stray from Rhiandra. The dragons won't harm you, as long as she is by your side, but if not... who can be sure?"

Leif was relieved to have the wizard's blessing, however grudging. "I'll take care, master."

He turned to his father, who offered him a close embrace. Whatever lay ahead, Leif would carry with him the loving affection that had grown between them over the past months. He felt honored that Elvinor was entrusting him to serve as the elven emissary to the estranged dragons, and hoped he would be equal to the task.

"Before you go," said Elvinor, "I have something for you, my son." He lifted a silver cloak from a chest and draped it over Leif's shoulders. It was as light as a feather. "Don't let its weight deceive you," said the elf king. "The cloak is woven from seiden, a fine grass that grows only in Mithralyn and is harvested by faeries under the full moon. It will serve to keep you warm on your northbound journey." He then reached into the chest once more and drew from it a sword. "And I want you to have this as well."

Leif accepted the weapon and slid it free of its scabbard. The blade radiated a wondrous light. It was so beautiful he couldn't imagine sullying it with blood.

"Thank you," he said softly. He saw there were runes inscribed on the blade. "*Tàn ddraig elduri,*" he murmured, then looked up in wonder.

"Yes," Elvinor said, "this sword goes by the name of *Dragon's Fang*. A most appropriate choice for you. It was my first blade, and my father's before me."

"Thank—thank you for thinking me worthy of it, Father," Leif said when he'd found his tongue. "I will cherish it always."

Master Morgan clapped his hands together. "A seiden cloak a*nd* an elven blade—I confess I'm feeling reassured to know you'll have these protections with you. I guess all is settled then." He raised an eyebrow at Elvinor. "What would you say to a proper elven banquet for our young adventurer before he and the dragons depart?"

"What is your pleasure, Leif?" the king asked. "Roast pheasant, marigold ice, and butternut stuffed cabbage rolls? The morels are in season as well."

Leif grinned. "I'll miss Mithralyn's larder."

"We shall feast tonight," Elvinor promised, "and again when you return home."

Home. Leif realized he *had* grown to think of this mystical realm as a home. He belonged here in a way he never had in Tonis Vale. *All that's missing to make Mithralyn perfect,* he thought, *is Gran.*

In truth, there was one other person whose presence would complete his happiness, but he doubted Maura felt the same way about living among the elves. Perhaps that was why she needed to stay in Drinnkastel. To find out where *she* truly belonged in the world.

He only hoped it would be someplace not too far from him.

* * *

When Leif arrived the next evening at the glade, having bid his father and the wizard farewell, he found Rhiandra alone. He listened with a sinking heart as the bluewing explained why.

"Ilyria is not returning with us to Belestar. She has seen something ominous in her dreams, and fears she will attract danger to you if she comes along. She worries, too, that our siblings will think she has been abandoned by her bindling, which will make a mockery of our purpose. It will be up to us, you and I, to present a convincing case that it is safe to bind again, and to remind my siblings that with binding comes something we have sorely missed: a heartfelt connection with humankind." Her tone held both pride and affection, and Leif glowed with pleasure, knowing Rhiandra shared his deep sense of kinship.

"I don't think Maura has abandoned Ilyria," he said, more confidently than he felt. By now the late king had been interred, and the transfer of power to his Nelvor successor had proceeded without incident. There was nothing more to keep Maura in Drinnkastel—nothing except her own desires.

Leif knew he should inform his father and Master Morgan of this change in plans, but he suspected they would reconsider their blessings on this journey north if they knew Ilyria was not going. It was best to depart as soon as possible. It would take them over a week to reach Belestar as it was, for they would have to lie up during the daylight hours to keep Rhiandra concealed until they reached the open seas.

As the last light faded from the sky, they took flight over the night-shrouded land. Crouched astride Rhiandra's broad back with the wind streaming in his face, Leif was grateful for his new cloak and for the sunstone he wore inside his tunic. Dragonflight was a chilling experience even in the mildest of weather, and beyond the borders of Mithralyn, autumn had arrived.

Leif was excited to finally see the great frozen land at the top of the world that his grandda had told so many tales about. Of course, Grandda hadn't known it was the home of dragons; his stories about the mysterious isle of Belestar, and the treacherous seas that surrounded it, involved great white bears twice the height of a grown man and enormous tusked sea cows with oily pelts that sang to ships as they passed.

After the first night of flight, they sheltered on an unscalable peak under the shadow of Amueke, the highest mountain on the Isle. Clouds covered the skies to the south, but northward the wide Eisendell Valley spread before them. Somewhere down there was the bridge Leif and Master Morgan had crossed a lifetime ago. From his perch above the world, Fynn grinned, recalling how frightened he'd been.

When they crossed from over Branley Tor into Valeland, he begged Rhiandra to circle west toward Tonis Vale before they rose above the Mynnyd Range. Even though there was nothing to be seen of the shrouded land below, he felt comforted knowing he was closer to his old gran than he'd been for nearly a year.

"I'll be back for you one day, Gran," he whispered. "I promise."

Before dawn of the fourth day, they passed the northernmost tip of Drinnglennin, Rhiandra racing against the light to reach a small island where they could shelter until darkness fell again. Leif doubted any human had ever set foot on this rocky outcrop strewn with shells and sea wrack. *And surely none would want to linger here,* he thought, not with the continuous din of birds' whistles and shrills piercing the air.

Rhiandra left for a brief time to hunt, then returned, folded her wings, and almost immediately fell into a deep slumber. Leif knew he should try to sleep as well, but he couldn't imagine the possibility in the midst of the unceasing noise. So instead he set off to explore, provoking great flocks of birds to rise and wheel above him, shrieking their displeasure. Shards of broken eggshells were everywhere, as were countless abandoned nests. When Fynn scrambled over a rise and burst into a colony of lolling sea lions, he was so startled that he slipped into the shallows, shouting as the freezing water flooded his boots. The seals roared in response and humped into the sea.

Fynn removed his sodden boots, then stretched out in the sun to wait for them to dry out. He managed to doze a bit in the golden afternoon light, but the birds and the blustering wind scouring the island kept him from true sleep.

As the day waned, he made his way slowly back to Rhiandra, allowing the treasures of the tide pools to distract him along the way: sea stars, purple-shelled snails, golden slugs, and tiny creatures he dubbed "sea dragons" for their long snouts and curling tails. Wide swathes of fiery orange lichens adorned the rocks near the shore, and a spreading meadow lay inland, crowned with delicate white and yellow flowers that bent and swayed in perpetual dance with the swirling air.

By the time he'd returned to the sleeping dragon, his pockets were spilling with shells and pebbles, petals and strands of wrack. He spread his bounty out on the ground to admire it.

But his pleasure faded when he realized this might be one of the last times he would experience a day such as this, a sweet echo of the life he'd left behind in Tonis Vale. He was no longer a child without care for the morrow. Being dragonfast entailed more than soaring through the clouds, and the vow he'd sworn placed a sober responsibility on his shoulders.

Beside him, Rhiandra stirred in her dreams, reminding him there was also much to look forward to. In repose, the bluewing was impossibly beautiful, and Leif felt his heart swell as he drank in her magnificence. Her azure scales shimmering with reflected flecks of light, as though she was clad in shards of the sea itself, and she emanated a vibrant energy, even in sleep, to which he thrilled, his blood singing. He felt both awe and tenderness for every part of her—her razor-sharp talons, her delicate frilled ears (about which she was exceedingly vain), the single, pearled horn curving up from her forehead like an elegant crown, and her long, sinuous tail.

Who would have believed that this was the turn my life was destined to take?

Leif knew he should be feeling proud and brave and honorable and all of those other traits associated with the dragonfast who had gone before him, but he still feared he was woefully unprepared for the calling. He'd learned to wield a sword and shoot a bow in the months he'd spent in Mithralyn, but he'd always prefer setting a new song to memory or deciphering the runes of an elven tale to the supposed glories of battle. The truth was, he didn't feel so very different from the boy he'd been the day he'd left Valeland with Master Morgan. Despite his heart's blooding and the successful completion of the trials the dragons had set for Maura and him, becoming dragonfast hadn't miraculously transformed him into a warrior.

The words inscribed above the lintel of the wizard's cottage sprang to his mind. *The sharpest weapon is a finely honed mind.* He knew the truth of this now, for in Mithralyn, he'd learned the value of knowledge. His father's library had opened up wondrous worlds to be explored between the pages of books. And he had taken heart in Master Morgan's parting words to him.

"You're better prepared than you may think," the wizard had proclaimed. "More importantly, your heart is true, to yourself and those you care for. Be guided by it, and you cannot go astray."

Watching the sea birds circle, Leif wondered if a steadfast heart would be enough to convince Rhiandra's kin to bind and return to coexistence with men and elves. He would have felt much more confident of success if Maura had been with him. He didn't want to think it, but it did feel as though she'd abandoned them.

That evening, they resumed their journey earlier than usual. No vessel could survive the rough waters of the White Sea in this season, so there was little fear that Rhiandra would be spotted. As she winged through wispy clouds, Leif closed his streaming eyes against the bitter wind.

They flew on for hours. At this point they'd come so far north that Rhiandra could continue flying even into the grey dawn light, for no human lived in this part of the Known World. She dropped low over the sea to spare Leif from the increasing cold, and he saw a necklace of islands below, the spangled sun igniting their cataracts and glittering lakes through pale veils of fog, the sea frothing against their cliffs banded with smoky mist.

On they flew, over majestic blue glaciers from which thundering rivers spumed, bearing massive plates of ice on their roiling backs. Leif spied great whales humping across the sea toward warmer waters to bear their young, and skeins of white geese winging south.

Over the following days, they stopped only long enough for Rhiandra to feed, alighting on juts of rock striving up out of the churning waters. Leif had a good store of waybread and dried fruits in his pack, but he ate sparingly all the same. He quenched his thirst at frozen pools they found along the way, using the heat of his sunstone to warm the ice so that he could crack through it. He saved the skin of elven crabapple wine—a healing elixir and pleasant stimulant—for a time when he might have real need of it. There was no telling how long it would be before they returned to Drinnglennin's shores.

He'd begun to compose songs in his head about the wonders of the White Sea to sing with the elves. It had occurred to him that he might not make it back to Mithralyn, but the closer they got to Belestar, the more he allowed his elven side to rule his spirit. They would find a way to meet whatever challenges lay ahead. Rhiandra was with him, and surely, they would come to no harm from her own kin.

When Rhiandra finally announced their destination was near, Leif felt a thrill of excitement tinged with fear. He had known they must be close, as it never really became day—dawn brought only a dusky twilight for a few hours before full darkness fell again. But the announcement sparked within him a rising urgency. Soon he would be in the presence of unbound dragons, which meant they would be far wilder and fiercer than Rhiandra and Ilyria.

On the final break in their journey, he lay curled contentedly at the dragon's side. "How shall I address them?" he asked. "Your sisters and brothers?"

"You will say nothing until I have properly introduced you," Rhiandra replied sternly. She wrapped her long tail around him, as if to shelter him from an imagined threat, but the pale smoke spiraling from her nostrils signaled a placid mood.

"Tell me again about the others," he urged.

Rhiandra gave an indulgent snort. "Again? Very well then. The eldest is Isolde, and she is a silverwing. She is the wisest of us all, although some of my siblings would like to think otherwise—especially Gryffyn, who shared her egg."

"Gryffyn is grey," said Leif.

"As is his temperament. He is ever resentful that Isolde emerged before him."

"But why?" Leif asked. "If I had a twin sister, I would delight in sharing everything with her. Besides, I thought it made no difference, that among dragons none has authority over another."

"This is true, but a firstborn's prominence is recognized nevertheless. After Gryffyn—"

"Comes Emlyn," said Leif, warming to the topic, "and she is a greenwing. She has a fierce spirit. Without her courage, her last dragonfast, Obinon, would have fallen to Skrimfil, a raging monster with the head of a demon and the body of a scorpion!"

"Perhaps *you* should be telling *me* about my kin," Rhiandra suggested dryly.

"No, no!" Leif protested. "You reveal something new each time. I won't interrupt again."

Rhiandra made a doubtful rumbling. "Aed is the fourth born, and only Zal is bigger than him. Aed's fiery red scales reflect his fierce nature. He loves nothing better than to hunt and kill."

A chill ran down Leif's spine. "What does he hunt?"

"Not the likes of you, young one, have no fear. Dragons have never preyed on men or elves." Rhiandra ruffled and stretched her leathery wings. "Next comes Ilyria, then Syrene, who is held in highest regard, followed by Una, Menlo, Ciann, and Zal. I am the youngest of the eleven, as you know. Una is blue-green like the sea, and after Ilyria, the most sensitive. Menlo is as deep as his indigo scales, and Ciann as pure as his white. Zal..." Rhiandra paused, and her breath darkened. "Zal is by far the most rapacious of my clutch. His distrust of other species makes him the most dangerous. You are not to go near him."

Leif needed no more urging to avoid the black dragon. "Is Syrene so highly regarded because of her clutch?"

Rhiandra nodded. "She is the only one among us who has been fruitful. Her clutch is the first since the dawn of the After Age, and its survival is our only hope for the continuation of our species."

"Will the eggs have hatched by now?"

"Ilyria thinks if they had, she would have seen this in her dreams. It's possible that we must wait many years. It all depends."

"You mean, because dragon young will not hatch unless it's safe? All the more reason why your brothers and sisters should bind."

"Not all would agree with you. Syrene, more than any of them, has reason to distrust humans. Her mate, Stondin, as you will recall, was slain by a maddened horde of Delnogothians in the Before. This, she will never forgive."

This tragedy, Leif knew, had occurred during the massacres on the continent that brought on the close of the last age, when magical creatures, including humans, were relentlessly hunted down and slaughtered. According to Master Morgan, ignorance and senseless fear had been at the root of this horror, just as it was in the more recent persecution of the å Livåri.

"Did Syrene ever bind?" Leif asked.

"She did indeed. But with the arrival of her clutch, she has chosen to forget this." Rhiandra's breath steamed in the cold air. "Dragonfast rarely survive their dragons, and few mortals understand the terrible loss we suffer when our bindlings pass from the Known World."

This was news to Leif. He was Rhiandra's first binding, and the thought of her suffering after he made the Leap prompted him to throw his arms around her neck. "I don't want to be the cause of any pain for you. I will always love you, and live in your heart, even beyond death."

The dragon's filigreed wing gently descended to cover him. It was the first time Rhiandra had enfolded him so, and together they savored the pleasure it brought them both. The air was bitter cold, but huddled against Rhiandra in his elven cloak, Leif had never felt so warm. Before long, he fell into a deep, restful sleep.

It was still pitch black when Rhiandra nudged him awake. "We don't have far to go now, and I would have this parley over and done with." She blew a short blast of fire into the smudged sky, a sure sign of her disquiet.

When she lowered her head again, Leif reached up and brushed his fingers over the frill of her ear. "All will be well as long as we're together," he promised her. "Before you know it, you'll be free to fly wherever and whenever you please." A sudden thought made him smile. "We'll go to Valeland and you can meet my gran!"

If the dragon had doubts about the outcome of their meeting with her siblings, she didn't share them. Leif leaned his forehead against hers and felt the warmth of her brimstone breath on his cheeks, then clambered onto her back.

They were one day away from Belestar.

* * *

"Wait here," Rhiandra cautioned Leif, "until I come for you."

Her counsel was unnecessary, for there was nowhere to go. The vast island of Belestar was mantled under a thick cover of snow and ice. From the small cavern where Leif sheltered, he could see no living thing. To the far horizon, the world was only black and white beneath the light of the full moon. But he knew that, somewhere out there, the last dragons were waiting.

He understood why Rhiandra had to set off alone to seek her kin. She would have to answer for not returning sooner to Belestar, and she did not want to present Leif until their certain displeasure was appeased.

Long hours passed while he waited for her return, but he spent them happily engaged tinkering with a song he'd been composing along the way. He was quite pleased with the lyrics thus far, and knew he could count on Frandelas and Galen to help polish it up once he returned to Mithralyn. He was just trying to decide which had a nicer ring to it—*daring* Leif or *dashing* Leif—when he heard the familiar sound of rushing wind that announced Rhiandra's return.

He slipped out of the cave and scanned the spreading sky, but could see nothing beyond the luminous moon. The sound rolled toward him, growing in volume until he realized it signaled more than one dragon in flight. Instinctively he stepped back under the shadowed ledge, and not a moment too soon. Two enormous dragons catapulted out of the north and shot past, leaving a trail of billowing vapor in their wake. His quickened breath filled his ears as the rumbling of the severed air faded. In the stillness that followed, Leif felt a sudden dread. What had spurred the dragons to streak across the sky as though the hounds of Blearc were on their heels?

Staring up at the indifferent stars, Leif pulled his elven cloak closer against the whining wind, but it couldn't warm the chill that crept into his heart.

CHAPTER 9
Morgan

At Elvinor's insistence, Morgan lingered in Mithralyn after Leif and Rhiandra departed for the far north. Thus it was that he learned that Ilyria had remained behind and was still secluded in the great golden wood. This was alarming news, for without the guidance of the older, wiser dragoness, the chances that Leif and Rhiandra would convince the other dragons to bind were surely diminished. Morgan feared they were heading into grave danger—but the matter was now out of his hands, and he would have to put faith in Leif, as the lad's father had done, and the young blue.

While in Mithralyn the wizard took time, at last, to mourn the passing of his sovereign. In his prime, Urlion Konigur had been a sound ruler of the realm, and for this, Morgan would always honor him. Over the years their friendship had endured, despite occasional disagreements and the wizard's long absences from the Isle. But now that the reign of the Konigurs had come to an end, Morgan had to determine how he could best serve Drinnglennin and its new young High King.

Morgan knew little of this son of Grindasa to whom he'd sworn Maura, Leif, and Halla's fealty. The Nelvor clan had proven untrustworthy in the past, yet it was possible that young Roth would break the mold. After all, the Tribus had settled on him, and Maura, too, must have seen much in him that was admirable, otherwise she wouldn't have insisted on remaining in Drinnkastel to show her support. Still, Morgan couldn't shake his uneasiness over the accession of a Nelvor to the Einhorn Throne. The clan's rapacious love of power had not appeared diminished at the time of the Twyrn. And he hadn't forgotten that Nelvorbothian guards had searched for him in the streets of the capital after Urlion's death. The question remained as to why.

After careful consideration, Morgan resolved to return to Drinnkastel, proclaim his own allegiance to King Roth, and ascertain that all was well with Maura. He had dedicated most of his life to the service of the High Kings of Drinnglennin, and now, more than ever, his counsel should prove useful. He also wished to meet with the Tribus regarding the Nelvorbothian attack on Restaria. An all-out war with the Helgrins could easily be the unfortunate result of this ill-advised aggression, but Morgan could offer advice on how to preserve the decade-long peace. King Roth would need to reaffirm Drinnglennin's alliances with Gral and Albrenia, without becoming embroiled in their infighting. Morgan would encourage the young king to act as an arbitrator to resolve any differences between the fractious states, for should the rumors that the Albrenians and Aksel, the yarl's nephew had joined forces against King Crenel prove to be true, it boded ill for the fragile stability of the entire Known World.

Morgan pondered his remaining obligations. Urlion's long-lost second wife and their son had perished in the terrible ravaging of Restaria, so at least this search could be laid to rest. But he had still to uncover the truth about Urlion's enchanter and see him or her brought to justice. And he had a promise to Nicu to follow up on: to discover what had become of those missing à Livåri who hadn't ended up as slaves in Albrenia. The wizard had learned from Whit that Nicu was alive and well on the continent, fighting to free their captive kinswomen, but many more à Livåri men and women had simply vanished.

Morgan also had to face the unpleasant task of informing Lady Inis that her daughter had declined to become the first lady of Cardenstowe, and had instead taken up with a band of rebel å Livåri across the sea. He had a reasonable idea of how this news would be received.

When the day came at last for the wizard to depart Mithralyn, Whit was nowhere to be found. Morgan had succeeded in convincing him to stay on a while longer, but the young lord had been avoiding him ever since Morgan had revealed that his duel with Lazdac had cost him his powers. Whit clearly felt he'd been deceived, since Morgan had led him to believe he himself would be instructing him. At this point, Whit had probably decided that a wizard so foolish as to surrender his powers had nothing of value to teach him anyway.

Before the wizard departed, he left a book for Whit with the elven king. He could only hope would make some amends for his failure to teach the lad himself. It was a risk to share its contents with a wizard of Whit's talents, but one Morgan felt he had no choice but to take.

He then set off, taking a ship down the coast. His journey to Chelmsdale-on-Erolin was without incident, but when he arrived at Port Taygh, he found his old friends in a state of uncharacteristic agitation.

"Thank the gods you've come, Mortimer," said Maisie, drawing him quickly through the door. "We've a right hill of correspondence from your friends around the Isle, and there's more coming in every day!"

When Horace joined them in the garden, the big man thrust a bundle of papers into the wizard's hands. "These are the ones we think are most pressing." Drops of sweat beaded the man's brow. "I've been at the stoves," he explained. "I'll get us some refreshments while you look those over, then I'll share the other news I've gleaned since last we met."

Horace returned shortly, bearing a tray of almond-stuffed olives, ripe coilhorn cheese, ginger preserves, and steaming hot flatbread. As Morgan sipped a glass of *mulate* wine, his friends detailed the trouble brewing in all directions. The wizard wasn't surprised by their catalogue of concerns, but he found it disheartening all the same.

"Glornadoor and Karan-Rhad are one season away from famine on a massive scale," Horace reported, "unless the lords there lay by a third of their harvests. The crop yield this year in Palmador has been poor, due to the rivers spilling their banks, and in much of the southern realms, the new plantings were washed away by torrential rains. Cardenstowe hasn't yet recovered from the flooding they experienced last spring, and the old farmers say to expect more of the same across the west in the coming weeks."

"Here in Lorendale, we've been spared the worst of the wet," Maisie added. "But rumors fly that we can expect a rain of Helgrin arrows at any moment. Many of the common folk living along the coast have abandoned their fishing boats and farms, and they've flocked inland to set up makeshift homes outside Lorendale's walls. Lady Inis and young Lord Nolan are having a time of it trying to convince their people there's no threat of imminent invasion. They've even sent soldiers to fortify the coastal towns. What began as an exodus to seek safe haven in Lorendale Castle is beginning to look more like a siege."

I shall have to arrange for assistance for Lady Inis, Morgan thought, adding this to his list of concerns. "What can you tell me regarding the whereabouts of the å Livåri?"

Horace sighed. "I'm afraid we've run into a thorny hedge there. There's a sizeable encampment down in Glornadoor, but other than that, all we've been able to turn up is ransacked camps, abandoned wagons, and a few bodies—all of them either old folks or babes." His face hardened. "The bastards!"

Morgan nodded in grim agreement as he sorted through the letters on his lap. "So it remains a mystery to be—" He stopped short when he spotted a familiar seal, a silver doe, on a thin missive. He held up the letter. "When did this arrive?"

Horace frowned in consideration. "I believe it was two days ago."

Morgan broke the seal, scanned the closely written page, then rose to his feet.

Horace heaved up from his seat as well. "Here—where are you going, Mortimer?"

"My apologies," said Morgan. "Urgent business, by order of the Tribus. I'll pack up the rest of the correspondence, then be on my way at once."

But Maisie protested, pointing out that Holly, at least, deserved a few hours' rest before making the three-day journey north to the Tor of Brenhinoedd—and as long as Morgan had to wait for the little horse to recover, why did he not partake in some refreshment himself? So he accepted his friends' offer of a steam bath, savored a bowl of Horace's ginger-infused fish chowder, and drank several goblets of Maisie's fine wine. Then, after giving strict instructions to be wakened before the candle had burned by half, he retired to his chamber and fell dead asleep.

He left Port Taygh in the wee hours and followed the coastal road. It seemed to him there was less traffic on the road than there should have been. The few wagons he passed were empty, and their drivers shared the same gaunt, hungry look.

He reached Stonehoven at midday. At the Braeburn Inn, he found a coach awaiting him, as had been promised in the thin missive. The discreet but eminently recognizable T scrolled on its doors ensured that he would meet with no challenge along the Great Middle Way through Nelvorboth to the capital. Morgan confirmed that his coachman knew their destination, then tethered Holly behind the carriage and climbed aboard. The coachmen gave the command for the horses to walk on, and they lurched into motion.

The cabin's interior was opulent, with soft seat pillows and a velvet-pleated ceiling replete with gem-studded stars and crescents. Violet silk covered the walls, complementing the rose curtains that hung over the windows. Morgan settled in comfortably and took advantage of their leisurely pace to ponder the reason for this summons passed on to him by Gilly. Did Urlion's enchanter suspect Morgan had uncovered their treason? Whoever it was who had placed the enchantment on the late king, they had to be a wizard of great power, with access to Urlion. This almost certainly implicated one of the Tribus. But Morgan couldn't be certain; the strain of breaking the spell he'd been under for all those years had killed Urlion before Morgan could learn who had betrayed him.

Morgan was well aware he might be heading into a trap, but there was no way he could ignore a call to the capital without raising the suspicions of the one he meant to expose.

It would all become clearer soon enough.

Someone had thoughtfully placed a food basket on the floor of the coach, and he had a flask of Maisie's *mulate* in the pocket of his cloak. After enjoying a light refreshment of cold chicken and briny pickles, he settled back and allowed the rhythmic swaying of the carriage to lull him into a deep, dreamless slumber.

It was the last unbroken sleep he'd enjoy for many days to come.

* * *

When Morgan awoke, the carriage was at a standstill. He was at once on his guard, for he couldn't possibly have slept all the way to Drinnkastel. Considering that his driver had simply stopped to relieve himself, Morgan eased the window curtain slightly open.

Moonlight seeped into the compartment, accompanied by the song of crickets and the mossy scent of recent rain. Wherever they were, the carriage was far from any town. *Far from any witnesses as well*, he thought darkly.

95

He didn't intend to wait meekly inside the carriage for whatever lay in store. With an agility that belied his years, he flung open the coach door and leapt to the ground, brandishing his staff before him.

He found himself sparring with air. The coachman was nowhere to be seen, and the pair of greys pulling the carriage had been released from their traces and presumably led away. Thankfully, Holly was still tethered at the rear. The pony pricked her ears, and Morgan lay a reassuring hand on her muzzle.

They were no longer on the Great Middle Way; indeed, the road was barely more than a track. It seemed he had simply been abandoned here—the question was why? Had his driver, instructed to do away with him, lost heart and fled?

A sudden light bloomed between the trees. He was to have an answer to his questions soon.

"Now, my girl," he murmured to Holly as he untied her, "it's possible that trouble is coming our way." He stroked her velvet nose as he watched the light bobbing toward them. "I've still got a few tricks up my sleeve, but should anything befall me, you're to find your way to Mithralyn, do you hear?"

The approaching light concealed its bearer in shadow, and Morgan prepared himself for the possibility of an attack.

A familiar voice called softly. "Before you accuse me of melodrama for bringing you to such a secluded place, you must hear my reasons."

The light was abruptly extinguished, and the following darkness was so complete that Celaidra moved into Morgan's arms before he could stop her. Gently, he held her away from him, and at that moment the moon appeared from behind the clouds to reveal her beautiful, strained face.

"I would never dream of calling you melodramatic, my lady," Morgan said with a smile, "but perhaps these reasons would be better shared somewhere more private?"

Celaidra took his arm. "There is a small croft just ahead."

Morgan was not surprised to find the cottage they entered set up with all the comforts a noble lady might require, including a crackling fire. Only when they'd crossed the threshold did Celaidra release him to pour them each a goblet of fine summer wine.

The wizard accepted the glass she held out to him, and saw her hand was trembling. "My lady? You are unwell?"

The elven princess shook her head, but sank slowly into a chair by the fire. "My illness is of the heart," she confessed, "although it is somewhat eased now that you are near, Mortimer." She set down her glass to push back her hood, revealing her lustrous hair. "I was so worried you wouldn't receive the message I sent through Sir Gilbin, and now I regret the danger responding to it has placed you in."

Morgan waited in silence for her to explain.

"You were ever a good listener." Celaidra's smile was bittersweet. "I'll get right to the point of my urgent summons. We did not debate long on who should succeed Urlion. Audric put Roth forward as the obvious choice, and even Selka, although sullen as usual, offered no argument." She lay her head back against the cushions and lifted her gaze to the low ceiling. "At first, it all seemed to be going as Audric had predicted—a remarkably smooth transition. Lord Roth was crowned High King, and on the same day, the leadership of the Tribus transferred from Selka to Audric.

"His first duty as High Elder was to formally introduce us to our new sovereign—which meant revealing to the new king the elves' presence in Drinnglennin. Under the Konigurs, I trusted that my people's existence here would continue to be a secret known only to our king, you, and the Tribus—and more recently to those you sheltered there this past year—but with King Roth... I fear the worst."

Morgan sat forward. "He plans to expose the elves?"

Celaidra shook her head. "No, no. Our young prince expressed delight that we still inhabit the Isle, and he assured me

Mithralyn will remain a secret, just as it has since the dawn of the After Age under the Konigur kings." She looked down at her hands, clenched tightly in her lap.

"And yet?" Morgan gently prodded.

Celaidra's amber eyes were filled with misgiving. "A recent appointment has given me cause to doubt our High King's assertion that magical folk are welcome in Drinnglennin. Gravlin has been removed as High Monter of the Elementa Temple, and replaced by Talek, a nephew of Nandor Nelvor. It seems Grindasa has long been a patron of his."

"Talek of Crydwyn? He's quite the zealot, is he not?"

Celaidra's lips formed a grim line. "He's long advocated for stamping out all magical practice in the realm. We were stunned when Roth selected such a man to lead the Elementa Temple."

"Perhaps the appointment is meant to appease Princess Grindasa?"

"Queen Grindasa," Celaidra amended. "She began to style herself thus immediately following the coronation."

Morgan frowned. "Are you saying you fear King Roth will be monarch in name only?"

Celaidra's little shrug evolved into a shiver. "It's too soon to tell. Roth seems an intelligent man, and he's already captured the hearts of Drinnkastelites, particularly those of the ladies. His fine face and figure have them practically swooning. The people have long been starving for a vigorous young ruler and the return of a lively, elegant court. And now that King Roth plans to wed, it's expected he'll produce an heir as soon as possible. The people crave stability in the succession, after these long years of uncertainty."

"Roth is to take a wife?"

Celaidra blinked twice. "Surely you knew? Your Maura, of the dragonfast, has accepted his offer of marriage. The formal announcement will be made tomorrow."

Morgan was careful to conceal the frisson of alarm her words set off. "I see. Has Maura... Does the High King know about the dragons then?"

"Not from me, and since there's been no mention made of them at council, I suspect not from Maura either. Not yet, at any rate. But if they are to wed, of course he'll soon learn of them."

Indeed, thought Morgan, for Maura bore the same concentric circles on her breast as Leif had on his. "It seems I'll have to go back with you to the capital at once."

He made to rise, but Celaidra seized his hand.

"You mustn't dare, Mortimer! I haven't told you the worst of it. Under no circumstances are you to come to Drinnkastel."

"And why is this?"

Celaidra dropped her voice as though she feared the walls had ears. "It's known you were the last person to see our former High King alive."

"Yes, that's true. I was with Urlion when he made the Leap."

"Someone saw you leave his quarters. My dear, I've come to warn you that you must flee. A warrant has been issued for your arrest. The king's guards are seeking you, and word is spreading across the realm of your supposed offense."

Morgan already knew the answer, but he asked the question all the same. "What is this offense?"

Celaidra's grip on his hands tightened. "Regicide, Mortimer. You've been charged with the murder of Urlion Konigur."

CHAPTER 10
Whit

Even since he'd learned about Master Morgan's lost powers, Whit had found it impossible to meet the wizard's eye. He told himself it was because Master Morgan hadn't held up his end of the bargain that had brought Whit to Mithralyn in the first place. But in his heart, he knew that wasn't the real reason. The truth was, the wizard's tale reminded him too much of what had happened to him in the High Priestess's musty chambers in Altipa. Whit suspected he'd come close to meeting a similar fate, and every time he thought of that frightening day, his blood turned to ice.

He was glad now that he'd never told Master Morgan of his own near-miss with blood-binding. If no one ever spoke of it, he could almost pretend it had never happened. He'd already sworn Cortenus to secrecy, and the tutor had mercifully made no further mention of the incident.

So it was that after pining for Master Morgan's return for many months, Whit now found himself strangely relieved when the wizard departed.

It marked Whit's own time to take his leave of Mithralyn as well. While his stay with the elves had been elucidating, he'd never felt like he belonged there, not in the way Cortenus clearly did, as evidenced by how quickly his tutor had seized on Whit's suggestion that he remain for a while longer in Mithralyn. The lure of Elvinor's library was largely responsible, and Whit wouldn't be surprised, if he were ever to return to Mithralyn, to find Cortenus right where he'd left him, poring over ancient manuscripts and sipping honeyed blackcurrant tea.

Cortenus's only concern was about Whit's traveling alone. Whit promised to hire some swords along the way, though he had no real intention of doing so. He possessed enough wit and magic to fend for himself on the road, and it had been far too long since he'd been able to keep his own company. The past months living in the midst of so many elves had been wearing for a wizard who had more serious interests to pursue than engaging in playful repartee and long nights of music, dancing, and aimless merriment.

Elvinor bid him a fond farewell, which Whit found himself returning with equal sincerity. The elven king bestowed upon him several fine gifts, including the books Whit had gathered, and a slim, battered volume from Morgan. Whit frowned at the spine of the book. It was an outdated almanac, and he wondered if this was the wizard's way of suggesting he needed to improve his knowledge of agriculture, which didn't interest Whit in the least.

Once he was back in his chambers, Whit stuffed the book, unexamined, into the bottom of his pack.

He set out alone for Cardenstowe. Sinead fell into a steady canter and seemed as happy as he was to be on the road. Rowlan, Halla's destrier, was tethered behind her, for Whit had promised his cousin he would return the horse to Lorendale. Fortunately the two horses had shared a paddock in the elven realm, and the stallion offered no objection to being led by her.

They followed a southwesterly route that would take them across the Tor of Brenhinoedd. Whit intended to break his journey in Drinnkastel, where he hoped to see Maura and make himself known to King Roth. With the advent of a Nelvorian dynasty, whatever divisions had existed between the Cardenstowes and the former High King could now be put aside, opening the way, Whit hoped, for him to offer himself as a candidate to fill the next vacancy on King Roth's Tribus.

He had given this vision of his future much thought. A Tribus appointment would free him from the necessity of managing Cardenstowe and allow him to focus almost exclusively on his magic. And sharing this honorable position with two other wizards or sorceresses would offer him the opportunity to glean from them even more magical knowledge. He would live a secluded life, away from distracting and often unpleasant interactions with people in whom he had no interest. He could devote himself to learning, reading, and growing his already considerable power. It would be the realization of his ideal life.

The only obstacle, as he saw it, was his obligation to produce an heir for Cardenstowe. But he was sure he could think of some way to address this.

At least Halla could no longer be considered a suitable candidate for the next Lady Cardenstowe. As soon as his mother learned her niece had not only lived and trained in a brothel, but was currently a member of a band of rebel Lurkers, she'd have no choice but to eliminate the girl from consideration as Whit's bride. Whit only hoped knowledge of Halla's escapades could be kept in the family. His aunt and young cousins of Lorendale had enough on their trenchers to deal with at present, what with so many of their peasants clamoring for refuge from what many believed was an imminent Helgrin invasion. And Whit himself would no doubt be busy with more important matters once his official standing as a full wizard, conferred on him by Egydd when the mage gave him his staff of power, was made known.

Occupied with dreams of his bright future, Whit cantered out of Mithralyn feeling all was right with his world. The road was his alone, for the Fairendellians, a superstitious folk, clove to their coast. Now he knew it wasn't mere superstition that kept them away; elven magic had rendered this dreary moorland purposely inhospitable to discourage anyone from discovering their hidden sanctuary.

After passing mile after mile without meeting another soul, he began to entertain himself with magic of his own making. He whipped the wind to his will, driving the threatening clouds northward out of his path, then he tested his illusing, a difficult feat of magic he'd been working on for weeks. At first his reflection in the puddles left from an earlier rain revealed only subtle differences in his appearance, but by the end of the day, the face of a much older man, with heavy brows and a prominent jaw, gazed back at him.

Two days passed uneventfully before Whit crossed the border onto the Tor, leaving behind Fairendell's dull fields of drifting mist for green meadows undulating toward the horizon. His first sign of civilization was a campsite. At first the circled wagons, the laundry hanging on the line, and the chickens scratching in the dust all indicated that people were near at hand. But on closer examination, Whit discovered that the blackened stains on the earth were blood, and the overturned pots evidence that their owners' lives had been interrupted by violence. He suspected he'd happened upon the aftermath of Lurker kidnappings.

Although dusk was fast approaching and the encampment had a good source of water, Whit didn't linger. Instead he followed the stream until he found a sheltered grove a few miles farther on. After carefully checking both horses' hooves, he tethered them to graze and sat down to some elven fare.

Low clouds spooled by overhead as he prepared his bedroll. There was no scent of rain in the air, so he could expect a dry night's repose. This enhanced smelling of things was a recent addition to his magical repertoire. He could now scent out weather, water, all sorts of plants, and the proximity of various creatures, including humans—but not, to his chagrin, elves. Unfortunately this capability also had its disadvantages, for he was just as likely to pick up the odors of dung, toadstools, or people's unwashed bodies as he was herbs for his evening stew.

As he lay down to sleep, he focused on developing his skill to perform another magical feat: shade-shifting. Ever since achieving a level of competence in the discipline of scrying, his ability to be still had improved significantly, and tranquility was essential to mastering the imperatives. Master Morgan had explained that for this reason, the moments before sleep were the most fertile times to practice this elusive shadow work. And the wizard proved to be right. On several quiet nights in Mithralyn, Whit had already managed to move his own shadow several increments across the wall of his chamber.

In the secluded grove, Whit lay on his side, focused on his breathing, and stared at the shadows cast by his conjured fire. His breaths slowed and deepened as he mentally projected his exhalations farther and farther from his physical sphere, while drawing his inhalations deeper within it. He expelled a long, slow breath, and his efforts were rewarded: the flickering shadows of the fire leapt up to lick, like black tongues, the boulder to his right. Whit's pulse quickened as he held the shadows against the stone, watching them dance. It was the longest he'd been able to maintain any shade-shifting thus far.

Encouraged, he willed the shadow onward to arc first to the trees, then out of his line of vision. He forced himself to count to ten before turning to follow its progression in the direction his mind had sent it. He was sweating with concentration, but a warm glow spread through him as he directed the shadow, like a master conductor drawing forth a symphony from his orchestra. *This was what Egydd meant about becoming my own magic.*

When at last he released the shadow, he felt a surge of triumph. He had succeeded in performing the first of the imperatives! He envisioned the time, now certain to come to pass, when he could shadow-cast and glide across any space wrapped in his shadow. He'd seen Egydd do it once. One moment the mage stood in front of Whit, and the next he'd disappeared. Whit would have been unable to track the mage at all had he not known precisely what to look for: the slight ripple of air surrounding a shadow that looks denser and darker.

With a sense of deep satisfaction, Whit now took control of the fire's shadows again. He lost track of the time he spent playing in the small arena of light. At one point, something Master Morgan once said about the essence of shadows flitted through his mind. *They are more than a confirmation of our presence in this world; they're a reflection of our inner mystery— ever-shifting and ethereal.* Whit wished the wizard was with him now to witness his achievement. He even wondered what Halla would think if she could see him wielding such challenging magic. Knowing her, she'd probably find some fault with it.

How Leif would enjoy it though! Whit imagined the lad chasing after the shifting shade, while Whit kept it leaping just out of his reach. He laughed aloud at the thought, and Sinead snorted in mild alarm.

Unlike scrying, shadow shifting didn't leave Whit feeling drained. Still, he needed rest, so with reluctance, he released the wavering dark forms and lay back on his bedroll. Despite his excitement, sleep came quickly.

But with it came troubled dreams.

He dreamt of a great hall, at the center of which stood a crystal dome, covering an ancient book, its pages lined with runic writing. A figure hunched over the glittering glass, intoning an incantation. In a sudden burst of light, the crystal shattered, spraying shards of glass that flew into Whit's eyes, blinding him.

He cried out, awakening to large drops of rain pelting his face in the grey dawn.

"So much for my powers of scenting," he grumbled, pulling up his hood.

After partaking of a quick meal and breaking camp, he rode on. Several hours passed before the trail widened and began to wind upward. A whisper of water steadily grew to a rush; a cascade tumbled somewhere ahead. Whit wondered if the Argens, the river running through Drinnkastel to the Vast Sea, had overflowed its banks.

The road rose steeply, and Whit had to pace Sinead accordingly over its muddy, slick surface, Rowlan plodding along behind. He felt a growing impatience at the delay. At this rate, he estimated it would take them a full day, if not longer, to navigate the switchbacks, and another half day's travel to reach Drinnkastel. He had been to the capital once before, when he was quite young, and his only memory of the experience was of the mummers performing in the Grand Square. He recalled thinking the performers were working magic, and how his blood sang as they breathed fire, made nosegays and live doves appear out of sleeves, and pinched coins from spectators' ears. Indeed, it may well have been that performance that had first stirred the magic in his veins.

His excitement over visiting the capital was tinged by a queasy anticipation at the prospect of mingling with the crowds. He'd found fighting his way through the throngs of people in the Segavian bazaars and the milling masses of pilgrims in Altipa to be a most unsettling experience. He tried to reassure himself that it would be different in Drinnkastel, among his own people.

Sinead at last crested the rim of the escarpment just as the rays of the setting sun pierced the louring clouds. A skein of geese winged its raucous way south above forests ablaze with autumn foliage, and the sun-struck river wound through the trees, a ribbon of light flaming like liquid gold. He'd have to cross to its far side at some point, and from the sound of the rushing water, he'd need to find a ford, or better still, a bridge.

He was reminded of the river he'd walked along with Cressida under Mithralyn's towering trees. He wondered where the sylth was now, and if she had already shed her mortal shell to meld her spirit with her poplar tree. His loins stirred at the memory of her as a living maid in the arms of her lover, just as they had when he'd first witnessed her young knight draw her down on that bed of sweet grass so many centuries ago.

He gave Sinead a gentle kick, attempting to exorcise his yearning. He knew it was a natural impulse for a young man his age, but the idea of the actual *doing* of the whole business unsettled him. How exactly did one go about it, so as to get it right? Whit had grown up seeing many a stallion covering mares, bulls mounting cows, and dogs locked in what seemed an agonizing union. And more than once he'd come upon one of his father's vassals humping away with a serving girl in an alcove. But he'd always felt more disturbed than aroused by these encounters. He suspected this was because his parents had treated anything related to sex as unmentionable.

In fact, the closest Whit had come to a frank conversation about intimacy was when Cortenus broached the subject. They had come upon two crows emitting low, clicking rattles while puffing out their bibs and bowing in a mirrored dance with one another, and Whit's tutor remarked idly, "It's the start of a lifelong relationship for those two."

"Lifelong?" Whit remembered feeling incredulous. "How can anyone possibly tell them apart to prove that? They all look the same."

Cortenus chuckled. "Not to one another, they don't."

They stayed to watch the odd ritual, then the mating afterward, which lasted only a few seconds.

"That's it?" Whit said.

"That's it," Cortenus confirmed. "It's a wonder his lady stays loyal."

"Why do you say that?"

Cortenus gave him a sideways glance. "A woman desires a lover who devotes time to her, my lord."

This was something worth learning. "How much time?"

Cortenus pressed a thoughtful finger to his lips. "I suppose the best answer is: it depends on the woman. And it's not *just* time you must invest—you must learn to read her subtler signs as well. Does she long for tender caresses, or is she yearning for a passionate embrace? Does she wish you to whisper terms of endearment or something... bolder into her ear?"

"That sounds complicated," Whit grumbled. "How's a fellow to know for sure?"

"Ah, if I had the answer to *that*, I'd be hailed as the wisest man in the Known World."

"Well, the whole business seems very imprecise. What's so funny?"

Cortenus covered his smile with his hand. "Forgive me, my lord, but as much as you may wish it, the art of love-making cannot be defined as an exact science. You'll better understand once you've experienced it for yourself."

The conversation ended there, but now, five years on, Whit realized he was no wiser regarding these matters than he had been back then.

He decided he would have to rectify that soon.

* * *

As the day progressed, Whit began to pass homesteads and crofts. Although he'd dressed modestly for travel, the folk he met on the road all pulled respectful forelocks or stepped aside with a curtsey. After this had happened several times, it dawned on him that it was the wizard's staff slung across his back that commanded their respect, and he took care to arrange his features in a sage expression when he passed the next traveler.

It happened to be a round-faced fellow with a jaunty cap driving a wagon filled with bright yellow and orange gourds. The man looked trustworthy enough, so Whit ventured to inquire where he might put up for the night. After sleeping in the open for days, he longed for a hot bath.

"There's the Magpie's Mirror," the farmer replied, pointing farther down the road. "'Taint more than a mile west o' here. Fenella serves a fine lamb stew and a decent ale. Mind ye, she charges twice what ol' Sim does over at the Pickled Pot, but yer not likely t' find more than a morsel 'o meat in *his* sorry swill."

To thank the man, Whit handed him a coin. The farmer's eyes shone with pleasure as he pocketed it. "She runs a clean house, Fenella does," he said, then dropped his voice. "And if it please ye, master, ask fer Maeve—sweet as Langmerdor honey, she is."

By the time Whit realized what the farmer meant, the fellow had clucked to his mule and continued on his way.

Whit spurred past the wagon, barely sparing the man another glance, for in addition to a hot meal and bath, he now had a maid called Maeve on his mind.

* * *

At first glance, the Magpie's Mirror did not disappoint. The small, tidy inn, shaded by spreading fall-kissed maples, sat cozily tucked back from the road. Its white facade was chequered by black timbers, and it was capped with a neatly thatched roof with stolid stone chimneys rising on either end. Pots of bright purple freesia bordered the arched front door, and above the lintel a black-and-white bird was etched on a circle of burnished metal, which must have cost a pretty penny.

After surrendering Sinead and Rowlan to a stable boy with detailed instructions as to their care, Whit ducked into the pub. The place was larger than it appeared from the outside, and already a few of the locals faced one another across the well-scrubbed tables. The aroma of the aforementioned stew emanating from the kitchen made Whit's stomach rumble.

A girl was crouched at the hearth near the door, attempting to fan a fire to life—though Whit could tell by the billowing smoke swirling round her that she'd used green, wet wood. When the maid, sensing she was being watched, looked up at Whit with the air of a startled doe, he gave her a reassuring smile, then tilted his staff slightly toward the fireplace and murmured under his breath. In an instant, the smoke vanished, and bright flames set the logs to crackling.

The girl's mouth formed a small 'O', and she flashed Whit a look of nervous gratitude before scurrying away.

Whit surveyed the room to see if anyone else had witnessed his work, but no one was looking his way.

He succeeded in procuring the Mirror's best room for a groat, and the first thing he did upon entering it was ask for water to take a bath in its rustic tub. He had to fold his lanky frame into it with care, but at least the water was hot, and he'd had the forethought to pack his own soap. As he sat in the steaming tub, his thoughts drifted to sweet Maeve. Was she fair or raven-haired, petite or pleasingly plump? Imagining how it would feel to hold her against his bared chest, he felt himself quicken.

With an effort, he rose out of the tub and let the cold air quell his ardor, then dressed with care, selecting a pearl-grey tunic and black hose girded with a silver belt. On a whim, he left his hair, which had grown long in Mithralyn, unbound on his shoulders, deciding it made him appear more wizardly.

As he descended the stairs to the pub, he noted that several serving maids followed him with their eyes, and a few of the men cast him curious glances as well. He knew strangers were likely to be viewed with suspicion in these provincial backwaters, but he was confident his princely attire would discourage any unpleasantness. He'd felt at ease from the moment he'd crossed the threshold of the Magpie's Mirror.

A pretty girl placed a mug of cool brown ale before him, then took his dinner order. Drinking deeply, he felt the last of the rigors of travel drain away, replaced by a growing exhilaration. Tomorrow he would arrive in Drinnkastel, and surely then his future would be secured. Of course, he was already a lord of the realm, but this paled in comparison to the prospect of one day soon becoming a member of the Tribus. He felt a giddy thrill at the thought of obtaining the most august commission a wizard could hope for in a lifetime.

And before that, there was tonight... which offered its own exciting possibilities.

Whit glanced about the room, taking particular note of a group of laughing young women. Perhaps Maeve was one of them. Several of them were quite comely, particularly a petite blonde with a laughing mouth and skin the color of fresh cream.

His stew arrived, along with a half a loaf of dense, warm bread and a pot of sweet butter. The old man who'd recommended the Magpie hadn't exaggerated the stew's flavor. Whit quickly polished off the tender chunks of lamb, turnips, and carrots swimming in rich gravy, then used the heel of the bread to mop up the last savory drops.

He was working through his third mug of ale when he sensed he was under observation. Lifting his gaze, he met the frank stare of the pretty blonde. Emboldened by the invitation he read in her eyes, he rose and carried his tankard across to where she sat with her friends. The ladies all fell silent as he inclined his head toward the vacant space on the bench.

But instead of sliding over, the fair-haired maid frowned, and Whit felt a jolt of misgiving. The ensuing flitter of giggles from her companions made him feel even more a fool. For a long awkward moment he stood frozen as the girl's eyes swept him from head to toe.

At last she parted her sultry lips. "'Tisn't the custom here, sir, to approach a lady without an introduction." She remained

unsmiling, but a spark of amusement lit her eyes as more tit-
ters circled the table.

Whit made a swift, courtly bow. "Forgive me. I'm a stranger to these parts, and so cannot call on an acquaintance to
properly present me." He stepped respectfully back, preparing
to retreat in humiliation, but the girl reached out and laid a
hand on his arm.

"Then you must proceed alone. What is your name, sir?"
The tip of her pink tongue flicked against her upper lip as her
fingers caressed the fabric of his sleeve.

"I... Card—" A sudden caution made him hesitate.

"Master Card?" repeated the girl, with a raised brow. "I've
not heard this name before. Where is your home, master?"

She still hadn't invited him to sit, but as her hand rested
on his sleeve, he was unable to leave. He fiercely rued the impulse that now had him under the scrutiny of the entire pub.
"I'm from... the west."

"I see," said the maid primly. "Well, Master Card from the
west, what is your intention in approaching me?"

Intention? Whit cast wildly about in his mind for an appropriate response. If he could have extricated himself gracefully, he would have done so at once, for the girl was decidedly
pert, and on closer inspection, he noticed that her eyes were
set slightly too far apart. "I... I..." He glanced up as a barmaid moved past bearing a tray. "I merely wished to buy you
and your friends a flagon of wine."

This appeared to have been the right thing to say, for the
girl smiled at last and flicked her beguiling tongue again.
"Why, Master Card," she purred, sliding over to make space
beside her, "in that case, you are most welcome."

With an inner sigh of relief, Whit settled beside her.

A plump dark-haired girl raised her goblet to him and
said, "I'm Shel." She tipped her glass toward the blonde. "And
she's Cammie."

The other girls offered their names as well, but Whit was deaf to them, for beneath the boards, Cammie's warm hand had come to rest on his knee. To cover his surprise, he hastily raised his tankard and gulped down his ale. When he set it on the table again, Shel leaned toward him, displaying her ample cleavage, and announced, "Cammie's gettin' noozed t'morrow."

"Noozed?" he repeated. It came out as a croak, for Cammie's hand was now sliding up his thigh. Whit found he couldn't shift his eyes from Shel's breasts, which threatened to burst from her tightly cinched bodice with the next breath.

"Yoked." Shel gave him a sly smile. "You know—hitched. Jumping the broom. I s'pose a fine gent such as yourself would say pledgin' 'er troth." Her speech was slurred, either because of a regional accent or the amount of drink she'd consumed.

Comprehension dawned on Whit. He turned his astonished his gaze away from Shel's heaving bosom toward Cammie, who was engaged in a whispered conversation with the girl on her right. Her fingers continued their bold approach toward his manhood.

While he was attempting to digest the fact that the girl who was causing him such inappropriate pleasure was about to be married, a barmaid plunked a bottle that he hadn't ordered down in front of him.

Cammie's hand abruptly withdrew, leaving Whit feeling both bereft and relieved, for he'd been on the verge of exploding. He now felt a slight revulsion toward the minx and pitied her hapless groom. Such wanton behavior on the eve of their wedding foreboded a doomed marriage.

The barmaid seemed to be of a similar mind regarding Cammie's moral fiber. She glared at the girl with knowing eyes, reminding Whit uncomfortably of Mistress Merch, a nanny under whose tyranny he'd been forced to suffer for nearly a year.

"You lassies should see the bride-to-be home," the barmaid proposed, "as she'll want to be fresh for her big day." She pushed the bottle toward Shel, but her eyes never left the blonde. "You can take the wine with you—it's on the house." She dropped her voice, which now held a threat of menace. "If it's fiddlin' you've a penchant for, Mistress Cammie, surely my brother will oblige you with a bow."

Her expression was so fierce, Whit rose at once, and Cammie had the grace to blush as she slid hastily off the bench. Whit felt certain the barmaid had guessed what had been going on under the table. His own face burning, he mumbled his excuses and made for the stairs, only to remember he hadn't paid for his supper. Cursing, he felt for the coins in his pocket and found them gone.

"Looking for these?" said a familiar voice. The barmaid jingled the silver in her hand. "There's no need for *you* to leave, sir." She laid the coins on the table, then pulled out a chair for him.

After a moment's hesitation, Whit sat, and was startled when the maid took the chair opposite his.

"You're not the first who's been taken in by that connivin' slut," she said. "I'd ask Mistress Frenella to bar her from this place, if it wouldn't mean I'd never see my younger brother again. That doxie will be my sister-in-law by this time tomorrow." She pulled such a sour face that Whit laughed, and her expression softened. "Ah well, we'll not have you saying your time at the Magpie was unpleasant." She signaled a passing barmaid for another ale. "It's on me."

"That's not necessary. I—"

"Will accept the ale and enjoy it," she said firmly and smiled for the first time. He liked the way her eyes crinkled at the edges, and her dainty teeth. She was pretty, in an understated sort of way, with dark curls that fell to her shoulders and a charmingly turned-up nose.

He smiled back.

"I saw you come in earlier," she said, "with a staff 'cross your back. My mistress says you must be a wizard. Are you?"

Whit sat up a bit straighter. "Yes, I am."

The woman's eyes widened with admiration. "I've never met a wizard before." She stretched out a finger and traced the scar on his wrist, leaving a pleasant tingle in its wake. "So— you can do magic?"

"Y-yes," he replied, his eyes glued to her hand. "I can." He expected she would now ask for some proof, but instead she sat back and crossed her arms over her breasts.

"And what do you do, when you're not casting spells and such?"

Whit blinked. "Why… I—I learn." He winced inwardly, for it made him sound like a schoolboy.

She must have thought so too, for she rose from her chair. "Well, Master Wizard, if there's anything else I can get you, you've only to ask."

Whit shook his head. "No. That is…"

"Another ale, perhaps?" She shook her glossy curls, then planted her hands on the table and leaned so close to him that he could smell cinnamon on her breath and see flecks of green in her brown eyes.

"Ale, is it then?" she asked again. "Or would you perhaps care to learn… something new?" A slow, suggestive smile spread across her generous lips, making Whit's pulse quicken.

Another barmaid sauntering past their table gave her a playful nudge with her hip while eyeing Whit approvingly. "Good evenin' t' ye, Mistress Maeve. Looks to be a fine evenin' you'll be havin' indeed!" She winked at Whit, then continued weaving through the crowded tables.

Maeve was still staring deep into Whit's eyes, and he realized that an evening of disappointments had taken a sudden turn for the better. "Do you know," he said, his heart in his throat, "I believe I *would* care to—"

Maeve pressed a finger softly to his lips and laced her other hand through his. "Aye," she murmured, drawing him up from his chair and toward the stairs, "I thought you might."

CHAPTER 11
Borne

Four months had passed since Borne had taken command of Nicu's men serving under Latour, and he was well-pleased with their progress as trained fighters. *The men and the girl*, he amended, for despite his earlier misgivings, Halla was proving to be an exceptional member of the å Livåri company.

Borne found much to like about the young statuesque lady, including the fact that she made little of her looks, stunning as they were. Mature beyond her years, Halla demonstrated a quick wit and was the most pragmatic female he'd ever met. She took the men's rough humor in stride, and had clearly earned their ungrudging respect. She'd been highly educated, even by the standards of her noble status, and although she didn't share Borne's passion for poetry, she'd absorbed a considerable store of knowledge about husbandry. Apparently she'd helped her father's reeve manage Lorendale's estate.

She was certainly a direct lass; when she disagreed with something, you'd know the reason why. Borne respected that in a soldier serving under him, provided the concerns were valid—which Halla's always were. When she contested something, she had legitimate grounds and always offered a viable alternative. Because of this, she'd earned her place on Borne's council, along with Nicu, Mihail, and Baldo.

And the maid could wield a sword.

Nicu, too, was an impressive soldier. Which made it all the more surprising what a model apprentice-at-arms he'd proven to be. He'd surrendered the command of his unit completely to Borne and carried out orders without hesitation, which prompted his followers to do the same. He was highly intelligent and had an amusing, if at times biting, wit.

The only sticking point came when Borne learned that Halla and Nicu were lovers. Having two of his officers share a bed could spell trouble, should the relationship break down. But rather than risk creating bad blood between himself and the å Livåri leader, he'd decided to wait until one of them gave him a good, solid reason to object to this arrangement.

To date, neither had. They shared no lingering glances while they were out on raids, and Borne had never seen them touch. Halla rode as an equal at Nicu's side, but her standing was based on her prowess in the field, and not on whatever went on between the sheets. Indeed, if Borne hadn't learned of their affair from Gormett, he'd never have guessed there was more than a comradely connection between the two.

When he said as much to Latour over a game of chatraj, the marechal nodded thoughtfully. "Yes, it's an intriguing relationship, isn't it? If I were a younger man, I should be jealous of young Nicu."

Meeting Latour's piercing gaze, Borne replied, "If that's your way of asking me if *I* am jealous, the answer is no. Lady Halla is a beauty, but I view her like any other soldier in my company."

"And a fine company it's shaping up to be. You've worked wonders with the å Livåri." The marechal sat back, folding his long arms across his chest. "And so, shepherd, I've decided to take you where your service to Gral can be properly rewarded."

Borne moved his knight two spaces forward. "I didn't take you for the sort to frequent bordellos, Marechal," he said lightly.

Latour's smile disappeared. "I'm not," he replied coldly, "and you'd do well to remember it, especially once you've worn the holy robes of the Tertulites."

Abashed, Borne flushed. "Marechal, if I've offended—"

Latour chortled and reached across the table to grasp Borne's arms. "I jest, man! But no, we won't be seeking the favors of Gral's finest courtesans just yet." His eyes were fired with enthusiasm. "We're riding north tomorrow so that I may present you to one whom you've served with honor: our most high and excellent prince, His Majesty Crenel Etiene Fralour Du Regis, King of Gral. It's all been arranged. We'll leave for Lugeneux at first light." He leaned back to gauge Borne's reaction.

Borne set down the piece he'd just lifted. "But—what of my men?"

Latour waved his hand dismissively. "Have no fear. Your company shall continue harrying the enemy under the able command of Gormett. I've asked Ser Nicu to come with us, and his lady might as well too. The king will be sure to find her of interest."

Borne raised an eyebrow. "*Ser* Nicu? I fear our proud å Livåri would disdain that title, Marechal. He has a general aversion to nobility."

Latour slid his serf forward and swept Borne's knight off the board. "As do most who've been poorly served by their masters. The only reason we've avoided an uprising here in Gral is because the peasants are too weak from deprivation to take up their scythes and pitchforks against us." He sighed heavily. "We've a long road to travel before we can ensure that all of Gral's people—not only a privileged few—have enough food and protection to take some pleasure in life. I for one am determined to see this journey to its rightful end." He lifted a flagon and refilled both their glasses with ruby wine. "I had hoped you'd finish that journey with me, as you seem to have made yourself invaluable."

Borne looked up from the board between them. "*Had* hoped?"

"I received news today that might prevent my wish from being realized."

"What news, Marechal?"

"Of your homeland. A young lord of the House of Nelvor has been crowned High King."

At the mention of Roth, Borne felt something tighten in his chest. He wondered if Maura had already consented to be his queen, then roughly pushed the thought aside. *It's no business of mine. Not anymore.*

Latour was studying his face. "It seems I'm the bearer of bad tidings."

"Not at all. I imagine Roth of Nelvor will make a fair enough ruler of Drinnglennin." Borne moved his hawk, knocking over his opponent's king. "Usurped," he declared. Lifting his goblet, he drained it.

Latour bowed in defeat, then sat back, his hawk's eyes never leaving Borne's face. "You are acquainted with this King Roth? All the more reason for you to meet King Crenel. His Majesty will want to know all you can tell him about Drinnglennin's new sovereign. And he wishes to send envoys as soon as possible to ensure that our treaties still stand strong, which is the reason I'm likely to lose you."

Borne set down his goblet carefully. "I'll be happy to oblige your king with any information I have to share, but there isn't much to tell. Lord—that is, *King* Roth and I competed against each other on several occasions while I was in Drinnkastel." *And bested me in the most important fight,* Borne thought ruefully. He got to his feet. "If we're to leave at dawn, I must excuse myself, Marechal. There'll be instructions to pass on to Gormett."

"You may be excused after you've answered me one question, shepherd." Latour propped his boot on his knee and cocked his head. "You've achieved quite a degree of celebrity among the men—both your own and mine. Like me, they've come to trust you and seek your favor."

Borne shrugged. "I've had a good model in you."

Latour continued to regard him with his brooding eyes. "Why are you here, Borne? I mean, really? What is that made you leave the country of your birth? A young man with the intelligence and leadership you possess should have more purpose in life than to fight as a mercenary in a foreign land. What of your own people? Drinnglennin is in a precarious state of transition. Surely she would benefit from your gifts."

"I think not." Borne felt the stirrings of uneasiness and couldn't help returning Latour's gaze coolly. "I told you before—I like fighting. And with all due respect, I might ask the same of you. What decided you on the course you've taken? I know men who revel in war and rapine, and I understand why they seek a soldier's life. But you're not this sort of man. No one would gainsay that you're a brilliant soldier, but you take no joy in battle. Yet you've chosen to dedicate the best years of your life to the profession."

Latour gave a slow nod. "You are not far off in your assessment, my friend. But sadly, war is an inevitability in our world. It's the road to power, but also to justice. If men such as myself eschew battle, who will protect the innocent and less privileged from those who wage war without scruple? We must oppose such men, or their tyranny will prevail. When I ride into battle, it is to honor the oath I swore to protect my more vulnerable countrymen.

"But you're right: I do not love killing. Those who find it an amusement should be reviled. They are generally short-lived, in any event." He released Borne from his gaze then, and began to collect the pieces from the board. "You still haven't answered my question, shepherd."

Borne's uneasiness now bordered on annoyance. "What would you have me say, Marechal? I'm here because there's nothing for me in Drinnglennin."

Latour lifted the chatraj board and placed it in its satin-lined box. "Nothing? Or something you wish to leave behind?" He swept the pieces into his hand, and one fell to the floor.

They both looked down at the maiden at their feet. Borne bent to retrieve it and dropped it in with the other pieces. "It's the same thing, really, isn't it?"

"Ah," said the marechal, as he lowered the lid of the box, "but is it?"

* * *

The Gralian capital, Lugeneux, was located in the center of the country, just south of Le Sauncee, a massif that spanned all the way to the borders of Helgrinia and Delnogoth. Due west of the fortified city lay the Val de Verdel, where once the Known World's finest vineyards flourished—until years of ravaging by the rogue knights halted the production of the fine *mulate, rimara* and *piqpoul* grapes. Now the untended vines sprawled to the ground, for too many *vignorons* had lost their lives to the outlaws, leaving few to keep the vines from neglect. It was the same to the east of the capital, where once fields of wheat, rye, barley, and oats had carpeted the meadows. These days, the only land that was under cultivation was that which could be successfully patrolled—and this would be reaped only for the noble tables of Lugeneux. The peasants were left to subsist on gathered mushrooms and other wild food, supplementing their diets with fallen nuts and olives from the few groves that had thus far been spared the renegades' torches.

Only twice on the road to Lugeneux did Latour's small company meet with other living souls. The first encounter was with a group of ragged peasants, who melted into the woods upon the riders' approach. The marechal's calls of assurance did not bring them back, so he ordered some of their stores to be unloaded in the middle of the road before they rode on.

The second sign of life was less than half a day's ride from Lugeneux, when they overtook a wizened farmer with a wisp of white beard pulling a cart piled with household possessions. The young woman and three small children trudging alongside it looked to be on the brink of starvation, and gratefully accepted the provisions the marechal offered them.

When asked where they were going, the old man replied, "Lugeneux, lord. We hear there is bread there."

"Then you shall come along with us," Latour insisted.

Halla jumped down to assist the woman onto her horse, and Nicu took up the older of the two boys. The little girl rode with Du Charney. Borne settled the smallest lad in front of him, and the boy promptly burst into tears—which dried when Borne placed an apple in his small, grimy hands.

Borne guessed the boy had never been on horseback, so he kept his steed at a gentle trot. His young passenger kept glancing down at Magnus, who padded quietly alongside.

"The dog won't hurt you," Borne reassured him. "He's called Magnus. What's your name?"

The boy had the fruit pressed to his nose. "Amé," he mumbled.

"Well, Amé, you have more to fear from Lisse. Mind that she doesn't nip that apple away from you. She's tried it more than once with me."

The boy clutched his treasure to his thin chest and glanced furtively around.

"Lisse's my horse," Borne explained.

And sure enough, the mare's ears pricked up when the boy's teeth crunched into the fruit's crisp flesh. But she was to be disappointed. The boy devoured the apple in a few quick bites, core and all.

Nicu, who had been riding close enough to follow their conversation, drew his mount abreast of Borne's horse. "I'll have you know, Amé," he said with a conspiratorial air, "that our friend here mixes beer with Lisse's mash, and he can't sleep unless he's given her three kisses, one on each ear and the last on the tip of her nose."

Amé giggled, and the boy in front of Nicu smiled shyly over at Borne.

"You're just jealous," Borne replied. "My Lisse is a fine, fair lady, while your... what did you name your horse again?"

Nicu frowned. "I didn't name her anything."

"But she *has* a name," Borne insisted. "What is it?"

Nicu sniffed. "Pudette."

Both boys burst out laughing.

"I take it that it means something amusing?" Nicu growled.

Borne grinned. "Let's just say it's not something you'd want to call your sister."

They had come to the top of a rise, and from here they could see the pale towers and spires of Lugeneux on the far side of the spreading plain. As they drew nearer, Borne could make out gilded cupolas and gables interspersed between the flat-sided bastions in the castle walls. The wide moat encircling the city reflected the drifting clouds in its tranquil surface, making Lugeneux appear almost as though it were floating on air.

They let down their passengers just inside the city gates, and Amé waved shyly in farewell, his arm little more than a stick of bone. *A city of silver and gold,* thought Borne, taking in the ornate façade, *whilst outside her walls, her people starve.*

Indeed, everything about Lugeneux stood in stark contrast to the surrounding countryside. Here was a bustling community of ringing forges, well-kept stables, coopers, cobblers, taverns, and municipal offices. The fragrance of freshly baked bread wafted from the cookhouses, and rows of loaves cooled on stacked shelves without. The courtyards of the tidy barracks they passed resounded with the thwack of training swords and the calls of men-at-arms. Wherever Borne looked, he observed a degree of order he hadn't anticipated. Back in Drinnglennin, King Crenel was said to be a dissolute fop, and perhaps that was so—but those appointed to the running of his capital city were clearly diligent in its management.

Most of the nobles were mounted on richly caparisoned steeds. Others rocked in open, canopied litters borne by burly slaves. Although none of the slaves were à Livåri, Borne was aware of Halla's and Nicu's scornful expressions as they passed these palanquins.

The ladies wore billowing hats festooned with vibrantly colored feathers and streaming ribbons perched upon their piled-up tresses. The gentlemen also sported caps, from which sprouted incongruously long plumes, and Borne struggled to suppress his amusement at their short, padded doublets exposing bulges in their tight hose that defied belief. Most of the men and women carried little hawks, either on their wrists or hung in gilded cages from their litters.

"Shall we take notes," Halla asked, keeping her voice low, "on the grandeur of Crenel's crown city for our new monarch? Roth will have to melt down a few chalices if he wants his towers to glisten like these do."

Borne laughed. The Nelvors were infamous for their lavish reconstructions of Nelvor Castle over the centuries. "It will take some getting used to—not having Urlion as High King, that is. A Konigur has ruled Drinnglennin ever since the first of that name came south from Morlendell and, with his singing axe Moralltach, succeeded in unifying the lower kingdoms.

"I never knew the first Konigurs hailed from Morlendell," Halla admitted.

"Perhaps you're also not aware then that it was Reagh of Lorendale who first bent the knee to Gundauld the Great, giving him dominion over his realm as High King. " Borne grinned at Halla. "The other clans needed a little more persuasion."

"Which proves that Lorendalers were ever sensible," she retorted, then raised her chin. "What do you make of that?"

They had skirted the bustling markets of the city and were now approaching a massive temple crowned by a dozen spires spearing the bright blue sky. Its ornamental portico depicted finely wrought figures worked in gold; Borne guessed they played out the stories of the goddess Priscinae's many miracles. Tall pillars, their grooved surfaces twined by sinuous lizards, framed the entrance to the temple's interior; each pillar rested on the curved shell of a giant tortoise. Borne noted, however, that no magical creatures were depicted anywhere, for these were an abhorrence to the devotees of the Mother of Mothers.

Before Borne could respond to Halla's question, a stream of mules came trotting toward them, each bearing a grey-robed monk on its back.

"Ah!" Halla cried with delight. "Will you not go forward and greet your fellow brethren?"

Borne gave an emphatic shake of his head. "If they caught wind of my battlefield antics while wearing one of their holy robes, they'd most likely meet me with a sword's thrust."

"Oh, I doubt that. After all, you saved the day for their king with your bugling. Perhaps they'd just require you to play for them."

"I don't intend to find out." Borne raised his eyes to the towering spires. "I have a feeling those dedicated to Priscinae have a penchant for sharp, pointy things."

But Borne was not destined to avoid the monks after all. For when they halted in the path of Latour's party, the mare-chal signaled Borne, Halla, and Nicu to his side.

"As foreigners who will go before the king," Latour said, "you three are required to follow the Path of the Goddess through our great temple. This passage is for purification, and will lead you to the east gate of the palais, from which you will be taken to where you can refresh yourselves. I will send word to my sovereign that we have arrived, then return for you."

Latour spurred his horse forward without waiting for an answer. Borne and his companions dismounted and surrendered their mounts to a stable boy's care.

But Magnus proved to be problematic.

"The dog cannot enter the temple!" cried a fuming monk when the hound started after Borne up the temple steps.

Halla called to one of Latour's party. "Jules! Can you see that the commander's hound is returned to him after we make our progression?"

Jules, a young knight with a mop of blond curls and a wicked grin, made Halla a slight bow from his saddle. "It shall be as the demoiselle requests."

Borne hesitated a moment, then sent Magnus after Jules and turned to Halla. "Thank you for so quickly coming up with that solution," he said.

She shrugged. "Jules owed me a boon. I beat him in a wrestling match last week, and I'd forgotten to collect it."

Borne should have been surprised, but nothing about this unusual girl could be too far out of the ordinary to believe. He glanced over at Nicu, whose dark-lashed eyes surveyed Halla with an amusement tinged with admiration.

The three of them passed through the doors and into the temple, which was as magnificent on the inside as out. Ribbed domes, inlaid with bright silver, were supported by massive columns that branched out at their crowns like great stone trees. At the base of each pillar the Goddess Priscinae was represented in one of her incarnations: Mother of Mothers, Light of Hope, Sword of Faith, and Heart of Love. The statues were sculpted of some exotic stone more luminescent than pearls, and each pair of the goddess's ultramarine eyes stared coldly down at them as if in judgment.

Borne found himself wondering how such a colossal structure had been erected by human hands. What sorts of mechanisms must the builders have employed? He imagined these same artisans would be capable of creating devastating engines of war; it was a puzzlement that King Crenel had not pursued this means of keeping the Helgrins at bay.

Nicu's hand on Borne's arm broke his train of thought, and he looked down to see a treacherous opening in the floor at their feet, offering a glimpse of a gilded crypt.

"The former kings and queens of Gral, no doubt," Nicu murmured as they stepped carefully over the breach.

At the midpoint between the entrance to the temple and its exit at the east gate, another, wider hole gaped in the floor, exposing a macabre mountain of blackened skulls. Borne recalled that it was here, in the bowels of the Mother Temple, that the zealous Tertulite monks had cast the heads of all those they had murdered during the Purge. His stomach turned when he saw that among these desiccated remains were many smaller skulls, of both children and animals.

Nicu swore fiercely beneath his breath, no doubt sharing Borne's revulsion. The truly evil had not been those who wielded magical powers, but the religious fanatics who had annihilated them.

Borne raised his eyes to the nearest statue—Priscinae holding aloft a white sword tipped with crimson. Silently he cursed this cruel deity who had demanded the blood of so many innocents in exchange for her protection.

Halla flicked her head toward the exit ahead, and made a gesture that left Borne in no doubt of her opinion of the temple. He swallowed the laugh that bubbled up inside him, and they covered the remaining length of the aisle swiftly, the sooner to escape the goddess's stern scrutiny.

"Give me the old gods any day," Nicu muttered as they stepped out into the summer air. "I feel no nurture from this cold Mother."

"And no cleaner either." Halla wiped her hands on her tunic in distaste. "Priscinae has a cruel appetite for a goddess demanding purity."

A gate of golden filigree spiraled up before them, crowned with the fiery sun of Gral. The sentinels guarding it stared straight ahead, as if oblivious to their presence. Borne was about to remark on this, when he saw the reason why.

A dozen armed guards had appeared and closed ranks behind them. One of them, a pinched-faced man with a short, pointed beard, saluted Borne, then swept a disdainful gaze over his two friends, although they wore the uniforms of Latour's army as well.

"Commandant," said the man, "before you come into the radiant presence of His Majesty, I must ask you and your"— he scowled—"*companions* to surrender your arms. They will be returned to you once you leave the Chambre du Sol."

Borne had expected as much. He and the others unstrapped and handed over their swords.

The pinched-faced guard waggled his fingers impatiently at Nicu. "I'll take the knife you have in your boot as well, *cachon.*"

With a growl of fury, Halla's knee connected with the man's groin. The officer crumpled to the ground with an anguished groan, and with a clatter of steel, his men drew their swords.

"*Hold!*"

Latour was stalking across the courtyard toward them. He thrust his way through the soldiers and saw the felled man.

"What's going on here?" he demanded.

A guard with a pitted face pointed at Halla. "The… the woman—she attacked Ser Purvis without provocation!"

"Without provocation?" Halla hissed in her now impeccable Gralian. She attempted to kick Ser Purvis again, but Borne forestalled her. "Tell him what you called our comrade, cur!"

Latour shifted his attention to the injured knight, who had regained his feet with the help of his men. "Well?" said the marechal.

Ser Purvis, still doubled over, attempted a bow. "I... Marechal, I had no idea he was one of your party," he said, untruthfully. "I..."

"He called me *cachon*," Nicu said.

The marechal's face darkened, and he brought the back of his hand across Ser Purvis's face with force. "You will apologize for this insult to one of the king's most ardent defenders, *and* I will have your sash for violating the code between brothers at arms."

Ser Purvis wiped the blood from his torn lips. "But... but, Marechal! The man is a—"

"He is a respected member of my company." Though Latour spoke quietly, his expression was thunderous. Ignoring the wounded man's stammered apology, the marechal addressed the other Gralians. "The rest of you—sheathe your weapons at once!" Then he spun toward the gate, and the sentinels leapt to open it.

As the doors swung wide, the marechal turned to Borne. "We shall speak later about the girl," he said, then strode ahead.

Nicu looked unfazed, but Halla was still smoldering, prompting Borne to lay a hand on her arm. "I suggest you put on a more amenable face, Halla. You're about to meet the most high, the most powerful and excellent prince, His Majesty Crenel Etiene Fralour Du Regis, King of Gral."

"Do you tell me?" Halla replied, between gritted teeth. "Well, if he's expecting a curtsey, he'll be disappointed."

Nicu took hold of her other arm. "Come now, Lady Halla. Can you not reprise the brilliant role you played in the markets of Altipa? I feel certain it will be better received than the one you felt you had to assume just now to defend my honor."

"He called you a dirty pig! What would you have me do?"

"Nothing. I've been called much worse."

"Nicu's right, Halla," said Borne. "We're guests here at Lugeneux, and the best impression we can make is none at all.

More importantly, we represent the first company of å Livåri to ever legally bear arms, and as such we must conduct ourselves with the utmost decorum. Latour put his faith in us, and I know none of us wishes to risk losing his good will."

Halla looked between them, sudden doubt in her eyes. "Is that what I've done?"

Borne started forward, leading her along. "I don't think you've done anything," he said, "that a gracefully executed curtsey can't rectify."

CHAPTER 12
Halla

"Blearc's blood!" Halla glared over her shoulder at the skinny maid attempting to lace her into the implement of torture she had reluctantly donned. "If you pull any harder, I shall pass out cold!"

The mousy girl gave her a reproving look. "If you wish to fit into the gold gown, my lady, you need the corset."

Halla grabbed hold of the offending garment, pushed it down over her hips, and kicked it aside. "In that case, I'll wear the silver."

The maid made a face. "But this gown's design is in the latest style! The silver dress is from last season."

Halla raised her arms and waggled her hands impatiently. "I don't care if it's from the Before. Just get me into it so I can go to dinner. I'm starving!"

With exaggerated regret, the girl lifted the shimmering sheath from the bed and helped Halla pull it over her head. The maid's sour reflection in the looking glass left Halla in no doubt of the fashion blunder she was committing. She snorted loudly at the thought, which clearly did nothing to improve the maid's assessment of her.

In truth, Halla's assessment of this version of herself wasn't much better. For days now she'd been playing the part of Lady Halla, and it wasn't agreeing with her any more than the overly rich food served at Crenel's table. But she'd had no choice. After the incident with Purvis, Latour had been insistent that she assume the tedious existence of a noblewoman. Not only had the marechal's censure been stern, but he'd even gone so far as to suggest that were she not to confirm her noble status, she might face charges.

So Halla had exchanged her sword, hose, and boots for borrowed gowns and slippers, and she'd been formally received by the ladies of the court—which entitled her to many tiresome hours of embroidery, music, and singing in their company. At first, most of the ladies gave her a cool reception and then chose to ignore her. Others made no more than the thinnest of efforts to disguise their disdain of the Isler in their midst—Lady Mineux, chief among them. Widespread tittering ensued when the pernicious raven-haired beauty, disparaging Halla's height and the size of her feet, wondered aloud if the demoiselle was, in fact, truly one of their fair sex. After months in the country, Halla had a good grasp of Gralian, but the venomous lady either did not realize or care that Halla understood her rude comments. The only bearable part of this dull routine was the scandalous gossip Halla was now privy to, for it revealed the true nature of these calculating women and kept her on her guard.

But the unpleasantness ceased the day the Comtessa Didriana singled Halla out for conversation. Didriana was the king's mistress and the most powerful lady of Crenel's court. When she observed how Halla shrugged off Lady Mineux's insults, the comtessa decided to bestow her favor on the foreign girl, and suddenly Halla found herself everyone's darling—which was arguably a worse fate, for it placed her in His Majesty's inner circle.

King Crenel, a short, bandy-legged man, rested his speculative gaze on her with disturbing regularity. Halla already knew from the wagging tongues of the court ladies that Crenel had slept with most of them. When he learned that she had recently turned a year older unheralded, he seized the opportunity to make a spectacle in her honor. Halla, fearing he would demand something of her in return, attempted to discourage the idea, but the king would hear nothing of it.

"Here in Gral, when a demoiselle turns seventeen," Crenel insisted, "she is introduced into society. Your debut must not be neglected. We shall have a fête, my little rose!"

Halla laughed inwardly at the sobriquet, for she was a head taller than the king.

That very celebration was to take place this evening—hence the intensity of the maid's remonstrations over her choice of attire. Halla's mood was petulant. She glared at herself in the mirror while the maid slowly plaited her hair, then lost patience after only a few tiny braids had been completed and abruptly dismissed the girl.

No herald had as yet appeared to escort her to the celebration, but Halla decided she didn't care to wait on him either. She stalked through the palace halls on her own, reasoning that if she arrived at the ballroom early, perhaps she could avoid a scrutinized entrance. But as she approached the Grand Chambre, the rumble of voices punctuated with laughter informed her that she would not be the first guest.

Steeling herself for an evening in which she would be the center of unwanted attention, she drew a deep breath and entered the crowded gallery. She saw in a glance that the hall had been lavishly decorated, even by Gralian standards. Crimson wall hangings descended from the high ceiling to the floor, tied at intervals with golden tasseled cords. Candelabra lit the gilded mirrors and chandeliers with sparkling light, and the expensive scent of vanilla bean emanated from flickering tapers. Halla's stomach rumbled its disappointment when she saw that there were no tables laid; it was to be dancing first and dinner after, in the strange Gralian style.

The court ladies were dressed in the most elaborate costumes Halla had yet seen. Their low-necked gowns were of the finest silks and satins, worn over frilled petticoats that peeked out from their full skirts, and their gems winked and sparkled in the candlelight. Comtessa Didriana wore a priceless cluster of diamonds and rubies at her throat, and the other demoiselles were only slightly less richly adorned. All the women wore their hair piled high, the better to display both their jewelry and their high-bodiced breasts.

And the men were every bit as decoratively attired as their ladies. Halla thought their lace ruffled shirts and puffed embroidered sleeves looked rather silly, as did the skirted velvet waistcoats they wore over them. When she'd first arrived in Lugeneux, she'd burst out laughing at the exaggerated codpieces that protruded from their hose, and had had to pretend to a coughing fit. Overall, the gentry of Gral seemed inordinately preoccupied with the appearance of things. She found this reprehensible in light of the poverty their peasants were forced to endure.

Still, passing among them, Halla felt a moment's misgiving at having left her hair unbound. The only ornament she wore was the ring Bria had given her, hanging from a slender chain around her neck. Nevertheless, she walked toward her host with her head held high, as her mother had taught her. She wished she had someone at her side, but she knew better than to seek Nicu among the guests; he'd made it clear he had no interest in the ball.

She could guess where he was instead.

Ever since their arrival, the ladies of Crenel's court had taken an extreme interest in both Borne and Nicu—especially Nicu, who, as an á Livári, was viewed as an exotic amusement. Halla admired the adeptness with which Borne deflected the ladies' attempts at flirtation—and did so without causing them loss of face—but Nicu clearly reveled in the attention, and Halla would have to have been incredibly naïve not to know where the bold repartee he exchanged with the demoiselles would eventually lead. She'd even overheard the women placing bets as to who would succeed in bedding him first.

She found herself burning with jealousy at the thought of Nicu in the arms of another woman. But she'd learned long ago that å Livåri men and women moved freely among sexual partners until they were wed, and she wasn't fool enough to think her lover would be any different in this regard. He'd certainly never promised exclusivity. Still, she hadn't been prepared for the hurt his dalliance was causing her.

Occupied with these glum thoughts, she didn't become aware of the hush around her until she reached the royal dais. Latour, seated beside King Crenel, gave her an approving smile, and she became aware that the eyes of other guests were equally appreciative. Perhaps her attire wasn't so unfashionable as her pert maid believed.

Flushing, she dropped into a deep curtsey. When she straightened, it was to see that the king had descended the dais and was holding out his hand.

"You shall do me the honor of the first dance, my dear," Crenel declared.

At once, the players stuck up a *juliana*, the graceful, swaying dance that was the current favorite of the court. Halla far preferred the daring *churi* of the å Livåri, or the lively leaps of the elven *leandera*, but at least the steps of the *juliana* were simple to follow. She wouldn't embarrass herself or, far more importantly, the king.

The king was a practiced dancer, and led her through the steps so skilfully that she didn't even have to think about them. But when the *juliana* came to a close, Halla saw that she would have no rest, for he released her to partner with a seemingly endless flow of his courtiers, and she soon lost count of how many men whirled her around the ballroom.

As yet another partner released her with a courtly bow, Halla saw the portly Comte Flaseur stepping forward to claim her for a second dance, his hennaed curls bobbing around his shoulders like fat sausages, the musk with which he'd doused himself preceding him. Halla's heart sank. His clumsy footwork had almost crippled her the first time round, and she wasn't sure her toes would survive a second assault.

But before the comte reached her, someone took hold of her hand from behind and she was spun into the arms of a tall, blond gentleman. It took her several seconds to recognize her savior as Borne. She had only ever seen him in uniform, or garbed in the simple black tunics he wore when not on patrol, but tonight he was dressed like a prince. A handsomely cut blue coat covered his simple silk shirt that opened to reveal his powerful neck, and his matching hose showed his muscular legs to advantage.

Borne flashed his damnable dimples. "Ah, I see you approve. May I say you are also looking irresistible this evening, my lady? Comte Flaseur appears in the depths of despair that I beat him to you."

"Thank the gods," breathed Halla. "If you hadn't rescued me, I'd have dropped to the floor and slithered like a snake from the room."

"An intriguing image, considering that gown." Borne closed his cornflower eyes as if to more fully appreciate it.

Halla gave him a discreet punch. "Wipe it from your salacious mind," she threatened. "The next blow will be aimed lower. Now take me somewhere I can sit without being incessantly bowed over."

With a courtly incline of his head, Borne tucked her arm proprietarily under his and drew her from the dance floor. "A glass of wine, perhaps?"

"I'd rather an ale. Better still, can we not just leave?"

"Not without insulting our royal host. This is your evening, Lady Halla." He looked beyond her. "And your beaux are not easily discouraged."

The cloying scent of musk moved Halla to action. She gave Borne's arm a brisk tug, and they escaped to the relative quiet of the balcony.

"A clandestine tryst!" whispered Borne as she drew him under the overhanging greenery and out of sight of the courtiers. "Should I fear designs on my virtue?"

Before Halla could think of a quelling response, he hoisted himself onto the stone ledge at their backs and asked, "Can you bend in that sheath?"

In answer, Halla levered herself up beside him.

"Follow me." Borne helped to her feet, then led the way along the wall to the end of the ledge.

Halla pushed an escaped braid away from her face. "Now what?"

"Sit," commanded Borne, and leaping down, he deftly lifted her off the wall.

Halla peered into the darkness and made out a set of stairs leading downward. "Where are we?"

He raised a cryptic brow. "Patience, Jelzahba."

Used to his obscure references to literary figures, she didn't bother to ask who Jelzahba might be.

Her attention was caught by the sound of fountains playing. It accompanied them down the steps and under a series of arching trellises. Here the grounds opened up, and Halla drew a breath of delight. A rippling lake spread before them, and on a small island at its center stood a house constructed entirely of glass, shimmering with a strange, starry light. A wooden bridge led across the water to the island, its railings adorned with half a dozen clusters of grotesques. Their grimacing visages may have been intended to discourage intruders, but to Halla they were wondrous.

"Come." Borne took up her hand.

As soon as they stepped onto the bridge, jets of water sprang up from the polished surface of the dark lake. Through the spray, Halla saw strange creatures slowly rising from its depths.

"They're mechanical," said Borne. "Whoever designed them was a genius. They used some sort of hydraulics."

Halla, who shared Borne's fascination with anything to do with engineering, clapped her hands as the emerging waterworks were revealed to be stately birds with bills that opened and closed and wings that rose and fell. She started forward to examine one of them more closely, but Borne placed a forestalling hand on her arm.

"We have to time it just so," he cautioned.

He drew a small stone from his pocket and tossed it a few paces ahead. When it hit the bridge, the nearest mechanical bird swiveled and spouted a stream of water at its exact location.

Borne sprinted over the bridge, and Halla, with a laugh, kicked off her slippers and scampered after him. She caught up with him when he paused to toss another stone. This time, the slats beneath it collapsed with a splash.

Halla gasped. "How did you know that would happen?"

But Borne was already leaping over the gap. His landing triggered the mechanical grotesques lining the railings, and as he leapt back to where Halla stood, the grotesques—which Halla could see now were apes—sprang into action. The creatures rattled along the railings, emitting simian shrieks and swinging their long, curved arms. Had Borne continued forward, they would have surely knocked him into the water.

When the apes' arms fell still, and the beasts themselves began to slide back to their original positions, Borne assisted Halla across the gap, and together they raced over the bridge.

But just before they reached the end, Borne pulled them to a stop. Halla looked up expectantly at him, and saw he was counting under his breath.

"On my signal," he murmured.

Halla poised herself to run. But instead of leaping forward, Borne hollered "Duck!" He tugged Halla to her knees just before a cunningly hidden paddle swung at the empty space where their heads had been.

"You'll love this part," Borne whispered.

He was up and off again.

A great roar thundered behind Halla, propelling her after Borne. She cast a frantic look over her shoulder to see a mechanical lion rise up through the hole in the bridge, water spilling from its back. Though she knew it wasn't real, she felt her blood pounding through her veins.

Borne was waiting ahead, his hand outstretched. He pulled her onto the island as the lion surged forward, its metal jaws closing with a jarring snap just inches from her.

"By the gods—"

But Borne's finger against his lips silenced her. Still holding her hand, he led her silently toward the glass-cased belvedere.

At the sudden and startling sound of an organ groaning to life, Halla bit her tongue so hard she tasted blood. The glass house went dark, and Borne pitched another stone at it. Halla braced for the shattering of glass, but instead a mirrored shield sprang up from the ground, sending the stone ricocheting into the lake. Simultaneously, buckets of water and flour emptied from the eaves of the house, followed by a drifting cloud of feathers that added to the pasty mess.

Halla burst out laughing. "Gods' blood! Who was the delightfully mad man who contrived this?"

Borne dropped onto a narrow bench beside the belvedere. "Woman. The mad woman was Queen Delaphoise, great-grandmother of his most high, most powerful—"

"Please, spare me all the honorifics," Halla said, sinking down beside him.

"Ah, but Delaphoise was deserving of them. Under her rule, the lesser kingdoms of Gral were unified in much the same way that Gundauld the Great brought together the realms of Drinnglennin."

"Him again," Halla groaned, then caught her breath as fissures of light began zigzagging within the glass house.

Borne shook his head in wonder. "I'm still trying to figure out how the lightning is done."

Halla released a happy sigh. "Thank you for... this. It's bloody brilliant! The best birthday present I could have imagined."

When Borne didn't respond, she gave him an elbow in the ribs. "Don't worry—I'm not about to get all dewy-eyed and cloying."

"I'm glad," he said, rubbing his side. "I shouldn't like to be the cause of any discord..."

"Between Nicu and me, do you mean?" Halla hoped she didn't sound bitter. "No, it's not like that with us." She bent down and retrieved a pebble at her feet. "I imagine you know as well as I do where he is right now."

Borne's dimples disappeared. "Does it bother you?"

Halla shrugged. "The demoiselle Margreitte set her sights on him the moment she saw him. They all did. He's a beautiful man. And no, it doesn't bother me, or at least not so much." *Perhaps*, she thought, *if I say that often enough, it will come to be true.* "Fidelity isn't really part of å Livåri life, at least not until marriage."

"But you're not å Livåri," Borne pointed out. "And, forgive me, but I assume Nicu is your first lover. I thought perhaps—"

"You thought wrong." She tossed the pebble into the muddle of flour and feathers rather harder than she had intended. "Does it shock you that I accept this? Or is it giving my maidenhead to someone like Nicu that you find hard to fathom?" She stood up and looked down at him. "I don't see why it should. I lead a soldier's life: I train, I fight, I risk death every time I ride into battle. Why shouldn't I partake of the same pleasures all of my comrades enjoy? Why is a girl's virginity considered sacrosanct and the loss of it out of wedlock to be shameful, while a man's sexual exploits are a cause for congratulations?"

Borne held up his palms in surrender. "Peace, my fiery warrior—I'm on your side. I've never heard a woman pose this view, but of course you're right."

"Then the women you've listened to are either too cowed by others' expectations or they're dishonest."

"Or perhaps I just never thought to ask their opinions on the matter. I shall be mindful of this in the future."

His words tempered Halla's anger. She sat down again, and they listened to the strains of viols and lutes wafting over the grounds.

"What about you?" she asked, when her heartbeat had returned to normal. "I've never seen you with a woman in all the time we've been riding together. I know for certain you've not been without opportunity."

Borne looked down at his clasped hands. "And how could you know that?"

Halla glanced sideways at him. "The ladies of the court are throwing themselves in your path at every opportunity, as you well know."

"And how do you know that I haven't accepted their advances?" he asked lightly.

"Because women gossip. So do men, for that matter, every bit as much as women, especially about their commanders. You'd be surprised what I've learned about you."

"Such as?" His guarded tone belatedly warned her she was on thin ice.

"Nothing too personal," she assured him. "You bathe too often for a man, you talk in your sleep, you—"

"I what?"

"Talk in your sleep—*when* you sleep, that is, which isn't very often. Most nights you make notes in your secret book about everyone in the company. I assume it takes up the time you could be spending with a wo—" She bit off what she'd been about to say when she saw his expression.

"Who told you about the book?" he demanded. "Nicu?"

142

Halla attempted a shrug. She hadn't meant to cause anyone trouble. "Nicu, Baldo, Chik—I can't remember. What does it matter? It's just idle talk." She pretended not to notice the grim set of Borne's mouth. "Surely this doesn't upset you?"

"Not in the least," he replied, rising to his feet. "We should get back. You will have been missed by now."

They crossed over the bridge in silence, and Halla found herself wishing for the commotion of the marvelous contraptions to ease the tension she now felt between them. She deeply regretted her casual mention of Borne's book; it had clearly offended him and now overshadowed all the pleasure of their escapade.

At the foot of the staircase, she ventured to lay a hand on his arm. "I'm sorry," she said. She felt his taut muscles relax slightly, and when he turned to face her, one dimple was on display.

"For?"

Halla sniffed. "My lady mother always said it's in terrible taste to repeat gossip."

He laughed then, but it had a hollow ring. "I think my mother once told me something along the same lines. In any event, you can assure the men I'm not writing about them."

Halla gave a little nod. "It's none of my business, but… am I right? Does your writing have something to do with why you don't have a woman?"

"You're right." Borne stepped aside to let her precede him. "It's none of your business."

CHAPTER 13
Fynn

In Fynn and Grinner's dreary cell, the weeks crawled to months. Judging from the fleeting daylight showing through the bars high on the wall, the winter solstice couldn't be far off.

During the long hours of the night, Fynn often lay sleepless, occupied by random, troubling thoughts that spun cobwebs of despair. He wondered if any Restarians had survived the massacre he and Teca had escaped, and what had become of Flekka, his mother's fine Albrenian mare. Sometimes, remembered snatches of silly conversations with Einar made him smile to himself in the dark, until he recalled that his friend's voice was likely silenced forever.

Fynn worried about Grinner too, fearing that the å Livåri's destiny had somehow become tied to his own. There'd been no court hearings for either of them, no information as to what fate they could expect. It seemed the world had simply forgotten their existence.

"Most like they reckoned we'd finish each other off," Grinner suggested with a wry smile.

But Fynn thought it more probable that they were both expected to die in here, and until they did, their warders would carry on with their orders: two bowls of gruel and a pail of water a day, with fresh rushes once in a moon cycle. He doubted they could survive indefinitely on the poor fare. Grinner had developed a worrisome cough from the dank, cold air, and a puncture Fynn had given himself in the heel of his hand with the wrong end of his spoon was slow to heal, the skin around it reddened and tender.

They did their best to keep each other's spirits from flagging. Grinner made clear he hated to speak of his past, but he hungered for stories about Fynn's childhood in the distant northern world of Helgrinia, so completely different from the harsh life the å Livåri had endured.

"Ye say the snowdrifts stood o'er a man's head? And great elkers pulled yer sledges through 'em?" Grinner chivvied Fynn to describe the icicles, as thick as young trees, that hung from the eaves of the longhouses, and the ice stars that formed in perfect symmetry on the windows of their manor. How it got so cold a man's breath would freeze in his beard, and wet clothes left hanging out overnight would crack and split. Grinner had seen dustings of snow before, but he'd grown up in the southern part of the realm and avoided the north of Drinnglennin in the winter months. "The one time I ventured up tha' way in the cold season were last year, and I nearly ended up at the end of a swingin' rope."

In recalling Restaria for his friend, Fynn found he couldn't avoid speaking about his family. The memories he related about his loving home brought a smile to Grinner's lips, and gave Fynn a glimmer of comfort through the pain.

On the day he finally told Grinner what had become of his mother, the å Livåri teared up. "We both knowed sorrow," he said, clumsily patting Fynn's hand. "What of yer pa an' yer brother? Do ye ken they was killed by them raiders, too?"

"I don't know." *And I never will,* Fynn thought bitterly.

But lying awake that night, his hand moved to the little pouch of bloodteeth tucked under his tunic, and he realized there *might* be a way to find out what had become of Aetheor and Jered. If he were to eat part of one of the mushrooms, might he not be able to dream-cast like Old Snorri? The tale-weaver had traveled to Cloud Mountain to beg for the gods' help; perhaps Fynn could do the same.

For several days, he wrestled with the obstacles in this path. For one, Old Snorri had eaten his mushroom cap in the presence of Wurl, the sacred tree. It might be that Fynn was too far away from the great oak to dream-travel across the sea, and the mushroom would only serve to poison him. And if he were to attempt a dream journey, he'd have to let Grinner in on his plans. That worried him. While he trusted the å Livåri to do him no harm while he dreamt, he wondered if the lure of a drug, even one that could kill outright, might be too great a temptation for his friend. What if Fynn were to awaken and find that Grinner had tried to dream-cast as well, and had died for his effort?

Of course, if Fynn got his own dosage wrong, he would never know.

But halfway through a sleepless night, he sat bolt upright, recalling that Old Snorri had gone to Gral to find the corpse of his father. Surely that meant that Fynn could dream himself a great distance as well.

As the days passed, thoughts of dream-casting occupied more and more of Fynn's time. Waiting out the end of his days in ignorance seemed a fate every bit as grim as death. He had to know if Aetheor and Jered still lived. *And if they do not*, he thought, *I'll have two more deaths to avenge.*

Eventually, the sheer monotony of his existence made his decision for him, and he revealed his intentions to Grinner. He was surprised to learn that the å Livåri knew of the powers some mushrooms held, although upon examining the blood-teeth, Grinner confessed he'd never seen their likes.

"No question they're poison, tha's fer sure. I've eaten loads o' wild victuals, and I know t' avoid any wit' red spots on 'em. Are ye sure this Ol' Snorri weren't chaffin' ye?"

"He was most serious when he told his tale," said Fynn. He supposed he should feel guilty for breaking the promise he'd made the old man never to share his story, but Fynn figured under the circumstances, Old Snorri would forgive him. "I'll know for certain tonight. I've decided I'm ready."

For the first time since Fynn had known Grinner, he saw fear flicker in the å Livåri's dark eyes. "Don' do it!" Grinner pleaded. "Don' leave me 'ere alone!"

"I'll only take a tiny bit," Fynn promised, attempting a reassuring smile. "Old Snorri survived after eating half a cap, and he did it twice." He broke off a small portion. "See? I'll only eat this much."

"What if they gone off?" Grinner countered. "They look right parlous t' me."

"That's only because they've been dried." But Fynn felt a stab of doubt. His mother had told him herbs become more potent through the drying process. *Will a quarter of a cap be too much?* He stared at the dusty spores on the underside of the crimson-spotted cap, then dropped it back in the pouch. He tried not to notice how his fingers trembled as he tucked the little bag under his tunic.

He rose to his feet and began to circle his friend. "I'll wait until tonight, so you won't have the whole day to fret away. We've still got hours to kill. Let's see if you can take me down today. I've won the last two bouts."

But Grinner refused to wrestle. He spent the rest of the day rolled up in his filthy cloak, only rousing himself when their dinner was pushed through the door. Even then, he slurped his gruel without comment, and when his bowl was empty, he set it down and turned away.

"Don't be like that, Grinner," Fynn pleaded to the å Livåri's rigid back. "I'm counting on you to help me."

"It's naught t' do wit' me," Grinner muttered.

Fynn crawled around so he could see his friend's face. "You can have the rest of my dinner," he said, holding out his bowl. "I think it's best I don't fill my stomach beforehand."

Grinner stared stubbornly past him.

Fynn saw he'd have to try another tack, even if it was risky. "Imagine that you had a chance to find out what happened to Petra. Wouldn't you seize it?"

"I know what happened t' her," Grinner said flatly. "Crennin took 'er."

Fynn sank back on his heels. "I'm sorry. But what if you didn't know… wouldn't you want to?"

Grinner shrugged. "I s'pose," he said, his voice tight in his throat.

"All right, then. It's the same for me. I *have* to know what's happened to my father and brother. Can you understand?" He waited until Grinner met his eyes. "It'll be well, you'll see. And maybe, just maybe, while I'm dreaming, I'll find a way for us to get out of this gods-forsaken gaol as well."

Grinner grunted, then reached for Fynn's bowl. "Just so long as it ain't boots first."

* * *

The mushroom cap tasted, not unpleasantly, of warm earth, and a hint of heat lingered on Fynn's tongue after he swallowed it. Lying on the rushes, he listened to his heart thundering in his ears.

I have to hold Father in my thoughts, no matter what. After I find him, I can try for Jered as well.

"Did ye do it?" Grinner whispered from the darkness.

"Yes."

Fynn heard his rueful sigh. For no reason, it struck him as funny, and he laughed.

"That were fast," Grinner muttered. "Yer already feelin' it?"

"I don't think so." Fynn's heart was still pumping hard, but he put that down to the fact he might have just caused his own death.

Don't let your thoughts go there.

He rolled on his side to face his friend. "Tell me about Dveld… while I'm waiting. What was it like?"

The rushes rustled as Grinner shifted toward him as well. "Dveld were… it were the best and the worst o' worlds. That first time in the forest, Petra and me, we chewed just a leaf apiece. I recollect the sound o' Petra's laugh, like a bell struck after years o' silence. I felt warm all over, like I could jus' curl up an' sleep, but I were too… happy. We set by a little creek watchin' and listenin' t' the water runnin' o'er the stones. It seemed hours passed, and still the sun were hangin' high in the sky. I weren't hungry no more, an' I dinna care 'bout nuthin'—not even that bitch Margred. 'Twere like light runnin' through me veins, fillin' me belly an' the forest all wit' golden honey."

A coughing fit took him, and Fynn reached over blindly to pat his back. When his friend could speak again, his voice was hollow. "Then we fell, an' fell hard."

A shiver ran up Fynn's spine. "What do you mean, you fell?"

"When the crennin begun t' wear off, 'twere like all the light were sucked from the woods, and it growed dark, the darkest o' dark. Petra started in cryin', and 'tweren't nothin' I could do t' comfort 'er. A great black hole were gnawin' at me insides, a hunger tha' pained me somethin' terrible, like an evil wind burrowin' in me gut, settin' up a howlin' in me head and clawin' at me belly. We didn't know it then, but 'twere the beginnin' o' the end fer anythin' good fer us."

The desolation in Grinner's voice made Fynn wish he hadn't started the conversation. Was this the fate that awaited him?

As if reading his thought, Grinner said, "It shouldna be like tha' wit' the mushroom. Margred chewed 'em from time t' time, wit' one o' 'er blowsy slut friends. They always talked bosh about seein' things' what weren't there, but the mushrooms didna take hold o' them like the crennin done."

Fynn opened his eyes as wide as he could. "Seeing things? You mean, like haunts?"

"Nah… more like rainbows an' lights trailin' off their fingers… just ravin' claptrap, were all."

Fynn lifted his hand and waved it in the dark. He didn't see anything, and didn't feel different than usual, except for maybe a slight heaviness in his arms and legs. He lay listening to his breath, and despite his long-held resolve not to, he longed for his mother. If the bloodteeth killed him, maybe he'd meet her again, in some afterlife, and feel once more the soft brush of her lips on his brow. Perhaps, since she wasn't a Helgrin, she too had been barred from Cloud Mountain. He could almost smell the jasmine scent she'd favored, and hear her low, musical voice calling to him.

A sharp elbow dug into his side. "Ye still here?"

"Ummm," Fynn murmured, reluctant to shift his mind back to the cheerless cell.

"I be 'ere waitin' fer ye, when ye get back," Grinner said quietly.

Fynn smiled, but he couldn't think of a reply. Trying to form words somehow seemed too hard. *It doesn't matter,* he thought, although about what he couldn't say. The heaviness in his limbs had been replaced by a floaty, light feeling, as though he'd slipped from his body into the air. There was something, though—something he was meant to do. He forced himself to concentrate, sifting through the fogginess, and finding again the words he needed, he repeated them over and over in his mind.

Father. Let me dream of my father.

* * *

He was still lying in the dark. The mushrooms hadn't worked. I must have eaten too small a portion, *he thought. His stomach churned, and he rolled up to a sitting position—only to realize the floor beneath him was bare of rushes. Reaching blindly in a circle around himself, he could find no trace of the dry grasses that covered the floor of the cell.*

"*Grinner?*"

His own voice echoed back to him.

His hand fell on a wooden box, and searching it with his fingers, he discovered its lid was slightly askew. He slid it open and felt the objects inside. A stone. A cold, flat piece of metal. It took him a moment longer to identify a stub of candle. And finally, a twist of cloth.

A tinderbox.

With trembling fingers, he made a net of his tunic and put the metal, stone, and cloth into it. Carefully, he stood the candle upright on the tinderbox. It took him three strikes of the metal on the flint to get a spark, and another two to connect it with the char cloth. When the candle was lit, he raised it above his head and looked around.

He sat in a windowless room under a low vaulted ceiling. Thick columns formed a wide aisle down the center of the chamber, and all around him, cold stone faces gazed down on him from high pedestals. Fynn rose to examine the statues, touching his candle to the sconces lining the stone wall as he passed under their glittering eyes.

If they were gods and goddesses, they were not those of the Helgrins. The first was a female with a great hawk perched on her shoulder, her sapphire eyes so exactly like his dead mother's, they forced a cry from him. The next stood in a sculpted fire, his feet twined by sinuous serpents, his ruby eyes glowing, a raised torch in his fist. There followed a goddess with a gentle expression, a wreath of leaves crowning her flowing tresses—then another, this one with emeralds for eyes and the tail of a fish, a pearly conch shell hanging from her slender, scaled waist.

The last statue was of a god who clearly reigned supreme over the others, for he was nearly twice their size. In one of his massive hands he clutched a huge iron club, and in the other outstretched palm rested a golden orb. His diamond eyes glittered like cold stars.

Tall arched doors rose behind each of the statues, all of them sealed except for the one behind the final colossus. It stood slightly ajar—a clear invitation for Fynn to pass through.

What brought Aetheor Yarl to this eerie place? *Fynn wondered.*

He sensed the answer must lie on the other side of that door.

He pushed against it, expecting to meet resistance, but it swung open easily, revealing a smaller chamber with no other exits. Fynn lit the sconces by the door, then looked around.

Inlaid into the floor was a mosaic of a wolfish beast with talons and a long, knotted tail. The same creature was embossed on stone boxes set into recesses along the walls.

Fynn's knees buckled as the realization of where he was—and why—struck home.

This was a tomb.

There could be only one reason why his dream-cast had brought him to this place. In one of these stone coffins, Aetheor, Yarl of Helgrinia, must lie.

Fynn's beloved father was dead.

He threw back his head and let loose a howl of grief. For how long he wept, only the gods knew, but once his tears were spent, he ground the heels of his hands into his eyes and got to his feet once more. He hadn't forgotten the uncertain outcome of Old Snorri's quest. The taleweaver had woken from his dream too soon and was doomed to spend the rest of his days in an agony of doubt, wondering whether or not he'd succeeded in sending his father to Cloud Mountain. Fynn knew his own dream could come to end at any moment, condemning him to the same fate. He'd already failed his father in so many ways, and would not squander this last chance to earn redemption. If his father's bones lay in this strange place, he would gather them and see that they received the proper rituals.

Grimly, Fynn approached the first of the recessed boxes and read the name and dates etched in the stone.

Gundauld 02-59 AA

He continued to circle the vault, his heart in his throat, stopping at each tomb in turn. Several repeated the same given names, but with a later date. All the surnames were the same. This was no Helgrin resting place.

Dread crept into Fynn's bones. He must have cast the dream wrongly—for how would his father's remains have ended up here?

When at last he reached the final tomb, he saw that the etching on it was recent, dated a moon after Restaria had been attacked. It was made of a darker stone than the others, and its smooth surface reflected the candle's light. The sigil on this vault was different, too. Not only was it much smaller, it was incomplete, ending abruptly at the creature's waist. Fynn reached up to touch the wolfish face, and. his breath caught in his throat.

With trembling fingers, he drew the pendant from around his neck and held it up to the dark stone.

Where it completed, perfectly, the other half of the sigil.

In nameless horror, Fynn tried to pull his hand away, but it was held to the stone by some dark force.

"Where is my father?" he cried, struggling to free himself. "I beg you! Show me!"

In answer, the etching on the tomb blazed alight, seared by red fire. Fynn fought to wrench his fingers away, but to no avail, as he was forced to accept the terrible truth.

He now knew, in all certainty, the reason his mother had made Teca bring him to Drinnglennin, why she had insisted he wear the broken pendant, and why he could never, no matter his prowess in battle, become the greatest of Helgrin warriors.

Because his father was not Aetheor Yarl.

His father, the man from whose seed Fynn had sprung, was buried here in this very tomb.

The name etched above the sigil was Urlion Konigur.

CHAPTER 14
Maura

Doesn't his throat slit like any other?

Maura had tried to forget that chilling conversation between Roth and his mother, and for a time, she had almost succeeded. Roth's impeccable behavior toward her made it seem impossible that he had ever said such a thing; he treated her with gallantry, affording her every courtesy and showering her with lavish gifts and honeyed words. On the day of his investiture as High King, which she'd witnessed seated beside her future mother-in-law, she felt her heart swell with pride and affection for the young and dashing new sovereign.

But his words could never truly be forgotten. Slowly but surely, she found herself re-examining her perception of Roth, and as she paid closer attention, a different side of his nature began to emerge. It started with little things that revealed a heartlessness in contrast to the gentle knight she'd thought him to be.

For instance, when the Nelvors took up residence in the castle, Roth immediately dismissed the household who'd served the Konigurs for generations, turning them out without recompense and replacing them with servants brought in from Nelvorboth. When Maura expressed her concerns for the displaced folk, Roth dismissed them out of hand, saying it was customary for the new sovereign to bring in his own people, so as to surround himself with those he could fully trust.

After that, he set about "retiring" a number of elderly nobles from court. Although he assured Maura it was their wish to return to their own realms, she'd overheard some of his courtiers laughingly congratulating him on weeding out the "fusty goats."

Then there were the evening meals. When Urlion was High King, they were decorous if rather dull, but under Roth they had evolved, at least for Maura, into a coarse trial to be endured. The accompanying entertainments were now raucous and in increasingly questionable taste. There were no longer recitations from the classics, for Urlion's old bard had been one of those loyal servants who was dismissed, and no one was brought in to replace him. Bawdy songs rather than ballads were now heard by the diners, and a horrid fool reeled between the tables making lewd comments and lascivious gestures. Copious amounts of mead, wine, and ale were consumed, and it was becoming a common occurrence to see one's supper companion face down on his trencher, dead drunk.

Maura took to excusing herself as soon as the last course was cleared. She had a legitimate reason, for her headaches had returned, and for once she was glad to be able to plead them as grounds. But even though she avoided the worst of the evenings' antics, she couldn't ignore the whispered reports of what went on in her absence. Indeed, given how loudly Sir Lawton boasted of their late-night revelries in the city, it was impossible to pretend ignorance.

Yet despite all the frenetic merriment, Roth seemed less and less content. Maura initially put his growing moodiness and occasional outbursts of temper down to the strain of his new, demanding role. But she couldn't help wondering if he'd always had this hard, restless edge, and he was simply no longer bothering to hide it from her.

She hoped to speak frankly with him about her concerns for his well-being on the royal progression from Drinnkastel to Nelvorboth, as he'd decided to continue the celebration of his coronation there. And though Maura wouldn't be able to take part in most of the festivities—she was still wearing mourning weeds—she looked forward to having him alone on the journey so that they could talk.

But her hopes were dashed when he handed her up into the carriage and she found that Grindasa and Lawton were already occupying it. She didn't care to broach such delicate topics in their presence, and even her attempts to engage Roth in casual conversation were unsuccessful. He seemed distracted—indeed uninterested—in anything she had to say.

Things were no better at Nelvor Castle. Roth set off with a hunting party early the first day, leaving Maura to fend for herself. She spent much of the time walking through the famed gardens, trying to sort out her feelings. In addition to her frequent headaches, she was now plagued by loneliness, and she had begun to long for Ilyria's presence, as she had in the first months of their separation, as well as for Leif's easy companionship.

It was on the second day of their stay in Nelvorboth that she chanced to overhear a terse exchange between Roth and the intimidating Lord Vetch from behind one of the grounds' many pavilions.

"Explain to me how this was allowed to happen," Roth said. His voice, though low, still managed to convey his outrage.

Lord Vetch launched into an explanation about a boy who'd been taken in the raid on Helgrinia. It had to be the same boy Grindasa mentioned, Maura realized. The boy who spoke fluent Drinn.

Doesn't his throat slit like any other?

"Maura?"

Maura spun to see Grindasa approaching, and she lifted her skirts to hurry the queen's way. The last thing she needed was for Grindasa to learn she'd been eavesdropping on her son. But as she and the queen drifted back toward the palace, Maura wished she could have heard the end of the conversation between Roth and his commander.

The next morning at breakfast, she was alone with Grindasa when the queen let fall the incredible news: Master Morgan had been declared an enemy of the Crown.

"Surely there's been a mistake!" Maura protested. "Master Morgan has served the Einhorn Throne for years, and he was a trusted, lifelong friend to my uncle."

Grindasa gave her a scathing look. "Which proves that all wizards are oath-breaking vermin! Morgan was the last one to see my poor Urlion alive. He was observed leaving the king's chamber and to me it's clear as a summer's sky: the wizard took his life. I would think you would want this kingslayer brought to justice every bit as much as my son and I do." The queen raised her kerchief to her dark-lined eyes and dabbed at invisible tears. Then she tilted her head as if a thought had just occurred to her. "But then, it was Morgan who brought you and your odd friend to Drinnkastel, wasn't it? The one who looked a bit... well, I did wonder if his blood was tainted. I thought he might be part Lurker."

Maura was rendered speechless by the queen's condemnation of wizards and å Livåri in just a few venomous breaths. Was Grindasa also hinting that she knew something about Maura's own antecedents? And if not, what would the queen do if she ever learned that her future grandchildren would carry that blood, mingled with that of a dragon?

"That boy disappeared at the same time as the wizard," Grindasa mused, with narrowed eyes. "Perhaps he was an accomplice in Urlion's murder."

"What an absurd idea!" Maura snapped.

From the sudden outrage in the queen's eyes, Maura saw she'd gone too far.

"I mean—"

Grindasa set down her knife with deliberate care, then swept from the room in livid silence.

Maura looked down at her clenched fists. She decided she was too angry over the woman's ridiculous accusations against

Master Morgan and insinuations about Leif to worry about what this bitter exchange might cost her. She was tired of being on her guard all the time around people she had hoped would be her new family.

Throwing aside her napkin, she left her breakfast untouched and went in search of Roth. She would insist on a serious conversation with him—at once, before her resolve deserted her.

She found him in the stables, dressed for riding in a new black-and-silver coat cut in the continental style. He didn't look altogether happy to see her.

Maura didn't mince her words. "Your mother has been so kind as to inform me you've declared Master Morgan a traitor and a murderer. She went so far as to suggest that Leif was involved as well." She gave a little choked laugh of incredulity. "You can't honestly believe that either of them had anything to do with my uncle's death?"

Roth continued to adjust the girth of his horse's saddle. "I know you like to believe the best of everyone, my dear," he said, stepping back from the charger and signaling to a groom to lead the horse to the courtyard, "but in this you are mistaken. Others better equipped to uncover the truth are certain my father was poisoned."

"What others?" Maura demanded.

When Roth didn't reply and attempted to pass her, she laid a restraining hand on his sleeve. He looked at it pointedly, and when he raised his eyes to hers, they were glitteringly cold.

"My Tribus," he said curtly.

"Perhaps," Maura retorted hotly, "your Tribus should ask Master Tergin why he was giving Urlion melia berries."

Several of the stable boys glanced over at them, and Roth shrugged off her hand.

"Perhaps," he replied, keeping his voice low, "I would be better served to wonder how *you* came by this knowledge?"

Before Maura could recover from the shock of his implication, Roth spun on his heel and left the stables. She hurried after him in time to see him swing up into his saddle.

"I can see the travel has left you overwrought, my dear," he said, wheeling the charger, "so I will overlook your impudence." He gave her a polite, cool smile. "In the future, however, do not try my patience with regard to this matter." Then he gave his horse a sharp kick, leaving her to the furtive looks of the grooms.

Maura sought the refuge of her chamber, where she sat staring blankly at what might have once been a favorite tapestry. The weaving depicted a scene of a lady astride a silver mare, reaching down to accept an open book from a courtly prince. Beside them, a minstrel fingered his lute while a small dog danced on his hind legs. Snow-capped mountains rose in the background, surrounding a white, spired castle out of a faerie tale.

A lovely scene, thought Maura bitterly, *of a perfect romance in a perfect world.* But perfect was just a flight of fancy. Her own world, which she'd recently thought so close to perfection, had come crashing down around her with seven words.

Doesn't his throat slit like any other?

CHAPTER 15
Leif

The cold light of a billion stars lent no warmth. Leif's feet were numb and the tip of his nose felt as if it might chip off at the slightest sniff. It had been three long nights since Rhiandra had departed, and he felt certain she hadn't planned to leave him alone for so long in this forbidding land. Something had gone wrong.

When the first sliver of light appeared on the fourth day, Leif took stock of his remaining stores. He had a dozen rounds of waybread and enough dried fruit to last him another week. After that he'd be in real trouble, for there was nothing to forage on this ice-bound island. And he had another, more immediate worry: the power of his solaric stone was fading, and he could no longer light fires with it. The few hours of twilight that made up a day in this place weren't enough to renew its powers. The cloak Elvinor had given Leif would keep him from freezing, but even the fine elven weave couldn't keep the icy fingers of the gusting wind from finding their way down his neck or up his sleeves. Already the chill had crept into his bones, and even though he kept his gloves and boots on at all times, his hands and feet had gone numb. It was likely he'd gotten frostbite, though this was far down his list of concerns; he'd no doubt succumb altogether to the relentless cold before he started losing toes and fingers.

Rising to stomp his feet and clap his shoulders, as he had done repeatedly over the last hours to stir his blood, Leif considered his options. He could either continue to wait where he was, in the hope that Rhiandra would return, or he could go in search of her. But if he left and she came back, she might find it difficult, if not impossible, to trace him.

Leif nibbled a slice of waybread, watching as the thin bright line riming the edge of the world widened. It came down to this: the idea of sitting idle in the cavern until his food ran out simply wasn't one he could stomach. It was one thing to die, but to do it by starvation…

The gruesome prospect decided him. He would head due north to find the dragons, for Rhiandra had told him they lived high on the far pole of the Known World.

Leif shouldered his pack, stepped out of the cave into a biting wind, and set off across the crusted snow. He would have only a few hours before darkness descended again, so he set a brisk pace to make the most of them. Despite the cold, it felt good to be moving, and his spirits began to lift.

Belestar was white and grey and black, and he wondered how any living thing could bear to dwell in such dull isolation. Of course, dragons had always avoided the bustle of cities and contact with humankind, but centuries of living on this lonely island must have grown wearisome. Leif's thoughts drifted to Valeland, with its dark firs and woodland meadows of purple wildflowers, beauty he'd once taken for granted, and he wondered if he'd ever see such vibrant colors again.

Although the first hour of the march was over flat terrain, jagged ice blocks loomed up in his path with increasing frequency, and he was gradually forced to slow his pace. As he picked his way carefully around these obstacles, he kept his eyes peeled for the dark lines that signaled weak ice, for a sudden fracture could send him plunging to a cruel death. He also kept his ears attuned for signs of life. Now and then he would hear a roaring in the distance, a deep, unsettling resonance that carried to him from what he hoped was afar. He didn't care to meet any of the ferocious ice bears said to share this isle with the dragons.

Occasionally he sensed he'd lost his bearings, and he wasted valuable time stopping to debate if he should backtrack or alter his course. The third time he felt like he'd strayed, having lost the pale sun under heavy clouds, he slumped down in near-despair. He was a fool to have set out like this. He had perhaps another hour before night fell once more, and there was no sign of shelter. He had already come too far to consider turning back, even if he wanted to.

It occurred to him that he might not survive the night.

His steaming breath slowed, and he was just about to rise once more, to trudge onward for however many steps he had left, when he felt a warm pulse against his chest.

The stone.

In the months since Master Morgan had presented him with the solaric pendant, it had never before signaled to him on its own accord.

He tugged the stone from the inner folds of his cloak. Though it was usually translucent, it now glowed a dark magenta. Leif gazed at it in wonder and was struck with a sudden inspiration.

Rising, he held the stone at arm's length, then made a slow circle. Nothing happened until he'd completed the turn, at which point the stone gave a soft pulse of light. He repeated his circling several more times, starting from different orientations, and the results were always the same: the stone pulsed with light when he faced a certain direction. Could it be that it served as a compass of sorts?

He took several steps in what he believed to be an easterly direction, then turned in place again. Three quarters of the way round, the stone lit up once more.

It *was* a compass. And it was guiding him north.

Heartened, he carried on.

Another hour passed. His neck ached from constantly looking down to watch for treacherous fissures and shifting ice. When he did glance up, the distant rise ahead remained just that—distant. Although several hours had elapsed since he'd started out, he appeared to be no closer to the higher ground. The sky was darkening, the temperature was dropping, and Leif was too weary to go on. He'd have to bundle up and do his best to stay warm until the sun rose again. At least the stiff winds of earlier had now ebbed.

That long night as he lay curled in his cloak, he saw the windlights for the first time. They began as pale greenish-yellow flashes that unfurled into ribbons of pink light against the dark sky, reddened at both ends—as though they had been dipped in the ichor of the gods. The stone against his chest radiated with sudden heat, so he drew it out—and to his delight, it pulsed in time to the rhythm of the sky's silent symphony.

Perhaps if Rhiandra were flying in search of him, she would see its tiny beacon.

The thought reminded him of his gran, who had always left a candle in the window of their little croft on nights he returned home from Master Morgan's cottage after dark. In his mind's eye, he could see her feeding sticks to the fire, then rising slowly to stir the hot broth thick with carrots and barley and onions she'd prepared for their supper. He hoped she'd gotten someone to help her stock in enough wood, and that her knees hadn't gone too stiff. They'd troubled her in the colder months of recent years.

If only he had been able to take his gran with him when he'd gone to Mithralyn. The leaves of the forests would be golden there now, as they were when Leif first arrived in the elven realm. How quickly the year had passed. And how much his life had changed since Rhiandra had pierced his heart with her talon. He'd left the little village of Tonis Vale and crossed over the mountains to Fairendell, where he'd met his father, the king of the elves. In Mithralyn, he'd made the first real friends he'd ever had. He remembered as if it were yesterday sitting by Maura's bedside after she'd been found unconscious at the sentinel stone, her heart pierced, as his had been, by a dragon's talon. And from the moment she opened her violet eyes, he'd known she was a true kindred spirit.

Leif gave a rueful laugh, his breath a puff of vapor in the still air. That's what he'd believed at the time, anyway. Recalling their bitter parting still made him feel wretched.

He dredged up happier memories of his time in the capital. The best of these had been the jousts, especially the one between Roth and Borne. Borne was the better of the two contenders, and he'd turned out to be a decent fellow as well. *I wouldn't have minded so if Maura had ended up with him, a fellow northerner. But the Nelvorbothian?* Leif wrinkled his cold nose with distaste, recalling the scent Roth wore. *As if he had to cover up an underlying stink.*

And I've gone and sworn to protect the man!

He rolled onto his side with a sigh. It was more likely he'd die here in this frozen land, and be forgotten by them all.

No. I can't think like that. I'll find Rhiandra—I just need to keep going north.

He closed his eyes and lay listening to the groaning ice. It sounded like a lament of coming doom.

* * *

Two exhausting days later, the distant peaks looked only slightly closer than when Leif had first set out. His extremities were numb, his body weakening. He'd finished the last of his dried fruits, and was down to five rounds of waybread. Still he plodded ever northward, trying not to dwell on how little time he had left.

Surely Rhiandra will come for me before I die, he thought, but he lacked his earlier conviction. If she'd been trying to find him, she would have done so by now. A terrible specter of his beautiful bluewinged soulmate, broken and torn by her siblings' cruel teeth and talons, had begun to haunt him. He felt certain he would know if she was dead, but he couldn't think of any other reason for the dragon's extended absence.

By the end of the third short day, the mountains to the north appeared a little closer. The ice had leveled out, and there were fewer crevasses to negotiate, so he threw caution to the wind and continued walking after dark, carrying the solaric stone like a radiant talisman before him. Rest was a luxury he could no longer afford; he must either find Rhiandra soon, or perish. And he was determined to find her, even if it was the last thing he did. If he was going to make the Leap, he had to know first what had happened to her.

As the hours dragged by, Leif felt the tendrils of despair gaining a stranglehold on his thoughts. He'd failed everyone. He'd left his gran heartbroken. He'd let Master Morgan and Elvinor down. His last words to Maura, who'd shown him only kindness, had been harsh. And now he was going to die a stupid, pointless death, leaving Rhiandra, heart of his heart, behind in terrible grief.

It was a mercy that exhaustion eventually emptied his mind of any thought beyond putting one foot in front of the other. In a daze, he tramped on to the cadence of his labored breathing, his eyes on his feet, which he could no longer feel.

He never saw the darker shadow lying in his path. He simply stepped into air and dropped through the cleft in the ice like a stone, thudding against the unyielding walls that tore at him with jutting teeth as he wheeled, blind and breathless, into the abyss.

* * *

There was light, but no air. Leif struggled to breathe, gripped by stabbing pain in his chest and gut. Gasping, stubbornly fighting his panic, he willed his lungs to inflate. When they finally obeyed and the terror began to subside, he lay for uncounted moments, staring up at the rising walls of ice through which he'd plummeted. It seemed impossible that he'd survived such a long fall.

He groped beneath him and found the reason why. His hand met a pliant pile of deep fur that had cushioned his landing. It was the only reason he hadn't shattered every bone in his body.

He pushed himself into a sitting position and gingerly tested each limb. Although he ached all over, and had trouble finding a spot that wasn't bruised, no bones were broken. He let his pack slip from his throbbing shoulders onto the luxuriant pelts, found his wineskin, and drank deeply. If he'd hurt anything internally, the elven elixir would help him mend. Then he lay back down and was still for a time, just grateful to be alive and warm. He was almost too warm, for his eyes kept drifting closed. *Don't sleep,* he warned himself. For all he knew, he'd fallen into an ice bear's den. He fervently hoped this was not the case.

As the elixir worked its magic, he surveyed his surroundings, for this subterranean den into which he had fallen was lit, but not from above. The treacherous rift through which he had fallen was lost in darkness. But then, where were the light and heat coming from?

He rolled onto his stomach and crawled across the island of furs until he found the source. A wide, deep bowl had been hollowed out in the pelts, and a crimson fire blazed at its heart, surrounded by scalloped golden shells. It burned silently and without apparent fuel. Leif sensed magic at work.

And in the midst of the fire stood four gilded stones, half as tall as he was.

He gasped as he realized where he was. "Syrene," he whispered.

What he'd mistaken for shells were scales—thick, golden, dragon scales—and what he'd thought were stones were in fact eggs.

The shed scales of Rhiandra's golden sister had formed this nest for her precious clutch.

Leif's heart gave a horrified lurch, and he scrambled to his feet. A mortal presence anywhere near these eggs would not be tolerated, not after the lessons of Chaos. If he were discovered here, his life would surely be forfeit. He had to find a way out of the nest before Syrene returned, as he was certain the dragoness would give him no time to explain himself.

Still, he couldn't resist approaching the nearest egg. He stepped forward, reaching out, his hand drawn as if by a will of its own. Against his chest, the solaric stone pulsed with heat as it fed on the fire, but he felt no burning sensation.

Transfixed by the flickering golden glow, he paid no heed to where he placed his feet. His boot sank deep into the scales, pitching him forward, and he felt the sharp scales slice into his palms as he fell headlong into the fire.

The pain in his lacerated hands kept him from realizing, at first, that he was not burning. He was on his hands and knees, right in the heart of the flames, and yet… they did not harm him.

The rhyme of the dragonfast sprang into his mind.

"Immersed within the elements,
The dragonfast acquire
The essence of the inner sphere—
Water, air, earth and fire."

The essence of the inner sphere.

Leif pushed himself to his feet, staring in amazement at the flames licking painlessly against him. His skin remained unmarked and cool. Why had Rhiandra not told him that being dragonfast would make him immune to fire?

He held out his bloodied palms and watched the crimson drops hiss into the flames, sending up sprays of light like the faerie dust in Grandda's tales.

Emboldened, he stroked the gilded shell of the nearest egg nestled in the embers, and laughed with delight as it quivered under his hand. He wrapped his arms around the egg, feeling a surge of joy such as he'd only known flying with Rhiandra.

The egg gave a sudden jolt, knocking him against another, which began to vibrate as well.

A sudden, terrible roar echoed through the chamber.

Leif spun around, expecting to see an enraged dragon crouched behind him, poised for a kill. It was then he spied another aperture, this one a dark funnel spiraling upward. It was empty.

The sound had come from the crevasse above.

Which meant the tunnel offered a way out—the only one. If he was to escape, he'd have to go up it before Syrene came down.

Leif slipped from the flames and shouldered his pack.

He peered into the dark tunnel, dreading where it would lead him. Taking a deep breath, he straightened his shoulders. Syrene was surely up there. But then, he reminded himself, so was Rhiandra.

He glanced down at his pendant—now blazing with pure, golden light—then began to climb.

CHAPTER 16
Morgan

"Get away, yeh stinkin' mumper!" The burly man shot Morgan a disgusted look, then pushed past him on the narrow lane. Morgan drew his filthy cloak close against the buffeting wind. He'd grown used to the smell of the thistle oil he'd been rubbing into his skin every morning, which made him reek of a combination of cat piss and rotting meat. Most folks crossed to the far side of the street when they caught a whiff of him, and certainly no one cared to strike up a conversation with a ragged man surrounded by a cloud of pong. Which was, of course, the point.

Morgan clutched his recent purchases against his chest and ducked into the seedy tavern where he'd taken a room. A boy with a smudged face was sweeping out the cold hearth, but he leapt to his feet on the wizard's approach, burying his nose in his sleeve.

Morgan handed the lad a farthing. "I'd like water and soap brought up. And if the water's hot, you'll get another of those."

After the boy had trundled up with the last of the steaming buckets, Morgan stripped off his foul garments and had his first wash in days. Feeling much refreshed, he donned the new clothes he'd bought, then lay down on the lumpy mattress. Staring up at the knotty ceiling, he wondered once more if he'd find what he sought in this southwest outpost of the Isle.

A letter from Barav, his informant in Findlindach, had been among those Morgan had received at Port Taygh, and Barav had directed him here.

My people will be wintering in Glornadoor. If anyone's learned what's become of the disappeared, it will be my cousin Lehr. He's a master of ferreting out what others would keep concealed.

On this advice, Morgan had purchased a mule and headed south. He'd been sorry to part with Holly, but with a price on his head, he couldn't risk anything that might cause him to be recognized—including his long-serving pony. He'd left her with Celaidra, who'd promised to deliver her to Gilly.

Following Barav's instructions, Morgan traced Lehr to Gloorhilly, a port town situated on Glornadoor's southwestern coast. The moors on its outskirts had served as a wintering haven for the å Livåri in years past, and Morgan was relieved to learn from a surly innkeeper that a community of wagons had again gathered there this year. He set out at once to find it, but as soon as he veered onto the rough headland track to approach the camp, he was challenged by a cadre of narrow-eyed å Livåri. Even after he presented the letter from Barav, the men kept their hands on the dirks at their belts. Morgan suspected the scar-faced fellow he'd shown it to couldn't read, so he produced the ring Barav had given him as additional proof of his good will. That at least extracted a vague promise.

"Lehr isn't here," said the fellow, pocketing the silver trinket, "but if you tell me where you're staying, he'll find you."

Two days had passed since then, and Morgan had resigned himself to another trek out to the moors if Lehr didn't appear by the morrow. In the meantime, it was prudent to keep to his room. He'd been declared a kingkiller, with a considerable reward offered for any information concerning him and an even more generous one for his capture.

Despite this, it had been a difficult decision not to proceed to Drinnkastel as he'd originally planned. But in his clandestine meeting with Celaidra, the sorceress had vehemently discouraged him from doing so.

"At the moment, King Roth wants your head, not your oath of allegiance. You can better serve the realm if you keep it," she argued. "Surely you have other pressing business to which you can attend? What of your quest to discover what's happening to the å Livåri? While you're investigating their disappearance, Audric and I can try to persuade our lord king that there is no concrete evidence for these charges against you. In time, perhaps we can find a way to clear your good name."

Morgan raised an eyebrow. "Audric, but not Selka? Does she hold me culpable for the murder of my king?" He gave a small, mirthless laugh. "Yes, of course she does. Just as she believes I stole the *Chronicles*."

Celaidra sighed. "When Selka sets her mind, none can dissuade her. You know she's never been an ally of yours, and since Urlion's death, she's grown more temperamental than ever. Just before I stole away to meet you, I heard her exchanging bitter words with Audric."

"Words over me?"

Celaidra shook her head. "I don't think so. Selka swept from the room the moment I entered, but I could have sworn there were tears in her eyes. Proud, cold Selka, weeping! Can you imagine?"

The elven princess knew nothing of Morgan's vow to find Urlion's betrayer, but he still found her reasoning hard to fault. Urlion was dead, and uncovering the spellcaster would not bring the late king back across the Leap. The missing å Livåri, on the other hand, might still be among the living.

And Celaidra had reassured him regarding Maura. "The girl is aglow with happiness. I seriously doubt she'll want to return to Mithralyn, at least not until after the wedding. Please, Mortimer. Attend to whatever affairs you can far from Drinnkastel. I promise you, I will send word if you are needed. We cannot afford to lose you. And I could not bear it if we did."

So Morgan acceded to Celaidra's plea. In truth he had always found it nigh impossible to deny the princess anything. On only one occasion had he ever done so, and the pain it caused both of them had been almost too much to bear. He'd long wondered what he might have made of his life if he'd listened to her. If he'd spent that summer night with her in his arms, as she'd begged him to.

Instead, he'd gone in search of Lazdac.

Morgan closed his eyes, attempting to quell the memory. Dwelling on regret brought nothing but heartache. And even though he'd lost all that he desired by turning a deaf ear to Celaidra's entreaties, his rash act had resulted in some good. His old mentor, Audric, had been selected to serve in Morgan's place on the Tribus, and the realm had benefited from his steady guidance, along with that of Celaidra and Selka.

And Morgan's choice had a silver lining that was not to be discounted. Over time, it had taught him the lesson of humility.

It had been a long process, that learning—and had come at great cost. After falling from on high, defeated by Lazdac and left with only the natural magic with which he'd been born, Morgan fled Drinnglennin to lick his wounds. For years after, he roamed the world, only lingering in places where he discovered someone or something worth knowing.

In Delnogoth, he spent a winter at the court of Grand Prince Rikur, from which he sought out the hidden mountain eyrie of the beautiful Valblissa and her sister, Baba Vrodya, the last sorceresses of that vast, frozen land. He spent many a night beside their fire, trying to convince them not to pass over the sea. "Magic will again be welcome in the world," he insisted.

But Baba Vrodya spat into the fire. "I will no longer waste my gifts here, to be repaid in the coin of ignorance and fear."

Valblissa remained silent, but the next time he climbed to their sky-high abode, the ash in their hearth had long since grown cold.

He traveled on by sledge over the tundra to the frozen falls of Solono, then sailed the great Fatlakova River south on an ice boat that hissed over the frozen water with the speed of the wind. The river ended at the Mvalthian Pass, through which a road constructed by the departed dwarves of Mittegoth ran on to Sâri Topci, Mittegoth's crown city. There he was welcomed with high honor by Izia, the *kathuna* of Kovatev, and acceded to Izia's plea to accompany her when she went to treat with the nomads of the Amukent Steppes. It was on those windswept plains that he encountered Tochar, perhaps the greatest mage of the far east, who later perished along with so many others in the last Purge.

In Far Taraia, Morgan traveled with the å Livåri, for this was their native land, and learned their language and ways. When they migrated west, Morgan continued east, ranging alone for many months over the Great Kyraki Mountains. Crossing the Tharkum Desert, he witnessed the hunting hawks of Helnig boiling over the snow-capped peaks in search of prey, and the summer migration of wildevacs, the great horned ungulates whose herds numbered in the hundreds of thousands.

From there, his wanderings took him south to the abandoned temples of Bhahtgat, spreading for miles across the Deeyann Plateau, swathed in perpetual mists and inhabited only by bats and wild pigs. The holy shrines were believed by some to have been the home of long-forgotten gods. Beside their gilded pagodas, the wizard slept under skies so full of stars, they blazed white in the dome of the heavens.

In Near Taraia, he trekked down into the Canyon of Glass, so named for its sheer walls of mica. There he gazed upon the massive geyser that rose daily out of a steaming river, and he bathed in its burbling waters, said to heal the broken spirit, though they did little for his.

He rafted the Kuratek between towering cliffs carved out over millennia by the rushing slate-blue river feeding the Hykanian Sea. When he came to Tell-Uyuk, he discovered that the imperial seat of Olquaria offered much to detain him—in particular, the House of All-Knowing. In this humble abode, the wizard passed his days sitting cross-legged on a rug, listening to the teachings of the *al-imtirta*, the most learned scholars of the land, and joining in lively discourses on geometry, philosophy, astronomy, and literature.

Then one day, Rusul-Lax, the great sage, invited Morgan to his home, where he was introduced to Al-Gahzi, the Basileus's supreme military commander and a dedicated scholar in his own right. Through Al-Gahzi, word reached the palace of this foreign *bazdir*, the title given to a highly learned man, and Morgan was duly summoned to an audience with His Imperial Majesty, Radan Basileus. After that fateful meeting, Morgan became a regular visitor to the palace. He was given a house in Kuca Zarich, a prestigious sector of the city reserved for foreigners who had found favor with the emperor.

Morgan was often in Al-Gahzi's company, and a deep bond of friendship grew between them. The commander opened his home and heart to Morgan. They hunted often together, using magnificent hawks from the royal aviary, they sparred fiercely with staves in the Olquarian style, and they spent many hours debating all manner of topics, from irrigation practices to the ordering of the heavens. When marauding Jagars threatened to overrun the western border of Olquaria, the two men fought side by side to drive the barbarians far to the south of the Lost Lands, where they could do no more harm.

Upon returning to Tell-Uyuk after their successful campaign, Al-Gahzi urged Morgan to marry his sister, Namatay, and found his own dynasty.

"Radan Basileus wishes you to remain among us, Morgan, and you are already as close as blood to me and my family. You cannot have failed to notice that you have found favor with my sister as well."

Namatay was both beautiful and intelligent, and Morgan would have been honored to take her to wife. But she deserved better—a great prince or landed lord, not the over-prideful son of a farrier who'd squandered his gifts. Besides, he knew he could never give her his heart, for it had long ago been lost to another.

Still, Morgan had come to terms with the bitter fruit of his terrible folly and had accepted his reduced role in the order of the world. So although he did not marry, he decided he would stay on in Tell-Uyuk indefinitely, gleaning and sharing knowledge at the House of All-Knowing.

But this was not to be his destiny, for it was not long before the sparks of ignorance and fear were fanned into the flames that would sweep from Albrenia eastward across the continental kingdoms and empires to Herawa on the Temonin Sea. The fever of another Purge burned, and all those deemed "different" would soon be forced to flee or perish before it. It was just such a Purge that had brought about the Fall of the Before, when all magical creatures—dragons, unicorns, basilisks, wolfwargs, alphyns, and gryphons—and folk outside the race of man—dwarves, elves, djinns, goblins, sylphs, sprites, faeries, merfolk, and giants—had been pursued by this deadly fire of hate. Only this time, the hungry inferno craved a different fuel, and the å Livåri became its favored kindling. They perished by the thousands, and if King Gregor of Drinnglennin had not offered the survivors sanctuary, it would have been a complete genocide.

Robbed of this terrible victory, the sanctioned leaders of the temples of Priscinae, Velicus, and Horiastria turned their vitriolic prejudice on the learned instead, who counted many a wizard and sorceress among them.

Thanks to Radan Basileus, Morgan was protected from the first crazed wave of killings in Olquaria. But he was not spared the horror of witnessing the Purge's rapacious sweep through Tell-Uyuk—and he could do nothing when the House of All-Knowing was barricaded from the outside and set alight.

In one night, the world lost the greatest sages of the Known World.

After that, for Morgan, bitter and heartbroken over the murders, the allure of the city was lost.

Then the last Helgrin War broke out, and Morgan felt called upon to return to the west to defend the isle of his birth. He was no longer able to raise the Shield of Taran, but he had a strong sword arm and a lethal way with a stave. So he went home.

Upon his return to Drinnglennin he found that although memories of Master Morgan the *virtuos* had faded, the disgrace with which his name was linked lingered on. Even simple folks would tell you it was Morgan, the only wizard forced off the Tribus, who'd set alight the great library of the Alithineum and stolen the *Chronicles*. Despite his sullied reputation, Morgan believed he still had something to offer, yet found his services, in any form, were unwelcome.

It was Urlion who restored his sense of purpose. When the High King caught wind of Morgan's whereabouts, he summoned him to Drinnkastel. Urlion gave him a place of honor, asking Morgan to ride at his side into battle as together they drove the Helgrin invaders back. Urlion succeeded in bringing peace to the realm, and Morgan found a way to be of service once more.

For this, he owed much to the last Konigur king.

Now Morgan had dedicated himself to a different purpose—one that had brought four young people together in Mithralyn's forest, where three of them swore an oath to support Urlion's heir. Soon one of them would marry the man who'd been named as Urlion's successor, perhaps, in part, because of her vow.

A Nelvor king who was likely behind the charge of regicide against him.

Since Morgan's return to the Isle, he'd done all in his power to see that Drinnglennin remained a tolerant and stable realm, that it did not succumb to the fear and bigotry that had infected so much of the rest of the Known World. He'd been aware of the risks to Leif, Maura, Halla, and Whit when he brought them into this political turmoil, but that didn't make the burden of responsibility for their fate any lighter to bear.

And bear it he must, for he would not alter his course, not for them or anyone else. No matter the cost, he would ensure the reinstatement of Owain Konigur's legacy. which had made Drinnglennin a haven of tolerance for all.

The rumbling of kegs across the floor in the tavern below prompted Morgan to his feet. At least his business in Gloorhilly might result in saving, not threatening, lives. He would try again to see Lehr.

He was fastening his cloak when there came a sharp rap on his door.

"Who's there?"

When there was no reply, Morgan reached for his staff. The sound of retreating footsteps drew him out of his room in time to see a man disappearing down the stairs—a man with a tail of black hair running down his back in the á Livári fashion.

Morgan followed him out of the tavern, then north on Wilkes Lane. From there, his quarry turned left, making for the town gate leading out to the moors. The á Livári never looked back, but continued along the rutted road until it rounded the headland and the way narrowed to a trail.

The scarp jutted up from the slate-grey sea, and the waves, fetched with whitecaps, railed against the bluffs below and foamed over the sand. The wind tore at Morgan's cloak and ashen clouds billowed over brown grass laid low by its bluster.

He thought he saw a sail on the horizon, but it might have been a trick of the flat, pale light.

In the brief moment he glanced at the water, the man he'd been following vanished.

Morgan walked on. The path began to descend, and he stayed close to the wall of rock on his left. One false step would send him pitching down to a cruel death. One false step—or a push. He tightened his grip on his staff.

At the next turn, he saw the å Livåri waiting in a narrow aperture in the cliff face, the wind whipping his cloak around him. He bore a distinct likeness to Barav, only older and stockier. When he stepped back to make way for Morgan to join him, the wizard offered the traditional Livårian greeting.

"*Oranat zava chuskoh.* Lehr, I presume?"

"*Patrut sunt oranat va chuskoh.*" Lehr leaned forward to brush Morgan's cheeks with the kiss of peace, then opened his palm and offered its contents. "You must be a true brother of my cousin. He would not have parted with his dragon ring otherwise."

Morgan smiled as he lifted the twist of silver from Lehr's hand. "I shall see that it is returned to him. You received my letter?"

Lehr nodded, then blew on his hands to warm them. "You wish to know what I've learned about the disappeared of our people. *I* need to know what you plan to do with this knowledge."

Morgan met his dark gaze levelly. "If they still live, I vow to do all in my power to bring them home."

Lehr looked doubtful. "All that you can?" He leaned back against the rock wall. "I know who you are, Master Morgan. Once, you might have accomplished this feat, but now? It's said you lost your powers."

"How I achieve my objective is my business. Do you know where the missing are, or who's abducting them?"

"What do *you* know?" Lehr countered.

"That some of the young women have been transport-ed to Albrenia, where they are being sold as slaves. That the very old and the very young have been slaughtered here in Drinnglennin. I know nothing of what has become of the oth-ers."

Lehr shifted his gaze to the dark, roiling water. "Two moons ago, a madman washed up on this beach you see be-low us. He was brought to our camp by a local fisherman—he was å Livåri, you see, and the fisherman thought he was one of our clan. He wasn't, but we took him in all the same. From his terrible wounds, it looked like he wouldn't last long, but we figured if he could tell us what had happened to him, we could at least avenge his death.

"The poor wretch lay on his stomach on the litter he was brought on, writhing in agony and begging for the mercy of death. In truth, I was tempted to grant his wish. The skin had been flayed off his back and hung in raw, pale threads, his right eye had been gouged out, and he'd lost much blood. How he survived in the sea…" Lehr shook his head, his mouth grim. "Our wise woman set about doing what she could to ease his agony, and for days he slept under the influence of crennin." He flicked a defiant look at Morgan.

"I'm aware of crennin's medicinal powers," said the wizard.

The hard set of Lehr's features relaxed slightly, and he con-tinued his tale. "One morning, I was holding a cup of willow bark tea to his lips when a flicker of sanity lit his eye, and he spoke for the first time. '*Craith*,' he whispered.

"At first I thought he was asking if we'd found a hound with him, but when I started to tell him he'd been brought alone, he shook his head. 'Me,' he rasped. '*Craith*.'

"This was his name?"

Lehr shot Morgan a reproachful look. "No å Livåri mother would call her son 'Dog.' But it was what the man called him-self." His eyes were cold. "After he told his tale, I understood why. And once you hear it, you may well want to reconsider your oath to bring our people home."

"No matter what, I shall not."

"We shall see." Lehr fixed his gaze on the chop and swell of the pewter water, as though collecting his thoughts. "Craith told me that a month before, he'd taken work on a merchant ship bound for Olquaria. The captain was a kinsman of his, and all the crew were å Livåri." Lehr turned and spat into the darkness behind them, as to rid himself of a bitterness on his tongue. "It wasn't until they'd set sail that Craith learned they'd gone *gresit*."

Morgan felt a cold dread mingled with anger. To go *gresit* meant to betray one's own.

Lehr saw by his expression that he understood. "This kinsman told Craith the hold was filled with wheat, silver, and arms to trade for gold, fine cloth, and spices in Tell-Uyuk. It was only once they were far out to sea that Craith learned the truth—that the cargo below was the blood of his blood: å Livåri men, women, and children."

Lehr drew his cloak closer against the whining wind. "Craith insisted he could do nothing, for he feared if he protested, his kinsman would simply throw him down into the hold and sell him along with the rest. So he watched and waited for a chance to free himself and the others. He knew nothing of the sea. But he was attuned to the cycles of sun and moon and stars, and he knew that for days on end they sailed not to the east as the captain had promised, but ever to the south."

"South?" echoed Morgan.

Lehr ignored the question. "One day, a thin line appeared on the horizon, signaling they were nearing landfall. Craith described the air as hot and heavy, pressing down on them so that it was hard to breathe, and said the ship moved sluggishly over the water. All day and through the night, Craith watched the growing silhouette of a port in the distance, and when the orange sun rose, it revealed a wide harbor, in which great carracks and galleons, more than he could count, rocked at anchor. The carracks carried twenty-four cannons just on their broadsides, the galleons ten times as many. He smelled fresh pitch and new wood; he was certain none of the vessels had yet made their maiden voyage. Beyond the swaying forest of masts a field of great barges lay anchored, loaded with various buckets and wheeled bases, levers and massive slings for the construction of mangonels and trebuchets, and there was no doubt in his mind that they had arrived at a city preparing for war.

"Once their own ship anchored, Craith was ordered to herd the å Livåri into small lighters to ferry them to shore. It was then that he saw the horror that would haunt his dreams for the rest of his days."

Lehr flicked his fingers to ward off evil. "There were... creatures."

Morgan felt his skin crawl. "What manner of creatures?"

"Possessed of human speech, but not human. 'Horned ones,' he called them, with scaly, gray skin and half again as tall as any man. They swarmed the port and carried our captured kinfolk away.

"All the long voyage back north, Craith was plagued by nightmares filled with the piteous cries of those they'd left behind, and he cursed himself for a coward.

"On the night before they made landfall in Drinnglennin, the captain ordered a barrel of ale to be tapped. Craith, tormented by guilt, got drunk and found his courage at last. He lashed out at the captain, swearing he'd see him brought to justice. For his insolence, Craith was flayed, then his kinsman gouged out one of his eyes and ordered what was left of him cast into the sea. By the grace of the gods, Craith surfaced to find a rope dangling off the stern of the ship, to which he tied himself fast.

"When they drew close to Gloorhilly's harbor, he cut himself loose. The sea carried him to shore, where the fisherman found him and brought him to me."

"What became of this man?" Morgan asked.

The å Livåri pushed himself away from the wall. "He died a few hours after telling his tale. We gave him the proper rites."

Horned ones. Morgan felt his throat tighten with anger and dread. *So Lazdac has done it, and gods help them, the* å Livåri *have somehow provided him with the means.*

"So now, master wizard," Lehr said, folding his arms across his chest. "Are you still standing by that oath?"

Morgan's expression must have given the man his answer, for Lehr's own shifted to reflect a faint hope. "Is it enough," the å Livåri asked, "for you to find them?"

Morgan looked out over the sea, which was now the color of lead. The scent of an approaching storm hung on the air.

"It will have to be."

CHAPTER 17
Whit

From the start, Maeve made it easy for Whit. "Is it your first time?" she asked, stepping out of her dress in his narrow room. She was naked underneath it, and Whit could barely find breath to answer, so taken was he by the sight of her alluring curves.

Yes," he managed to whisper.

"Good." Maeve moved closer, smiling as she unbuckled his fine belt. "Then I'll have no bad habits to correct." She drew his tunic over his head and took his hand, her warm eyes sparkling. "Are you ready for your lesson, Master Wizard?"

"Indeed," he said, falling with her onto the bed. "I am always ready to learn."

* * *

When Whit rose again, the moon still hung high in the sky. He stood at the window, watching the silvery orb slowly arc toward the shadowed trees. Only when it had slipped from view did he realized how cold the room had grown.

With a murmur, he rekindled the glowing embers in the hearth to roaring life.

From the bed, he heard a gasp, followed by a low, musical laugh. "Prettily done," Maeve purred.

He turned to see her arms stretched languorously above her head, the bedding falling away to reveal her firm breasts.

"But I'd prefer something else to warm me," she added.

He crawled obligingly back under the covers.

This time, he lasted long enough to make Maeve cry out twice. Lying breathless against his chest, she said, "True to your word, you are, sir—a fast learner." He felt the curve of her cheek against his as she smiled, and felt a burst of gratitude.

He was just drifting off to sleep again when she reached up and stroked his face. "I have to go," she whispered.

Whit's stomach rumbled, and they both laughed.

"I'll see a proper breakfast is sent up. You'll be wanting some fuel for that fire within you," Maeve teased.

Whit buried his nose in her hair. "Then you must stay to kindle it."

But she slid from his grasp and into her dress. "I've a wedding to attend," she reminded him, pulling together the stays of her bodice. She leaned over and brushed his lips softly with her own. "I'll not forget this night, and I'd like to think you won't either. They say a man never forgets his first."

"Never," he vowed. He tried to draw her back into the bed, but she danced away with a laugh. Blowing him a soft kiss, she slipped out the door.

Whit lay drowsing, a smile on his lips, when a rap on the door jolted him fully awake. He pulled on his crumpled tunic before admitting a boy bearing a fragrantly steaming tray. Maeve had been true to her word as well. She'd sent up fresh bread, runny eggs, and thickly sliced bacon, which Whit took back to bed and ate with relish. After a quick ablution, he dressed and went down to have Sinead saddled.

He rode out to the accompaniment of chirping birds and rustling leaves, and found himself humming a tune often played in Mithralyn. He felt buoyant, with a world of possibilities ahead.

He had at least a half day's ride between him and Drinnkastel, so used the time to consider what he would wear to his audience with the High King—Cardenstowe's black and yellow, of course, and the fine belt he'd inherited when his father had died, with the golden crow buckle. He'd need to see a barber beforehand, though.

The pounding of approaching hoofbeats snapped him out of these musings, and a score of riders were upon him in the space of a few breaths. The men wore unfamiliar silver livery, trimmed with crimson, and their well-bred mounts sported costly trappings. Whit felt slightly less apprehensive when he spied the monter riding with them. *Not robbers, then.* Still, he kept his hand on his sword as they milled around him.

"Identify yourself, sir," demanded a solid man with close-set eyes.

"It's you who've accosted me," Whit retorted. "If you mean no harm, give me your names."

"Why don't I shorten that insolent tongue of yours instead," snarled a rough-looking man with coarse, orange hair and a bulbous nose. He pulled a dirk from the scabbard at his waist.

"Hold, Saywen! The whelp has the look of a lord about him." The heavy man's smile didn't reach his eyes. "As to who we are, our colors speak for us."

"Not to me."

The man puffed out his barrel chest. "We serve High King Roth, and wear the red panther proudly."

Whit now discerned the crouching feline on the man's breast. "I beg your pardon, sir. I've been… away. I didn't know King Roth had adopted new heraldry."

"Well, now you do, Sir…"

"Lord," Whit amended sharply. "Lord Whit Alcott of Cardenstowe. As it happens, I'm on my way to the capital to have an audience with His Majesty."

He didn't much care for the effect his words produced. The sturdy man exchanged a cryptic look with a tall knight who'd ridden up beside him. The newcomer's hair was jet black, and sleek as an otter's.

The heavier man offered Whit a slight bow. "My Lord Cardenstowe. I'm Sir Ewig Ghent, captain of the King's Guard. It's fortunate we've met on the road. As it happens, King Roth is not in Drinnkastel. He and Queen Grindasa are currently in residence at Nelvor Castle. We'll be happy to escort you there."

Whit frowned. "Nelvor Castle? I think not. I've other business to take me to Drinnkastel as well. I'll await the king's return there."

"Surely none more pressing than swearing Cardenstowe's allegiance to your sovereign." Sir Ewig was no longer smiling. "Your absence has been noted, sir, but I'm sure now all can be put to rights. If you'll just come along with us." His expression made clear he would brook no objection. "Nelvorboth is quite pleasant this time of year—you'll see for yourself, my lord." And with that he spurred to the head of his men, leaving Whit glaring in frustration at his back.

Sir Ewig's men had closed ranks around Whit. A tall knight detached himself from the circle and urged his horse forward, making Whit a courtly bow. "Sir Harlin Korst, at your service, my lord. I shouldn't consider refusing Sir Ewig's kind offer of an escort, if I were you."

Whit's irritation had turned to anger. "Why am I am being forced to go to Nelvorboth against my will?" he demanded.

The skeletal monter kicked his mule closer as well. "Come now, my son. You said yourself you wished an audience with the king. Are you not in fact a kinsman of his? King Roth takes the bond of blood very seriously."

"As do I," Whit replied. "Drinnkastel is on my way to Cardenstowe, where my mother awaits me. I've been gone many months and have responsibilities to attend to there."

"Your first responsibility is to your king," Sir Harlin said evenly, "and Cardenstowe seems to have been managing without you for the past year. As I recall, my lord, you weren't at the Twyrn." His look was coolly speculative. "Indeed, Cardenstowe remains the only realm that has not sworn formal fealty to our new High King, because you were not to be found. May I ask where, exactly, you've been all this time, my lord? Your lady mother claimed even she didn't know your whereabouts. It was thought you might have taken ship for the continent with Sir Glinter and his band of mercenaries. It's lucky you didn't; Glinter and his crew sailed against the express orders of the Crown."

Whit was alarmed to hear his mother had been questioned about him. "I was in the north," he replied stiffly, "in the company of Master Morgan. Perhaps you've heard of him?"

"Lord Blearc, preserve us!" the monter cried.

"Heard of him?" Sir Harlin gave an incredulous laugh. "Every soul in the land knows of the wizard's perfidy! Derrlyn, Saywen, to me!"

Two powerfully built men, armed with rough staves, trotted forward and scowled at Whit.

"Secure this man and guard him closely!" Sir Harlin commanded.

Whit swore as Saywen—the man who had threatened him with his knife—grabbed hold of his arm. The other man, an even more unsavoury-looking fellow with a protruding jaw and pockmarked skin, eyed Rowlan and gave a low whistle.

Whit tried to urge Sinead out from between their mounts, but Sir Harlin grasped the mare's bridle.

"What's the meaning of this?" Whit demanded. "I am a peer of the realm!"

His loud protest brought Sir Ewig riding back. "You refuse to come to Nelvorboth?" the captain demanded.

"The young lord here says he was away in the north," Harlin replied, "in the company of *Master Morgan*."

A slow, delighted smile spread across Sir Ewig's face. "You will tell me, at once, where this Morgan is hiding."

Saywen started to wrap a rope around Whit's wrists, and Whit attempted to pull away. "What do you think you're doing?" he cried.

"Answer my question," Sir Ewig demanded.

"I've no idea where Master Morgan is! We parted in the north days ago."

"Where exactly?"

Whit was so incensed he couldn't think straight. He needed a moment to gather his wits. He could easily set the rope alight, but in doing so, he risked harming Sinead and spooking Rowlan. More importantly, he sensed that to use any magic in front of these men would be ill-advised.

"Where did you leave the wizard?" Sir Ewig repeated.

"Are you deaf? I said in the nor—"

The knight's blow took Whit full in the face, and he saw stars before his eyes.

"See here, Ghent!" Sir Harlin cried. "We've no proof the young lord was involved in that treason."

"Any who consorts with wizards bear the taint of these heathens," the monter intoned. He narrowed his eyes at Whit, his loathing palpable.

Whit held his jaw, trying to make sense of what he was being accused of.

"And we've no proof that he *wasn't* involved, either!" Sir Ewig growled. The captain leaned toward Whit, who smelled onions on the man's breath. "I claim you as my prisoner, Whit of Cardenstowe. You'll answer to King Roth himself for your treachery."

"What treachery?" Whit cried.

But Sir Ewig had already wheeled his horse.

"Saywen," said Sir Harlin, "see that his lordship comes to no further harm." Then avoiding Whit's eyes, Sir Harlin rode after Ewig.

Saywen was still ogling Rowlan. "Tha's a fine horse, tha' is."

"The destrier is the property of Lady Halla of Lorendale," Whit said stiffly.

Saywen leered at him, revealing dark, broken teeth. "Then what 'er ye doin' wit' 'im?"

Whit leaned over and spat blood in answer. It would be better to say as little as possible to these men. If he was suspected of some foul crime, it wouldn't do to link Halla or Lorendale to him, any more than their bonds of kinship already did. In any case, he didn't owe these ruffians any explanation.

The man called Derrlyn screwed up his eyes at Whit. "Like as not, 'e stole 'im. Is tha' the way of it?"

"Looks like 'is lordship's lost 'is tongue." Saywen leaned over and took hold of Sinead's reins. "He stands to lose more 'n that, soon enough." He gave an ugly laugh and kicked his horse to a trot, with Whit in tow.

* * *

Whit spent the long ride south in a state of vexed frustration. The knights kept their distance, leaving him in the company of the louts, Saywen and Derrlyn, and Whit passed the time plotting all manner of revenge to inflict on them. He was sorely tempted to use magic to effect an escape, but the monter's decrying "the taint of heathens" had sounded a disturbing note, reminiscent of the ignorance and prejudice that had held sway on the continent ever since the last Purge. The use of magic might further mark him as guilty, beyond his mere association with Master Morgan.

The wisest course of action seemed to be to bear the discomfort of the journey and share his grievances over this rough treatment personally with the High King at Nelvorboth.

However, this didn't rule out *all* magic use—only that which would be identified as such. He couldn't, for instance, illuse to make himself appear to be a goblin, but he *could* savor the sound of Saywen's screams upon waking to see a gigantic hairy spider on Derrlyn's face, and he fully enjoyed Sir Harlin's curses when his horse was discovered to have thrown all four shoes.

Sometimes Whit didn't even need magic to get his small revenge. When Ewig insisted on accompanying Whit as he went to relieve himself, Whit led the knight into a cluster of planter's bane; the knight clearly didn't know to avoid their poisonous leaves. Whit later had to hide a smile when Sir Ewig began to relentlessly claw at his crotch, muttering darkly about poxy wenches.

Whit didn't spare the monter, either. He suffered a nasty burn on his tongue while drinking broth that somehow refused to cool one evening. *That's a taste of the taint of heathens for you*, thought Whit spitefully. *And once I've seen the king, you'll all regret causing me this inconvenience.* The blow to his cheek had split the skin, and though he'd been able to clean it, if it left a scar he would present it as evidence of the mistreatment he'd suffered.

Crossing Nelvorboth, they rode through forested land and alongside rolling meadows much like those of Lorendale and Cardenstowe. The farms they passed all appeared quite prosperous, and they began to overtake great wains brimming with apples, beets, and cabbages, as well as carts of squealing pigs and honking geese bound for market.

It was late afternoon when they rounded a bend and Nelvor Castle appeared in all its splendor. Whit had heard it said that it rivaled Cardenstowe and Drinnkastel as the mightiest of Drinnglennin's fortifications, and although he believed his own fortress to be superior, he had to admit Nelvor was an impressive sight, especially in the long light that made it glow golden on its hilltop perch. He recalled that it had originally been built as a motte-and-bailey with three wards, but its wooden fortifications had long since been replaced by stone, and each successive lord had added something more, seeking to leave his own stamp on the lofty seat of the largest Drinnglennian realm. Kenwyn Nelvor had constructed a luxurious palace at the heart of the city, and his great-grandson Ennon had torn it down to build an even grander one in the following century. The infamous Gelfin had later commissioned expansive gardens that sprawled over five hectares, and the grounds included intricate mazes, a jungle of sculpted animal statuary, and a multitude of pools and floral displays.

The most recent renovations had been made by the late Nando Nelvor, who'd brought in Albrenian architects to reconstruct the private apartments to suit the taste of his foreign bride. Master Cortenus had described these as "extravagant," and he had cause to know; before coming to Cardenstowe, the learned man had tutored one of King Roth's cousins at Nelvor.

The approach to the castle was via a long avenue bordered by majestic castanyas, beyond which lay an expanse of manicured grounds. Under other circumstances, Whit would have been excited to visit this legendary palace and to explore the surrounding town, but now his thoughts were occupied with his upcoming audience with the High King, under circumstances that were far from desirable. He'd rehearsed what he wanted to say, but by the time they clattered under the arched gateway into the main courtyard, his mind had gone blank. Despite the chill in the air, he felt sweat trickling down his back.

Whit's escort circled to the left of the original motte and entered a ward, its ornate curtain wall a stark contrast to the ancient tower. Red-and-silver banners set along its allure furled and snapped in the gusting wind.

A storm's coming, Whit thought glumly. He knew it was illogical to take this as a bad sign, but he did just the same.

They threaded their way through crowds of people crossing the ward, and came to a halt in front of the gilded doors to the temple, whose soaring spires Whit had admired from a distance. The lout Derrlyn hauled Whit off Sinead's back, and Whit was forced to watch, with a sinking heart, as the mare and Rowlan were led away. He could only hope they'd be well cared for until this ridiculous misunderstanding was cleared up.

"We shall give thanks for our safe passage home," intoned the monter from the top of the temple stairs.

But when Whit made to follow the others inside, the holy man glared at him.

"Do not think to sully this sacred space!"

Although he had no interest in the gods, Whit protested. "I've done nothing that should bar me from the temple."

"So say you," Sir Ewig growled. He waved his two hench-men over. "Stay with him until we return. And see that he's here when we come out, or you'll be dancing on shortened legs."

The guards seemed to take the knight's threat seriously, for they swung their staves menacingly in Whit's direction. Whit ignored them—and did his best to ignore as well the curious glances from those passing by.

You are Lord of Cardenstowe, and a wizard of power, he reminded himself, lifting his head high.

Heavy drops of rain began to splat onto the cobblestones, and the crowd scattered. Soon the courtyard was empty of all but Whit and his two captors. Whit started for the cover of the recessed temple doors, only to have Saywen's pole block his way.

"Sir Ewig said you was to be here when he came back," Saywen said, waggling his stave in Whit's face.

"'Here' being the operative word," Whit replied scathing-ly. "He meant 'present,' not wallowing in a downpour like a drowning toad." *You dolt,* he added silently.

A flash of red drew his attention to one of the archways. A lady, wrapped in a bright lapin shawl, stared out at him. To his surprise, she drew up her hood and ran out into the deluge toward him.

"*Whit?*"

Pushing his sopping hair back from his brow, he looked at her blankly for a moment before he realized who she was. "*Maura?* What are—"

"What happened to your—"

Maura laughed, then sobered as she took in his bound hands and the two guards. "By whose orders do you hold this man?" she demanded of his captors.

"Sir Ewig, m'lady. He said we was to wait here with the prisoner." Saywen tugged his forelock, clearly ill at ease addressing a noblewoman.

"Surely not in the pouring rain!" Maura pointed to the sheltered passageway she'd just vacated. "You will take Lord Whit under cover at once." She lifted her now bedraggled skirts and preceded them, and her confidence that they would follow was rewarded.

Once they were all under shelter, Maura frowned at the two ruffians with disapproval. "I'm sure there's been some mistake," she said. "I know his lordship, and I'm certain the king will not be pleased to learn he's been ill-treated in any way."

"No, m'lady," said Derrlyn meekly. "I mean, yes, m'lady…" The man was visibly shrinking under her stern gaze.

Maura raised her chin with regal hauteur. "I would have a private word with his lordship."

"We're under orders to guard 'im," Saywen protested.

Maura's violet eyes flashed. "Surely you can do this from a few yards' distance. The man can't go anywhere." Without waiting for a reply, she drew Whit farther down the passage.

Her face now reflected concern. "Tell me quickly. Why are you here, and as a prisoner?"

"I was waylaid on my way to Drinnkastel, where I intended to swear fealty to King Roth. Then I made the mistake of mentioning to his men that I'd recently been in Master Morgan's company. What's our wizard friend done that's made consorting with him a crime?"

Maura paled. "You haven't heard? Master Morgan has been accused of murdering my uncle Urlion."

Whit couldn't believe his ears. "What? But that's nonsense!"

"Of course it is, but as he was the last one to see Urlion alive, it has been convenient to lay the blame of the High King's death on him."

"Well, it looks like I've put my foot in it, then. But who made this ridic—"

Maura glanced over at the guards, who were flicking their anxious eyes between the temple door and the two of them. "I'll tell you all I know later, and vouch for you to Roth, only... how shall I tell him we met?"

"Roth? You're on a first name basis with our High King?" This was encouraging news. "Well, I suppose that's on account of your being dragonfa—"

"Shhhh!" Maura took hold of his arms and turned him with surprising force so that her back was to his keepers. "He doesn't know about the dragons. No one does, except for us. I decided to wait until our wedding day to tell him."

"Your wedding... You're to wed the *High King*?"

"It was my uncle's wish, according to Queen Grindasa. And you know I took an oath to serve Urlion's rightful successor."

"Serve him, yes, not *marry* him! You do know the Nelvors aren't known for keeping *their* pledges."

A flicker of apprehension in Maura's eyes directed Whit's gaze to a tall, well-built young lord striding in their direction along an adjoining walkway, trailed by half a dozen courtiers. He was immaculately dressed, and he would have been quite handsome if his fine features weren't contorted by a scowl.

The man was directing his ire at a bald officer by his side. "I thought I made it clear. How is it that this matter has *still* not been dealt with?"

"Your Majesty," the older man murmured, "we'd hoped the boy's imprisonment would have come to a natural end by now. You know of the curse—" His steely gaze swept ahead and held Whit's for an instant before he added in a low voice, "This discussion is best pursued behind closed doors, sire."

"Blearc's bones, Vetch! It's not for you to decide where we speak. Bugger the curse—I want it done!"

Whit's heart gave a sudden bump. This was the High King himself in such a rage! It did not seem the ideal time to make introductions, but the king had seen Maura and Whit and now swept toward them.

"My lady." He turned to Whit. "And who might *you* be?"

Maura dipped into a curtsey. "May I present Lord Whit of Cardenstowe, my lord? He's come to pledge his fealty."

The king's eyes lit with interest. "Cardenstowe—the mysterious missing lord! We are wondering why it has taken you so long to do your duty to your sovereign." He frowned at Whit's bound hands.

Belatedly, Whit offered a deep bow. "I've... I was away in the north, sire. In truth, I was on my way to Drinnkastel to make my oath, but there's been... a misunderstanding..."

"Lord Whit is a great scholar, my lord," Maura said brightly. "I'm sure he can be of service to you." A day ago, her suggestion would have been music to Whit's ears, but under the present circumstances, he felt a deep disquiet in the king's presence.

"Lady Rhea said her son was away, studying with *Master Morgan*, Your Majesty," said Vetch.

Whit felt a thrill of alarm. Had Vetch himself questioned his mother?

King Roth regarded Whit with pale, speculative eyes. "Is this true, Cardenstowe? Are you too a wizard?"

"I… I am, sire."

For the first time, the king smiled. "You see, Vetch? The gods are good. They've sent a solution to our little dilemma— curse or no curse. Have these bonds removed. Lord Whit should be brought to my chambers, once he is presentable." Then he turned on his heel and strode back the way he had come.

Maura cast Whit the briefest of glances before following in the king's wake. Whit read a clear warning in her eyes. Watching her go, he felt chilled by more than the gusting wind.

* * *

Whit's meeting with the High King was brief but harrowing. Roth got straight to the point.

"You have raised our doubts about your loyalty, Cardenstowe."

"Your Majesty—"

"Silence!" the king thundered. "You will speak when we command it. Where is Morgan?"

"I have no idea, sire. We parted some time ago."

"Did he tell you what he had done?"

"Sire?"

Roth's face flushed with impatience. "Did he tell you about murdering my father?"

Whit suddenly realized how much danger he himself was in. He picked his next words with care.

"I spent only a brief time in Master Morgan's company, Your Majesty. I knew nothing of this charge."

"Yet you admit to consorting with Morgan, and you've failed to swear your allegiance to us in a timely fashion." Roth glared at him for a long moment, and then seemed to come to a decision. "If you would prove your loyalty, there *is* one sure way. I have need of a wizard."

Whit felt a flood of relief. "Then you have found him," he replied confidently.

The strain around the king's eyes mouth relaxed as his slow smile transformed his now handsome face. "There is a boy in Toldarin, a nobody, who is falsely claiming to be Urlion's legitimate son. Pure lies, of course, but at this time when we are newly invested, even such nonsense can be a threat to the stability and security of the realm." He raised his chin, as if daring Whit to refute this.

"Yes, of course, sire."

Roth picked an invisible thread off his satin sleeve. "The imposter must be silenced." The king flicked his fingers, and Whit's newfound pluck faltered. There was no mistaking Roth's meaning. "I'm told magic leaves no trace."

Whit was shocked speechless, and in the stillness, Roth narrowed his eyes. "Is this beyond your abilities? If so—"

"No, my lord, it is not." Whit dropped his eyes to a spot on the floor between them. Had he just agreed to kill for this man?

"I'm glad to hear it. In that case, we shall overlook your association with the murderer Morgan, and your tardiness in presenting yourself to your king. You may retire to your chamber. See that you stay there. Once I have consulted with Lord Vetch, he will fill you in accordingly."

Dismissed, Whit found himself standing alone outside the High King's chamber. They hadn't assigned a guard to him, although he supposed someone would soon be sent to make sure that he had returned to the room in which he had previously changed his soiled clothes.

He could hear the low voices of Commander Vetch and the king, but couldn't make out their words. Knowing they were likely still discussing his promised service, Whit saw an opportunity too good to pass up.

He walked purposefully down the quiet corridor to the next door in the hall. It was locked, but after listening carefully outside it for a moment and determining the room was empty, a murmured request and a flick of his wrist got him inside. Then it was simply a matter of listening through the wall, for the king and his commander's voices were now clearly audible to Whit's highly attuned ears.

"If the people were to learn of this boy's existence," Roth seethed, "it would mean the ruin of all we've worked for!"

"It's not certain he's Urlion's lawful son," Vetch replied.

"It's not certain he isn't, either. You said he wore a necklace that might prove his claim, which you inexplicably neglected to take from him."

"I-I thought there was no safer place for it then with the lad, rotting in a cell."

"Safer still if he were dead—another bone I have to pick with you. Have you put Lord Belnoth off?"

"He's still asking questions about the boy and badgering me to let him speak with him."

"His interest in the lad has complicated matters, sire. If the boy should die in his cell, along with his cellmate, it will raise questions."

"And his disappearance won't?" Roth snapped.

"Not if it appears he escaped, my lord, and *then* vanished."

"How will we know if the wizard actually does the deed?"

"Have no fear, sire. I'll send the two soldiers we discussed, the ones who require disciplining, to see that Cardenstowe keeps his word."

"And you've plans to deal with them as well?"

"Rest assured, my lord. I shall meet them personally on the road upon their return, to confirm the deed was done. I'll send the wizard on to you. After that, I'm afraid these men will meet with an unfortunate accident."

"Who will you tell them the boy is?"

"Leave this to me, sire."

"Very well. I know I can count on your loyalty, Vetch. And having the wizard bound to me through his part in all this should prove very useful in the long run."

Roth's words sent a chill down Whit's spine.

He realized he'd been right about the storm being a bad omen. It portended a tempest of another sort, and he was caught in its eye.

CHAPTER 18
Borne

The gyrfalcon was a bloody distraction. Borne didn't see how the others could concentrate on the council's discussion with the incessant jingling of the bells attached to its tresses. But His Majesty King Crenel insisted the restive bird accompany him everywhere, even to meals. The previous evening, a large pastry served at the royal table had been cut open to release live skylarks, and the hawk had hunted down fleeing birds right there in the dining hall. The larks' droppings had fouled Borne's stew, and even the king's ermine robes had not been spared.

Today the gyrfalcon was hooded as it paced restlessly on its perch. Borne supposed he should be grateful that the king's gathered advisors had not brought in their birds as well; all the court carried the blasted things around like lapdogs. The demoiselles paraded about with little merlins clutching their gloves, while the gentlemen favored the more formidable peregrine. But only the king could possess a silver gyr, the largest and rarest species.

Not for the first time, Borne wondered why he'd been invited to join this council. Latour's presence was understandable, but what call was there for his Drinnglennian underling? He supposed he should consider it an honor, surrounded as he was by the royal household's most prominent members. The Constable of Gral, Comte Walerin, to whom Marechal Latour was directly responsible, was seated across from Borne, his close-cropped grey hair and weather-etched face mark-

THE DRINNGLENNIN CHRONICLES

ing him as the oldest man present. Comte Jeane Respay, the Lord Chancellor, sat at the king's left hand. The dashing raven-haired lord, less than half the age of Walerin, was charged with the daunting task of overseeing the kingdom's unwieldy judicial system. Borne remembered studying this tangled web, based on the primacy of customary law, under Master Lorian, the same tutor who'd taught him his impeccable Gralian.

Crenel's High Steward, Artrois Roann, was seated on Latour's right. The comte was cousin to the king, and one of the most influential men present. He headed the imperial household and thus enjoyed more of his regal kinsman's company than the others combined. Only Fra Quimpe, Monter on High and the goddess Priscinae's holiest servant, and Comte Montchaurt, the king's financial comtetroller, held more power.

Thus far, Montchaurt had dominated the discussion, reviewing in tedious detail the lavish expenditures for the renovation of the king's water closet. While Borne found the engineering of its air circulation and drainage of interest, he'd heard more than enough about the padding of the privy's seat and the quality of the linens available to His Grace for cleansing his royal ass.

"How can the marechal serve such a popinjay?" Borne had asked Du Charney bluntly a few days earlier, after enduring an astounding lecture on fashion and etiquette from one of His Majesty's dressers. He held up a pair of narrow boots with bright red heels, supposedly all the rage at court. "Am I really expected to wear these, and *be sure* to slide my left foot in front of my right before I sit down?"

Du Charney, Latour's second, raised an expressive eyebrow. "In answer to your first question, Marechal Latour serves the *Crown*. And you mustn't think of ill of His Majesty. King Crenel came to the throne as a child, and was made a pawn in his elderly uncles' pursuit of their own advancements. Once the last of these vultures died, one can forgive the prince for giving himself over to all the amusements previously denied him—pageantry, gambling, hunting, hawking, and dalliances with pretty women. Some will say he's overfree with the coin of the realm, and often deaf to wiser counsel, but since he came of age, his advisors have met with more success in reining in his spending."

Borne laughed. "Did these advisors sanction depleting the treasury so His Majesty could indulge in the complete renovation of Lugeneux?"

"King Crenel must have *some* entertainments," insisted the comte. "He is a restless, capricious prince. When he was denied his beloved grand processions across the realm, it was necessary to provide him with an interest that also benefits Gral."

"More's the pity. If he were to go on procession now and see how his people suffer, perhaps he'd have more care for them."

"*You* should have a care how you speak of the king," growled Du Charney. "One forgets sometimes your youth, and that you come from that uncivil Isle over the sea, for which I hold your insulting tongue accountable."

"I beg your pardon, my lord," said Borne contritely, "but you too must find it frustrating to witness the squandering of Gral's assets at the expense of the peasants. I fear Drinnglennin will veer in the same direction now that Urlion's made the Leap. Not that our late sovereign did very much to improve the conditions of his subjects over the past decade, or to protect the legacy left us by his father. King Owain championed the rights of all Drinnglennians, including the å Livåri. Yet now these people are being persecuted in my land, as they once were here."

"Your High King gave his people peace," said Du Charney, skirting the issue of the å Livåri, whose maltreatment in Gral was yet another blot on the country's honor. "Peace, above all else, is what we too are striving for, and we pray Latour will achieve it. Without peace, none of us—noble or peasant—can hope to improve our lot in life."

Borne tossed the crimson-heeled boots into the corner. "How did it even come to this juncture, with the lawless knights?"

Du Charney made a most ignoble noise. "You'd be better off putting that question to my lord Respay, but in simple terms, the problems stem from the Old Law. For years, King Crenel's vassals could invoke their right to independently withdraw from military conflicts if they needed to protect their own castles and lands. They invoked the right regularly when the Helgrins began making their inexorable inroads into our sovereign territory, sometimes slipping away right before battles.

"Crenel was infuriated that his knights were putting their own interests before those of the nation, so he declared the Old Law void and threatened to strip titles and land from any knight who left his military duties to defend his home. The king's decree raised an uproar, prompting some nobles to band together in revolt and declare themselves independent of the throne's jurisdiction. Hence, they became renegades." He shook his head with regret. "It's only since Latour convinced His Majesty of the need for a royal army, solely in service to the throne, that we've begun to restore the people's faith in the Crown's ability to keep order in the land."

Borne wondered now if restoring the people's faith was even possible.

He was drawn out of his reverie when the council's consideration finally shifted from privies to matters of war.

"You will be pleased to learn, Your Grace," the Constable of Gral was saying, "that many of the dissenting knights are at last honoring their vows. Baffette and Trevigion have both petitioned for your royal pardon. In exchange, they will lead armies of their own vassals into the next major assault on the Helgrin invaders."

"While the merchants of Lugeneux lounge by their fires," grumbled the king.

"The merchants are not trained for war, sire, or legally allowed to take up arms," Fra Quimpe reminded his sovereign. He tucked his vein-marbled hands into his trailing sleeves and hunched his heavy shoulders, although a fire blazed in the hearth and his great bulk should have prevented him from feeling a chill.

"Well, perhaps they *should* be permitted weapons, in this time of need!" snapped Crenel.

"Your guildsmen are occupied with valuable trade, sire," Latour pointed out, "and they pay for the privilege. Without their steep entrance fees for guild memberships, which go directly into the royal coffers, and their favorable loans to the Crown, the kingdom would have been bankrupted long ago."

Borne had observed such exchanges between his marechal and the king on several occasions now. Crenel, for all his frivolous habits, had so far demonstrated the good sense to listen to Latour's counsel. And why shouldn't he? Under the marechal's command, all but a lingering vestige of the anarchy that had ravaged Gral for the past decade had been crushed. Only a handful of rogue bands were still at large, and Latour hoped Gormett would succeed in ferreting these out before they returned to the camp at L'Asedies. In the very near future, Latour would be free to turn his brilliant and punishing attention to liberating the Helgrin-held lands along Gral's northern coast.

The king scowled as he heard his marechal out, but didn't press his petulant argument further. Beside His Majesty, the gyrfalcon rocked on its perch, emitting a high, mewling plea signaling its boredom. Borne empathized with the bird; he was feeling much the same. Stifling a yawn, he realized his name had been spoken—twice—by the king.

He dropped his hand from his mouth and straightened. "Sire?"

The king sprawled in his chair, his thin fingers stroking the gyrfalcon's breast. "My marechal informs me that you are personally acquainted with Drinnglennin's new High King. Can you allay our concerns regarding him?"

Borne blinked. "Concerns, Your Majesty?"

"We are surrounded by enemies," Crenel complained. "The Albrenian king is almost certainly engaged in secret talks with the Helgrins, and the stirrings of the barbarians in the far south are rumored to be supported by both our hostile neighbors. The emissary to our court from Segavia went home several months ago on what he termed 'personal business,' and has not returned.

"It's long past time to renew our once-strong ties with the Isle. Lord Hudde, Drinnglennin's last ambassador, retired to Drinnkastel half a dozen years ago, and Urlion never saw fit to send a replacement."

"We did receive Konigur's assurances that Drinnglennin's pledge of alliance would stand, Your Majesty," Walerin said.

"Bah!" scoffed the king. "Empty words! They haven't kept the Helgrin wolves from our shores! Our pleas for help from Urlion fell on deaf ears!" He eyed Borne speculatively. "I understand you are not yet sworn to service to this King Roth."

"The only oath I am bound by," replied Borne, "is the one I took upon entering the marechal's company, Your Highness. I owe allegiance to no other at present."

And this was true. Oaths of fealty were taken by a vassal to his lord, and generally rewarded by a grant of land. Borne was no vassal, and although he'd inherited Bergsehn when his parents perished, Lord Heptorious had never required a vow of fealty from him.

"Then we shall proceed." The king rose abruptly from his chair, his advisors surging to their feet around him. Crenel strode on his bowed legs to the center of the room, Walerin and Latour close on his heels.

To Borne's surprise, Latour signaled for him to join them.

"It is my marechal's wish that your service to the Crown be recognized," said Crenel, once Borne stood before him. "In this, I am happy to oblige him."

"With your permission, sire," said Constable Walerin. Receiving a royal nod, the man drew his sword and placed it in His Majesty's hands.

"Kneel," commanded the king.

Stunned into silence, Borne obeyed.

"By the Grace of our Lady, Priscinae, Mother of Mothers, and the power vested in us through Her Sanctity and through our royal blood, we are pleased to bestow upon you, Borne Braxton, the Office of Herald, and all the privileges to which this rank entitles you."

It was only when Borne felt the weight of the constable's sword on his shoulder that he believed what was happening. He was not only a commoner; he was baseborn. Yet with two strokes of the blade, his status in life had been redefined.

"Rise, sir," Crenel commanded.

Borne bent low so that the much shorter king could drape the silver-and-gold sash across his shoulder, and he remained bowed down to receive His Majesty's three kisses, in the Gralian fashion.

After these salutes, Borne dropped again to one knee. "Sire, I am honored and... speechless."

A satisfied smile curved Crenel's thin lips. "You have your commander to thank, Sir Borne. The marechal assures me your dedication and the contributions you've made to defeating our enemies have earned you this position. He also tells me you're highly intelligent. Is it true you're classically educated and that you are fluent in Olquarian?"

Borne glance over at Latour, wondering at this turn in the conversation, but the marechal was studying his hands. "Yes, sire."

The king stroked his pointed beard and gave a thoughtful nod. "I was considering you as a replacement for the departed

Lord Hudde, but my advisors tell me your lack of a generations-old noble birthright makes you an unsuitable ambassador to Drinnglennin."

Borne breathed a silent prayer of thanks for this. "It's true, Your Grace. I'm the son of a shepherd. In any case, an appointment to this post would have to come from Drinnkastel."

"If I may speak, Your Majesty," said Latour.

With a nod from the king, Latour turned to Borne, his eyes lit with something close to amusement. "As herald to His Majesty, sir, you are duty-bound to accede to King Crenel's commands."

"Of course," Borne said, but he knew now to be wary.

The king paced to the window, then turned to look up at Borne. "We have urgent need of your services, regardless of your antecedents. You shall be ensured safe conduct and can expect to be welcomed in accordance with your high standing in this court."

Borne's mind had seized on "safe conduct." Was the king sending him away?

The gyrfalcon shrieked, and Crenel, turning, held out his hand so that Roann could tug a heavy gauntlet over it. Then the steward removed the falcon's hood, revealing the bird's liquid brown eyes. It gave a series of rapid chirps before fluttering over to land heavily on the king's glove.

"Comte Walerin and Marechal Latour can fill you in on the details of your mission," said the king, stroking the silver bird's feathers. "Come, Marthé," he crooned. "We shall ride out now. My lady needs to stretch her wings."

Respay, Montchaurt, and Roann followed the king from the room, leaving Comte Walerin to outline King Crenel's plans for his newly appointed herald.

Hearing Walerin's proposal, Borne felt his jaw drop. "You want *me* to represent His Majesty in Olquaria? But I'm a foreigner, and know nothing of diplomacy, sir!"

"Comte Balfou is leading the delegation," said the constable, "and he has many years of experience with the Basileus's court. Indeed, Emperor Zlatan has shown the comte great favor. At this time, however, Zlatan Basileus has need of an elite corps to train his army in the use of modern armaments.

"Olquaria has always remained neutral when conflicts have broken out between her neighbors, near or far. King Crenel has been courting the Basileus for some time now to consider a new alliance. Our lord hopes to win a firm commitment of military support from Zlatan, should we come under attack from Albrenia."

Fra Quimpe interjected his thin voice into the discussion. "I shall select an appropriate monter to join your party. Although we are not permitted to spread the Holy Word of the Mother in that heathen land, our emissaries are allowed to worship privately within the foreign compound. Your souls shall not suffer from neglect while you are away."

My soul is the least of my worries, thought Borne. "What exactly can I contribute to this expedition?"

The constable tented his fingers before him. "According to the marechal, you are not only a fine soldier, but also a professional trainer of men. As King Crenel's emissary, you will lead a company comprised of some of my best fighters as escort for the delegation. Once in Tell-Uyuk, you will employ these men to instruct the Basileus's forces in modern strategic warfare. Your company will include experts in the use of crossbows, siege engines, and cannonry. In addition, you personally will have another, more discreet role."

Latour's heavy-hooded eyes gave Borne no clues as to where Walerin was leading.

"You speak Gralian like a native son," continued the constable, "and we are not a people known for the mastery of other tongues. No one will suspect you of possessing fluent Olquarian."

Borne sat back in his chair. "You want me to be a spy."

Walerin exchanged a glance with Latour, who shrugged and said, "I told you the fellow is clever."

Borne appealed to his commander. "What about the å Livâri corps, Marechal? I've made a commitment to Nicu and his men."

"Which you've honored, as they've honored their commitments to me," replied Latour evenly. "They'll be released to return to their own concerns, taking with them the training and arms to which we agreed."

Borne tried and failed to think of another argument that would keep him in service to Latour. He'd come to admire the marechal more than any other man he knew, save Lord Heptorious, and had hoped to stay on with the Gralian company once they'd fully subdued the rebels. If this wasn't possible, he'd thought to join Nicu in the fight against the enslavement of his people. Now, in the space of a few minutes, both options had been taken away, and another assignment forced on him.

Walerin pushed back from the table, clearly assuming the matter to be settled. "There are arrangements to be made. We'll meet again as soon as all is finalized. Until then, gentlemen."

The monter rose ponderously to his feet and raised his doughy hand in benediction. "May the Mother of Mothers and Sword of Faith sustain you, and grant you success in His Majesty's name." Then he trundled after the constable, accompanied by the sound of his wheezing breath and his long skirts sweeping the rushes.

* * *

Out in the courtyard, Latour clapped a silent Borne on the shoulder. "Come now, my friend," he said. "Why so glum? You've succeeded in exchanging your shepherd's crook for a sword, and your herd of coilhorns for an army. *And* you've obtained the status of nobility, Sir Herald!"

"I don't see what good it will do me. You don't seem to care much for *your* birthright, *Comte* Latour."

"It's true that I prefer my earned title of Marechal," Latour conceded, "but that doesn't mean I don't value the advantages with which my family name provides me. Without it, I could never have risen to this rank." He cuffed Borne lightly on the chin. "Admit it," he demanded.

"Admit what?"

"That you're already tantalized by the prospect of traveling to the exotic city of Tell-Uyuk."

"I haven't had time to even begin considering it!"

"Well, let's get you started over a flask or two of *mulate*. We've much to celebrate."

Borne couldn't help but take Latour's enthusiasm as an affront. "You seem positively jubilant to be rid of me," he grumbled.

Latour shrugged. "I'm a practical man. I was unlikely to keep you in any event, and I'd rather lose you to the further service of Gral than to a rebel band of å Livåri." He laughed at Borne's expression. "You are surprised, Sir Herald, that I suspected your future plans?"

Borne could only shake his head.

"Don't worry," said Latour. "I'm sure you'll find much to intrigue that inventive mind of yours in the East."

"*Tanah velkrie vela dar, vole rellen me'taksa mar,*" Borne replied.

The marechal frowned. "I beg your pardon?"

"It's a line from *Heart Songs for Hegamah* by Olkim bè Halour."

"Who's that?"

Borne clicked his tongue disapprovingly. "Only the greatest poet who ever lived. Do you learn nothing about the world beyond your parochial borders?"

Latour cuffed him again, this time with more force. "Mind your step, *sir*," he cautioned. "I take it this bè Halour is Olquarian. What do the words mean?"

Borne grinned. "It's difficult to translate, but it refers to the exquisite charms of the love maidens of Tell-Uyuk."

With a shout of laughter, Latour threw his arm across Borne's shoulders. "I told you—you're halfway there already, you bastard! Now, let us go and salute that flashy new sash of yours in true Gralian style."

CHAPTER 19
Halla

Halla ran her hand over her dripping brow. The sun had climbed high above the mesa, and the growing heat was relentless. She would have pulled off her tunic as well if she weren't wary of her fair skin burning.

"By the breath of Alithin," she grumbled, plucking the cloth away from the sweat pooling between her breasts. "I'd give my teeth for a whisper of wind." She scowled at Nicu's amused expression. "This Albrenian spring is brutal. It feels more like high summer!"

She raised her waterskin to her lips but drank sparingly, for there was no telling where the next watering hole might lie. As far as the eye could see, the rust-brown land stretched, arid and flat as a trencher, save toward Delnogoth, where distant mountains wavered in the hazy heat.

Halla, along with the rest of the å Livåri contingent that had remained in Gral, had been released from Latour's service three weeks ago, and they were now in the far east of Albrenia with Mihail and his freedom fighters. Nicu's second-in-command had been busy in their absence, and had rescued scores of å Livåri women in the past months. The company had recently uncovered a lucrative slave trade operating in nearby Estelbau, but on the several forays they'd made into the market town, they'd seen none of their own people up for auction—only Goths and eastern tribespeople.

It was good to be back at camp with her comrades—where there was no need to play the lady. Halla fell easily back into the routines of training, foraging, and going out on raids, but one thing had changed. Despite what she'd told Borne about accepting her lover's dalliances, Halla had not returned to Nicu's bed after the party Crenel held in her honor. Over the remaining months of their service in Gral, she'd maintained a cool, polite distance. Nicu's response was at first amused, but when she continued to avoid him, he began excluding her from his daily briefings. It seemed her behavior had stung him in return. That tension had eased somewhat now that they were back in Albrenia, though, and she hoped they could return to a semblance of their early camaraderie. She missed his companionship.

When scouts reported that new shiploads of å Livåri women had arrived in Segavia to be put up for auction, Nicu gave the order to prepare to move south. But then the morning before they were to break camp, another scout returned with the news that a large military operation was being carried out less than a day's ride to the west, and Nicu sent four men out for a closer look. Now, as the hours crept by, Halla could tell he was on edge waiting for the men to return. In between sharpening his knife with short, sharp strokes, he would periodically rise and pace, running his hand absently through his thick curls. And with good reason: it shouldn't have taken the men so long to complete their business. When Hus struck his ladle against his battered pot to signal their supper was ready, Nicu swore under his breath.

"I suppose we might as well eat," he muttered.

Halla gave a small groan. The men had killed a boar earlier, and the gamey smell of the stew Hus had concocted had been making her feel nauseated all day.

Nicu raised an eyebrow. "Not hungry? You barely ate your morning porridge either."

"You go ahead. I'm too hot to eat." She leaned back in the shade, willing the sun to hurry its descent below the horizon.

But when Nicu came back, he was bearing two bowls.

213

She accepted one, albeit reluctantly, knifed up a piece of the gristly grey meat, and frowned at it. "If I hadn't seen Hus dress the boar, I'd swear this stew was made from those burrowing rats." She leaned over and dropped the meat into Nicu's bowl, setting her own aside with a grimace.

Nicu paused with his knife halfway to his mouth. Halla, following his gaze, saw a small cloud of dust in the distance. She reached for the hilt of the sword slung on her back. "Shall I alert the others?"

Nicu sprang to his feet. "No. That's Chik's horse. I just can't tell if he's on it."

Halla squinted. "I can't even see a horse."

A slow smile spread over Nicu's lips, although his eyes remained riveted on the approaching riders. "You forget that I'm descended from dragons," he said, citing the old å Livåri legend.

Born of the dragons of Tarm, she recalled. She'd heard the tales from Bria and Florian by their campfire. She wondered what Nicu would say if she told him she'd ridden astride a real dragon's back.

The horses were close enough now for her to count four of them—all with riders. Nicu strode out to meet them, and as the å Livåri converged and leapt from their saddles, they exchanged the wrestling embraces and insults that passed for warm greetings among men.

"It took you long enough," Nicu grumbled, leaning over to sniff at Mihail's tunic. "You reek of sow dung. Have you been rolling again?"

"I smell a sight better than you, you loll-sacked skamelar!" Mihail threw a mock punch at him.

Nicu grinned and turned to clap Chik's shoulders. "Come. I want to hear at once what you learned about these military manueveurs." He glanced over at Halla. "You too, *Åthinoi*."

Halla felt a small bubble of pleasure welling up inside her. He hadn't called her that since they'd stopped sleeping together.

"I'll see to the horses first," she offered.

Chik's gelding was especially footsore and thirsty. She walked him a bit to cool him before letting him drink his fill. "Later I'll give you a good brushing," she murmured as she led the piebald to a patch of shade.

When the horses had been cared for, she joined the others in the relative cool of the lean-to and found the men still on their feet. "What did I miss?" she asked, scanning their faces.

Nicu's eyes were ablaze with excitement. "It seems King Jorgev's high commander is in the region."

Halla felt her stomach clench. "Seor Palan?"

"The very same." Nicu knew all about Halla's connection with Seor Palan de Grathiz, the man who'd commissioned her purchase and sent her to the Casa Calida to be trained as his bed slave.

Her hands balled into fists. "When do we ride?"

"Patience, Åthinoi," Nicu said. "We'll need to do some more scouting first."

But Halla's blood was already singing in her veins. *"When do we ride?"*

* * *

The Albrenian commander had chosen his base well. His army was encamped on an oasis of grassland, the only green for miles around. Halla knew from her time with Latour that Palan had been conducting field drills along the border with Gral for some time. "Flexing his muscles," was how the maréchal had described it, but judging by the size of his force, it looked more like Palan was shaking his fist.

She and Nicu had ridden under cover of darkness to meet up with Chik, Mihail, and Jibin, who'd gone ahead to observe the army several days before. Now, as the sun made its way over the horizon, Halla peered out from the scraggy under-brush, her eyes drawn to the *adarrak*, the first she'd ever seen, at the center of the milling riders in the camp. These great horned horse were of a rare breed found only in Albrenia. Some believed them to be descended from unicorns, and now Halla saw why. The *adarrak* stood over seventeen hands high, and had two knobbed bones protruding from the ridge of his forehead. His thick, black mane was twined in a crisscrossed web over his regal neck, and his full tail was braided as well. Both were laced with golden ribbons that swept the ground. The creature was draped in a cloth of royal blue, winking with sapphires and topazes worth a king's ransom.

The tall man sitting the ornate saddle was in full uniform, the sash and badges of his supreme office on prominent display.

Halla narrowed her eyes at the sight of him. "Devil's whoreson," she hissed.

Beside her, Nicu gave a soft laugh. "Your former owner, in the flesh." Seeing her expression, he cautioned, "Don't make me regret giving in to your pleas to come along. You're to keep that lethal knife of yours sheathed."

Halla glared at him. "I didn't plead. You asked me to come."

"Only because I knew you'd follow in any event."

He was right, of course.

As they watched, the commander dismounted and tossed the reins of his fine horse to a waiting squire. Halla had to clench her itching fingers to keep from drawing an arrow and putting it through the Albrenian bastard's throat. He was soon lost among his milling men, but she assumed he was headed toward the tall peaked tent rising from the center of the camp, its bold blue-and-gold banner flying above all the others.

On Nicu's signal, the å Livåri backed away and returned to the thickly brambled hedge shielding them and their horses from view.

"There must be over a thousand men in the camp," Nicu said. "Mostly infantry I'm guessing, but still…"

Halla could tell he was reconsidering the feasibility of their plan. They'd faced a full army when they were backed by Latour and his Gralian force, but now the company's size limited them to smaller-scale raids.

"We're not going to engage with all of them," Halla reminded him. "Only Palan."

"We're not going to engage with Palan either," Nicu replied. "We go in and take him, then offer terms to King Jorgev for his release."

Halla failed, once again, to hold her tongue, even though previous efforts to convince her comrades their expectations were pure folly had fallen on deaf ears. "You're asking for the release of hundreds, maybe thousands, of å Livåri in exchange for *one man*," she protested. "You think you can negotiate something like that with a king? Jorgev will not only refuse—he'll throw the full force of his royal army against you. It would be better to just slit Palan's throat and slip away unscathed."

Nicu shook his head. "We've been over this. If we kill Palan and run away, we'll have nothing to show for it, no leverage to use. And Jorgev will still end up sending the might of his forces against us. You're letting your personal enmity for the man rule your head, Halla. Palan is worth a great deal to our cause—but only if he's alive."

"And if King Jorgev refuses to free the å Livåri slaves?" she persisted.

"Then we'll demand gold," Mihail said. "Enough gold to buy their liberty."

"But—"

"Leave it, Halla," Nicu said, his voice stern. "That's an order."

"At least let me go with you to take Palan. My waiting here serves no purpose."

"It does if you have to carry news of our capture back to the main camp."

Halla scowled, though Nicu was in fact trusting her with a critical role. If the Albrenians captured the å Livåri, they'd make sure to extract the location of any comrades before taking their lives. It would be up to Halla to warn the others to move, lest the entire company be caught unawares.

Nicu's stern expression softened. "Don't look like that, Åthinoi. If Palan follows his usual routine, we shall seize him and be miles away before he's missed. The Albrenians are within their own borders. They aren't expecting any trouble. Palan's so certain of their security he hasn't even bothered to post sentries."

"It's an incredible stroke of luck that he's a creature of habit," Mihail said. "Every day at sunset, he goes alone to bathe in the *wadi* on the western border of the camp. After his bath, he sits by the water for as much as an hour in prayer. No one ever disturbs him."

Chik grinned. "We'll take the bastard while he's communing with his goddess. Tonight, there'll be no moon—nothing could be easier."

Halla had to admit that the plan was so simple, it might just succeed.

They had hours to kill before the daylight faded. After a light meal of grapes, cheese, and hard, spicy sausage, Chik, Mihail, and Jibin found a patch of shade and stretched out in it. They'd need to sleep now, for they'd face a hard night's ride after the kidnapping.

Halla was too restless to join them, and she was relieved when Nicu produced a deck of cards.

"Fancy a game of Bloody Flux?"

Halla nodded, and as she was ordering her cards she asked, "If this ransom is pulled off, and your people freed, what will you do then? I mean, after it's over."

Nicu threw down a ten. "Nothing will be over. We've still to find out what's happened to those who never made it to Albrenia."

Halla took his ten with her knave. "So where will you look for them?"

Nicu shrugged. "I guess I'll go back to Drinnkastel—see if the wizard has turned anything up."

Halla stared hard at her cards. She felt guilty about not telling Nicu about her connection with Master Morgan. Even when Nicu told her about the wizard's part in finding Maura's brother, Dal, she hadn't said a word. It was just too complicated. She'd have to explain she knew Maura as well, yet leave out any reference to Mithralyn and the elves, not to mention the dragons.

"What about you?" Nicu leaned back on his elbow and eyed her speculatively. "Since you're so dead set against wedding your cousin and playing lady of the manor?"

Halla shrugged. "I don't know." It was the truth. The prospect of returning to Drinnglennin certainly didn't excite her. Even if she escaped a marriage to Whit, her mother would likely try to force her into another of advantage to Lorendale. "I don't think I'm ready to cross back over the Erolin Sea."

If Nicu was disappointed, he didn't let on. "Latour would probably have you back, or you could petition to join Borne's royal commission and travel to the East. In fact, I think you'd prefer that; à Livåri are born with wanderlust running through our veins."

Halla grinned at his inclusion of her as one of them, and he returned her smile with a disarmingly gentle one of his own. Something in the way he remained gazing at her made her heart quicken.

"You're like no one I've ever known, Åthinoi." He reached out and tucked a strand of hair behind her ear. "Most will look at you and see no further than your beauty. And that's a pity, because it distracts from your greater assets."

Halla looked down at her cards to cover her surprise. "If you think I'll spare you because you're spouting pretty words, think again." She plucked her Grand Dame from her hand and covered his King. "*Bela!*" she pronounced as the round fell to her.

But Nicu had folded his cards and his gaze had not wavered. "I'm sorry," he said, his voice low.

Halla didn't pretend not to understand him. "You have nothing for which to apologize. We took no vows."

"That is so. And for this too, I am sorry." His eyes were like black pools, so deep she thought she might drown in them. She looked down at his fingers, which had curled around her own as he lifted her hand to his chest. Beneath his dusty doublet, she could feel the steady rhythm of his heart.

Nicu leaned forward until his forehead rested against hers. "I have burned for other women," he murmured, "but always, once the fire was quenched, I was as I had been before. Not so with you, Halla. You appear to be made as other women, but you are not. You left me with something beyond the burning."

Halla untwined her fingers from his hands and gently pushed him back until she could see his face once more. In his smoldering eyes, there was something she had not seen before.

He gently pulled her closer again until his lips touched her brow, then he moved them to her ear. "Emptiness, Åthinoi," he whispered, "that's what you've left me with—emptiness that can only be filled by you. I would wake to feel your breath on my cheek again, and to hold you throughout the night; to hear you laugh, to run and ride and dance with you. I would have you as my wife."

Breathless, she had no words with which to reply, but let her lips give him her answer.

* * *

Waiting had always been hard for Halla. Waiting for her father to finish meting out justice before coming to ride with her, waiting for the interminable embroidery lesson to end so she could escape to the sparring grounds. Waiting in vain, once her brothers had usurped her place in Father's heart, for him to remember that once she had been his dearest child.

Nicu and the others had ridden out at the sun's set. "If we're not back within two hours," Nicu had told her, "leave our horses and ride to the main camp. Should something go awry, perhaps one or more of us can escape." He chucked Halla gently under the chin. "Such a frown, Åthinoï! All will be well, and we'll bring you your former master in chains. You'll enjoy that, won't you?"

But she wasn't thinking about Palan now. The stars that formed the White Ship had already sailed high in the night sky, the Serpent was descending, and still they had not returned. The gnawing worry in the pit of her stomach had long ago bloomed into dread.

Something had gone wrong.

But if it had, wouldn't she have heard shouts, or men riding out to ensure there were no others, like her, waiting with the horses?

Halla's hair lifted in the rising wind, and bits of grit and pebbles began to strike her face. A storm was coming out the east. The dry leaves on the hedges rustled and puffs of dust swirled and eddied over the ground. The horses grew restive— Haize flicked her ears and raised her lip to scent the air, and Nicu's grey snorted, shying from the gusting wind.

Halla rummaged in their saddlebags for anything that might protect them from the dust-filled air. She found several soiled tunics, and set to work with her knife to fashion covers to protect the horses' eyes and nostrils. While she was wrapping the last one on Haize, the stars suddenly disappeared and the temperature plummeted.

Halla's heart gave a jolt as the wind surged to a roar, giving voice to the towering wall of darkness that roiled toward them across the land. Stones were now hurtling at her from all directions, and the horses squealed in terror and pain.

She tied a strip of cloth over her own mouth and nose, then pulled her hood down over her face, curled into a ball, and waited for the storm to sweep her into its gritty maw. She kept her eyes squeezed shut, and held her breath for as long as she could, but still the dust found its way into her lungs, making her choke and cough. If the horses were still whinnying, she couldn't hear them; her ears were filled with the racing wave of angry, churning wind.

She lost track of how long she huddled under its assault, but after what seemed an eternity, the storm's howl diminished to a whine, and it was over as suddenly as it had begun. Venturing to lift her hood, Halla saw that the stars had returned to the heavens, and the horses were still there. She rubbed the grime from her face and tended to the animals, soothing them with her hands and voice as she removed their wrappings and examined them for injuries. They were covered, as she was, in a fine coat of dust, but miraculously were unhurt.

The storm had prevented Halla from following Nicu's orders to return to camp, but Baldo, who was in command there, was no fool. By now he would have assumed that their plan to kidnap Palan had failed, and the å Livåri would have moved on. They did not need her to warn them. Still, as a good soldier, she knew she should mount Haize and ride like the hounds of Blearc after them.

But leaving was not an option. She could still feel the warmth of Nicu's arms encircling her. She wouldn't, indeed couldn't, desert him. If Nicu and the others had been captured, she was their only hope of escape.

She knew she must act.

Yet it was beyond foolish to try to enter the camp right after rebels had attempted to waylay its commanding officer. There were sure to be sentries posted now.

So how do I get past them?

She thought ruefully of the fine silver gown that King Crenel had insisted she take with her, now balled up in her pack back at the å Livåri camp. Not that it mattered—even if she had the appropriate attire to try to bluff her way into the Albrenian camp, how would she explain the presence of a lady alone in the near wilderness?

Think. What would Nicu do in your place?

No flash of inspiration came. She would just have to follow her instincts.

She untethered the horses so that if she too was captured, they might find their way to water and new caretakers. Then, tightening her sword belt, she headed toward the enemy camp, offering up a silent prayer to any god listening that she would find her comrades still alive.

If they weren't, Palan was a dead man.

CHAPTER 20
Fynn

Fynn opened his eyes to harsh light that shot a bolt through his brain. Gasping at the pain, he squeezed them shut again.

"Water," he croaked, for his mouth felt like it was lined with leather, but all that came out was a strained breath. "Grinner?" This time he managed a garbled sound.

The cold voice that answered was not that of his cellmate. "He lives."

"Grinner?" he mumbled again.

"Shut yer trap." A different voice this time. He recognized it—it belonged to Strawman, the guard with the pale, spiky hair. "Or should I shut it fer him, me lord?"

"Carry him out and put him in the cart," ordered the first speaker, "and make sure you're not seen."

"Where's Grinner?" Fynn whispered.

"Gag him if he makes another sound."

Fynn heard retreating footsteps echoing against the stone, then he was hoisted like a sack of grain and slung over Strawman's bony shoulder. He wanted desperately to find out what had become of his friend, but the thought of a cloth stuffed into his parched mouth forced him to hold his tongue.

Swinging upside down, he ventured to open his eyes again. He saw only the stone floor passing under him. Strawman grunted as they started up the stairs, and the clumsy oaf was heedless to Fynn's cry when his head struck the wall.

A bolt slid and keys rattled, and they were out into the cold. Fynn drew a deep, hungry breath. After the long months underground, the fresh air was almost enough to quench his terrible thirst.

Within the space of ten steps, he was dumped onto the hard slats of a cart. For only a moment he stared up at a midnight-blue sky peppered with glittering stars; then a tarp was thrown over him, blotting them out. The canvas smelled of damp earth, and he felt a thrill of terror. *This must be what it feels like to be buried alive.*

The cart listed as someone settled onto it, then lurched forward. "One peep," Strawman hissed, "and I'll bludgeon ye cold."

As they rumbled over the cobbled streets, Fynn's foggy mind began to clear. He had cast a dream and survived it, but what he'd learned in the process made him wish he hadn't. Old Snorri had sworn that a bloodtooth vision was always true. Which meant Fynn was not the son of Aetheor Yarl. But why had Fynn's mother never told him this? Had she been afraid Aetheor would somehow find out as well, and make Fynn a thrall?

Fynn's heart ached for the loss of the birthright he'd so treasured. *No wonder I'm such a craven,* he thought bitterly as he bumped along in the bed of the cart. No Helgrin blood ran through his veins. His real father was one of the enemy, a man Fynn would never even know, for according to the dream, he was dead and buried.

Coming here to his mother's homeland had deprived him of everything he cared about. Now he had no family at all. He should have died in Restaria, ignorant of the loathsome truth his dream had revealed.

To make matters worse, while he'd been dreaming, something had happened to Grinner. If his friend was dead, Fynn was to blame.

His fingers crept to the small sack hidden under his tunic. At least he still had the means to end his misery once and for all.

Eventually the cart rolled to a halt. When the heavy tarp was lifted, Strawman's broad face loomed over Fynn's.

"Not a sound," the warder reminded him, shaking his truncheon.

Fynn let himself down from the cart, his legs rubbery beneath him. Tall houses lined the deserted street, so he knew they were still in the city.

Strawman kept a meaty hand curled round the collar of Fynn's ragged tunic as the gaoler half-dragged him up the steps of one of the houses. The door swung silently open, and they crossed the threshold into a dark corridor.

A stern voice addressed them from the shadows.

"You will forget this house and this night's work, else your life is forfeit. Leave us."

Strawman needed no further encouragement.

When the door closed behind the gaoler, a man draped in a dark cloak emerged from the gloom. "Can you walk?"

Fynn nodded.

The stranger stepped aside and gestured for Fynn to go ahead, pointing toward a thin ribbon of light showing beneath a door at the end of the corridor. It led into a musty room where a single candle burned on a sideboard.

Two men, both wrapped in heavy cloaks, awaited them.

"Come over to the light, boy," said the taller of the two. His auburn hair was combed back from his high forehead, and the sharp, pointed beard on his long face put Fynn in mind of a fox.

Fynn stepped forward, and the shorter man, with long grey hair and wiry whiskers spouting from his chin, leaned over to study his face. "Why, he looks like... " He glanced over at his companion, his expression one of surprise.

"Never mind who he looks like," said the other. He jerked his chin at Fynn's escort. "You'd best get on with it."

This directive was met with a heavy silence. When the man behind Fynn at last spoke, his voice was low. "I'd prefer to be alone when it is done."

Fynn didn't care at all for the sound of that. He edged back and turned slightly so that he had all three men in his line of sight. He saw then that the one who had met him at the door was young—younger even than Jered. His dark hair was neatly tied back, and he was dressed all in black, except for the silver buckle on his belt. Unlike the other two, he wore no sword, but in his grip he held a long, twisted staff.

"We're to bear witness," said Greybeard, "to see that it's done."

"That it's carried out, *my lord*," the young man amended coolly.

The offender inclined his head. "My lord."

"You're aware of the curse said to befall the murder of one with royal blood in his veins? It may well extend to any who cold-bloodedly stand by while such an abomination is carried out. Besides, the magic is complicated. I can't guarantee that it won't produce unpleasant... reverberations." The staff-bearer lifted a suggestive eyebrow, and his companions exchanged an uneasy look.

"I suppose we could wait outside the door," conceded Foxface, "and view the body afterward."

Fynn had been pondering the mention of magic, but now his heart began to race. *The body?*

Greybeard remained adamant. "Vetch said we were to see it done, with our own eyes."

So Vetch had finally decided to have Fynn done away with, and had sent a wizard to do the job. Death by magic. It struck Fynn as a fate even worse than drowning. A brave Helgrin prayed to die with his sword or axe in his hand.

But you're no Helgrin, remember?

He cast a swift glance at the door, weighing his chances of dodging around the wizard to reach it.

The young man laughed. At first Fynn thought he'd read his thoughts, but the wizard's wide grey gaze was focused on the others. "And what do you two think your lives will be worth," he said, "after witnessing the murder of Urlion's son?"

Fynn's heart sank. So the bloodtooth vision was true.

Foxface gasped and Greybeard's eyes widened. "Wha—the lad's an imposter!"

"It would be easy enough to prove that, wouldn't it?" said the wizard. "So why order the boy's death? Look at him... or do your eyes deceive you?"

The two men gaped at Fynn, and Foxface went suddenly pale.

"If I were you," said the wizard, "I'd get on my horse, flee to the harbor, and find a ship departing on the next turn of the tide to somewhere far from the Isle. And I wouldn't look back." He smiled pleasantly, but his eyes held danger. "I hear Gral is hiring mercenaries. Perhaps there, you might escape the long arm of your commander."

Greybeard scowled. "What about you?"

"I have nothing to fear. Lord Vetch knows that my part in this deed ensures my silence. Indeed, it will further prove my loyalty to His Majesty. Perhaps he would thank me if I took care of you two as well."

Both men's hands went to their swords, but the wizard was quicker. With a strange cry he raised his staff, and an ear-splitting *crack* rent the air. Greybeard and Foxface scrambled across the room, the force of their pounding boots making the candle wobble. Greybeard clawed at the latch and flung the door open, and in the next moment, both men were gone.

Fynn was under no illusion as to what was to happen next, but he was determined to face it head-on. Ignoring his shaking knees, he forced himself to square his shoulders and lifted his chin. He may have lived as a coward, but he refused to die as one.

To Fynn's astonishment, his executioner held out his hand. "I'm Whit. You can relax—I mean you no harm. If you're who they think you are, we're actually related by blood—on my mother's side," he added, with a sudden vehemence.

If the wizard planned to murder him, he was going about it in a strange way. Numbly, Fynn extended his own hand. "Fynn," he said, still anticipating the fatal flash of light that would put a lie to the wizard's words.

"Very well, Fynn. My little performance just now may have bought us some time, but we'll need to be on our way. Once we've put a few miles between us and Toldarin, I can explain more. Will you trust me?"

Fynn didn't see that he had a choice. He nodded. "Are you really a… "

"Wizard? Yes. But as I said, you needn't worry. I've never killed anyone by magic, or any other means." He frowned. "Though I suppose it *will* come to killing, soon enough." Seeing Fynn's expression, he added, "I don't mean you. This way."

In a daze, Fynn followed him to a door on the opposite side of the room.

"*Gadewch fod golau*," Whit murmured. A light sprang from the head of his staff, revealing a narrow staircase winding downward into darkness. "I'll go first. Have a care, and hold on to my cloak."

The strong scent of apple wafted toward them as they descended into a cellar lined with old oaken casks. Fynn's thirst reasserted itself with a vengeance. "I need something to drink."

Whit raised an eyebrow. "Have a fondness for cider, do you?" He rummaged inside his cloak and pulled out a small flask. "Try this instead, but just a few sips, mind you."

Fynn brought the flask to his parched lips and took several deep gulps. The liquid tasted of honey and berries and summer all at once, and filled him with warmth.

Reverently, he handed the flask back to Whit. "Is it magic?"

"You might say that." The wizard tucked the bottle back into the folds of his cloak. "It's brewed in the north by... friends of mine."

Without warning, the light disappeared, and in the sudden dark Fynn heard a bolt slide. He realized he was no longer frightened; perhaps the magical draught had quenched more than his thirst.

They passed through a door and emerged onto the street that ran behind the house. Whit immediately set off at a run, and Fynn had to scurry to stay on his heels. They made for two horses tethered to a ring on the stone wall—one white, one chestnut.

"Up you go," said Whit, hefting him onto the white horse's back. To Fynn's surprise, Whit then swung on to the same horse, sitting astride behind him. "Hold tight!"

Fynn wrapped his hands in the horse's mane as it shot forward; the larger chestnut barreled along behind her.

The air smelled of brine and fish, reminding him of home. He cast his eyes to the stars and saw the Anchor, Vron's Hammer, and the Maiden wheeling above; they felt like old friends returned to him after a long absence. Although the cold rushed through his tattered tunic to the core of his bones, he welcomed it. He was grateful to be alive—and free.

Shortly, they slowed to a canter, making a number of twists and turns through the city streets before the wizard reined in on a narrow lane. Only then did he notice Fynn's shuddering.

"Dylar take me for ashes!" Whit cursed. "You're freezing, aren't you?" He swept his voluminous cloak over Fynn's head. "Stay as still as you can under there. The town gates lie just ahead, and I want to be remembered as leaving Toldarin alone."

Fynn guessed the cloak must have come from the same friends in the north as had the drink in Whit's flask, for in the short time before the horses drew to a halt again, his trembling ceased and he could feel his fingers and toes again.

"Leaving us so soon, my lord?" a voice boomed to his left.

"My movements are my business."

Fynn hoped the porter wouldn't be angered by such a brash reply. The last thing he wanted was to be returned to his dismal cell. He held his breath until he heard the rattle of the grille winding open, and the horses trotted on. They were out of the city.

Almost at once, the horses picked up their pace. They raced on for what seemed like hours before finally slowing to a walk. When Whit pulled the cloak from over Fynn's head, the day had broken to a world rimed with frost under low, heavy clouds. Nearby, a brook ran over dark stones, frothing with white foam.

"Where are we?" Fynn asked.

Whit swung him to the ground and dismounted after him. "Unfortunately, we're still in Nelvorboth, but a stop is required. The horses need rest, and to be watered and fed."

Fynn raised a hand to the mare's snowy neck. "What's its name?"

The wizard patted the horse fondly. "*Her* name is Sinead."

"Grace," Fynn said, for it was a runic name. He watched the mare step lightly down to the brook, and decided her name suited her.

He trailed after her and knelt down on the muddy ground to drink his fill. The water was so cold it burned his hands and throat, but he didn't care. After the brackish stuff in his prison bucket, it tasted nearly as good as the nectar in the wizard's flask.

When he got to his feet, he turned and met Whit's disapproving eye. He looked down at his dripping sleeves and the clods of earth caked on the knees of his tattered breeches.

The wizard gave his head a slow shake. "It's lucky for you I never travel without a change of clothes." He withdrew several neat rolls from Sinead's saddlebags. "If it weren't so cold, I'd insist you wash first. I've already gotten several bites from whatever bloodthirsty creatures have taken up residence on you."

Fynn pulled his soiled tunic over his head, then donned the fine blue linen shirt Whit handed him in its place. He had to cinch the borrowed breeches with a belt and roll their cuffs, for the wizard was a tall man, but they fit him better than he thought they would. He must have grown a fair bit while he was in prison.

"Hang on," Whit said, digging out another cloak from Sinead's pack. "I'd forgotten I had a spare."

Fynn draped it over his shoulders, and it felt wonderfully warm.

The wizard then pulled a slab of ham, half a loaf of bread, and an apple from the saddlebags. Fynn ate slowly, aware that his stomach might not accept such long-denied fare, simple as it was. He was certain that food had never tasted so good. By the time he'd finished eating, most of the fog that had inhabited his brain since he'd awoken from his dream-cast had dissipated, and his curiosity about Whit and the whole business back in the abandoned house surged to the fore of his thoughts.

"Why did Lord Vetch want me dead all of a sudden, after all this time?" he blurted out. "And why did he ask *you* to do it?" Fynn leaned back on his hands.

Whit stabbed up a slice of apple and held it out to him. "As to your first question, I thought perhaps you could tell me the answer to that. Where did you grow up?"

Taken by surprise, Fynn gave a little cough and said, "In the east." *Across the sea*, he added silently as he accepted the slice of fruit.

"And your mother? Where is she?"

When Fynn remained silent, Whit gave a little nod of understanding. "I'm sorry."

Fynn swallowed a bite of the apple with a hard gulp. He didn't want Whit's pity, or anyone else's.

The wizard took a long drink. "Where did you learn runic?" he asked, offering Fynn the flask. "You knew that Sinead means grace in the old tongue."

Fynn felt his jaw drop, for Whit had posed his question in Helgric. "*You* speak Helgric?"

Whit gave a small shrug. "I read runic fluently, and the Helgric language is based on runes. It's a modified form of the ancient Old Tongue, which a wizard needs to learn if he wants to study the ancient texts." He scanned Fynn's face. "Have you studied with a wizard? Is that how you came to know it?"

Fynn laughed. He didn't see any reason to lie. "I speak Helgric because I was raised in Helgrinia."

Whit laughed. "Sure you were." He caught himself and frowned. "You're serious? I don't understand. If your father..."

"I grew up believing my father was a Helgrin." Fynn turned away, for the pain of knowing he wasn't Aetheor's son was still too raw.

Whit must have noticed his discomfort, for he shifted the topic of conversation. "What's Helgrinia like?"

"It's beautiful," Fynn said wistfully, "with silver lakes and tall trees that would dwarf any of these around here. The forests are filled with elk and boars and cave lions, and in the far north, the great white bears rule the land." He hugged his knees against his chest, warming to the memories of his homeland and happy to be speaking his first language. "Fish swarm in the rivers, and in the summer, so many birds come to nest, they're beyond counting. We feast on swan and ptarmigan then." Remembering felt both good and bad at the same time. He could almost smell the balsam firs that had risen like towering sentinels around their manor. "My father went north after Midsommer every year, to hunt hrossval, the giant tusked seals." Fynn flushed. "Father... I mean Aetheor... he was—"

"Aetheor? *Aetheor Yarl* raised you?" Whit had switched back to Drinn, his grey eyes wide with disbelief. "You—the son of Urlion Konigur?"

Fynn wasn't sure what to make of the young wizard's sudden agitation. "Why does it matter?"

Whit continued to stare at him. "Do you not know who your real father was—*what* he was here in Drinnglennin?"

Fynn shook his head. He wasn't sure he cared to know anything about the man buried in the cold crypt of his dream. *He was never a true father to me,* he thought stubbornly.

The wizard gave him a long look, as if considering saying something more, then rose and began circling the small clearing, speaking under his breath and drawing lines in the air with his staff. When he finished whatever it was he was doing, he dropped back down beside Fynn.

"We'll rest here for a few hours." Whit leaned back against a tree, closed his eyes, and fell asleep at once.

Fynn was aware that Whit hadn't answered his other question—about why Vetch had chosen him to be Fynn's murderer. He wondered if the wizard had laid some sort of spell to keep him within the confines of the circle, or if the muttering had been for the purpose of keeping ill-wishers out. He supposed he could test it, but he felt weary beyond measure. He wrapped his new cloak around him and curled up on the mossy ground.

It seemed only a moment later that he felt a hand on his shoulder.

"We must go."

Whit was already mounted by the time Fynn struggled to his feet. Judging by the sun's position, they'd slept for several hours.

"Where are we heading?" Fynn asked groggily.

"South." Whit held out his hand to pull him up before him.

Fynn eyed the other horse. "I can ride."

234

"That may be, but my friend Rowlan is particular about whom he allows on his back." After Fynn was mounted in front of him, he added, "We'll have to stay off the main thoroughfares. I'm taking you to Stonehoven. No one will think to look for you there."

It gave Fynn a queer feeling, knowing that there was a possibility he was being hunted. For whatever reason, Vetch had ordered his murder, and would likely renew pursuit if Whit's deceit was discovered.

"Will you be staying in Stonehoven with me?" he asked.

"I'm afraid not. The High King will have returned to Drinnkastel by now, and I'll have to go there to report your 'death.' With any luck, my two companions in Toldarin took my advice and fled the country without reporting in."

"What if they didn't? What if Lord Vetch suspects you of hiding me?" Fynn thought grimly of Grinner. He didn't want to be responsible for more trouble.

"That's my concern, not yours." Whit clucked his tongue at Sinead, and they started down the trail.

They rode in silence, following the brook as it crossed the broad fields, where they were visible to any riders traveling the same road. Fynn felt better when their path veered into woodland again. As the hours passed, he drifted in and out of sleep, and once he nearly slipped off the horse before Whit pulled him upright. They rode into darkness and through the long night, the horses churning stout-heartedly onward.

Just as the sky was pearling to pink, they crested a low rise to see the pale sea spreading before them. Whit reined Sinead in, keeping to the shelter of the trees, presumably to scan the stony beach for any possible dangers. The crescent-shaped bay looked harmless enough, as did the distant spires of the town perched on its edge. On the sea, ships' masts tilted through the drifting fog. It took a moment for Fynn to realize that the acrid smell in the air was caused by burning, and that it was smoke, not fog, that hung over the water.

And then he saw the boats clearly.

With a cry of astonishment, he flung his leg over Sinead's back, leapt down to the ground and then—shouting and waving his arms—raced toward the town.

Fynn heard Whit calling after him, but he didn't waste breath to answer. The stones clattered beneath his thin boots as he flew onward as fast as his legs would carry him, his heart pounding in his chest, his breath steaming before him, his spirit alight with joy.

For the ships that were laid to anchor were Helgrin longboats, and one of them was *Ydlyia*, the flagship of Aetheor Yarl.

CHAPTER 21
Maura

Maura's happiness over discovering Whit in the courtyard at Nelvor Castle was short-lived. That same evening she learned he'd been sent away, as Roth coolly informed her, on "the king's business." She'd been bitterly disappointed, as she'd hoped Whit might talk some sense into the king regarding Morgan. She also craved news of Ilyria, Leif, and all the others she'd befriended in Mithralyn. Only the fear that any association with her would cause trouble for Whit had restrained her from asking Roth when he might return.

For it was clear that Maura had fallen out of favor with her fiancé.

On the return to Drinnkastel, Roth rode with his courtiers. Since Grindasa, recently returned from Nelvorboth, had chosen to remain behind in Nelvorboth for another week, Maura traveled back with Heulwin, who was made ill by the rocking carriage and moaned the entire way. And when they reached the capital, Maura continued to feel outside the Nelvor circle. She encountered them only at meals—during which Roth treated her with a polite formality, while Roth, more often than not, greeted her coolly and then ignored her.

Perhaps that was for the best. On the one evening when she did draw the High King's attention, it was not the sort she would have wished. He tossed back goblet after goblet of wine at supper, eyeing her from time to time with a disconcerting gleam in his eyes. Fearing some unpleasantness to follow, she pleaded a headache and left before the boards were pulled.

Much later, Roth came to her rooms and banged on her door, demanding to be let in. And he was not alone—Maura could hear Sir Lawton egging him on. She remained silent, trembling in her bed, until they'd gone.

Increasingly, sleep eluded her. The week in Nelvorboth had made clear to her that she didn't really know the man she'd agreed to marry. She'd allowed her judgment to be clouded by her desire to make Roth the prince of her dreams and to create with him a new family to replace the one she'd lost. She'd come to realize the life he had to offer, glamorous as it might be, was not one she cared for, and she had to figure out how to extract herself from this future—the sooner, the better.

One night, tossing and turning, she decided to risk a visit to her uncle's library. Books were her sanctuary now, and she hoped to read herself to sleep. She threw on her robe and slipped out of her chamber. The torches had burned low in the west wing, but knowing the corridors well, Maura didn't bother with a candle. At this time of night, no one would be about.

She arrived at the east wing without incident and was heading toward the library when the door at the far end of the passageway swung open. A low, feminine laugh emanated from the High King's apartment.

Maura instinctively darted behind the large sculpture of Mihfar the Good, an ancient monter reputed to have been beloved by the gods for his deep devotion. Concealed in shadow, she heard the murmur of Roth's low voice, and her first thought was that Grindasa, recently returned from Nelvorboth, had been bidding her son goodnight.

There was no reason, except for the late hour, why Maura shouldn't be in this corridor, but all the same she feared detection. Holding her breath, she watched a flickering light approach, then pass, offering her a glimpse of a fair-haired woman, clad in a filmy gown that left little to the imagination.

In a state of numb disbelief, Maura slipped from her hiding place to follow the candle-bearer. She didn't give any thought to what she would do if the woman turned around.

Roth's visitor stopped in front of one of the guest chambers, opened the door—then raised her eyes to look directly at Maura, a mocking smile on her sultry lips, before slipping into her room.

Maura fled on down the corridor, and by the time she'd bolted her own door behind her, she was caught up in a torrent of anger and hurt. And more than either of these, she felt amazed at her own naivete.

Bitterly, she forced herself to recall how methodically Roth had courted her; how early on, he'd ensured that her name was linked with his, beginning with his bold request to wear her token during the Twyrn jousts. After that had come the invitation to the most highly attended temple service of the year, where all the nobles of the court saw Urlion's niece at the side of the dashing Lord Roth. The Nelvors had urged her to come often to Casa Calabria, and encouraged her to consider herself one of the family. How cunning of Grindasa to send a petition to the Tribus, requesting Maura announce Roth's selection to succeed her uncle, putting to rest any lingering doubts that Maura might feel she had a more legitimate claim to the Einhorn Throne. After all, Urlion had recognized her, and not Roth, as his kin.

I was just a means to an end all along.

Even the announcement of their engagement had been carefully timed. Then, once Roth was proclaimed High King, all the urgency to prepare for the wedding had fallen away, and with it any semblance of romance. The ceremony had been postponed until the spring—and perhaps...

Maura felt a stirring dread, remembering the calculating look in Grindasa's eyes when she'd dared to defend Master Morgan, and the coldness in Roth's tone when he'd asked her how she knew about the melia berries.

Perhaps a marriage between them had never been a part of the Nelvor plan. Perhaps something would occur to prevent the wedding from ever taking place.

But most telling had been the expression she'd seen on Roth's lover's face. She hadn't looked like someone caught betraying a friend by entering into an incestuous relationship with her own cousin. She wore the same sly smile as Maura's mother had that long-ago day in the kitchen while caressing the unborn children in her womb—the babes who had by now replaced Maura and Dal in Cormac's heart.

Indeed, Maitane had looked like a cat who'd been at the cream, smug triumph written all over her face.

* * *

The following day, Maura kept to her rooms, at one moment dreading a visit from Roth—or worse, his mother—the next wishing the king would appear so that she could assail him with all the venom churning inside her.

When a scratch finally came on the door, she opened it with clenched fists and her heart in her mouth. But it was Heulwin, bearing a letter addressed to her in an unfamiliar hand. Accepting the missive without comment, Maura stepped aside to let the maid in to tidy the room.

Moving to the window, Maura examined the letter's seal. At first glance, it looked like her late uncle's sigil, until she noticed the alphyn stood rampant and faced to the right. She broke the wax and scanned the few lines scrawled on the slip of parchment. Tears sprang to her eyes as she read, and she was glad that Heulwin was occupied with smoothing the bed.

Maura tucked the paper into the pocket of her burgundy surcoat, sending a silent prayer of thanks to any gods who might be listening. She knew she shouldn't let herself hope too much, for what was on offer might well be damnation rather than deliverance. Still, the timing of it made it seem a godsend.

Once she felt composed enough to speak, she said, "I'll need you to send my regrets for dinner, Heulwin."

Heulwin straightened, her brow creased with concern. "I thought as much, m'lady, seeing those dark rings under your eyes. Is it the headache again?"

Maura gave a small nod. At least her sleepless nights lent credence to her lie. "You needn't bring a tray either, Heulwin. I'm going directly to bed."

As soon as the maid departed, Maura plumped two pillows under the bedcovers, in case the girl looked in later. Then she waited until she was certain Heulwin had left their corridor before she slipped out after her. She knew that in the west wing she had little fear of discovery, but negotiating the wide hall separating it from the royal apartments and guest residences might prove difficult.

When she got there, though, the hall was empty. At this time of evening, all those who stayed in the king's part of the palace—Nelvor kin and a growing number of their Albrenian relatives—were no doubt in the Grand Hall, beginning the first course of another long and raucous supper. She hurried across the marble floor, then darted on to the familiar corridor where the storeroom was located.

When she slid through its door, she saw that someone had lit the two sconces on the wall, illuminating the clutter of curious objects. Her eyes swept over heavy leather-strapped cases and miniature enameled boxes, an old wooden cradle heaped with dusty poppets, tarnished shields and plumed helmets, and other odd bits of armament, including a full suit of armor fashioned for a child. Vases made from porcelain, pewter tankards and silver chalices, and drinking horns carved from bone stood on the floor or along the shelving. A jumble of unopened crates was pushed to one corner.

She remembered Leif's assumption, that these were gifts to the High King that had found no favor, and thus had been carted here and forgotten. Maura would have wished Leif now at her side had it not been for the ominous suspicion voiced against him by Grindasa.

Better he's safely in Mithralyn, she thought, stepping over a roll of dusty carpets.

She scanned the wall for a peephole, and it gave her a queer feeling, knowing that she was likely being observed. Otherwise, how would anyone be aware of her knowledge of this room?

To steady her nerves, she drew out the piece of parchment and read it again. *Come to the storeroom in the passageway to the tourney grounds at seven bells. Behind the mirror, you'll find a friend.* It was not the startling message, but the signature beneath these lines that had convinced her to accept the offer of aid.

She located the mirror easily enough, although she had to navigate her way around a gruesome gargoyle to reach it. Then it was simply a matter of easing behind the glass and ducking into the narrow tunnel behind it.

It opened onto a corridor identical to the one off which her own chambers lay. For a heart-sinking moment, she thought she'd somehow circled back there, but then she noticed that the wall torches were on the opposite side of the hallway, and the tapestry, depicting a seated lady in a golden field cradling a unicorn's head in her lap, was one she'd never seen before.

Where are you, friend? she wondered, and then gave a little jump as the door just opposite her creaked open. When no one emerged, she smoothed her skirt and crossed its threshold.

The richly appointed room made her catch her breath. Gold-scrolled chairs framed a mahogany side table to her right, upon which stood a jade porcelain vase spilling with wild purple orchids. Wrought in iron on the wall was the coat of arms from the wax seal on the letter she'd received, its white alphyn against a field of red. Half a dozen arched mirrors reflected the light from the candelabras, which perfumed the air with lemon and jasmine. Magnificent paintings hung between the sconces, a feast for the eyes, their vibrant hues only achievable with malachite, verdigris, and ultramarine. And on either side of the canvases were shelves, stretching from the high ceiling to the floor, on which books—hundreds and hundreds of them—resided, their spines illuminated with leaf of gold, their hammered covers inlaid with precious gems.

Enchanted, Maura advanced toward a raised hearth before which a low divan and several ornately carved chairs were placed. Above these, filigreed birdcages, delicate glass windbells, and hanging sculptures revolved slowly in the warm air. Plush lapin rugs in bold red, magenta, and azure covered the floor, and she recalled the bales Cormac had sent off each year to be woven for the royal house of Konigur. Perhaps some of their wool had found its way here, to this beautiful suite.

She was far enough into the chamber now to notice another room, and the woman, dressed as if for a formal court evening, standing framed on its threshold. A gold circlet rested on her fair brow, crowning her honey-kissed hair. She wore a pale green samite gown slashed with rare cloth of gold and hemmed with miniver, and the skirt swung gently from side to side as the woman moved to close the distance between them.

Maura stood, arrested, for it was like looking into a mirror of her future, down to the deep violet eyes. Belatedly, she dipped into a low curtsey.

"Princess Asmara," she murmured.

The princess opened her arms with a pleased smile. "You shall call me Aunt, child. Come, let me embrace you, as I've longed to do ever since my brother brought you to court."

As if in a dream, Maura entered into the arms of her father's only sister.

Releasing her, Asmara held Maura at arm's length. "Let me look at you properly. All these months I've had to make do with peering through curtained glass or from behind a heavy veil."

Maura took the opportunity to reciprocate. Up close, she could see tiny lines at the corners of Asmara's mouth and eyes, and creases on her brow beneath her artfully applied powder. But her full lips and the sparkle in her amethyst eyes belied her age, for Asmara was of the long-lived Konigur line. She still had a lithe figure, and the low-cut neckline of her gown offered more than a glimpse of firm, unblemished breasts.

"Let us sit, niece," the princess said. Hooking her arm through Maura's, she drew her to the chairs and sat opposite her. Asmara's eyes never left Maura's face, and Maura felt herself flush.

Asmara noted it with a laugh. "Forgive me if I stare, my dear. You're all that's left to me of my brother Storn, and I would drink in that which I see of him in you. As much as I despised my elder sibling, I loved the younger. And I confess, looking at you is like a window into my past."

Their resemblance to one another gave Maura a queer sort of happiness. It was proof that her mother had at least not lied about her father, as she had about so much else. "Now I understand why Urlion knew I was his niece," she said.

"We share the same coloring, it's true. Storn's hair was black as tar. But you have his mouth and his arched brows."

"What was he like, my... my father?" It felt disloyal to call someone other than her papa that, but she supposed Cormac had likely forgotten her by now.

"Storn was as lively and gay as ever a prince could be," Asmara replied. "Oh, he was a mischievous boy, for sure, but his larks held no malice. He kept all manner of pets—parrots, dogs, even a monkey at one time. But Marigold was his favorite—a little grey squirrel with tufted ears. She wore a belled collar so he would always know where she was. Most of the time she sat perched on his shoulder." She laughed at the memory. "Such a dear, dear boy."

A hint of melancholy tinged her smile. "Of course, by the time he reached manhood, Storn's favorites took another form, with flowing hair and rosy lips. The ladies of the court fell over themselves trying to win his favor, and he bestowed it liberally. He was beautiful, my brother, and a devilish charmer with his dancing green eyes."

Beautiful. That's how Maura's mother had described him, even after he'd seduced her, and then discarded her while she carried his child.

Something of Maura's conflicted feelings must have shown on her face, for Asmara laid a hand on her arm. "There was no harm in him," the princess assured her. "But our mother died soon after he was born, and he was coddled and indulged by us all. He always had a generous nature—unlike Urlion." Her voiced hardened as she uttered the name. "They were as different as the sun is to the moon. Storn was the best of us, although he worshiped our brother all the same. He never saw Urlion's flaws."

"But you did?"

Asmara's violet eyes flashed. "Urlion was a tyrant! He never let me forget, not for a moment, that he was the firstborn. From my earliest memories, he bullied me, lording his position over me. If he'd had his way, he'd have used me as a pawn in his quest for power by marrying me off to a foreign prince, then banishing me from my homeland forever. He cared nothing for my happiness, nor anyone's else's—only his own."

Maura found this hard to believe of the gentle, if sometimes querulous, old man she'd grown to know and love.

The princess raged on. "I might have pitied Leficia, his long-suffering wife, but she too was blind to Urlion's true nature. She perfected the art of pretended ignorance of his many affairs, and would hear no word spoken against him. After she was long dead, and I learned what he'd done to that poor child, I hated him even more. I—"

She stopped short, a flicker of alarm replacing the anger in her eyes. "You must forgive me, my dear, for ranting on about old grievances."

Maura wanted to ask what had happened to the "poor child" to whom her aunt had referred. But she hesitated. Her departed uncle had been ever kind to her, and she wasn't ready to hear more ill spoken of him.

Asmara gave Maura a sweet smile and patted her hand. "In any case, I've put all that behind me now. I am at peace in my life."

If her words rang false, Maura understood why. She didn't think she could ever forgive Daera for what had happened to Dal, and for deceiving them all about her past. "It must have been difficult to find your way to this peace," she said quietly, "if Urlion succeeded in denying you happiness."

The princess arched her brows. "Denying me? Ah, but in this you are mistaken, my dear. I thwarted his plans by taking my vows. *I* emerged the victor, for I defeated his purposes and served my own."

Asmara sat back and folded her elegant hands on her lap, a sudden gravity in her expression. "You must be wondering why, after all this time, I asked you to visit me. I'm afraid you are in danger, Maura, and I want to offer you my help."

Maura felt a jolt of alarm upon hearing her aunt confirm her own suspicions. "I'm grateful," she replied carefully, "but may I ask what provoked this fear?"

The princess regarded her frankly. "There's little that occurs in the castle of which I'm not aware. Although I remain, for the most part, in seclusion, my source is, shall we say, well placed. For example, I know that you've learned of the High King's dalliance with Lady Maitane. I hope this hasn't caused you too much pain?"

Maura was startled by this admission. Was it possible there'd been a witness to what had happened the previous night? "I intend to break off our engagement," she said stiffly.

"And you have good reason to," Asmara agreed, "but I doubt it will be that simple. It won't serve the Nelvors' interests if this indecent affair is made public. They'll want to prevent that at all costs. No, if you want to be released from your pledge, there will have to be another reason for abandoning the wedding plans. And it's best that you come up with one before *they* do. Otherwise you might find yourself quickly married off to one of their sycophants. And that's if fortune smiles on you. Grindasa has always been a schemer, and if you are not already, you must be on your guard against her. She will feel no compunctions about contriving to make you appear guilty of some infraction... something that would make a marriage between you and King Roth impossible under the law."

"Like a close-kin relationship?" Maura suggested hopefully.

Princess Asmara waved a dismissive hand. "Kings can marry where they choose. No, I'm thinking more along the lines of a charge of regicide."

Maura felt the blood drain from her face, and wondered if this was what Roth's mention of the melia berries was leading to. "I would never have harmed Uncle Urlion, and neither would Master Morgan or Leif. You must believe me."

"I have no doubt, my dear. But there are those who will be willing to support such a claim made against you, if it furthers their own advancement with the Nelvors, no matter what the truth may be. That is why you must offer them another way to achieve their ends." The princess leaned forward. "There is one, but it will not be an easy choice for you."

Maura straightened. "What do you propose?"

"That you take a vow to the goddesses, as I did. I would welcome you here, and you would lack for nothing for the rest of your days, I promise you."

She's lonely, Maura realized. And who could blame her? Asmara had lived in isolation behind these walls for decades. And although the luxurious apartments bore no resemblance to the austere temples where acolytes of the goddesses usually resided, the thought of spending the rest of her life in a gilded cage didn't appeal to Maura in the least.

In any event, it wasn't an option open to her. "I'm already bound by another oath," she replied.

"You mean your acceptance of Roth's proposal?" The princess took up Maura's hands and squeezed them encouragingly. "This can be easily rescinded."

Maura shook her head. "This binding is not one to be broken."

The sparkle dimmed in her aunt's eyes. "You are the daughter of a Konigur prince. You are not required to serve a Nelvor usurper. I beg of you, by the blood we share, take the sacred vow!"

"I can't." Maura gently withdrew her hands from Asmara's grasp. "But… there may be another way."

"What do you have to offer the Nelvors that will prevent them from howling for your blood?" the princess demanded.

Maura didn't flinch from the stern gaze so like her own. "The blood I share with another."

CHAPTER 22
Leif

The climb to the top of the tunnel seemed to take Leif several lifetimes. More than once, he lost his grip on the golden scales embedded in the icy walls and slid back over hard-earned ground until he could stop himself to climb again. He dreaded meeting Syrene at every turn, her talons flexed to tear him to shreds, but although he could hear occasional angry roars, no dragon appeared.

By the time Leif neared the surface, his gloves were reduced to shreds and he was faint from hunger, but when at last he saw the shadowy flickering of a fire's light above, a warmth spread over him that had nothing to do with its flames, and he forgot his raw hands and rumbling stomach.

Rhiandra was near.

Still, knowing this didn't completely dispel Leif's worry. His dragon was seemingly unharmed, yet something had prevented her from coming back for him. He was about to find out what.

When he came to the mouth of the tunnel, he found his way blocked by the blue tail of a dragon. He heaved a sigh of relief, and his heart leapt at the sound of Rhiandra's voice, speaking in the Old Tongue.

"I must return to Mithralyn at once. Ilyria is at risk, I tell you!"

"Zal and Menlo will see that she comes to no harm, sister. They must be with her by now."

"Our brothers will bring Ilyria back with them," said a third voice, "and then we will decide what must be done. It is best for you to wait in Belestar until we are all together once again. You had a long flight to get here; surely you wish to rest."

Leif crept closer, so close that he could reach out and touch Rhiandra's shining scales if he wished. But he didn't. He'd learned what perceptive beings dragons were, especially with regard to each other, and he felt certain she knew he was there. There must be a reason she hadn't acknowledged his presence.

"But we're *not* all here together!" Rhiandra's voice sounded strained, as if this discussion had been going on for some time. "Gryffyn and Aed flew off not long after I arrived, Una. And where is Emlyn? Where is Syrene?"

There was a distinct pause before Una answered her. "Emlyn disappeared a week ago; we thought she might have gone off in search of you as well. As for the drakes, surely you will remember they are often away for weeks, hunting on the far side of the isle. But Syrene will be back soon from her feed; she never leaves the clutch for long. When she returns, one of us will bring you something to eat."

"Why should I not go to feed on my own?" Rhiandra demanded. "Do you really intend to try to stop me, and keep me here against my will?"

"We're safeguarding our future," countered a new voice, this one lower in register than the others. "Your presence is required for this decision. You and Ilyria left once before, to bind, despite our grave reservations. We cannot risk you flying off again back to Drinnglennin and your bindling before we have reached consensus." The dragon gave a derisive snort. "Although I don't know why you'd want to, since your dragon-fast is too cowardly to accompany and support you."

Fynn knew then that Rhiandra hadn't told the dragons he was here in Belestar. He couldn't see the logic in this, especially as his absence weakened their argument for binding.

"You know nothing of my bindling, Menlo," Rhiandra protested.

"I know enough to decide not to bind myself," the drake retorted. "Perhaps if this elf-boy were as brave and steadfast as you purport, I might choose differently. But clearly the elves are as indifferent as humans are to the survival of our kind."

This was more than Leif could bear. He laid his hand on Rhiandra's tail and ran his fingers along it as he emerged from the tunnel. But when he reached up to climb onto the dragon's back, he found himself instead pitched to the ground. He rolled onto the ice and scrambled to his feet to see that she had reared and spread her wings. She was using her body to shield him from the view of the other dragons.

"Behold! Syrene comes!" Rhiandra's lashing tail swept Leif further from the fire. Then he heard a whispered hiss meant for his ears alone. "*Go!*"

Leif wasn't about to creep off into the shadows. They would make their case together, as they'd agreed. He stepped boldly into the open.

But his dramatic appearance went unnoticed by the other dragons, who were all watching their golden sister's approach. Only Syrene, the magnificent creature winging toward them, saw the intruder in their midst. Her roar caused seven dragons to swivel their heads in his direction.

"Your bindling!" A great white drake, who could only be Ciann, shifted his smoky gaze from Leif to his sister. "Why did you not tell us he was here, Rhiandra?"

Syrene hurtled to the ground and thundered toward them. "How *dare* you bring that creature to this place!" she bellowed, flecks of green and silver glinting in her narrowed topaz eyes. She was nearly double the size of the other dragons.

"Calm yourself, sister," said a sea-green female. *Una, the eldest.* "This is the son of Elvinor Celvarin."

"My dragonfast," said Rhiandra, and Leif heard the mixture of pride and anxiety in her voice.

The golden dragon continued to glare at him, and he felt more than a faint alarm when he saw the black smoke streaming from her nostrils. Although every part of his conscious mind screamed at him to flee, he forced himself to take a step forward, trying his best to conceal how frightened he was.

"I've come on behalf of King Elvinor Celvarin," he said, mindful of the need to address the dragons with formality. "My father sends greetings, and bids me remind you that elves have ever held dragons in great esteem." He spoke slowly, dredging up the words he'd memorized under the elven king's instruction. "The time has come for man and elf and dragon to live again in harmony on the Isle of Drinnglennin."

He had been looking at Una, but now he ventured a glance at Syrene. He wished he hadn't, for there was no mistaking her burning disdain. He blundered on. "The winds of... of change are gathering strength, and the last stronghold of... in the Known World will... all of us... will need... will need all of us to..."

It was no use; under Syrene's fierce gaze, the lofty speech he'd so carefully rehearsed had deserted him.

Rhiandra tried to come to his rescue. "King Elvinor provided sanctuary for Ilyria and me."

Her words gave Leif the breath of space to remember what he'd meant to say. "And I'm to... I'm to... extend the same invitation to you all." He turned in appeal to the other dragons, who appeared only slightly less threatening than Syrene. "If you would come... if it *pleases* you to come to Mithralyn, we will offer you all a safe haven on the Isle while you seek bindlings."

For a long moment, the only sound was the thin whistling of the wind. Then Ciann spoke. "Why should we wish to seek bindlings, if to do so puts us in danger? You say you represent your father's people, but what of your mother's? I can smell the mortal within you." His nostrils flared in distaste. "We may be able to put our trust in the elves, but by what authority do you speak for mankind?"

Isolde, the silver dragon, gave Leif a more conciliatory reply. "We are pleased by your father's greeting and his gracious offer, but skeptical of this vision of harmony. If we are to reveal ourselves to man once more, which we have not done since the fall of the Before, we must be assured it is safe to do so. Indeed, are the elves prepared to do the same, and risk exposing themselves again to the intolerance of ignorant humans?"

Leif strove to remember what Elvinor's answer had been when he'd posed much the same question. "It's true that some men wish to brew trouble anew. Old alliances are being broken and dangerous new ones forged. There are reports that the Jagars' new *vaar* is preparing for war. The time has come—"

Ciann cut him off. "And you speak of harmony?" The drake ruffled his wings impatiently. "With every word you utter, I become more convinced that *nothing* has changed."

"Are you not listening?" Rhiandra hissed. "Drinnglennin will inevitably be drawn into these new conflicts. If she should fall, there will never be another chance for us to return to the world. The last place where man, elves, and dragons might again coexist will be lost. And if that happens, we are doomed to living and dying on Belestar for all eternity." The smoke from her nostrils was now as dark as Syrene's. "Our sister Ilyria has gazed long into the flames. She has seen what is to become of the world should these malevolent forces prevail. It is an evil beyond imagining. But she has also seen a glimmer of hope, a light against the foreboding darkness. There are many more good men than bad, and we know the quality of the elves. If we all join forces and lend our power to—"

A blast of fire rent the sky. "Here is my light—the light of vengeance!" Syrene roared. "You were not yet born at the time of the Purge, Rhiandra! You cannot know what we suffered as we counted our dead! Where were your *good men* and *fine elves* when we were being shot out of the sky or netted and butchered?" Syrene brought her snout within inches of her youngest sister's. "What is your bindling doing here? How could you be such a fool as to risk that which *for certain* holds the key to dragon survival?" She narrowed her gilded eyes at Leif. "For all we know, he could be a wizard."

Leif hastened to reassure her. "Oh, no… I don't know any magic, truly I don't. Once, I'd hoped Master Morgan would teach me some, but then Rhiandra chose me. If I were a wizard," he pointed out, "I could have magicked myself here to find Rhiandra. But I couldn't… because I'm not! I had to walk for days across the ice, and then I fell into a crevasse back there"—he waved vaguely toward the south—"and had to climb up through that…"

Too late, he realized his mistake. Syrene's eyes widened, and Leif hastily dropped the arm he'd raised toward the tunnel.

With a growl of fury, the goldenwing reared and sent a blast of fire barreling toward him.

Leif tried in vain to scramble away from the flames, but they engulfed him all the same. A terrible bellowing arose, and he heard Rhiandra cry out in fear and rage.

But even she fell silent when they all saw he had suffered no harm. *Why?* he wondered. *They know I'm dragonfast, and fire cannot hurt me.*

"He *is* a wizard!" Ciann cried, lunging toward him with bared teeth.

Leif reeled out of reach a second before the drake's jaws snapped closed, then bolted for the tunnel. He heard Rhiandra's roar of anguish above the pandemonium of the dragons' pursuit. She couldn't hope to protect him against the wrath of all her siblings combined.

As he dove into the mouth of the tunnel, he wondered how it had all gone so terribly wrong. *Now they think I'm after the eggs,* he realized as the roaring grew angrier. There was no time to explain he wouldn't harm the clutch; he'd be torn to a pulp if he hesitated long enough to try.

His feet skidded from under him, and he careened blindly downward at dizzying speed, like a turtle on its back. He had a few seconds' lead, and the tunnel was only wide enough for the dragons to pass in single file, but the sound of them hurtling after him was terrifying, even more terrifying than his fall.

He realized his only salvation would be to get among the eggs. *When they see I did nothing to them, it will prove I mean no harm.*

The rising heat from below told him when he was almost to the cavern. He dug his heels into the slushy ice, trying to slow himself, but it was not enough; he catapulted into the air.

He landed with a shattering crash, and a thousand needles pricked his skin. He looked down at his hands to see that they'd been pierced by countless tiny golden splinters.

It was only then that he realized the unspeakable horror of what he'd done.

He was in the nest, wreckage strewn all around him.

His fall had shattered Syrene's eggs into a thousand shards.

A cry rose in his throat as the dragon mother burst out of the tunnel, her siblings behind her.

Leif scrambled to his feet amidst the broken shells.

"*WHAT HAVE YOU DONE?*" Syrene thundered, her outrage sending icy stalactites crashing down around them.

"I didn't mean to!" Leif cried, backing away. "I'm sorry—I didn't—!"

"*Sorry?*" Syrene bellowed. Then she raised her head and let loose a terrible, howling wail, a sound Leif knew would haunt him even across the Abyss.

Behind the golden dragon, the others had fallen silent, the black smoke from their nostrils pluming around them.

"I never meant to hurt them!" Leif sobbed, edging to the far side of the nest. "I swear! They were Rhiandra's kin, so nearly mine as well… I would *never* have deliberately caused—"

His plea was cut short as his feet met with thin air. The drop wasn't far, but his head struck the ice with a crack, and the world went black for a moment. He struggled back to consciousness, and in his swimming vision, he saw a galaxy of Syrenes spinning in orbit above him. His ears rang with a strange chittering as he steeled himself for the gnash of her terrible teeth. The *chirring* grew louder, and now there was a low rumbling as well. All the dragons circled around him, gathered to witness his just punishment for his unforgivable crime.

Rhiandra was the last to come into his wavering field of vision. He wished he could beg her forgiveness, but he was beyond words. She would not wish to hear them anyway.

With a sharp pang of loss that cut far deeper than any knife, he saw that it was not sorrow that lit Rhiandra's golden eyes, but anticipation. Her frilled ears were raised, and pale smoke wisped from her flared nostrils. She'd be free of him now, and able to bind with someone worthy of her. Someone who wouldn't fail her, as he had.

Thus Leif Elvinor fell to the fate to which he had been born. When the first talon pierced him, he screamed in agony, and then screamed and screamed again, as one by one, the last dragons of the Known World exacted their revenge for the doom of their kind.

CHAPTER 23
Morgan

"Grendel! 'Nother ale!"

Roarin' Regis slapped a grubby coin down on the tavern table. Grendel peered at it and tossed her auburn curls.

"That copper won't pay for a sip, Master Regis, let alone another mug." She stepped back to let a hooded customer pass. To the barmaid's surprise, the newcomer took a seat across from the drunk and placed a silver skell next to Regis's penny.

"We'll have two, please," he said in a low voice.

When Grendel returned with the frothy mugs, the newcomer took possession of both and disappeared into the back of the pub. Roarin' Regis rose unsteadily to his feet and lurched after him.

Grendel looked over at Gilly, the owner of the Tilted Kilt, who removed his stained apron and headed toward the warren of rooms in the tavern's interior. ""Mind the till, Grendel," he called over his shoulder, "and see that we're not disturbed."

Regis looked up as Gilly entered the hidden room behind the storeroom's sliding panel. His brown eyes were unsurprisingly clear and bright, the ale before him untouched. The hooded man with him remained hunched over, his long fingers wrapped around his own mug.

"You'd better have a good reason for being here, Regis," Gilly said gruffly. "This room is not to be used for your private business."

The stranger drew back his cowl. "What about the business of the realm?"

"Gods' bones and breath!" Gilly cried, yanking the panel closed behind him. "What are *you* doing in Drinnkastel? Your life's not worth a ha'penny if you're recognized!"

"On the contrary," Morgan replied, "I believe it's valued at a thousand pieces of gold."

* * *

The tavern keeper ran a hand over his bald pate as he sank down opposite the wizard.

"It's no laughing matter, Mortimer. I'd hoped you had the good sense to flee across the sea by now."

Regis leaned back and crossed his arms over his stained tunic. "Our Master Morgan's not one for fleeing. And no one knows he's in the capital. I'd have heard if they did."

"But how did you get past the sentries at the city gates? They're searching every wagon and questioning all who come through." Gilly leaned forward and dropped his voice. "You aren't practicing again, are you?"

Morgan shook his head. "Alas, no, Gilly. I haven't suddenly recovered my magical powers. But I never lost those of my brain. There are ways to enter Drinnkastel that don't require a guard's inspection."

"The question is, why would you want to," said Regis, "what with the price on your head and all?"

Gilly's eyes narrowed. "You're going to give yourself up to them, aren't you? Why, Mortimer?"

"So our friend Regis here can collect the reward," Morgan replied, keeping his tone light. "Now Gilly, don't look at me like that. I have a plan. It's not ideal, but if it gives me the opportunity to convince the High King of the dangers that lie ahead, it's worth the risk."

"Why do *you* have to do the convincing?" Gilly demanded. "Why can't I tell His Majesty?"

"Lazdac is on the rise." Uttering the words, Morgan felt a chill enter the room. "I can't say for sure when he will act, but there've been too many signs to ignore. If he's back in full possession of his powers, there is not a sorceress or wizard in Drinnglennin who can hope to prevent him from unleashing whatever evil he has in store for us all.

"Our only hope is to convince the High King that Lazdac poses a dire threat to the realm. If I can persuade Roth to muster Drinnglennin and to send envoys to Albrenia *and* Gral—indeed, to every ruler in the Known World—to join forces with us and strike first, our combined strength may be enough."

Gilly slammed his palms down hard on the table. "Damn it, man! Are you daft? Unless you've got Grindasa's ear, you've not the ghost of a chance of swaying our king. *She* is the power behind the Einhorn Throne, *and* the one calling loudest for your head!" The publican leaned forward. "As for young Roth, have you not heard? He's threatening to put an end to the twelve kingdoms' autonomy. He's got Nelvorbothian soldiers and those cursed Albrenian mercenaries billeted in the castles of our most eminent lords in the lesser realms. All for 'security's sake,' or so he claims." His face twisted in distaste. "And he's pressing a host of female cousins on those same lords' unmarried heirs—another ploy to strengthen the dominance of the Nelvors. There's even rumors that he plans to marry one of them himself."

Morgan frowned. "But I thought he is betrothed to Urlion's niece."

"That he is. But Lady Maura hasn't been seen in public for several weeks now." Gilly lifted his chin toward Regis. "Our friend here's heard rumor she may have fallen under some sort of suspicion herself."

This was worrying news. Morgan had hoped Maura could lend her influence to rally the High King to arms. He assumed that by now King Roth knew of the dragons, and that his bride-to-be was dragonfast. It was possible this was not the case, but if neither Maura or Celaidra had revealed this information to Roth, he had to wonder why. Besides this, Morgan feared for Maura for her own sake. The girl was clever and strong, but no match for a hardened schemer like Grindasa.

Regardless, Gilly's news signaled trouble. Morgan would have to try once more to reason with the new High King. If he failed in this endeavor, the only course left was to rouse the Tribus to action. They were well aware of the havoc a Strigori-led invasion would wreck on Drinnglennin, and surely the prospect of this catastrophe should unite them in encouraging the king to repel it. Defeating the dark wizard would likely come at a terrible cost, but if Rhiandra and Leif met success in Belestar and the dragons agreed to bind, they had a chance.

Morgan did not delude himself, however. It was a very slim chance.

His two companions were looking at him expectantly. Morgan lifted the untouched mug of ale before him in salute. "The time has come for me to meet our new sovereign," he declared. "Don't look so grave, my friends. You're about to collect a lot of gold for my capture! Surely we can drink to that."

Neither man made to raise his mug, but merely watched, with mournful eyes, as Morgan drained his own.

* * *

Dawn was gilding the sky when Morgan donned fresh robes for his first audience with the Nelvor High King. After a hearty breakfast of smoked sausage and duck eggs, compliments of the Tilted Kilt, the wizard and his two friends set off. Regis had shaved and discarded his ale-stained tunic for one of crisp linen, over which he wore a yellow doublet. His thinning brown hair, which usually obscured his face, was neatly brushed back. No one would recognize him as the resident drunk of the Tilted Kilt.

Gilly wore the rose and grey of Morlendell with the black bear rampant stitched on his breast. He carried his famed silver-hilted sword, dubbed the Bridge for sending so many enemies across the Abyss. Despite his advancing years, Sir Gilbin looked every inch the champion astride his black courser.

Although Gilly had offered Morgan a horse, the wizard insisted on riding his sturdy mule. "I'm your prisoner, remember. There's no need to mount me on a fine palfrey."

"I might be escorting you to your own funeral," the old knight growled, "but I'll not call you my prisoner!"

"Very well, then we'll say I turned myself into Regis, and you agreed to accompany me for my own safety."

His old friend's doleful expression didn't alter.

They rode in heavy silence, save for the horses' clopping hooves against the cobblestone; the streets were surprisingly empty. It was just coming on midday when they reached the Grand Square, yet there were many fewer vendors than Morgan recalled from previous market days.

When he remarked on this, Regis shrugged. "The farmers have less to sell now. The Nelvor king's demanded a third of everything the peasants raise to feed his growing army. He's also increased the number of landsmen required to serve in this force, leaving too few sons to work their fathers' land. And to add salt to the wound, the chief monter's asking once and a half the usual yearly tithe owed to the temple coffers."

"If we're not careful," muttered Gilly, "we'll find ourselves in the same sorry state as yon Gral o'er the sea. Already resentment's brewing among the lords of the north. Almost all the high court offices have gone to Nelvors or to houses traditionally allied with them through generations of marriage— mainly Tyrrencaster men. And the port at Toldarin is awash in foreigners, newly arrived from Albrenia to 'defend' us from the Helgrin wolves, who, according to our High King, would otherwise be roving in packs over the Isle. Worst of all, far too many of the officers under Vetch are now Albrenian—in the Drinnglennin Royal Army!" He shook his head in disbelief. "Can you believe it? When the lords who still have their balls protested, they were ignored." He gave a disgusted snort. "The only upside is that Vetch's nose is so far out of joint he can smell his own—"

A squadron of approaching soldiers in the crimson and silver of the new royal house silenced him. Morgan recognized their leader as one of the angry Nelvorbothians who'd been in the audience the day of Nicu's scathing parody of Grindasa's house. Maura's brother had been murdered by one such as him.

Gilly spurred his stallion forward to shield Morgan from the soldiers' view, and they met with no challenge as the guard rode past. They were near the inner castle gates now, and could hear the crank and clang of the iron grille being raised.

A pack of hounds streamed toward them, followed by a dozen or more noblemen and ladies garbed for the hunt. The three men drew their mounts to one side, and Morgan scanned the aristocratic faces for a glimpse of Maura as the party trotted by amidst laughter and banter. He saw no sign of her. Only a regal blonde with full lips and sultry eyes briefly met his gaze. Some of the pearl buttons of her silver-and-red bodice had been immodestly left undone, drawing the eye to the curve of her shapely breasts. When she caught him looking at her, she gave him a brazen smile.

One of the cousins? Morgan wondered as they proceeded to the gate.

"Sir Gilbin of Morlendell," the old knight at his side proclaimed gruffly to the gatekeeper. "I have business with His Majesty regarding the wizard Master Morgan."

The two guards took note of Gilly's princely garb and his high-bred stallion. Regis stared arrogantly ahead as though born with a silver rattle in his hand, and not the gutting knife of a fishmonger. Neither of the soldiers recognized Morgan.

The older of the two pointed to where a narrow-faced noble in hunting attire waited, with marked impatience, for the white mare being led toward him.

"You'd best see that gentleman, m'lord. The High King has finished hearing petitioners for the day, but Lord Lawton is His Majesty's Master of the Chamber. He'll know best how and when you might get an audience."

Gilly gave a stiff nod, then kicked his horse over to the now-mounted Lawton and effectively barred the lord's path.

Lawton scowled at him. "You would do well to move your horse out of my way, sir," he demanded in an icy tone. "I'm late as it is."

Morgan urged his mule to his friend's side. "I think my lord will thank Sir Gilbin if he does not. Master Morgan," he said, with a cordial bow of his head.

Lawton's jaw dropped, revealing his unsightly crooked teeth. "You're—"

"Here to see King Roth," the wizard said. "We're hoping you can help us arrange this."

* * *

Guards were summoned to take Morgan to the throne room while the master of the chamber went in search of his sovereign. Gilly and Regis tried, and failed, to accompany the wizard, and Morgan could hear Gilly's protests all the way down the long corridor from the inner courtyard.

Marched into the majestic hall, Morgan was brought to stand before the Einhorn Throne, the ancient seat of Drinnglennin's kings. It was a work of wonder, wrought from the horns of the magical forebears of coilhorns. Like so many other marvelous creatures, the last einhorns had vanished at the fall of the Before. The rare horns were overlaid in places with rose gold, and the wide cushioned seat was covered with silver lapin fur. Three steps, symbolic of the three members of the Tribus who supported the High King, led up to the throne, and a wheel of gold, divided into twelve parts and etched with the sigil of each of the lower realms, served as its backrest.

Morgan recalled vividly the last time he'd stood before this seat of power. King Owain had sat in it then. It was the only time the wizard and Urlion had been together in this majestic room. The occasion had been the then-boy prince's investiture as Owain's heir. Princess Asmara, who must have been around ten years old at the time, stood straight and still off to the side during the entire ceremony, except when she had to whisper a cautionary word to her fidgety younger brother. Storn was barely out of clouts, and the lengthy rites had bored him nearly to tears. Morgan wondered how differently things might have turned out if the Konigur reign had not terminated with Urlion.

It seemed to be taking Lawton some time to locate King Roth. Morgan didn't mind; he studied the fine tapestries depicting the former kings and queens who had heard petitioners and passed judgments in this ancient hall down through the centuries. Although faded with age, the gold threads in the weavings still glistened in the light of the candelabras.

His gaze moved to the great chalice at the left of the Einhorn Throne. Encrusted with jewels and standing as tall as a man, the Chalice of Brennhines had been presented to Princess Ceenguled by her husband, Prince Kasworan, the last of the Brennhines kings. Morgan's eyes fell then on the Paros, the enclosure of linden wood that shielded the Tribus from view, to the left of the throne. He silently admitted to a pang of regret, seeing this reminder of the time he'd counseled his kings from behind the screen.

The sound of rapidly approaching footsteps signaled he was about to receive his own taste of royal judgment. The tall, handsome Nelvor who entered the room was accompanied by a dozen of his courtiers, among them several Albrenians. They were followed by Lord Vetch, with Princess Grindasa on his arm.

Queen *Grindasa,* Morgan mentally amended. *I'll need to remember that.*

The young king's expression was stern as he strode to his throne, and Morgan could see he had little of his father in him, regardless of whether he'd been sired by Nelvor Nandor or Urlion Konigur. Both had been dark-haired, while Roth's locks were fair. The reek of wine accompanied his sauntering entourage, and the bruised smudges under Roth's pale blue eyes suggested he'd made some less than clever choices the night before.

Well, he'd have that in common with Urlion at least. That and his height.

Vetch dismissed Morgan's escort with a wave of his hand. The murmuring courtiers fell silent. The wizard kept his gaze respectfully lowered, awaiting His Majesty's pleasure. The soft sound of another door closing assured him the Tribus were also present, behind the screening Paros.

"You are the wizard Master Morgan?" King Roth's voice was strong and ringing.

"I am, Your Majesty." The wizard raised his gaze and lowered himself to one knee. "I have come to swear my fealty to you, sire, as I did to three Konigur kings before you. On my honor—"

"Ha!" Grindasa lurched forward, her hands clawed before her. "You have no honor, *regisscido!*"

Lord Vetch leapt to restrain the queen, then led her gently back to stand at the foot of the throne steps. She offered no resistance, but her ire-filled eyes never left Morgan's face.

The king's own expression was stony. "I have no wish for an oath of loyalty from you, old man. You stand accused as a traitor to our realm, the murderer of our beloved father and sovereign, Urlion Konigur."

So. This is how it is to be.

"Your Majesty," Morgan replied, keeping his voice even, "your father died of natural causes. I will gladly tell you all you wish to know regarding my last audience with him. But first, I must speak with you and your Tribus in private, on a matter of grave concern to the realm. If you will give me—"

"You are not in a position to make demands, master!" King Roth's ice-blue eyes flashed. "You are on trial, and I am your judge. You will be accorded an opportunity to offer your defense, should you choose to do so, as it is the right of even the lowest criminal under the law. Otherwise, you shall show respect during the proceedings, and speak only when requested to do so."

An elderly man dressed in the robes of the lord chancellor cleared his throat loudly. It took Morgan a moment to recognize the round-faced, owl-eyed official as Thameth Wynnfort, the second son of old Ulfur Wynnfort of Tyrrencaster. The last time Morgan had laid eyes on Thameth, he'd been preparing to take his vows as a monter to the Elementa. He must have done so, for the five-headed star hung from the heavy chains across Wynnfort's chest. Could it be that Roth had given a monter one of the most powerful offices in the land? If so, this was a flagrant violation of the separation of temple and state decreed in the Law.

Wynnfort looked as though he was as ill at ease with his unsanctioned position as Morgan was. "Your Majesty," the lord chancellor said in his reedy voice. "The prisoner hasn't yet made his plea."

Roth frowned, and the creases in his brow deepened when a sharp rap came from within the Paros.

Morgan released a grateful breath. The knock signaled that one or more of the Tribus wished to advise the king. Now Morgan would be granted the opportunity to put his arguments to them, and once they all learned of the dire state of affairs, Celaidra and Audric, and likely even Selka, would support him. Together they would able to convince Roth of the danger Lazdac's growing power presented. Once this had been achieved, Morgan felt confident he could defend himself against the trumped-up charge of murder.

Surely Roth will heed his Tribus, even if he doesn't trust me.

"It seems I am to receive counsel." The king did not trouble to conceal his irritation. He descended from the throne and stalked toward the small chamber that adjoined the Paros. The wizard had often sat at the round table within it. "See that the prisoner is secured," the king called over his shoulder.

Roth's courtiers eyed one another uncertainly, and despite the circumstances, Morgan couldn't help feeling a wry amusement. The guards had been dismissed, and none of these young men looked eager to sully their hands with the menial task of binding a criminal.

Lord Vetch likely considered himself above the task as well, but he hadn't risen to power without a clear understanding of the requirements of duty, regardless of how unsavory they might be. "My lords," he said, in a voice pitched perfectly to convey both authority and respect, "I will attend to the prisoner. It is likely our king will be some while in counsel. May I suggest you take your ease in the king's salon, until such time as this assembly reconvenes? Refreshments can be organized—Ewart, see to this."

The squire behind him departed to carry out his lordship's order. The young courtiers filed out after him, no doubt relieved that they wouldn't be forced to stand around awaiting the king's return. Lord Wynnfort hesitated for a moment before following, wringing his fleshy hands as if they had a life of their own.

Vetch turned his attention to Grindasa. "My queen, will you not retire to your solar as well? I fear the strain of this rogue's sudden appearance has been too much for you." Morgan heard something more than obedience in the commander's tender tone, and wondered if the lord high commander served the lady in more ways than one. Grindasa, recently returned from Nelvorboth, had been notorious in her prime for her long list of sexual conquests, including the several years she was mistress to Urlion. That affair had ended in bitter disappointment and a pregnancy, the wizard recalled, but at least Nandor had accepted the babe as his own.

And now Grindasa's gotten all she wanted from Urlion through her son: the title of queen and a guiding hand on the reins of power. That is, if she isn't already driving the royal coach herself.

He'd never trusted her, especially since she'd clung so tightly to her Albrenian roots. Now this stubborn adherence could prove even more dangerous. If she should urge the young king to break with Gral over the border disputes between this eternal ally and Albrenia, all hope of a unified front against Lazdac would be lost.

Grindasa allowed the commander to escort her to the door, but not before she cast a look of loathing in Morgan's direction. Then Vetch and Morgan were alone before the Einhorn Throne.

Morgan held out his wrists helpfully, but Vetch merely scowled. "Make a move, and you're a dead man," he growled, his hand resting menacingly on the hilt of his longsword. "I rather wish you *would* try to escape. It would save us all a wearisome trial. I'll give you a clean death, which is more than you deserve. The penalty for killing a king calls for a merciless end before you descend into the Abyss." His black eyes glittered speculatively. "I admit to being curious to hear *why* you did it. Tell me, and I'll make a quick end to it."

"You make it sound as though my conviction on this ridiculous charge is a foregone conclusion."

Vetch's laugh was venomous. "Surely you don't believe you can convince the king and Tribus of your innocence. You were seen leaving the late king's chambers only moments before Urlion was found dead."

"By whom, I wonder? Those who should have been guarding him? I found the king alone and unattended. Where were his heralds? And Master Tergin?"

Where was Maura? he added silently. Urlion had said he hadn't seen his niece that day. "I was with Urlion when he died, but as to whom is to blame for what killed him—"

"Yes?"

"I do not know the answer," the wizard admitted.

The sound of a door closing behind the screen heralded Roth's return. His gaze shifted between Morgan and Vetch. "Where is Wynnfort?"

The outer door swung open. "Here, sire," said the lord chancellor, who must have been listening at the door.

"Shall I recall the courtiers and your mother, sire?" asked Vetch.

"There is no need," Roth replied, resuming the throne.

The wizard's heart lifted. The Tribus had offered wise counsel, and they could now sit together to plot a course of action.

"Upon the advice of my Tribus," the king continued, "and in their presence, this trial shall proceed. Lord Vetch, you will serve as witness for the court, and Wynnfort shall deliver the sentence." For the first time, the young king's lips curled into a smile. "You seem surprised, Master Morgan. Did you think that because you once held a place on the Tribus, you would receive preference from those who more honorably serve on it now? If so, you were mistaken. So, master, do you confess to the murder of Urlion Konigur?"

"Before I enter my plea, Your Majesty, may I ask what your Tribus advised?"

"You may not." King Roth's reply was as cold as a crypt. "The next words you utter will be your confession. Otherwise, Lord Commander, you will cut out the prisoner's tongue."

When no knock came from within the carved panels of the Paros, Morgan knew then he would find no support from that quarter. Had they all been in league with regard to Urlion's enchantment? What else could explain their silence?

"Ahem... you will answer... ahem... His Majesty's question, Master Morgan," Wynnfort said.

"I do not confess to this crime," Morgan declared loudly, as though the room were filled with observers. "Nor will I ever. I did nothing intentionally to harm King Urlion. But I did tell him the truth, and it proved too much for him to bear. I fear my king died of a broken heart."

"Or a poisoned one?" Grindasa, recently returned from Nelvorboth, had slipped back into the room from an antechamber on the right of the hall. She crossed to stand opposite Wynnfort at the foot of the throne. "You see, my son? He does not deny it!"

"Ahem... my lady, the prisoner has been instructed... ahem... not to speak unless he wishes to confess." Wynnfort looked as if he was literally washing his hands of the entire business.

"Who dies of a broken heart?" The king shook his head in disbelief. "A poor defense, master. Surely you can do better." But he couldn't resist asking the question Morgan had planted in his thoughts. "What truth was this of which you speak, so powerful as to slay a king?"

"It had to do with the cause of his illness," Morgan replied. "It was for my king's ears alone."

"*Here is your king!*" Grindasa cried, pointing to her golden-haired son.

Vetch's sword was halfway out of its scabbard. "You will answer the question!"

Morgan bowed his head. "Very well. I told King Urlion that I had discovered he had a—"

"Silence!" Roth thundered, all color drained from his regal face.

Even Vetch froze at the fury in the Nelvor's voice, and Morgan observed a charged look passing between the commander and his king.

"This traitor has as much as confessed, Your Majesty," Vetch said. "He provoked Urlion's death. We don't need to hear more of his lies in an attempt to conceal his perfidious act."

They know, Morgan realized. *They know something, either about the enchantment or about Urlion's wife and son.* The knowledge settled on him like a stone.

Roth leaned forward, gripping the arms of the Einhorn Throne. "Take this kingkiller to the low dungeons, and see that no one has access to him. No one! Is this understood?"

Vetch seized Morgan roughly under one arm and propelled him toward the door. "You've just sealed your doom, you old fool," he muttered. "I took you for a wiser man."

Morgan cast one final look at the Paros before leaving the hall. "Sadly, so did I."

CHAPTER 24
Whit

Moving stealthily through the narrow port lanes, Whit cursed himself for a fool. While Fynn dashed down the beach, Whit had wasted precious time staring after him like a dimwit. And by the time he'd come to his senses, it was too late; by then, Fynn had already drawn the attention of the Helgrins, who reached him before Whit could spur Sinead after him. It seemed the boy had made the choice to return to the people with whom he had grown up. And from the back-thumping that ensued once they took charge of Fynn and made their way to the shoreboats, the lad had been clearly recognized as their yarl's son.

But Whit had seen what the boy, in his haste to reach the Helgrins, might not have. Their longboats were flying the fiery eye, not the white bear of Aetheor. These raiders were not his foster father's people.

Whit needed time to think about what this all portended. He backed Sinead deeper into the cover of the woodlands, and watched as several shoreboats were launched into the water, one of them carrying Fynn in the direction of the flagship. His heart gave a lurch as a distant shout rang out over the water. Fynn was on his feet in the pitching boat, fighting to free himself from the grip of one of his companions. The man yanked him down hard on the seat, then struck him full in the face.

This violence finally spurred Whit to action. He would not leave Fynn in the hands of these men. They might be the

272

boy's countrymen, but they weren't his people, and they clearly weren't his friends.

A rescue wouldn't be accomplished easily. Whit would have to get through the remains of the town, steal one of the remaining shoreboats, and go after him—all without being seen.

He leapt down and hastily stowed his pack, then put out a sack of oats for the mare and the stallion, whom he left untethered. If the horses weren't there when he got back, at least he'd know whoever had taken them would have feed.

If he got back.

His heart pounded in his chest as he crept stealthily out of the woods and onto a narrow street running parallel to the harbor. Little remained of the town he'd ridden into with Master Morgan, Halla, Wren, and Cortenus over a year ago. The Helgrins had made their indelible mark. Most of the houses were still in flames, and the heat was nearly unbearable. Bodies were sprawled on the cobblestones, telling a grisly tale of swift, brutal deaths. All of the corpses were missing thumbs, many of them limbs as well.

The sharp crack of splitting wood warned him only just in time to spin out of the path of a falling timber. It hit the ground in a cloud of ash and smoke, making him cough and choke. Anything that could burn—thatch, the dry timbers of the old houses, wood piles, and even manure heaps—had been put to the torch. The smoke mingled with the rusty tang of blood and sour bile, making his gut churn.

At the sound of men's voices, Whit's heart gave a jolt. The fiery inferno gave him nowhere to hide. All around him, roofs were caving in, sending swarms of sparks skyward, as if signaling his whereabouts.

He closed his eyes and turned his mind inward, seeking the well of power he harbored within, and for the first time, he attempted to cast his shadow out of real need. He deepened his breathing, compressing time and space in his inhalations, then released them as he exhaled. His heartbeat slowed and steadied, and the sense of his own shadow took shape in his mind.

Opening his eyes and expelling a long breath, he cast the shadow forth.

Whit felt a surge of pleasure as it took shape before him, followed by distress as the shadow immediately began to fade. He understood then why Morgan always said there was no place for conceit in magic.

Focus. Breathe.

The shadow darkened once more, and he moved into it, entering a landscape cast in gradients of grey. It felt like he'd slipped into a second skin, but it didn't cling, didn't hinder his movements. He felt *expanded*, as if his physical being had rippled outward to form an envelope of air surrounding him. Then his body fully merged with the shadow, no longer contained within it, and he felt light and agile, almost weightless as he glided across the ground.

He mentally gathered the shade again and cast it forward. He leapt with it, double the distance he'd thought possible, rushing through the air within the cloaking shadow, then leapt again, making his way down the burning lane.

Occasional scattered screams rent the air, but even more harrowing were the sudden silences that cut them off. He thought of Maisie and Horace, the gentle souls with whom he'd planned to leave the boy, and wondered whether they'd fallen prey to the Helgrin wolves.

It was as he slipped between two warehouses that the fire had not yet begun to feed on that he at last chanced upon the living. He wished he hadn't. The first was a young girl huddled under a cart, clutching a still infant, its tiny thumbs severed, against her thin chest. The second was an old man propped against the wall and sitting in a pool of his own entrails, cradling a white-haired woman. He was still clutching the knife he'd used to mercifully slit her throat before the Helgrins could get to her. Neither saw Whit, wrapped in his shadow, as he stole past.

He forced himself to swallow his gorge and keep going.

He could see the harbor at the end of the alley now, and the dark, turbulent sea beyond. With more than fifty long-boats still ranged across the bay, and at least ten shoreboats beached on the strand, many of the invaders were clearly still roaming through the town. All the same, since everything was aflame, he presumed the Helgrins would soon return to their ships. As for Fynn, he was either already aboard the flagship, or dead and cast into the sea. The thought of the latter scenario aroused a sadness Whit could not have foretold.

And what then? If Fynn had indeed perished, Whit could return to the capital and report that he'd accomplished the gruesome task he'd been sent by Roth to do. For in a way, he'd done just that—he'd led the boy to his death. The thought repulsed him even more for having been done, even if unintentionally, in the service of King Roth. As much as Whit had hoped to sit on the Tribus one day, he had no desire to advise a sovereign who had, in cold blood, ordered the end of an innocent young life.

Whit recalled Roth's fine patrician face, his immaculate dress, and the air of entitlement he'd exuded while giving the order for murder. There was a time in Whit's life when the man's appearance would have impressed him, but all he had felt on that day was fear—fear for Drinnglennin. It was why he'd decided that he would go to Toldarin—not to kill the boy, but to protect him.

Whit didn't intend to be of use to King Roth. At present, he was beholden only to Cardenstowe, for in Roth's haste to send him to Toldarin, he had neglected to extract Whit's oath of allegiance. *When I pledge myself and my vassals, it won't be to that jumped-up Nelvor bastard—it will be to a king I can be proud to serve.*

Perhaps that king was Fynn. The boy might be the right-ful heir to the throne, and he might not, but he was clearly Urlion's son. Whit had seen many a likeness of the former High King in historical tomes, and the boy was the spitting image of Urlion as a youth. And now Whit had let this boy, the last Konigur, slip through his fingers and into Helgrin clutches.

Whit had reached the end of the alley. He peered out onto the harborside. Here, the dead mounted. It seemed as if every man, woman, and child in the city had been hacked down by Helgrin blades and spears. The raiders had been merciless.

He kept close to the warehouses lining the port, for the low buildings offered additional cover to keep his shadow from being detected. The storerooms he passed had been pried open, and bales of precious lapin fur had rolled out onto the cobblestones, bright humps against the grey of sky and sea.

He sensed the approaching Helgrins just before they emerged from a parallel street onto the harbor front, making for the remaining shoreboats. A few stragglers continued to collect booty, but most of the men began to launch the crafts into the waves.

As Whit hovered in the shadow of a warehouse, the smoke made his eyes stream. Ash fell all around him, and he found it hard to breathe, so hard that he began to cough. He quickly stifled the sound, but it was too late. To his horror, one of the looters lifted his head and stared directly at him.

"What was that?"

The man was ridiculously tall, even for a Helgrin, and built like an auroch. His fair, sweat-soaked hair hung to his shoulders, and a rough, shaggy beard covered the lower half of his face.

Only one of his two companions bothered to glance over. His hands were awash in blood. "Rats fleeing the fire," he sug-gested. Then he bent over a dead man to hack off his thumbs and add them to the blood-soaked bag slung over his shoulder.

"Solvi's hearing things," said the third. "He's still hoping to find a treasure as valuable as the one Jorson took back to the *Ydlyia*." He slipped a gold necklace over his head, where it glittered amongst a dozen others.

"Don't know what was so special about the brat," the thumb-collector grunted. He nudged a corpse over with the toe of his boot. "He'll just be another thrall."

"He spoke Helgric," Solvi said, looking away from Whit at last. "He claimed he was the son of the yarl."

The thumb-collector gave a nasty laugh. "He said he was the son of *Aetheor* Yarl, who lies unburnt at the bottom of the sea."

All three men touched their wrists, and Whit remembered reading about the runes the Helgrins tattooed on their skin to protect them from evil. Then his tickling throat closed. The flagship in the harbor flew the fiery eye, as he'd already noted. If Aetheor was dead, then who was yarl now? And what did this mean for Fynn?

"The tide is turning." The tallest man hefted his axe over his shoulder and lumbered toward two small boats that were beached on the sand. The others trailed in the big man's wake, stooping here and there to collect any remaining booty that caught their eyes.

Whit felt a rising panic. Soon they would take their plunder and row away. If he wanted to rescue Fynn, he'd have to go with them. But how? There were still hours of daylight left, and a shadow moving over open ground was sure to draw their attention.

He could swim after them once they were on the water, but he doubted he could manage shade-shifting while struggling with the icy chop, and even if he could, they'd likely have their sails up and oars at the catch before he was halfway there.

Use the elements at hand, a creaky voice whispered inside Whit's head. Egydd's usual advice, which he'd demonstrated often in their duels.

The elements at hand. Well, there was the sea and the wind. Surely he could make something of these.

The plundering Helgrins had apparently finished their business. They struck off down the beach toward the last two remaining shoreboats. Whit watched with mounting dread as the tallest Helgrin dumped his haul into one of the boats, then began to push the other, which was hitched to it, into the shallows. His companions stowed their own treasures and hurried to assist him, their boots crunching over the stones as they alternated between dragging and pushing the two skiffs into the water.

Still concealed at the side of the warehouse, Whit tugged off his boots and—with great reluctance—laid his staff beside them. He would have to cross a distance of nearly one hundred yards to reach the boats. And he'd have to do it undetected.

Drawing a deep breath, he cast his shadow in the direction of the water and flung himself over the clattering stones, the seaward wind covering the sound. He cast his shadow again, and then once more, drawing ever closer to the trailing boat.

Suddenly he pitched forward, flying headlong. His foot had caught on a piece of driftwood. As he struck the stones, his lungs emptied, and he lost hold of his shadow.

He lifted his gaze, fully expecting to see the three Helgrins pounding toward him with their axes raised. But they still had their backs to him, occupied with the boat launch. Both crafts were now afloat in the shallows, and the big man already had one foot in the leading skiff.

Scarcely able to believe his luck, Whit scrambled to his feet and lunged forward to put the trailing boat between him and the other two men. He barely registered the frigid water as he sloshed into it, too relieved to feel anything else.

When he reached the boat's side, he ducked low, forced his breathing to slow, and reached for his shadow. This time the magic flowed with ease. Under its cover, he ventured a peek over the gunwales. The last of the Helgrins was hauling himself aboard the first boat.

Whit whispered up a surge of water, sending a wave crashing over the occupied boat. The Helgrins shouted and ducked down instinctively, giving Whit time to clamber aboard the second boat, which had been reserved for carrying loot. He landed with a stab of pain, and looked down to see blood welling through a gaping hole in his hose. He'd been sliced by one of the men's plundered blades.

He heard the Helgrins sputtering from their soaking, then the slap of their oars.

Whit groped in his pocket for the flask of elixir. It wasn't there, and he realized it must have fallen out when he tripped on the beach. He still had his knife though, which he used to saw off a strip of his tunic—regretting the ruin of a fine linen shirt—then bound the gash.

When he raised himself to peer over the bow, his heart sank. The rowers were making for a longboat to the far left, not for the flagship and Fynn. He'd have to alter the skiffs' course.

Calling up wind required more finesse than a wave. It took Whit a precious minute to center his mind. Then he slowly emptied his lungs to bind the spell.

Dwal gwynd thoil dagat!

He envisioned the wind's dance over the water and the rising foam on the crest of the waves, then held the image in his mind.

His cloak billowed around him as the little craft rocked and reeled to the right. The Helgrins' shouts informed him their boat was reeling as well. He could hear the dip and drag of their oars as they tried to fight the will of the magicked wind.

Whit kept up a fierce concentration, peering over the gunnels as he guided the gusts to send them toward the ship flying the fiery eye. They began to close the distance to the flagship, slowly at first, but then accelerating.

When they came within a half dozen yards of the longboat, the Helgrins in the forward dingy cried out and braced themselves for a collision. Whit levered himself into the water, the shock of the cold sea making him gasp, and released the wind.

The two boats quickly slowed, and the rowers pulled hard on the oars to turn the dinghies to the port side of the flagship, while Whit struck out for the hull. Already his fingers were going numb, and the rest of him would soon follow if he didn't quickly find a way to get aboard the longboat. As he rounded the stern, he spied what he'd hoped to find: a set of rungs running up the ship's side.

Grasping the lowest rung, he hauled his trembling body out of the water, shivering in the stabbing, cold air. As he climbed, he drew breath into his aching lungs to cast his next spell.

Gwenyl pferd al gwinch y dal!

Wisps of mist began to drift over the sea, their tendrils thickening to dense fog. He heard shouting just above as the men exclaimed at the sudden weather. The fog engulfed the longboat in a matter of seconds, and under its cover Whit pulled himself up the last few rungs and aboard. He hit the deck and rolled under the gunwales, wrapped once more in his shadow's cloak.

Through the dense fog, he sensed the presence of other men, some only an arm's length away. *You're a fool, Whit Alcott,* he told himself, *if you're imagining this will end well.*

The surrounding fog meant he was almost as blind as the Helgrins who were bumping about around him. He pictured the layout of a longboat; he'd seen a few illustrations of them in various books he'd read. It would be less than two dozen feet wide, but over a hundred long. And these crafts had no cabins—the deck would be largely taken up with more than a score of benches for rowers.

From under the narrow gunwale, Whit could see only the cloth-wrapped legs of three Helgrins.

Across the water, a horn blared.

"Fell and the others are aboard *Fàlki*," said one of the men.

"Set the sail," came the command.

"In this murk? We can barely make out our hands in front of our faces. I've never seen such a brume come up so sudden-like. The men don't like it. Vadik says it smells of sorcery."

A gob of spit hit the deck inches from Whit. "Vadik!" the raspy voice scoffed. "That's the stench of his own belches the old fool's scenting. Our bard'll be seeing snakes in the rigging soon."

"Aye, he's likely buckled. He's downed more than a few claps of thunder, and so have the rest, Yarl. They've already tapped a second of the kegs we found in yon gods' house cellars."

Yarl! The rough-voiced speaker was Aetheor's successor. Surely this was who they'd brought Fynn to—but where was the boy now?

"Well, bung the keg up again," the yarl growled. "I plan to be long gone by moonrise."

"We'll have to row out of this pall before we raise the sail."

"Get to it then! Reider, give the signal to drop oars!"

A pair of legs darted past Whit's hiding place toward the bow. In a moment, the drum would be struck, and there would be no chance for escape once they put out to sea.

But instead of the drum, a shout of anger rang out, and a new pair of leggings stalked by. Dragging behind them were thinner ones, clad in Whit's own hose. He edged out to have a peek at Fynn, and it was only when he saw the boy's white face that he realized he'd let the fog of enchantment drift from his mind. It had served its purpose, and so instead of raising it again, he cloaked himself in his shadow so that he could observe the scene about to play out.

"The White Bear's cursed cub bit me!" the newcomer howled. The offended Helgrin was stout, with a nose that appeared to have been broken more than once.

Fynn struggled in the man's grip, his mouth a firm, determined line. Someone had stripped him of the elven cloak, and his face bore the marks of a beating. "Where's my father?" he demanded. "This is his ship!"

The man Fynn addressed was built low to the ground, and had the bulging eyes of a fish. A thick band of gold rested on his broad brow, and gold rings encircled his beefy arms. He smiled unpleasantly, revealing jagged teeth. "Your father's body lies under the sea, cousin. As for his soul, who can say?"

"You're lying!" Fynn shot back. "Jered always said you were a liar."

Cousin. This was Aksel Styrsen, Aetheor's rebellious nephew.

The smile fade from Aksel's thick lips. "Your brother was always an arrogant—"

"*What did you do to my father?*" The anguish in the boy's voice was heartbreaking.

Aksel shook his head with mock regret. "My uncle was with me when we set off on this raid. But before we made landfall here, we got separated, and your father and his men sailed into an Albrenian ambush. Fortunately, I myself am on good terms with our southern neighbors."

He must be lying, Whit thought. *Why would Albrenians be in these waters?*

Fynn stared at Aksel with a mixture of disbelief and fear. "But... these ships are all from Father's fleet. Where are his men? Why are *you* sailing the *Ydlyia*, his flagship?"

"She *was* Aetheor's flagship. Was, but is no more. As Aetheor Yarl is no more."

Fynn's sudden stillness was almost worse than if he'd wailed with grief. When he spoke again, his voice was tight. "And Jered? Where is he?"

"Ah." Aksel crossed his arms across his chest. "Now that I'd like to know myself. You've done me a great service, cousin, joining us so unexpectedly. I thought you'd died in Restaria, you and Aetheor's Drinnglennian whore. I imagine Jered thinks so, too. How happy he'll be to discover you still walk the earth! What do you think your brother might offer in ransom for the last of his kin? How many ships? How much of Aetheor's buried gold? Of course, I'll get it all in the end. But I need to flush out the other cub to put an end to the White Bear's line, and you'll do nicely as the bait."

Fynn stiffened. "Jered is no brother of mine. I'm not even Aetheor's son. My mother was carrying me in her womb when she was taken from Drinnglennin. I'm worth nothing to Jered."

How brave, thought Whit, *and how foolish.*

"I don't care if your mother was queen of the faeries," Aksel growled. "And don't expect me to swallow this claptrap. We make now for Frendesko, the new seat of all Helgrinia. I'll see that Jered learns you are my… guest there, and I will invite him to come to retrieve you." The yarl laughed unpleasantly, then lifted his bulging eyes to the mast. "The fog's clearing and the tide has turned. Raise the sail!" He shoved past Fynn without another glance.

Fynn twisted toward his captor, then brought his knee up hard in the man's groin. The Helgrin doubled over with a groan, and the boy wrenched himself free. Before anyone could stop him, he vaulted past Whit onto the gunwale and dropped into the sea.

Whit hurtled after him, swinging himself over the ship's rail, followed by the angry shouts of the Helgrins.

He hit the black sea with a splash. It felt even colder than before as he fought his way back the surface, then shook the water from his eyes. There was no sign of Fynn, and he wondered if the boy could even swim.

Something pierced the sea an arm's length away. Whit looked up to see Aksel notching an arrow into a longbow.

He dove under the water, the twang of the bowstring ringing in his ears, but no arrow punched into him. Had it found Fynn instead?

When he surfaced once more, he had a spell already on his lips. *Tynwych y d⊠ra thoil dagat! Water, spin if it please you.*

The sea began to churn around him, and he propelled himself in the direction of the shore, willing the water behind him to rise, holding the vision of a swirling funnel in his mind. The men on the flagship leapt to their oars, frantically attempting to row out of the emerging waterspout's path, and the *Ydlyia's* sail was hoisted amidst shouts and curses. It rippled and filled, rocking the longboat slowly westward. Her seven sisters already plowed the waves ahead of her, for they hadn't been hindered by Whit's magical fog.

A dark head bobbed up suddenly to Whit's left and just as abruptly disappeared again below the surface. The stark look of terror on the boy's face sent an echoing jolt through Whit's chest, and he flung himself over the waves to reach him.

Whit plunged down after Fynn, but he could see nothing in the dark sea. Still he dove, again and again, rising each time only when his lungs felt close to bursting. The fourth time he broke the surface, he was numb and lightheaded, and his chest ached as though he'd been stabbed in the lungs. The cold would soon overcome him.

He suddenly remembered a retrieving spell he had learn from Egydd. He released the windfunnel, for the longboats were already moving away across the bay, and cast the new spell.

Domsar tui min!

This time when he dove, he saw something shooting toward him from the depths, and Fynn collided with him in a tangle of flailing limbs. A flash of white pain exploded behind Whit's eyes as a kick caught his wounded thigh. Fighting to stay conscious, he grabbed hold of Fynn and hauled him upward. As they broke the surface, Whit's burning lungs filled with air, and he felt like weeping with gratitude.

But one look at the limp boy in his grasp swept that emotion aside. Fynn's eyes were glazed over, and the breaths from between his purple lips were shallow. If the cold had reached the core of his bones, he was a whisper away from death.

Whit wrapped one arm tightly around him and gathered his energy for another spell.

Thamal, den à dul qywlh y dal!

The spell was inexact, he knew, but his powers of concentration were fading fast. *Wave, carry me to the shore, if it please you.* He imagined the two of them atop the white crest, riding the surf to the beach.

They were lifted toward the shoreline, and Whit breathed a sigh of relief, a feeling that lasted no more than a second as his foggy brain wrestled with a new problem: how to slow the wave. It rose higher and higher, picking up speed, and Whit's gut twisted as he looked down from its crest, that now towered over the stony shoreline. From this height, they would be smashed like earthenware jugs on impact.

Whit's mind screamed for inspiration even as his thoughts grew more muddled.

Soft! What is soft?

An image of Maeve flashed through his mind, her alabaster arms stretched above her head as she writhed beneath him. With horror, he pushed the vision away, only to have Maura replace her, wrapped in her scarlet shawl.

The wave curled and began its descent. Whit tightened his hold on the lifeless boy as the grey beach rushed toward them, and cried out one last desperate spell.

CHAPTER 25
Borne

Borne gazed out over the great inland sea separating Olquaria from Delnogoth. Shreds of vapor swirled beneath a tentative sun, and in the shifting light, Lake Mazarine reddened from rich blue to deep magenta. It was yet another wonder along the way east.

The scent of roses mingled with the dank smell of the boggy wetlands. The late spring wind lifted Borne's hair, which had grown shaggy in the two months since his departure from Gral. He supposed he'd have to trim it before he came into Zlatan Basileus's august presence.

A sudden thrashing in the water warned Borne to retreat, and Magnus gamboled out of the shallows, spraying water in all directions. He grabbed the dog by the nape of his sopping neck and gave him an affectionate shake. "You great loon," he laughed, "you're still a pup at heart, aren't you?"

"Ah, Borne! There you are!"

Comte Balfou strolled up, keeping a prudent distance from the dripping hound. "Good news—I've received confirmation that we can sail today. If we'd come a few weeks later, it would have been too risky to attempt a crossing."

Ejder, their local guide, had already explained to Borne how in midsummer the winds sweeping the lake changed direction, bringing the *burzani* in from the west. When these hot, dry gales roared down from the Delnogoth steppes, they raised spinning funnels of water that swallowed everything in their path. In this season, even the Mazarinei stayed ashore.

The comte drew a deep breath. "No matter how many times I pass this way, the lake air never fails to delight!"

"It carries the promise of summer," Borne agreed. "While we were crossing the Valmoinnes, I confess I wasn't sure we'd survive to enjoy another."

Balfou gave a slight shudder. "Indeed. Particularly after Nagoret brought down that snow slide with his abominable singing. I remain convinced the gods were intent on silencing him once and for all."

Borne laughed, although at the time, it hadn't been at all funny. They'd escaped a frozen burial only because the slide started high enough above them that they'd had time to run out of the avalanche's path. All the men were spared, but two ponies had not been so fortunate. Luckily, they were not the beasts bearing gifts from King Crenel to the Imperial Basileus.

Glancing over at the leader of their delegation, it once again confounded Borne that, despite the weeks of hard travel, the comte's auburn hair remained sleekly groomed and neatly bound, and his attire impeccable. Today, Balfou wore a snowy white tunic and spotless hose, while over his broad shoulders lay a spectacular *seraser* cloak, interwoven with threads of gold and silver, a gift to the ambassador from Zlatan Basileus himself. Borne pitied Gaétan, the comte's diligent squire, who must surely labor long into the night, brushing and pressing his lordship's clothes to maintain their pristine condition.

It was Balfou's pride in his appearance that had caused Borne, at the beginning of their journey east, to mistakenly assume the comte was just another decadent fop of the Gralian court. But he'd quickly come to respect the man. In addition to being an authority on Olquarian society, Balfou had proven himself an experienced guide. He'd known which trails along their way would remain passable in the early winter snows, and apart from that one close call, he'd brought the company over the treacherous mountains safely.

"If we're about to sail, my lord," Borne said, "then I must excuse myself. The men must prepare for boarding."

Receiving Balfou's gracious nod, he made his way toward the long cedar piers jutting out into the lake. His troop was already assembled there, their belongings and weapons securely packed and shouldered. Borne suppressed a grin as D'Avencote, his aide-de-camp, planted a kiss on the forehead of his sturdy mountain pony, Aurelie, who had carried the Gralian over the treacherous passes of lower Delnogoth.

"Farewell, sweet Aurelie," D'Avencote crooned. He stroked the beast's muzzle gently before reluctantly releasing her to the trader.

They'd sold all the horses here in the lake port of Merthol, since Balfou had assured Borne that the Basileus would provide them with alternate transport from Rizo to Tell-Uyuk. In any event, Borne doubted that the vessels set to convey the embassy across the lake were suitable for the animals. The *joltoras*, as the boats were called, were woven from the giant sedge curtaining much of the Mazarin, and they were sealed with the sticky tar found in the ancient pits dotting the landscape. To Borne, they looked concerningly fragile.

The thirty men of the Gralian party required two *joltoras*. Boarding was accomplished without incident, save for one misstep that landed Nargoret—a florid, thick-set man with flaming red hair—in the reeking mire. His fellow passengers refused to let him embark until he'd stripped off his muddy clothes and rinsed them in the lake.

Once they had cast off, Borne settled beside Ejder and studied the *joltora's* craftsmanship more closely. Although primitive, it was strangely beautiful. The prow and stern rose gracefully, like a crescent moon on its back. The figurehead of the *Naza*, Borne's ship, was a water lizard with luminous green eyes; the *Pelin*, alongside them, bore the head of a *kabaga*, the giant turtle who swam in the depths of the Mazarine and basked on the *ulas*, the man-made floating isles of reeds scattered across the lake.

The *Naza's* captain was a wiry, wizened fellow with short, tightly wound grey curls. Like his crew, he was slender and long-limbed, with bright, almond-shaped eyes and sun-kissed skin. From his place at the rudder, he called out melodious instructions to his crew as they wielded their broad-bladed paddles to the soft cadence of their songs. Borne had already picked up a smattering of Mazarini, but wished he knew more. He would have liked to record their lyrics in his journal. These days he no longer composed or read poetry, for it gave him no pleasure, but he still carried his old diaries, along with a few volumes on military strategy, a bundle of maps, and an anthology of the Olquarian sages.

When they were well off the shore, *Naza's* single sail was hoisted, belling in the stirring breeze. The paddles were stowed as the captain set a westerly course to skirt the dangerous shoals on the lake's eastern shoreline. The *joltora* picked up surprising speed, skimming over the glassy water like the black terns dotting the lake.

Ejder pointed to a thatched watchtower on one of the *ulas* as they glided past. "My grandfather built that lookout," he proclaimed proudly. "It was his duty, and my father's after him, to warn our people when the Hanamah came raiding."

The Hanamah, a tribe inhabiting the vertiginous slopes to the east of the great lake, had once been the Mazarinei's inveterate enemies. As a result of generations of capturing each other's women, over time the two tribes had become deeply interbred. The year Ejder had been born, a truce was declared, and since then their exchanges had consisted of wares rather than wives.

The captain signaled to Ejder, who touched his heart politely before answering the summons. Balfou took the Mazarinei's place at Borne's side. "If this wind holds," the comte said, "we could reach Tamanti before nightfall. Otherwise we'll heave to and shelter by one of the *ulas* along the way."

Tamanti was one of the few natural islands on the lake, and lay about a quarter of the way to their destination. If they were to achieve such a distance in one day, they would arrive at Rizo within the week. It had taken them three to cover the same ground while crossing the rugged Valmoinnes.

"What should I know about Rizo?" Borne asked the comte, "other than that it's the guardian city of the Contara Straits?"

Borne knew Balfou needed no encouragement to speak of his adopted land; he'd served as Gral's ambassador to Olquaria for over half his life, and it was clear he'd grown to love it. His dark blue eyes sparkled with passion whenever he spoke of the eastern empire.

"Rizo? Why, it's the busiest port in the world, set at the crossroads between East and West. Her ships carry goods through the straits down to the Middle Sea, then on from there all along the coast. Rizo was the birthplace of Al Douwal, whom you well know was the father of mathematics, and of Gorgani Kazim, whose maps are still used today, as well as Bektash Kadari, the brilliant astronomer, and Rushdi Santai, the renowned poet of love. The city is four times the size of Segavia, a sleepy village by comparison." Balfou gave a dismissive wave of his hand. "But we won't be lingering in Rizo. The Basileus has requested we proceed with all haste to the capital. And while his northern port city is impressive, no metropolis can hope to match the magnificence of Tell-Uyuk!"

Borne recalled the priceless Kazim map with vignette borders and decorative cartouches that adorned one wall of Windend's library. Lord Heptorious acquired the ancient artifact during his campaigns with King Urlion on the continent. As boys, Borne and Cole spent hours studying that map, and had pestered their tutors mercilessly for tales of the places depicted on it. Had it been Master Dunford or Master Orlick who'd told them about the splendorous Tell-Uyuk, City of Seven Hills, with its gleaming white towers and wide avenues, all leading to the Golden Palace of the Basileus? Borne felt a dull ache in his heart as he remembered a time when Cole and Lord Heptorious had still been a part of his life.

"We must see that you experience this as soon as possible. What do you say?" Borne blinked. Balfou was looking at him expectantly.

"I'm sorry, my lord. What do I say to…?"

"To joining me for the annual exhibition of *yaraket*? It's really quite a thrilling event. I have a box in the *Censibas* just below that of the Basileus, and it offers an excellent view of the course."

It took Borne several seconds to recall that the *Censibas* was where the famous *eniyara*, the free runners, performed their *yaraket*. These artists of movement tested the limits of their athleticism through climbing, jumping, balancing, and running. While they normally practiced these feats out in the world, the *eniyara* held a yearly exhibition in the *Censibas*, an arena so vast it could accommodate the entire population of the free peoples of Tell-Uyuk, as well as the slaves they required to attend to them.

"I'd like that very much, my lord," Borne replied.

"Excellent!" Balfou rubbed his hands together in anticipation. "It's just one of many things you're bound to enjoy in the capital."

"I'm not sure how much time I'll have for leisure, what with training the Basileus's army in arms, and campaigning with them when required."

"Yes, yes," said Balfou, with another wave of his expressive hands, "but your eyes and ears can also serve Gral while in attendance at social engagements. A highly presentable young lord like yourself will surely find favor with the court."

Privately, Borne didn't know that he cared to find favor. He was still adjusting to his unexpected change of status from mercenary under Latour's command to herald serving the Gralian king. Of course, he couldn't have refused the honor bestowed upon him by King Crenel without giving offense, and Latour had clearly wanted this for him, convinced as the marechal was that linking Borne's fortunes with Gral in this way would prove to be beneficial to both Borne and the realm.

Besides, if Olquaria was all Latour and Balfou claimed it to be, there could be worse places for him to put down new roots. Time would tell.

Balfou seemed to be reading his thoughts. "Should the rumors prove to be true, regarding the shifting sands of allegiances on both sides of the Erolin Sea, you'll be well out of it here. The Basileus is sure to remain neutral, unless his hand is forced, and that is highly unlikely. Zlatan is a master of survival, as one must be to rule the infamous Imperial Court." He paused before adding, "May I speak frankly, my lord?"

Borne doubted the comte spoke any other way. "By all means."

"The prospect of conflict in the west is looming. Latour assured me that should Drinnglennin go to war, you won't abandon your post here and rush home to join it."

Borne met his searching gaze evenly. "I wouldn't have accepted this commission if I didn't intend to honor it, sir."

"Yes, yes, of course. I had no doubt!" Balfou's flushed cheeks suggested he was sorry he'd implied otherwise.

A sudden flapping drew their eyes to the sail, which had momentarily emptied of wind. As the crew scrambled for their paddles, the canvas fluttered and the *joltora* began a slow spiral in the indigo water. Shouts rang out from the sailors, and the previously placid captain leapt from his perch, shouting orders Borne didn't need to understand to discern their urgency. The men's paddles rose and fell, but the *Naza*'s bow continued to swing inexorably east.

Far off on the horizon, a massive cloud bank was rolling in, its base dark and flat as a griddlecake above the lake. The water beneath it had turned slate grey, and a blurred sheet of rain fell like a curtain between sky and sea. Racing ahead of the rain, a flock of winged black creatures flew in formation, and for a moment, Borne thought they were young dragons. But as they swooped overhead, he saw that they were swans, only three times the size of any he'd ever seen.

Borne's pulse quickened as a finger of water slowly snaked from the cloud to touch down on the lake's surface. The coil of water resembled a huge whirling top, like the ones Borne had played with as a child at Fernsehn.

It began to gyrate in their direction, the spout thickening and sending out steam as it picked up speed, trailing a visible wake.

"It's the *burzani*!" Balfou cried.

The crew gave up trying to row against the wind, and Borne leapt to help them reef the now buffeting sail while the captain wrestled with the rudder. The *joltoras* lurched into motion once more and raced across the lake, just ahead of what was now a blinding squall. Cresting waves crowned the lake with white foam that spilled over the gunwales.

A sudden deluge of water gushed down out of the sky, and some of the crew set to frantically bailing the *joltora*. Borne joined them, all the while tracking the path of the waterspout, which had veered to their port side. He pushed back his sopping hair and grinned over at Ejder, whose eyes had grown wide with fear.

"It looks like she'll blow by!" Borne called reassuringly to the Mazarinei, but it appeared Ejder couldn't hear him over the hiss of wind and water. He remained staring rigidly beyond Borne.

A wail rose up from the local men, and Borne turned to see what was frightening them so. Shielding his eyes against the rain, he made out a large *ula* rising like a giant turtle out of the aubergine lake.

"What is it?" he called to Balfou. "What have they seen?"

The comte's expression was equally stark, and for once he appeared heedless of the damage inflicted on his fine clothes by the wet. He murmured something too low for Borne to make out.

"What?"

"*Ile la Malfica.*"

Isle of the Witches. It meant nothing to Borne, but now he could see figures garbed in saffron robes lining the shore among the tall golden reeds. None of them appeared to be armed.

"Who are they?" Borne called, pitching his voice lower as well.

But Balfou only shook his head.

The waterspout had lost momentum and the rain was abating. To Borne, there seemed no need for such alarm. In frustration, he turned back to Ejder. "Come, man! The storm will soon be over. We can shake out the sail and be on our way."

Ejder lowered his face to his palms and moaned. "Too late... we are doomed!"

Borne could see that was all the explanation he would get from the terrified man.

He pushed past the guide and, seizing a paddle, thrust it into a crewman's hands. Then he leapt to the sail. Several of the Mazarinei hastened to help him remove the reef. With the shift in the wind, they should have started to come about already, but *Naza* seemed to have taken on a will of her own. She continued to stream toward the *ula*.

The captain abandoned the helm and made his way to the bow. Stretching out his hands in supplication to the watching people on the *ula*, he began an eerie keening. Borne caught the word "mercy," and then the crew lent their voices to the captain's lament, raising the hairs on his skin.

In frustration, Borne shook the comte's shoulder. "Balfou, for the love of Alithin, tell me what's happening! Who are these *malfica?*"

"The gravest hazard on the Mazarine," Balfou replied hollowly.

"Why? What do they want from us?"

"One of us," Balfou replied. "They will want one of us."

Borne stared at him. "For what purpose?"

"Vengeance. The *malfica* have held sway on this isle since the last Purge, after which those of their sisters who survived came here to seek sanctuary. Sometimes you can see them swooping over the lake, borne on the backs of great black swans. They've never forgotten those who lost their lives during that terrible time. They are still exacting restitution for their deaths."

This close to the *ula*, Borne now saw that all its inhabitants were female. A few were old and haggard, but many were young, and fair to look upon.

"Most of these women wouldn't have even been born at the time of the Purge," he protested.

"The *malfica* never forget."

The *Naza* had entered the shallows, and some of the women were wading out to meet her, chanting in a strange tongue that drew on no language Borne possessed. If they intended to do the travelers harm, he, for one, would not go meekly into their clutches. He grasped the hilt of his sword, but as he attempted to draw it, a strange lassitude overcame him. He recognized it for what it was—some sorcery of the witches' making.

Balfou had already slumped to his knees when Borne sank down beside him, fighting to keep his heavy eyes open. All around them, the Mazarinei sprawled to the deck.

The last thing Borne saw before he lost consciousness was the slender fingers of the *malfica* grasping the gunwales to pull the *Naza* to the perilous isle.

* * *

He awoke to darkness. He was on his back, and his hands and feet were stretched wide, bound by what felt like cord. The musky scent of incense and herbs mingled in the heavy air, yet he felt a chill. As his eyes adjusted to the gloom, he saw that his clothes had been taken from him.

He was not alone. All around the perimeter of wherever he was, shadowy figures ranged. One of them murmured, and a torch was lit. In its dancing light, Borne saw the women were also naked, their skin varying from alabaster to ebony. There were no bony, grey-haired hags among them; these women were all in the bloom of their years, with ripe breasts, full hips, and narrow pelts between their shapely legs.

In unison, they swayed forward, and Borne twisted to see if an axe was about to descend on his neck. It was only then that he saw the line of girls, too young to have flowered, observing with unfeigned curiosity whatever was about to take place.

"He is fine," crooned a dark-haired woman, running her liquid black eyes over Borne's body. "I claim the first seed."

"You claim nothing, Makayda." A tall, lithe beauty with black tousled curls and warm umber skin knelt at Borne's side. "I was the one who first felt the pull."

"It is so," said a third, whose golden hair matched the glow of her skin. She stared at Borne with hungry green eyes. "Hinata raised the first cry. He is hers by rights."

"Don't worry, sisters." Hinata smiled, and Borne felt her fingers brush across his loins. "This one has plenty for all. Indeed, he is overripe."

Borne heard the smacking of their lips as they gathered around him, stroking him with cool, provocative fingers. He felt himself grow hard.

"What do you want of me?" he demanded.

Hinata's low, throaty laugh stirred him further. "All that you have to give, *othanda*."

As much as he dreaded the answer, he persisted. "You mean to take my life?"

This drew more laughter. "In a manner of speaking," the golden witch replied.

"Don't frighten him." The woman who spoke had ivory skin and platinum hair that fell to her waist. Her breasts were small, perfect orbs, the nipples rosy in the growing heat of the room. "I, for one, don't want to carry his fear." She covered his hand with her own and leaned over to whisper in his ear. "We will harvest your pearls, *othanda*."

The warmth and heavy fragrance made Borne feel disoriented. *Keep them talking,* he thought. *Perhaps they can be reasoned with.* "I've been told it's vengeance you seek."

"Of course you have," replied Makayda. "It's a tale we've long cultivated to keep away unwanted visitors. It's served us well over the years. You'll have to judge for yourself the truth of it. What we desire, however, is continuance."

"Enough," Hinata declared. "Let us weave, sisters." She began to hum, and the gathered women took up a lulling chant, repeating strange words over and over again: "*Mu awan obin rinwa.*"

Hinata's perfect white teeth flashed at Borne, and he felt her gently stroking him. Realization dawned at last. His pearls.

The witch lowered her dusky lashes and exhaled a long, audible breath that was echoed by her sisters. Borne felt the heat of desire wash over him as she stretched out on his right, pressing her silken flesh against him while she caressed his cheek.

"Do you feel the pull of our loom, *othanda*?" she murmured.

Despite himself, Borne groaned.

Hinata's lips were so close to his he could taste the sweetness on her soft breath. She kissed him softly, and despite himself, he hungered for more.

"If we untie your bonds, do you give your word you will not fight us?"

"What do you plan to do to my companions?" Borne asked, although it was a struggle not to drown himself in the onyx pools of her eyes.

"Such discipline and devotion!" The witch's eyes sparkled wickedly. "The boats cannot sail without our leave. If we are satisfied—*fully* satisfied—you and your friends may proceed with your voyage still in possession of your wits... and your lives."

Borne surveyed the sultry creatures surrounding him. "In that case, ladies, you have my word that I will submit meekly to your requirements."

"Oh," Hinata purred, swinging herself astride him as the others loosened the ropes binding him. "There was never a question of your compliance, *othanda*." She languidly lowered herself onto him with a moan of pleasure. "But meekness is not required."

She felt like warmed honey, and then like fire. Borne's senses were filled with the scent of her musk. He felt himself responding to her slow, exquisite rhythm, the breathy sighs of her sisters spurring his growing lust. It had been months since he'd been with a woman, and although his mind might have resisted, his body did not.

Wrapping his arms around the witch-goddess, he deftly flipped her under him. For a breath, her eyes widened, but he kept them in perfect sync until she gave a low growl and arched her back to meet his thrusts.

Suddenly, Hinata cried out and pushed her hands against his chest. "I have caught!" she gasped. "Makayda!"

Hinata slipped away, and the brown-haired beauty eased under him. Borne seemed to have lost all will of his own, but he was in full possession of his senses. Indeed, his whole being tingled with a sensation hovering between ecstasy and pain.

When Makayda called out, a silver-haired witch took her place, and following her, the golden blonde with the sun-kissed skin. After that, Borne lost track of all those with whom he coupled, rising to their ravenous demands again and again, his body slick with sweat, both his and theirs. Wrapped in a tangle of limbs, the tang of sex filling his nostrils, he pumped out his seed to quicken in their voracious wombs. There was no time and no memory—only an insatiable hunger that drove him beyond what any mortal should have been able to endure.

It was only when the room filled with the blush of dawn that the witches released him from their loom of lust, and the women and girls rose to drift away.

At the last, only Hinata remained, her head upon his heaving chest. He listened to her long, slow exhalations, and his racing heart gradually slowed to match the beat of hers. Makayda and several others soon returned with cool cloths and a pungent salve, which they used to sooth the bites and scratches they'd inflicted on him. A petite russet-haired vixen, whom he recalled raking his chest until it bled, offered him sweet mead and a bowl of purple fruits that held succulent segments of heaven beneath their rinds. He ate them all, and a second bowl as well.

Hinata watched him with amusement, and when he had sated his hunger, the witch led him outside through the sway-ing reeds. Between the tall grass, he could see the two *joltoras* rocking in the shallow water. There was no sign of life on the boats, and Borne wondered if Balfou, their company and the crew were even still aboard. And Magnus. The hound would have come looking for him long before now if he was able.

"They're only sleeping," Hinata assured him, then led him down winding wooden steps to a perfectly circular pool. At her urging, Borne entered it. From the temperature of the water, he guessed the pool was fed by hot springs. He lay back and drifted, feeling the strain of the night's revelry drain away.

Hinata dove in after him. When she surfaced, water droplets spangled her curls with diamonds of light. "I see questions burning in those sky-struck eyes. You may ask me three."

Borne seized the chance. "I am curious as to how you've managed to survive since the last Purge."

"You mean, how we've been able to keep at bay those who would destroy us?" Hinata's beautiful mouth hardened. "Before the Purge, women like us lived in isolation, most often alone on the edges of villages providing restorative tonics and willingly treating any who came to us in need. Even then, we were only tolerated because of our skills with healing. We were never trusted, and we were reviled by the ignorant who saw evil in our singular gifts.

"But that was nothing compared to the distrust and loathing heaped upon us after the Strigori, cursed be their name, spread their poison across the lands. The dark wizards were both merciless and unassailable, feeding people's fear of anyone possessed of magic. When the Strigori at last fell from power, those who'd suffered under these cruel brothers craved revenge—and in the absence of the Strigori, we served as easy surrogates.

"For the crime of being different, we were tortured and mutilated, hanged, burned at stakes, and held under the water until we drowned. We were pummeled with rocks, the life pressed out of us with heavy stones. Those who judged us raped us, often unto death, and cut our unborn children from our wombs. We were branded with searing tongs, flogged, flayed, and dismembered."

The witch's eyes blazed with cold fury as she recited the torments witches had suffered through the ages, and Borne regretted having stoked this fire. But instead of lashing out at him as he feared, she dropped under the surface of the pool.

When she bobbed up again, her knowing smile was back in place. "No longer," she continued, "*and never again.* Those of us who managed to survive the terror of the Purge began to seek one another out. We banded together and made our way east under the guidance of Olena, a witch descended from the Mazarinei. Here, we found safety in our numbers." Her eyes took on a prideful light. "And Olena taught us her wild magic, so that we can commune with other living things. Not even the great wizards and sorceresses have this ability. And here in this coven of kindred spirits, our powers have grown. We weave our own wands from the reeds and have mastered many spells. Never again will any man have dominion over us. Although we were forced to step out of the Known World, we've created one more to our liking. All that we need is here—all, that is, except seed to perpetuate our kind. And this, we take as we please."

Borne could attest to that. "But how do you keep those who would do you harm from seeking you here with ill intentions? If a big enough army were to attack—"

Hinata's smile grew cunning. "You found us only because we wished you to. Our *ula* cannot be seen otherwise. Some who visit us never leave. Once they have served their purpose…" She laid her hand lightly on Borne's arm. "You needn't worry, *othanda. You* have pleased us."

Borne supposed this was meant to ease his fears, but the witch's subsequent sigh raised a frisson of alarm. "But?"

Hinata shook her head. "No 'but,' *othanda.* You are free to leave. It is only that I fear you may have spoiled us for whoever will follow. Perhaps you might sail this way again in a year's time?"

Borne sensed it was prudent not to rule out this possibility. "Perhaps. But before I leave, I still have one more question. Where are your men? I mean, if you have been breeding since the last Purge with those who answer the call of your loom, what happens to the boys you bear?"

"We sacrifice them on a night with no moon, and drink their blood." Seeing Borne's expression, she laughed. "I jest, *othanda*. We don't give birth to boys. We've found a way to ensure we have only daughters. Now." Hinata tilted her slender neck to one side. "I have a question for you. You are bound, *othanda*, heart and soul. Are you not?"

Borne didn't ask how the witch had guessed this. "It makes no difference. Even if it is so, she is beyond my reach."

Hinata's gaze rested on the surface of the water. "Yes," she said thoughtfully. "I see this. In any event, your destiny lies to the east."

"I hope so," he replied lightly, and he stroked across the pool and pulled himself up onto the grass.

Before Hinata left him back at the hut, she pressed a chain with a black swan pendant into his hand. "A gift from us. It is our pledge of thanks to you. If you are ever in need, you may return to us, and if we can help you, we will. But you must not remove it, else its value is forfeit." She slipped it over his head, then ran a light finger down his cheek and slipped away.

In the hut, no trace of the previous night's orgy remained. Instead he found a fine linen tunic, soft breeches, and a pair of boots. As he donned these, he couldn't help wonder whether they had belonged to a hapless predecessor who hadn't lived up to the witches' expectations.

When he stepped outside, he found himself alone, so he made his way as quickly as possible down to the beach. There was always the chance that the capricious witches might change their minds about letting him go.

In the shallows, the *joltoras* waited. They had not shifted, although no lines moored them.

Cursing softly under his breath, Borne waded into the shallow water, setting off a chorus of unseen frogs from within the whispering reeds. When he was halfway to the boats, he cupped his hands and called softly, "Balfou! Ejder!"

To his intense relief, Magnus barked excitedly, and then several heads bobbed up at the near gunwale. One of them belonged to the comte.

Borne plunged deeper into the lake, then struck out with swift strokes. By the time he'd reached the *Naza*, the crew had their paddles poised at the ready.

Balfou and Ejder hauled him aboard, their eyes bright with astonishment. "You're alive!" the comte cried. "How did you escape the *malfica*?"

Borne had no intention of describing what he'd experienced on the *ula*. He would do nothing to encourage others to invade the witches sanctuary. He scooped up a paddle and drove it into the water.

"I barely escaped with my life," he said, keeping his expression somber. "As to what they wanted, that tale must go with me to my grave."

CHAPTER 26
Halla

The sandstorm proved to be a gift from the gods. If Palan had posted sentries, the blinding wind drove them to shelter, which allowed Halla to slip unseen into the sleeping camp in the storm's aftermath. Her heart in her throat, she raced toward the largest pavilion, praying she would find Nicu there, still alive.

She was running full tilt when something scuttled at her feet, making her stumble and bite her tongue so hard blood flooded her mouth. She rolled over to see a viper undulating across her path. Lying still—exposed to anyone who appeared—she waited until it had moved on, then she did as well.

Dawn was still hours off, but a light was showing in Palan's tent, and she was close enough now to hear muffled voices within. A single remaining banner snapped above the pavilion, fraying Halla's nerves as she circled to the rear of the tent. There she found a jumble of wooden crates, which she edged behind to better listen to the conversation in progress.

"You've watched your comrades die, most unpleasantly, for refusing to disclose the whereabouts of your camp." *Palan.* Halla would never forget that arrogant, entitled voice. "You will suffer the same fate if you persist in remaining silent. But if you cooperate, I can be generous, and promise you a clean death."

Ice replaced the fire in Halla's blood as a high-pitched scream shattered the night. She smelled the stench of burning flesh.

"*Dal d å nimic då na vul, divolè!*" The strangled words were Nicu's. *I will tell you nothing, wormspawn.* Then all was ominously still. Halla leaned closer to the tent wall, and she was so intent on hearing Nicu's voice that she was oblivious to all else until rough hands seized her and wrenched her to her feet, twisting her arms at her back.

Halla kicked her heel back, but her captor dodged the blow. He spun her to face him and she saw he was a bear of a man. Beside him, another man held up a lantern. This one had the look of an aristocrat, with thick black hair and a close-trimmed beard ringing his narrow lips. He jerked back Halla's hood, and his jaw dropped.

"Bring her," he commanded the bear.

Halla was propelled forward, her arms pinned painfully behind her. She faked a stumble and succeeded in bringing her boot down hard on the big man's foot, but he merely grunted and levered her arms higher. The pain was so intense she feared she might pass out, but he suddenly released her to push her after the bearded man into the pavilion.

She barely registered the tall man's groping hands searching her and cutting away her scabbard. All her being was focused on Nicu, who hung pinioned between two stakes. A glowing iron rested on the brazier beside him.

Halla gave an anguished cry when she saw what they had done to him. The skin on one side of his beautiful face had been flayed off, and a black, bloody hole gaped in place of the perfect shell of his ear. Burns were seared into his naked chest, and the reek of scorched flesh filled the tent. His eyes, once so bright, held only desolation.

"*Cucè, Åthinoi?*" he whispered through his torn lips. *Why?*

"What have we here?"

At the sound of Palan's voice, Halla tore her eyes away from Nicu. The Albrenian commander was just as she remembered him, with the same menace in his mocking smile and ice-pale eyes.

"She's my captive." Nicu's voice was raspy and strained. "She's of high birth and worth a king's ransom. That's what we planned to do with her." s

The commander moved toward Halla with the grace of a leopard and lifted a strand of her filthy hair. She wanted nothing more than to spit in his face, but she knew Nicu would pay for her venom. Still, De Grathiz's eyes narrowed, as if he sensed her loathing. "Where did you take her?"

"In Altipa," Nicu said. "She was up for auction."

"I don't believe you. Even under the grit, you can see her beauty. She would have been snapped up on the block in Segavia." He nodded to the man by the brazier, and Nicu's face paled. "Think again, dog."

Halla edged slightly closer to Nicu. "You're right. I was sold in Segavia," she said. She'd just realized Palan's underling had neglected to check her boot. *If we are to die today, Seor Palan, then so will you.*

De Grathiz's eyes lit up with sudden recognition. "I *thought* we'd met before." He jabbed a heavily ringed finger at her. "It was at Casa Calida, wasn't it? Before you were so ungrateful as to flee the litter bearing you to my home. That ill-considered act cost your friend Kainja her life."

Halla felt the blood drain from her face.

De Grathiz turned to Nicu. "This wench is *my* property; I invested a considerable sum in her training. I should thank you for returning her to me, but the question is—in what condition?" He smiled ruefully. "If *you've* had her, she's of no use to me. She's tainted goods in that case, soiled beyond cleansing, for which I shall have to exact a special restitution."

"He never touched me!" Halla cried. "I swear it!"

"Let's find out how honorable your word is." Palan snapped his fingers. "Nemia."

From the shadows, a slender woman rose from a low couch, her honeyed hair hanging to her waist. Underneath her sheer tunic, her voluptuous body was clearly visible. "My lord?"

"See if her maidenhead is intact."

The bear gave Halla a push toward the couch, but the woman drifted forward and ran her hands over Halla's belly.

"There is no need, my lord," Nemia declared, her voice low and throaty. "The mare is breeding."

Palan's mouth twisted with distaste. "In that case…"

He raised his chin, and his henchman lifted the iron from the fire.

Halla's cry of protest was silenced by the back of Palan's hand striking full force across her face. She reeled back, but he grabbed the front of her tunic and pulled her so close she could smell the wine on his breath.

"For your lie," he hissed, rage in his frosted eyes, "I will send you somewhere that will make you long for the Abyss. But first you will witness this swine's death. We'll make sure it's slow, so that you can recount it in detail to his bastard." He tilted his head thoughtfully at Halla's expression. "Does this upset you? I would not wish you to think me heartless." He turned to Nicu. "Perhaps we should offer you a final entertainment, swine? Would you like your whore to show you what she learned at Casa Calida before we proceed with your punishment for taking what was mine?"

He thrust Halla to the center of the tent.

Halla wiped the blood from her split lip, still reeling from Nemia's pronouncement. *The mare is breeding.* Her heart caught in her throat as tears streamed down Nicu's ravaged face.

Palan smirked as he followed her gaze. "Ah, I see. Neither of you knew? Of course, a woman of *high birth* would be ignorant of the signs. A pity I didn't get to her first. I can tell you from personal experience what vixens well-born virgins turn into, once they get a man between their legs. They generally put up quite a fight, which makes it all the more interesting."

He shook a reproachful finger at Halla. "But you've gone and sullied that pure blue blood of yours with the scum of a Lurker." His nostrils flared. "Revolting—I can even smell him on you." He snapped his fingers again. "You will dance for us, Lurker's Whore, as Kainja taught you."

Halla's eyes were still locked on Nicu's. "*Fitar, dragost me moasă,*" she said. "*Nim pecarnu să natingă să imil.*"

Be strong, my beautiful love. Nothing he can do to us can touch our spirits or our hearts.

Nicu's reply was barely above a whisper. "*Promi că nev salv copul. E dorțna me moa.*"

Promise me you will save our child. It is my dying wish.

"Be silent!" Palan thundered. "If you speak in that filthy tongue again, I shall cut yours out." He signaled to Halla. "We're waiting."

When she remained stubbornly motionless, he inclined his head, his bright smile still in place. "You refuse? Very well. I think it is time for the knife now, Franco." The smile widened. "My man is a sculptor, and he will carve out a long, slow agony for your Lurker. The cur will die in any case, but there's still a chance to win him a merciful death. Otherwise, Franco will ensure that his worthless life is protracted in most exquisite pain."

Franco raised his blade, awaiting his commander's order.

"Please, my lord." Halla spoke through gritted teeth. It took all her force of will to resist flying at De Grathiz to strangle him. "What is your pleasure?"

The Albrenian's cruel eyes sparked with triumph. "*Our* pleasure, wench," he corrected. "You will dance, as the *floritas* do, for your foul-blooded lover and for me."

Franco waggled his blade and leered at Halla, then pointed its tip at Nicu's groin. She knew then that regardless of how compliant she was, Palan would make Nicu suffer terribly. He had left her with only one choice.

With trembling fingers, Halla untied her cloak and let it drop to the ground. She kept her face turned toward Nicu, as if only the two of them existed in the room, in the world.

Slowly, Halla, she imagined the *prima florita* of Segavia saying, *slowly, so as to mesmerize your man.*

She unbuckled her belt, swaying slightly as she did so, ignoring Palan's amused snort. Then, incrementally, she raised her tunic over her head, arching her back and thrusting her breasts forward.

All that was left to remove now was the linen wrapped over her breasts and her torn hose and boots. She felt all of their eyes on her, even Nemia's. Franco's mouth had fallen open, lust plain on his ugly face.

Halla lifted her arms and began to untie the knot of her hair. She could almost hear Kainja urging her on. *Roll your shoulders ever so slightly—yes, like that. Drop your chin and then raise it, and slowly shake that unruly mane loose.*

"*That's* better," Palan said. "Now the rest."

As desperately as Halla wanted to prolong the process, unwrapping the cloth binding her breasts took only a moment. To buy time, she writhed her hips enticingly as Kainja had done.

De Grathiz let out a slow breath. "Perfect," he murmured. "You were worth three times what I paid." He sighed with what sounded like true regret. "For that reason, I shall have to raise my remuneration." He raised his brows. "Franco?"

The henchman drove his knife into Nicu's gut. Halla screamed and lunged at Franco, but Palan caught her and held her fast, the crook of his arm pressed so hard against her throat it stopped her breath. She struggled in vain as Nicu looked down at the stain blooming on his tunic, then lifted his eyes to her. They spoke of all he could not find the power to say.

"Don't worry," De Grathiz said with a laugh, his sour breath hot against Halla's hair. "He won't die from that wound, at least not today, and likely not tomorrow either. Franco has much more in store for him. It will get worse—much worse— unless you cooperate. *Fully.*"

At the sight of the dark blood seeping from Nicu's wound, Halla felt all the fight go out of her. She'd witnessed too often the agonizing, slow death from a blade to the belly.

"That's better," crooned De Grathiz. He released her and gave her a little push in Nicu's direction. "You haven't yet finished your dance. If it fails to please us, Franco will give a little demonstration of his own. I hope the sight of a dismemberment won't give you night terrors... what with your delicate condition."

Franco fumbled with the ties of Nicu's breeches, and Halla guessed what was to come next. From the dark terror in Nicu's eyes, so did he.

She knew what she had to do, and she would have only one chance.

As she began swaying again, she was no longer aware of who was watching her. Her thoughts flew back to the days— so many days—spent with Florian in Lord's Wood. She could feel his hand on hers, the heat of his body as he stood close behind her, moving the knife in her fingers until she mastered the grip. Over and over again, he guided her through the flicking motion. Over and over, until it became second nature, until she could send her blade spiraling, with blinding speed, to hit its mark every time.

Franco tugged Nicu's breeches to his knees, and as Palan turned to savor his next assault, Halla bent forward.

The hilt of her knife leapt into her grasp, and in less than a breath, the blade spun through the air—to plunge, with deadly accuracy, into its mark.

She lifted her gaze from the knife to meet the eyes of the man whose life she had just taken. The ghost of a smile curved his lips—lips that had so recently pressed against her own. With his dying breath, Nicu whispered Halla's name.

CHAPTER 27
Fynn

Fynn kicked and flailed in a turbid sea that had no up or down. This was how the gods had always intended he would die. He had robbed them twice already, once during the *synda* that Midsommer's Day, and then again when Vetch wanted to throw him into Restaria's harbor with his pockets filled with stones. This time, the sea would have him.

Fynn struggled to free himself from whatever held him. Perhaps the serpents of Nagror already possessed his soul. He braced himself for gnawing daggers of pain, then his stomach clenched and he gagged and spewed. He gulped in the unexpected air, not caring that it reeked of singed hair, weak with relief at discovering he was still alive.

Hearing a groan—a very human one—he dared to open his eyes.

All color had fled from the world. All he could see was white fire raging within a row of grey buildings.

Then hands hauled him to his feet and dragged him toward the flickering light. Fynn tried to turn his head to see who held him, but breathing in and out was as much as he could manage. If it was one of Aksel's men, better the sea had taken Fynn. His traitorous cousin would use him to lure Jered to his death.

He tried to pull away, until a familiar voice said, "Don't fight me, Fynn. I need your help."

"Whit?" Fynn struggled to stay upright on the stony strand, but he couldn't feel his feet. "I'm trying, but I'm numb all over. And my... my eyes... "

"It's all right. There's nothing wrong with them. You're in my shadow." Whit's breath was labored as he heaved Fynn forward a few more paces. "Are you hurt?

"No... only... I smell smoke. Is my hair on fire?"

Whit gave a weak laugh. "That's the lapin fur. I summoned bales of it to the beach to break our fall. Some of them were alight."

Fynn stumbled over something and pitched forward, and in an instant, color returned to the world.

"Now that's a stroke of luck!" Whit cried. He bent over and picked something up from the stones. "You've found my flask!" He took a deep draught, then offered it to Fynn.

With his first swallow, Fynn felt heat pulsing through his veins, and his toes and fingers tingled back to life. He pushed himself to his feet, feeling surprisingly steady. "I can walk by myself now, I think."

They made for one of the warehouses, where the wizard collected his boots and staff. Fynn could only imagine how hard it must have been for Whit to leave his rod in order to come to his rescue. Not to mention that Fynn's impulsive race into the Helgrins' clutches had almost cost them both their lives.

"Where's Sinead?" he asked.

The wizard put his finger to his lips and hurried them along the crescent of the port. He stopped at last at the smoking ruin of a rambling house and stood in silence, surveying the shards of broken crockery and the big stone fireplace, which was all that remained.

"Were they friends of yours?" Fynn asked.

"Yes, I guess they were. In any case, they were good, kind people. I'd planned to leave you with them for a spell." Whit nudged a charred piece of wood with his boot, rolling it over to reveal a gruesome mask. "Where to take you now?" he muttered, then turned to Fynn. "What about your mother's people? Where did you say they came from?"

"Langmerdor. But my mother never spoke of them. I don't even know her family name." For the first time, Fynn regretted that he hadn't asked Teca when he'd had the chance.

Whit frowned. "Langmerdor's too far away. Vetch will soon have the roads watched, if he hasn't already." Suddenly the wizard brightened. "Trillyon. That's where we'll go."

Now that the elixir had cleared Fynn's brain, what he'd learned on the longship began to sink in. "I should have killed him."

Whit didn't need clarification. "Aksel might have been lying… about what happened to Aetheor."

Fynn heard a lack of conviction behind the wizard's words. "He has my—the yarl's longboat. Aetheor would never have let another man captain his *Ydlyia*, not even Jered." He swallowed the lump in his throat. "Aksel was telling the truth. Aetheor Yarl lies under the sea."

He wished he could promise to avenge Aetheor's death, but that obligation would have to fall to Jered, the yarl's true son and heir. The brother with whom Fynn shared no blood ties. And if Jered ever learned that Fynn was fully Drinnglennian, he wouldn't want anything to do with him. The realization made Fynn terribly sad.

They made their way back to the southern edge of the harbor. Fynn's stomach twisted at the rank smell of blood as they passed the worst of the carnage, even though he averted his eyes from the butchered bodies. He was ashamed of his weakness. *You should have known after Thorpe that no Helgrin blood flows through your craven veins.* He wondered if Aetheor had suspected it when he'd sent Fynn home in disgrace.

At the thought, a sob escaped him. He felt Whit's hand come to rest on his shoulder, and Fynn brushed away his tears. Thankfully the wizard made no comment.

As they approached the woodlands, Whit gave a soft whistle, and Sinead trotted out of the brush with Rowlan following docilely on her heels. Whit rummaged in the saddlebags and handed Fynn some dry clothes.

"I'm sorry I lost your good cloak," Fynn mumbled, wiping his nose on his sodden tunic.

"I imagine you had little choice in that. At least no one stole the horses while I was looking for you." Whit patted the white mare affectionately and offered her an apple, crooning to her as she nuzzled his hand. The stallion whickered softly, and Whit gave Fynn another to feed to him. Rowlan's warm breath against Fynn's hand was oddly comforting, and by the time he'd changed and had another glug from the flask, he'd stopped snuffling.

"We'll want to put some distance between ourselves and Stonehoven," Whit said. "When news of the Helgrin attack gets abroad, this place will be swarming with soldiers from both Lorendale and Nelvorboth."

Fynn didn't object. After all, he had nowhere else to go. No home to return to. No family. His mother was dead, as were both his fathers—his true father and the man he still thought of as one. His brother, if he lived, might no longer accept him; they weren't blood. He thought of Grinner, and wondered if his friend was even still alive.

What he did have, though, was this kind young wizard who, for his own obscure reasons, wished to protect him.

For now, that would have to do.

* * *

They headed west, setting a brisk pace while the road was good, then slowing once Whit veered onto a less traveled trail. At one point they plunged into the brush and followed an old gully to a copse before Whit reined in, signaling for silence.

Fynn hadn't heard or seen anything, but after a few tense moments, the wizard clucked his tongue and the horses clambered back onto the track.

A few miles onward, they came across an abandoned croft. Its roof had fallen in, but the adjacent barn was still intact. Inside it was dry, and there was a rough pit filled with charred logs. They were not the first to shelter there.

"Once I've seen to the horses and had a look around, I'll make us a fire," Whit said, then slipped out of the barn before Fynn could answer.

Wishing to be useful, Fynn scraped together some kindling, but he had no flint, so he had to wait alone in the gloom until the wizard returned.

It turned out that Whit had no flint either, and didn't need one; with a word, he had a flame licking at the wood. Despite its magic origins, it seemed an ordinary enough fire, warm and bright—until Fynn noticed that it wasn't throwing off any smoke.

"Do you want to eat?" Whit asked.

"I'd rather we talk," Fynn replied bluntly. "Why are you doing all this?"

Whit raised his brows with a little smile. "I've asked myself that same question many times over these past hours. It's complicated."

"We've time. You were sent to kill me—by Lord Vetch. Why didn't you?"

"I never planned to, but if I hadn't taken the charge, they would have sent someone else."

"They?"

Whit sighed. "Forgive me for not explaining all this earlier. I thought the less you knew, the safer you'd be. Lord Vetch was acting under orders from the High King himself. I was a witness to his command."

Fynn shook his head to clear it. "The High King? Why would *he* want me dead?"

"Because he sees you as a threat to his reign."

Fynn gave an incredulous laugh. "That makes no sense at all."

"It does, actually, if you can be confirmed as Urlion's bastard. Urlion had years to acknowledge Roth and never did." Fynn's confusion must have been evident, for Whit drew a hand over his weary face. "I should have made it clear before now who your father was. Urlion Konigur was descended from a long line of Drinnglennian royalty. He ascended to the throne when he was even younger than you are now, and ruled as our High King for nearly seventy years. Since Urlion sired no children in wedlock, when he died, the Tribus decided the Einhorn Throne would pass to Roth of Nelvorboth. The same Roth who ordered your murder, because of something Commander Vetch said you were wearing."

Fynn would have been sure Whit was making this all up, if it hadn't been for the dream he'd cast right before he'd been taken from his cell. The dream that had shown him, without a doubt, that Urlion Konigur was his true father.

Mamma had spoken his name with her dying breath, when she'd instructed Fynn to put on the chain with the pendant. *You must never take this off, or reveal it to anyone, save a loyal vassal of Urlion of Drinnglennin.*

And High King of the Isle, she'd neglected to add. Stunned by this revelation, Fynn wondered fleetingly if he was still dreaming. He wished he was, but the heat of the fire and Whit's somber gaze were too real.

"Did you serve Urlion?" Fynn asked.

The wizard blinked in surprise. "Cardenstowe pledged fealty to Urlion. My father fought at his side in the Long Wars."

Fynn reached under his tunic, drew out the pendant, and held it up to the light of the fire. "This is what Lord Vetch saw me wearing." His voice sounded far away to his ears, for his mind was still reeling over what Whit had just told him.

Whit's eyes widened. "The necklace King Roth spoke of!" He leaned over and studied the pendant. "It's the hind quarters of an alphyn."

"My... father gave it to my mother when he learned she was carrying me." It felt disloyal to call anyone but his Helgrin father by this name. To Fynn's shame, his eyes welled with tears.

Whit seemed to understand. "I'm sorry... about Aetheor Yarl."

Fynn rubbed his eyes. "He—he wasn't my real father." The words were bitter on his tongue.

"Aetheor raised you as his son. Nothing can take that away from you—not even death."

"I was a disappointment to him," Fynn said softly.

Whit gave a little laugh and stabbed at the fire. "I'm no stranger to a father's disappointment. Everyone fails someone sometime. Did your father never let *you* down?"

Fynn started to shake his head, then remembered the woman Aetheor had lain with behind the curtain in Thorpe, and how he'd done nothing to intervene when his men raped the woman in the shed. He saw again the bright surge of blood from the little girl's throat as she slipped to the ground.

After a time, Whit released a long breath. "I'm not sure I can honestly say I loved my father, or he me. He wasn't given to displays of affection, and what he most often expressed with regard to me was disapproval."

Fynn rolled to his side and propped himself up on one elbow. "Your father's dead, too?"

Whit gave a curt nod.

Fynn remembered what Whit had said about the possibility of the two of them being related. At the time, he'd figured it had only been to win his trust. "And your mother?"

"Alive and well, at least the last I heard," Whit replied. "It's through her that we're related to Urlion. I'm his grand-nephew."

Fynn blinked. "Grand? But that would mean—"

"He was an old man when he sired you. I would say close to sixty winters. But the Konigurs were ever long-lived."

Mamma had been sixteen when Fynn was born. It was hard enough to think of his mother with anyone other than Aetheor, but to imagine her lying with a man of such great age was impossible. His beautiful mother! Why would she have done such a thing?

Whit appeared to be thinking hard. "Do you have any idea what station in life your mother held in Drinnglennin?" he asked. "Was her family a noble one or—"

Fynn shook his head. "I told you—I was raised to believe Aetheor was my father. My mother never gave me any reason to think otherwise." Then the memory of Mamma's expression when she'd settled his Midsommer's crown on his brow came to his mind.

You look like your father, she'd said, and she'd been startled by his reflection in her looking-glass.

Then, when she was dying, she'd tried to tell him the truth. *Why did you wait so long, Mamma?* he thought bitterly.

"It's a pity," Whit said. "It would make it all much simpler if you knew their story. Is there anyone else who might?"

"Only Teca, and it's likely Vetch killed her."

Whit looked up sharply. "Who's Teca?"

"She was our thrall. When my mother was taken to Restaria by my father, Teca was too. She returned to Drinnglennin on the same ship that brought me, but we were separated at the port in Toldarin. One of Vetch's men knocked her down when she fought to stay with me."

"You don't know what happened to her after that?"

Fynn shook his head, remembering how Teca had crumpled to the ground, blood trickling from her mouth.

"And there's nothing else your mother told you about Urlion?" Whit persisted. "Think, Fynn. It could be very important."

Fynn could feel the weight of the wizard's will pressing on him. A memory surfaced, and he heard the echo of his mother's voice. *I wore the jewels my husband gave me on our wedding night... We took our marriage vows before the gods.*

"What is it, Fynn? What have you remembered?"

"My father—Urlion—he married my mother. They took vows before the gods."

"Blearc's beard!" Whit's eyes were strangely alight. "If this is true... Fynn, it means that you *are* the rightful heir to the Einhorn Throne of Drinnglennin."

Fynn frowned. "But—that's ridiculous. I don't want to be... and I *couldn't* be! I was raised a Helgrin! Even if what you claim were true, how could I rule a people I've been taught are my bitterest enemies?"

Whit leapt to his feet and began to pace. "By learning a new credo. This is your homeland, Fynn, not Helgrinia. Your parents and their parents, going back generations, were born here!" The wizard spun toward him. "*I'm* Drinnglennian. Do you think of me as your enemy?"

Fynn didn't know how to respond to that. The whole idea that he was heir to *any* throne was rubbish. His mother must have meant a different Urlion.

He distinctly recalled Teca's words: *On that fateful day, when your mother offered herself to the Helgrins.* Offered herself. Why would Mamma have left Drinnglennin of her own free will, if she'd been the queen of this land? It didn't make any sense.

Whit crouched opposite him. "This Teca—if she still lives, where would she go?"

Fynn took a moment to consider this. "I... I suppose she might try to find her way home." It seemed a strange thing to say; he'd always thought of Restaria as Teca's home, but of course that was stupid. She'd been a thrall there. Here in Drinnglennin, she'd lived a free life. "She was raised with my mother in Langmerdor, but I don't know where. Teca didn't want to talk about her past. Except…"

"Except?" Whit urged.

Teca *had* said something on the ship. She'd mentioned two places, but he could only remember one. "Thraven. They came from Thraven."

"Thraven!" Whit shot to his feet again. "If Urlion married her there, there should be some record of it in the local temple. It would be proof you're his legitimate son!"

"But I don't *want* proof!" Fynn protested. "It makes no difference now anyway. Urlion's dead, and so is my mother."

"Of *course* it makes a difference! You're grieving now and confused, but soon you'll want to assert your rightful claim."

"I *won't!*" The vehemence of Fynn's retort caused Sinead to snort in alarm. She gave him a long look before settling back to her feed.

Whit dropped down beside him. "Listen, Fynn, I know this is all a lot for you to take in. It's a lot for *me* to take in. But it was one thing when Roth thought you were just one of Urlion's by-blows, as his mother Grindasa claims he himself is. It's quite another if you're the lawful offspring of the Konigur line. That's not something you can just ignore. You have… you have obligations to honor, just as I do, whether we like it or not."

He laid a hand on Fynn's arm. His expression was grave, as if what they'd both just learned had added years to his face. "I'll help you, Fynn. We'll figure this out. But we have to keep you out of the Nelvors' reach until we've evidence to support your claim. Your heritage must remain a secret, just between us, for the present. Will you trust me in this?"

Fynn nodded. As far as he was concerned, it could stay a secret for all time.

"Good. That's settled then." Whit stretched his arms over his head. "Let's get some sleep and then set off as soon as the light fades. With luck, we'll make Trillyon in three days." He threw a few more logs on the fire.

Fynn lay back down, his heart heavier than his eyelids. His father might have been a Drinnglennian king, but Fynn would have given all the royal blood in his veins to be back in the manor on the hill, living a happy lie as the Helgrin son of Aetheor Yarl.

CHAPTER 28
Maura

Maura had been in an agony of indecision ever since learning of Master Morgan's arrest. She longed to see the wizard, but any request to do so might be used to implicate her as an accomplice in this farcical charge of regicide. Wracking her brain for something she could do to help the old man, she paced in her chamber until the walls seemed to press in on her. When she could stand it no more, she fled to the stables.

No one challenged her as she galloped out of the castle grounds and on through the Gate of Havard. She promised herself that she wouldn't return until she'd come up with a plan of action.

She headed north across the Tor, then veered off the main road onto a track leading to the Brynglwan Moor. Here, the rocky path forced her horse to a walk. The moor might seem a lonely place to some, but its brown, windswept grasses and rugged stone outcrops suited Maura's mood, and the piping of the rosy-breasted stonechats was all the company she desired. A muted palette of cotton-tufted swards and rust-colored mosses covered much of the terrain, and juniper, sphagnum, sundews, and bilberry grew in abundance.

Maura slid off her horse to rub the leaves of the wintergreen, savoring its scent on her fingers. She thought of her lapins, back in Branley Tor, and wondered who was tending them now, using stores of herbs such as these to treat them when they fell ill.

Riding on, she came upon remnants of an ancient stone circle. It reminded her of the sentinel stone where she'd had her first encounter with Ilyria and she was tempted to just keep going north, back to Mithralyn. *Then Ilyria and I could go somewhere no one would ever find us.* But even as she had the enticing thought, she knew she wouldn't.

For Master Morgan, she'd sworn an oath to serve Roth, who had now imprisoned the wizard. She had no idea how she could help Master Morgan and still keep her word.

For a while, after she'd become dragonfast, she'd felt transformed into someone stronger and more resolute—in control of her own destiny. But she realized now that that had only been because of Ilyria. Without her dragon, Maura had reverted to being just Maura. Not even Maura Trok—lapin-tender, older sister to Dal, and dutiful daughter to her parents—but mixed-blood Maura. *The by-blow of a dead prince from an obsolete line and a deceitful Lurker mother,* she thought bitterly.

She drew a steadying breath of the cold, cleansing air. Her mother's duplicitous past would serve Maura in one way, at least. Maura merely had to tell Roth the truth about her Lurker mother, and that would put an immediate end to her ill-starred engagement. She would be clear of her predicament and could return to Ilyria. She would not forget that she had sworn an oath to serve Roth, should she be called upon to do so, but this did not require her to marry the man.

But she would not depart without Master Morgan. She had to find a way to make Roth listen to reason about the wizard, and if she failed in this, perhaps Asmara could help her. The princess might know of a secret passageway to the lower dungeons. If Maura could speak with him, he could tell her who to call on to advocate for him.

As the sun descended, Maura turned back toward the city. The pale light glinted off icy patches where the bog water had frozen, and a few flurries swirled down from the lowering sky. By the time she'd rejoined the main road, snow was falling thick and fast. She looked back to see that the trail up to the moor had already disappeared under a white mantle. There was no trace that she'd passed that way.

As if where she was right now was where her road began.

* * *

She sent Roth a message, asking him to meet her in the library. After his late-night attempt to force his way into her chamber, and with what she now knew about him and Maitane, she hoped the coming encounter would be the last she'd ever have alone with him.

To Maura's relief, Heulwin returned with his agreement, and shortly before the appointed hour, she made her way to the east wing, hoping the solace of her favorite place in the castle would bolster her confidence for what lay ahead. But when she heard approaching footsteps, she felt a rush of anxiety and snatched up a book to have something to occupy her trembling hands.

Before she could open it, Roth stalked in. He was dressed in a new riding costume, this one in dove grey with snowy lace at the throat and cuffs. If she'd harbored any doubts as to his present feelings toward her, they were dispelled when she saw his cold expression. His face, which she had once found handsome, now appeared stark and forbidding, the set of his lips grim. He stopped at a distance from her that seemed calculated to invite no intimacy.

She clasped the book before her and dropped into a deep curtsey. "Your Majesty. Thank you for granting me this audience."

Roth looked momentarily nonplussed by her formality. Had he expected accusations and tears?

"Lady Maura."

"I wish to speak with you about Master Morgan, my lord—"

Roth's mouth turned down at the corner as he cut her off. "You brought me here for this purpose? Let me make myself very clear: the wizard will burn, and there is nothing you can say or do that will alter this fact."

He turned on his heel, and as he stalked away, Maura felt a surge of angry frustration.

"There's something else," she called after him, and when he did not slow his retreat, she added, "something I have to confess."

Roth stopped then and turned toward her, a spark of interest lighting his eyes.

"To confess?"

"Yes. I… I once believed it would not matter to you, but I see now I was wrong."

She forced herself to raise her chin. "You see, you don't actually know all there is to know about my mother, Daera Trok."

A look of boredom replaced the flicker of curiosity, and Roth slapped his riding gloves against his palm. "Truly, Maura? This again? I've important affairs to attend to—"

With your cousin? she wanted to spit at him. Instead she said, "Hear me out—please, Your Majesty. I promise you won't regret it."

Something in her voice must have swayed him. "Very well. What is it?"

"You know that my mother is not of noble birth. What you *don't* know is that she is å Livåri."

Roth laughed, his incredulity plain to see. ""Really, Maura! What nonsense is this? Do you expect me to believe Prince Storn got a child on a *Lurker?*"

"He didn't know about her true bloodlines. Daera was orphaned quite young, and taken into the service of Sir Drenen of Tyrrin-on-Murr. My father met her while on a visit there."

Roth's mouth fell slightly open, and Maura could almost hear the wheels of his mind spinning. "If this is true..."

"It is the truth, my lord," Maura assured him. "If you wish to make inquiries, I'm sure someone at Meadowbrook Hall would remember my mother. She was released from Lady Harrien's service seventeen years ago to join Prince Storn's retinue."

Roth's expression shifted to one of revolted fascination. "Your mother was his *whore?*"

Maura stiffened, but she willed herself to sound remorseful. "I... I suppose she was, my lord." She was rewarded by the sight of Roth's unguarded delight. *He sees his escape from our betrothal. Now we can be free of one another.*

But then his expression altered. "You've committed a grievous crime, Lady Maura, in lying to your sovereign."

"I didn't lie to you," she protested. "I've just told you the truth of my own free will. I thought... before, I thought it would make no difference, not if you loved me."

Roth shook his head in a show of regret. "Maura, Maura. One forgets your youth and inexperience. But these are no grounds for excuse; I am gravely disappointed. Did you honestly believe that a true marriage of heart and mind could arise from a foundation of deception? Of course, in light of what you've just told me about your sullied lineage, one couldn't expect *you* to act with honor."

"But I have done!" Maura pressed her lips together against more hot words. Getting into an argument with Roth would only make matters worse. She attempted a more conciliatory tone. "I'm sorry I've so disappointed you, my lord. I understand that you cannot be expected to—that is, that we shall have to call off our engagement."

Roth's expression didn't lighten. "At least you can appreciate this much."

She chose her words carefully. "I suppose... we can simply say we are not as well-suited as we first believed, my lord."

After all, this was certainly true. "Then I shall withdraw discreetly from the court, until such a time as you have need of me."

"Need of you?" Roth scoffed. "What makes you believe I would ever again have need of you?"

"You make it sound like I meant to deceive you, my lord. You must believe I would never do such a thing."

Roth scowled. "Once, perhaps, I would have believed anything that sprang from those fair lips. But now? I have no idea who you are, nor what you may be—or have been—capable of." He tilted his head to look at the book in her hands. "For example, I would never have suspected your reading tastes to run in this direction." The hard, exultant look in his eyes made her feel cold all over.

"My lord," she said. "Roth—"

But the king was already headed toward the corridor. "I suggest you keep to your chamber." At the threshold, he paused long enough to look back at her. "I shouldn't like for your deception to become public knowledge through an unfortunate slip of the tongue. I shall send for you, once I've decided how and when we will make the dissolution of our betrothal known. Now, however, I must deal with your wizard."

As the ringing of his boots faded, Maura looked down at the book she still held and read its title. *Tales of Treachery*. Blindly, she thrust it back onto a shelf and fled the library.

Your wizard, he'd said. She'd only succeeded in making matters worse for her friend. But at least Roth had given her warning. She only hoped she would have enough time to heed it.

* * *

Maura stood outside Asmara's door in an anguish of indecision. The princess was not alone; from within her chambers the gentle strumming of a lute and muffled laughter drifted out into the hall. The princess's vows had placed her in cloister, but Maura supposed it was possible other monteras visited her from time to time.

She turned to leave, but the music suddenly stopped and the door swung wide. There was no one on the other side, so she stepped warily over the threshold.

The sumptuous apartment was exactly as it had been on her last visit, except for the ambrosial scent in the air. *That fragrance,* she realized, inhaling the mossy perfume. *I've smelled it before, but where?*

She heard a soft rustling and turned to see her aunt gliding toward her, regally attired in a crimson gown and cloth of gold overtunic, its sleeves embellished with lace and jewels. Her golden hair was twisted under a delicate netting and her cheeks were flushed with color. Without a word, she enfolded Maura in her embrace.

The warm gesture unleashed Maura's pent-up anguish, and a sob escaped her.

"There now," her aunt murmured, "what is amiss, my child?"

Maura drew a ragged breath. "I'm… I'm sorry. I… I don't know what came over me."

"Come to the fire, my dear. There's no need to apologize. You've been under a great strain for some time now."

The princess settled opposite her, her violet eyes reflecting her concern. "What has prompted you, niece, to return here on your own accord."

"I have to get into the low dungeons where Master Morgan is being held. Can you help me?"

Asmara's fair brow arched in surprise. "The low dungeons? That is no place for you."

"You don't understand. It's urgent that I speak with Master Morgan, before… before something happens to him."

Asmara reached for her hand. "You're frightened! What is it, child? What is it you must say to him? Perhaps I can get a message to him."

"Thank you, but I must speak with him alone."

Asmara shifted her gaze to the fire. She was silent for so long, Maura wondered if she'd gone into some sort of religious trance.

"I see," the princess said at last. She continued to stare at the flames, as if something in the flickering light spoke to her. "Very well. If it is to be done, it should be at once." Her expression grew pensive; she seemed to be listening to something only she could hear.

When she rose abruptly, Maura also got to her feet.

Asmara smiled at her, as if they'd been having a light and friendly conversation all along. "It seems there is an uproar in the Great Hall," she said briskly. "We must make use of the distraction. Wait here."

The princess disappeared into the inner chamber and shut the door behind her.

In the sudden stillness, the fire crackled and popped, spilling a cascade of sparks onto the hearth. Maura jumped at the sound. Her nerves were frayed almost beyond bearing, but she would soon feel better, once she saw Master Morgan and had his wise advice to guide her.

But when the bedroom door opened again, a tall, veiled woman stood on the threshold.

Maura felt a sudden sense of misgiving. "Llwella?"

The maid silently held out a cloak to her.

Maura reminded herself that Asmara trusted Llwella. She would have to as well. She slipped on the dark garment.

Without a word passing between them, Llwella preceded her out of the apartment and down a set of stone stairs. These led to a covered walkway beside an unfamiliar muddy courtyard. A freezing rain had begun to fall. The wind tore at her cloak as they started across the yard, and her kid boots were quickly soaked through in the slushy mire.

Bent nearly double, Llwella hurried ahead. Maura caught the mingled odors of hay and dung, and realized they'd come to the back side of the stables. Abruptly the older woman came to a halt, and Maura nearly ran into her as Llwella's fingers swept over the dripping stones. She must have found what she was looking for, because when she laid her palms flat against the façade, a section of it swung silently inward.

Llwella gestured Maura through into a darkened passageway.

A low light sprang up ahead, and she wondered if friend or foe awaited them. Llwella's hand rested on her back, gently urging her forward. With a growing sense of uneasiness, Maura followed the rapidly narrowing tunnel. The ceiling began to drop, and soon she was forced to her hands and knees.

"Is it much further?" she whispered.

Llwella's only reply was a soft, drawn-out "*Shhh!*"

As the walls closed in, Maura felt her heart contract, and she battled a surge of panic. But just when she thought she could stand the cramped tunnel no longer, she arrived at its end and emerged into a circular tower. A steep, narrow staircase led upward; there was no way down to any dungeons.

She turned back, only to find herself facing the hard, blank surface of an unbroken wall. The tunnel through which she'd crawled had vanished entirely, along with the maid. For a frenzied moment, she scrabbled at the stone, searching for a fissure with which to part it, as she'd seen Llwella do on the outer wall, but all she got for her efforts were torn and bleeding nails.

She leaned back against the cold stone, willing herself to calm down. The only way out was up the stairway. Was it possible that this was a trap—that Asmara and Llwella were in league with the Nelvor? She realized anything was possible. *Anything,* she amended glumly, *except escaping from this turret.*

She was a prisoner now, and the one most likely to have consigned her to this place was the man who wielded the highest power in the land. If Roth wanted her out of the way, he had every means to achieve that aim.

I should have returned to Mithralyn with Leif, she thought belatedly. But even if she had, she'd still be bound to serve Roth. The oath she'd taken was as unbreakable as her binding to her dragon, unless Master Morgan were to release her from it.

A muffled thud from above made her nearly jump out of her skin. "Is there someone there?" she called.

There came no answer.

There was nothing for her to do but climb the stairs and see for herself.

Keeping her eyes on her sodden slippers, Maura ascended, silently counting her steps until she reached the landing at the top of the tower. A solid pine door stood before her. Cautiously, she placed her palms against the wood and wondered if she would live to regret crossing this threshold—indeed, if she would continue to live to regret anything at all. At the thought, she wrenched her hands away, but the door had already begun to swing inward.

The interior of the modest solar revealed nothing sinister—a desk, stacked high with books, and two narrow chairs. The floor was spread with fresh rushes, and there was even a small hearth in which a merry blaze crackled. If this was to be her prison, at least she would be warm.

Then a figure stepped from behind the door, and for the second time that day, she was taken into an embrace.

CHAPTER 29
Morgan

"We shall have perhaps one hour, no more." Morgan drew Maura to one of the straight-backed chairs at the table. "After that, I will be returned to my cell in the dungeon and you to your chambers."

The wizard took the measure of the dragonfast maid. He discerned a newfound maturity and poise, but the pallor in her cheeks was concerning, and he noted how slender she'd grown. The separation from Ilyria was sure to have come at a cost to her.

"You have been missed in Mithralyn," Morgan said. When he saw a flicker of guilt cross Maura's face, he hastened to add, "I'm certain you had good reasons for your decision to stay here in Drinnkastel. Which reminds me—I understand congratulations are in order?"

He was surprised by her bitter laugh. "If you mean my engagement, it is newly broken off. The king will make our decision public when he feels the time is right."

So that accounts for her pallor. "I am sorry, my dear, if—"

"Don't be. We found we were not... well-suited." She looked down at her hands. "And there is, of course, Roth's revulsion of my å Livåri blood."

Morgan frowned. "You sound as if you don't blame him. The only thing that separates your mother from your father is the opportunity of their births. There is no difference in their blood."

Maura shrugged. "It can't be changed."

Morgan wished he had time to talk this through with her, but he had more pressing matters. "I want to tell you about how your uncle died."

Maura's fine brows shot up. "Surely you don't think I believe the ridiculous charges lodged against you?"

He gave her a little bow of gratitude. "I'm honored by your trust, Maura. But you see, in a way, I *am* responsible for the manner of Urlion's death. His illness was actually the result of his long struggle against a dark enchantment. When I told him this, he summoned the strength to fight it, and all the memories the spell had repressed came back to him. Alas, the shock of it all was too much for his heart to bear."

"My uncle was under a *spell*? Why would anyone do such a thing? Who *could* do such a thing?"

"Indeed, I hope I will be given the time I need to discover the answers to these questions."

"When I met Roth earlier," Maura said softly, "he said you're..." Tears welled in her eyes.

"I'm to be found guilty?" Morgan sighed. "I'm afraid this was a foregone conclusion, my dear. The High King has already given me the pretense of a trial, and I will likely pay the utmost penalty." He cupped her face gently between his hands. "Come now. All hope is not lost. You are not to allow regret to sap your spirit. You will require all your energy to meet the challenges awaiting you." He gave her what he hoped was a brisk, reassuring smile. "Now. How may I help *you*?"

Maura pushed back a loose tendril of hair. "I... I find myself in an untenable position. It's about the oath I took, back in Mithralyn. Once, I thought Roth to be a worthy man, and that the Nelvors might prove to be a loving family to me. That was before I realized that since the day I met them, everything they've done has been calculated to attain one goal alone—to put Roth on the High Throne and to found a Nelvor dynasty." When Morgan didn't comment, she plowed ahead. "Over the past weeks, I've witnessed a darker side of this clan. They've shown themselves to be ruthless and deceitful. Why, I've even overheard them discuss slitting a child's throat!"

Nothing the girl said was surprising. "What was this child's crime?"

"I don't know. Roth said something about Vetch coming across this boy in Restaria—what is it?"

Morgan found himself on his feet, a sudden warmth in his old bones as he seized her hands. "When? When did you hear this?"

Maura rose as well, alarm in her eyes. "Shortly after the coronation."

"Did Roth say anything else about the boy? Where he might be now? Think, Maura! It's of the utmost importance."

Maura frowned in concentration. "*He* didn't, but Grindasa did. The boy and his mother—she said Vetch brought them back to Drinnglennin because they both spoke Drinn."

Morgan felt a sudden misgiving. Old Snorri had shown them where the child's mother was buried. "Are you sure?"

Maura nodded. "Who were they talking about, master? Do you know these people?"

"No, but it's possible I know *of* them."

If the boy was with his mother, it meant he couldn't be Fynn. But Morgan intended to find him and be sure. Until then, he wouldn't tell Maura that the lad might be Urlion's lawful son—this was too dangerous for her to know at present.

"Thank you, Maura. You may have just given me the best news I could have wished for."

Maura gave an uncertain smile. "I'm glad. But—master, about my vow to serve and protect Urlion's heir... I wanted to ask you—to beg you—to release me from this oath. Under the circumstances, I find it—"

"Out of the question!" Morgan clapped his hands together, causing the girl to jump.

"I don't understand—"

"After what you've just told me, there is all the more reason to hold you to your vow."

"But I don't—"

The swoosh of something black flitted between them, cutting off Maura's protest. They both looked up at a small squeaking bat circling the turret. As Morgan listened attentively to its disquieting report, his newfound hope drained away, leaving a cold pit in his stomach in its place.

"Master Morgan?" Maura laid her hand on his sleeve. "Master, what ails you?"

"Grave tidings from Egydd," he muttered. "They concern us all, but you and Leif more than any." He covered her hand with his own. "You must be strong, my dear."

Her eyes darkened with fear. "What is it, master? Please—tell me what has happened to make you look so grim?"

"Dragons," he said, his voice hollow in his ears. "Dragons have been ravaging in the north over Valeland, Branley Tor, and Fairendell." He paused as the bat chittered on. "Some say there are two, while others report dozens."

Maura clutched at his sleeve. "Surely there's been some mistake. Why would Ilyria and Rhiandra reveal themselves after all this time and go ravaging? It's unthinkable!"

He nodded. "I fear something terrible must have occurred when Leif went to Belestar."

Maura stared at him in disbelief. "Leif went—what are you saying? He went to the dragons? *Alone?*"

"He had Elvinor's blessing, and mine, in the end. Leif and Rhiandra flew north to try to persuade the other dragons to bind."

"And you think he must have failed?" Maura hugged herself fiercely, as if by doing so she could somehow shelter Leif from afar. "I should have been with him. *We* should have gone with him, Ilyria and I!" She lifted her grief-stricken face to him. "This is my fault. If I had answered your summons, this could have been prevented. By staying here, I've lost another brother."

"We must find out the truth before we leap to conclusions, Maura." Morgan meant to comfort her, but in his heart, he knew that if Rhiandra was flying openly over Drinnglennin, this could mean only one thing. Bound to Leif, the bluewing was held to the boy's vow to protect king and country. But if Leif had made the Leap, she was now released from any promises she made when he was her dragonfast.

And if it was the dragons' intention to wreak havoc across the Isle, this was nothing short of a declaration of war against humankind and elves alike. All his carefully laid plans had come to naught. He had prevented nothing.

"Master, I must—"

A scratch on the door silenced her. Their time was up.

"A moment," Morgan called. He put his lips close to Maura's ear and whispered, "You must leave Drinnkastel at once."

Maura stared at him. "But you just said—"

Morgan laid a finger over her lips. "I said you are not released from your vow to honor and protect the one true king, and this still stands. I will explain everything, but this is not the time or place." He inclined his head toward the door.

"I will go to Ilyria," she whispered back.

"Yes. It's best you return to Mithralyn and enlist Elvinor's help in finding the boy Vetch mentioned. But have a care. Ilyria is still bound by your vow, but she may not be in accord with it—"

They both turned as the door swung inward, revealing the tall veiled maid. She beckoned silently to Maura.

With tears glinting in her eyes, Maura embraced Morgan. "I can't bear to think of what will become of you."

"Whatever it is should not alter your path," he said firmly. "Go now, child." He bestowed a tender kiss on her cheek and gently turned her toward the door.

She paused on the threshold. "I will try my best not to disappoint you again."

Her words made him smile, despite everything. "My dear girl—as if you ever could."

* * *

Morgan's eyes had barely adjusted to the dark of his dank cell when he heard the key grind in the lock once more. In the sudden torchlight, he blinked up at a thickset man with shaggy dark hair.

"You're to come with me," the stranger growled, then stood aside to let him pass.

"May I ask where we are going?"

The man did not reply, but once they climbed up to ground level and headed down a number of corridors, it became clear they were making for the throne room, most likely to hear Morgan's sentence formally proclaimed. Afterward, no doubt, he would receive his punishment straightaway. *A nice tidy business,* he thought, *swiftly enacted.*

There was no opportunity this time to enjoy the murals in the Great Hall; the chamber was crowded with courtiers and their ladies. As Morgan scanned their expectant faces, he experienced a jolt of alarm at seeing Maura among them. He'd hoped she'd already be on her way north. Instead she stood to the left of Grindasa, who held the position of honor directly below the Einhorn Throne. Drinnglennin's sovereign sat above them, an ermine-lined mantle of black fur draping his topaz-studded tunic. King Roth wore a golden crown set with rubies, and he clasped a jeweled scepter crested with a champlevé-enameled panther, its eyes, teeth, and claws wrought of gold leaf. A bold statement of sovereignty, if Morgan had ever seen one. Under different circumstances, such ostentation might have been amusing.

As the lord chancellor read out the lengthy catalogue of the wizard's supposed crimes, punctuated by incessant throat-clearings, Morgan gave his attention to Roth of the Nelvor. The king stared straight ahead, but his clenched jaw and whitened knuckles eloquently communicated his unspoken outrage.

Here is someone who could play any role suitable to the occasion, Morgan observed, which made Roth even more dangerous than the wizard had presumed.

Murmurs rippled through the assembly, and he realized Lord Wynnfort's droning had ceased. King Roth was staring at Morgan fixedly, clearly waiting for some reaction.

"I beg your pardon," Morgan said pleasantly. "I'm afraid I was wool-gathering. Could I trouble you to repeat that last bit?"

Wynnfort's jaw dropped. He shot an uncertain glance at the king, but it was Grindasa who exultantly called out the sentence that had just been passed. "You're to burn, old man, in righteous agony for your treasonous act! As shall any proven to be in league with you!"

"Ah." Morgan inclined his head in a slight bow. "I thank you for the clarification, Princess."

Grindasa's lips contorted into an ugly sneer. "Do you dare to mock your *queen,* wizard?"

Morgan calmly met her flashing eyes. "Never, ma'am. I have shown only honor to the lawful queens of Drinnglennin."

Grindasa lifted her chin, apparently debating whether or not he had just done her further insult. But before she could speak, the doors of the throne room crashed open and the throng drew in a collective gasp. Morgan recognized the disheveled young man on the threshold—it was Lord Lawton. Four more men raced in on his heels, all with eyes wild with terror.

"What is the meaning—" Lord Vetch had his sword half-drawn, but his demand was cut off by Lawton's strangled cry.

"A dragon! A dragon is flying over the castle, Your Majesty!" Several of the ladies screamed, and courtiers rushed to the windows to confirm this incredible announcement for themselves. The High King leapt from his throne with athletic grace and thrust his way through the crowd to the balustrade. "There!" A pallid man with a pinched nose pointed toward the north. "Gods have mercy, we are all doomed!"

Morgan remained standing before the throne, but he noticed the young lady from Branley Tor was gone. It was unlikely anyone would remark her absence in the cacophony of shouts and entreaties. Even when the lord high chancellor pounded his ceremonial staff of office on the floor, it was to no effect.

"Save us, Your Majesty!" a high shrill voice called out, and the plea was taken up by others.

Roth stared out the window, his petite mother sheltering in the crook of his arm. Unobserved, Morgan made his way to the windows. The sky was a benign, cloudless blue, empty of any threat.

Until a blur of bronze streaked directly overhead, its bellow of fury sending the frenzied lords and ladies reeling backward in horror. Only Roth, Grindasa, and Morgan remained to watch Ilyria veer and circle the turrets.

Roth's voice cut through the frenzied cries. "Call out the royal army, and all auxiliary troops! Prepare whatever armaments are necessary—cannon, catapults—whatever it will take to bring the beast down!"

The bronze dragoness had not yet loosed any fire, but she would do so if threatened. Morgan had just opened his mouth to counsel the High King to exercise caution when he noticed Roth's attention focused on a lone rider with autumnal hair galloping away from the Havard Gate. The faint echo of her horse's hooves clattered against the cobblestone as it raced toward the North Bridge spanning the river.

THE DRINNGLENNIN CHRONICLES

"I knew it!" Grindasa hissed under her breath. "The little half-cast *was* in league with the wizard all along—else why would she run?"

Roth spun around, his eyes scanning the assembly. "It can't be her—she was just here!"

Several of the bolder lords and ladies had returned to the windows. One of them, a slim brunette maiden, unwisely clutched the queen's sleeve. "Isn't that Lady Maura, Your Grace? Oh, gods preserve her! She's sure to draw the dragon's eye!"

Grindasa's rebuke died on her lips, and her eyes took on a speculative glint. "Isn't there a legend?" she said, turning to face the court. "About dragons and sacrifice? Perhaps..."

Beside her, Wynnfort cleared his throat. "I believe... ahem... my queen refers to the tale of Bryluen of Bronwenil, who... ahem... sacrificed herself to save Glornadoor."

"Actually," Morgan said, "I fear there you are in error, my lord Wynnfort. Dragons have never required human sacrifice. And Bryluen was no heroine; she was a foolish girl who was incinerated when she attempted to steal a dragon's egg from a nest she chanced upon. It was recorded thus in the *Drinnglennin Chronicles*. As for the idea that Maura—"

A fearsome roar drowned out his words, and all eyes followed Ilyria as she soared high above the castle. From this vantage point, the dragon would certainly spy the fleeing girl.

As soon as Morgan formed this thought, the great winged creature shot after the galloping horse.

"Blearc preserve us!" cried the same lady who had dared to lay hands on the queen.

A look passed between Grindasa and her son. Morgan knew what they were thinking: if Maura were to die now, it would eliminate the need to come up with an excuse to put her aside.

He watched as Grindasa artfully allowed worry to cloud her brow. "Oh, that poor dear brave girl!" she sighed, leaning heavily on the king's arm. Roth, taking his cue from his mother, looked gravely concerned. The members of his court edged closer as if to bolster him, although their eyes remained riveted on the dragon plummeting toward her quarry. Even Vetch stood spellbound at Grindasa's side.

Morgan seized the moment. Silent as a shadow, he melted back into the crowd. It was a mere few steps to the Paros; he slipped behind it and into the Tribus's inner sanctuary—the last place his enemies would think to look for him. As he entered this once-familiar territory, he heard a terrified cry rise up from the Great Hall, followed by a harrowing silence.

There was no time to lose.

CHAPTER 30
Whit

Sliding from Sinead's back, Whit felt the throb of every muscle. During the wretched, wet ride to Trillyon, he'd stolen only a few hours of sleep. All he wanted was a long hot soak in a tub, and then his bed.

Mistress Ella, standing on the threshold of the lodge, took one look at him and his young companion and began issuing a rapid series of instructions to the still-assembling household.

"Sigrid, see that his lordship's room is aired and fresh linens are on the bed. The young master...?" She raised her brows at the lad.

"I'm Fynn, my lady."

"Mistress Ella," she corrected him with a smile. "Master Fynn will take the blue room adjoining his lordship's." She cast a glance at Whit, who nodded his approval, and a tall, thin maid spun off to do her bidding.

The chatelaine turned to a pretty, dark-haired maid, whom Whit vaguely remembered. "Quina, ask Cook to prepare breakfast trays immediately, and if she would be so kind as to roast a goose for supper this evening. Hinman, Warf—you will see what else the gentlemen require once they've settled in their rooms."

She suggested Whit and his guest take their ease in the smaller sitting room while their chambers were being made ready. It seemed an excellent idea, and Whit sank down in a chair by the hearth with a sigh of pleasure. He'd passed many an afternoon reading in just this spot. Across from him, Fynn took in his surroundings. In the morning light, the boy's face was all planes and angles, and there were dark hollows under his hazel eyes. *He's in need of nourishment,* Whit realized.

Mistress Ella poured them both a mug of creamy ale. "You must wish for nothing more than to sleep, my lord. I apologize for the delay. If we'd known to expect you…"

Whit stifled a yawn. "It's all right, Mistress Ella. I should be begging your pardon—there was no one to send ahead."

The chatelaine nodded her understanding. "May I be so bold as to ask after Lady Halla, my lord? I couldn't help noticing that you brought her horse with you. I hope nothing has gone amiss with her?"

Whit shifted uncomfortably in his chair. He hadn't thought to prepare for this query. *No, nothing amiss in the least, Mistress Ella. Lady Halla was a slave for a while, training in a bordello. The last I saw of her, she was in Albrenia, armored for battle and riding with renegade Lurkers.* No, the truth wouldn't do.

"My cousin was well when last we parted." His voice sounded stiff to his own ears, but it served to deflect further questions.

"I should have known you were coming, my lord." Mistress Ella moved to the sideboard to set down the pitcher. "Something prompted me to tell Cook to bake this morning." She turned her bright smile on Fynn. "Do you like apple tarts, young master? I believe they're still warm."

Whit found himself smiling. "Even if he thinks he doesn't, he'll like these."

When the pastries arrived, still steaming, Fynn polished off four. Whit was finishing his third when the maid Quina entered the room and bobbed a curtsey. He recalled then that she was the one Halla had drugged before attempting to steal away from Trillyon. How long ago that seemed now.

"Your rooms are ready, my lord."

Whit levered himself out his chair. "I'll show you up, Fynn. If you'd like a bath before you sleep, the girl can fetch hot water now."

As Fynn rose to his feet, shouts rang out in the courtyard. Whit exchanged an alarmed look with Fynn, then reached for his staff. "Go upstairs with Quina. I'll see to this."

He was relieved to find no Nelvorbothian soldiers milling in the yard. Instead, two of the grooms were wrestling with a bedraggled stranger.

"Sorry for the disturbance, my lord!" Flax called over. "We caught this Lurker skulking 'round the back of the manor." The groom paused to get a better grip on the fellow. "Claims he has a friend here!"

Whit was suddenly jostled to one side as Fynn barreled past him.

"He's *my* friend!" the boy cried. "Let him go!"

The astonished grooms obeyed, and Fynn threw himself at the stranger.

"*Grinner!* You're alive!" He was laughing and crying at the same time, and the two of them thumped each other's backs, all the while exchanging a garble of Drinn, Helgric, and Livårian.

"How did you get out—"

"I thought you was dead!"

"You weren't there when I woke up!"

It began to rain, but neither seemed to notice. Flax looked uncertainly at Whit, who dazedly waved the grooms back to the shelter of the barn.

Fynn hooked arms companionably with the Lurker and led him over. Seeing the intruder's disfigured face up close, Whit felt a surge of distaste. Surely Fynn didn't mean to bring the vagrant inside?

"This is Grinner!" the boy announced. It was the first time he'd looked happy since Whit had met him. "He was my cell-mate."

The Lurker kept his head bowed and muttered something unintelligible.

This put Whit even more on his guard. The drifter might well be one of Vetch's creatures, sent to find Fynn, then report back on his whereabouts. Now that he was here, the Lurker mustn't be allowed to leave—but what were they to do with him?

Whit was so tired he couldn't think clearly.

Fynn was still beaming. "Grinner, this is Lord Whit of Cardenstowe. He rescued me when I was taken from—"

"Not here!" Whit cautioned sharply. "Your... friend can bed down in the barn while we get some sleep." *Where my men can keep him under watchful eyes.* "Once we're rested, he can tell us what's brought him to Trillyon."

"In the barn?" Fynn echoed. "If that's the case, I'm staying there too."

"Don't be ridiculous, Fynn! You're exhausted and soaked to the bone—again. You're likely to take a chill, if not something more serious, unless you get into a warm bed at once." Whit was aware he sounded like a scolding nurse, but he didn't care.

"As will Grinner. He's just as wet as we are." Fynn had a stubborn set to his jaw.

Whit felt himself sway with fatigue. He leaned on his staff, too weary to take up a fight with the boy. "Very well. I suppose Grinner can have some dry clothes and—"

"Stay in my room with me?" Fynn suggested.

Whit didn't like the idea of that at all. "May I have a word, please?" He drew the boy out of earshot of the Lurker. "I don't really think having this fellow in the same room with you while you sleep is—"

Fynn gave an incredulous laugh. "Grinner was with me alone for *months* in our cell, and never once did he try to harm me. If it hadn't been for him, I would have died in that horrid place." He crossed his arms over his chest. "I trust him with my life."

The boy's argument was compelling, as was his fierce loyalty, and Whit's own powers of persuasion seemed beyond his reach at present. "Very well," he said. "We'll find someplace inside for him to stay, but once I'm rested, I'll need to question him further."

"It's settled then," Fynn said. "He'll stay in my room." He led the shivering Lurker past a startled Mistress Ella and into the manor. In resignation, Whit followed them.

"Are we to have the pleasure of an additional guest, my lord?" the chatelaine asked, taking in the newcomer's ragged clothes. She wrinkled her nose. "You'll be wanting a bath, Master…?"

The Lurker, standing in a small puddle of his own making, was gaping at the portraits on the walls.

Fynn gave him a playful shove. "She means you, Grinner. Master Grinner, that is."

Grinner blinked. "I'm no master."

"You are in *this* house," replied Mistress Ella crisply, "and you *will* want a bath."

Under her stern gaze, the Lurker gave a diffident nod.

The chatelaine resumed her kindly demeanor. "Very good. May I suggest you all get out of your wet things? Hinman will follow to collect them and bring you a change of clothes." She turned to Whit. "With your permission, my lord, I believe some of your old garments in storage might suit our guests."

Whit nodded a weary consent.

"I'll see that another tray is sent to your room, Master Fynn," Mistress Ella continued, "for—Master Grinner, was it? *And* the bath water." With a neat curtsey, she bustled back toward the kitchens.

There seemed nothing for it but to follow her instructions. Whit trudged up the stairs with Fynn and the Lurker trailing behind him. Fynn kept up an excited prattle as they climbed. Grinner's arrival had brought him to life at last.

"You weren't there when I came out of my dream," Fynn was saying. "Did they hurt you? However did you manage to escape?"

Grinner seemed just as eager to share his side of the story as Fynn was to hear it. "After you went inta that dream o' yours, it seem t' me you wasn't breathin' no more. I thought ye were a goner, and there were no way I were stayin' in that stinkin' cell alone. So I made me a plan, I did, and set up a wailin'. The guards come runnin', and when I tol' 'em ye'd made the Leap, they opened the door right quick. I stood aside, all bowed o'er like me guts was afire. 'Ye poisoned us!' I hollered. The Owl, he went white as a sheet, and the two of 'em dropped t' their knees and tried t' rouse ye. It were then I made me move—nipped the keys right out o' Strawman's pocket, I did, and were out the door and swingin' it fast 'fore they ever marked it!"

Whit spied Quina and a tall, prim maid conferring quietly outside his bedroom door. He hoped they hadn't overheard the Lurker describing his breakout from gaol.

Seeing his attention directed their way, the women dipped in unison. The older one kept her gaze respectfully downcast, but Quina stole an owl-eyed glance at the Lurker.

Whit swung open the door to the blue room and Grinner gave a low whistle of appreciation, as if he was already calculating the value of any portable objects. Whit wondered if he'd awaken to discover Trillyon stripped of its silver and one less occupant in residence. He left Fynn and his friend and made his way to his own room, where he dropped on the bed with a groan. He was too tired to do more than tug off his boots and wet clothes, then crawl beneath the coverlet.

He was out like a pinched candle.

When he awoke, it took him a moment to recall where he was, and why.

Fynn.

He threw back the covers and leapt from the bed. The rosy light informed him the sun had set. Someone had removed his sodden clothes and boots, but he found a robe in the cupboard and threw it on. As quietly as he could, he opened the door joining Fynn's room to his. With a sinking heart, he saw Fynn's bed was empty, although the rumpled bedcovers indicated it had been occupied. Had the Lurker somehow managed to steal the boy away?

Whit was halfway down the stairs when a peal of laughter rang out from the sitting room.

"You don't have to gobble them all at once, Grinner!" he heard Fynn say. "No one's going to snatch them away."

The Lurker mumbled something in response.

Whit drew a calming breath to slow his racing heart. They were both still here.

He retraced his steps to dress, and met the tall chambermaid coming down the hall. She had been at Trillyon for some years, but her name eluded him.

"Good morning…" He raised a querying brow.

"Grelda, my lord." The maid dropped a practiced curtsey. "Mistress Ella sent me to see if you wished to come down for supper. I took the liberty of ordering hot water for you."

"Splendid." At the prospect of a bath, Whit's spirits lifted. He hadn't had a proper wash in three days, and some of the vermin Fynn acquired in prison had migrated to him.

He spent the next quarter hour scrubbing himself clean, then poured a final bucket of cold water over his head to clear away the last cobwebs of his long day's sleep. When at last he entered the sitting room in clean tunic and hose, he was rewarded with Mistress Ella's approving regard.

Fynn was seated across from Grinner at a chatraj board, the same one the chatelaine and Whit had battled over when he was a boy.

The Lurker frowned at the board with fierce concentration. "Can I slide this one side-wise?" he asked, lifting the archer.

Fynn pressed Grinner's hand down until the piece rested once more on the board. "No," he replied patiently, "at least, not by Helgrin rules. And remember—you can't lift a piece unless you're committed to moving it."

Whit winced inwardly at the mention of Helgrin rules. He stole a quick look at Mistress Ella, but she seemed intent on the knitting on her lap. With an inward sigh of relief, he settled on the low hassock and surveyed the board. "Is this your first time playing chatraj?" he asked the Lurker.

Grinner looked up then, his eyes narrowed. "Might be."

"Well, for a beginner, you've established a strong defense."

"It's not bad," Fynn conceded, "but he's no match for me." He lifted his falcon with a flourish, and plunked it down directly in front of Grinner's black monter.

Whit drew breath to protest, until he saw Fynn's discreet wink.

Grinner scowled at the board, grumbling as his fingers twitched above his pieces. "If I move here, you'll nab me serf." He blew a loud puff and his frown deepened. "But if I was t' take yer bird... hah!"

He seized his monter, swept Fynn's falcon from the board, then leapt from his chair and broke into an odd little gambol. "No match, did ye say?" he crowed, and Whit couldn't suppress a smile as the funny fellow capered around his chair.

Fynn was trying his best to look disappointed, but Whit could see he was pleased for his friend. *He has a kind heart,* Whit thought, listening to the silly banter between the two friends as they set up the board for a new game, *and he's loyal to a fault.* He was certain Fynn truly would have slept in the barn if Grinner had been barred from the house. The lad didn't lack courage, either: he'd bravely stood up to his murderous cousin Aksel, and although it could have cost Fynn his life, he'd denied his blood ties to Jered in an effort to protect the yarl's son. Hardly the acts of a coward, regardless that he'd named himself one.

Grelda arrived to tell them supper was served. Whit hadn't touched the tray in his room; he'd been too exhausted to eat. Now he was ravenous. The four of them trooped into the hall, where dozens of tall candles illuminated the hunting murals lining the walls. The Lurker stopped to gawk at them and had to be prodded along by Fynn.

Whit insisted another place be laid for Mistress Ella, and after a genteel protest, the chatelaine accepted his invitation. The goose was wonderfully succulent, its crispy skin peeled back to reveal rich fat and tender meat, and there was plenty of warm bread on hand to sop up the flavorful drippings. The ruby wine from Trillyon's own vineyards complemented the meal so well that they soon became quite merry.

Afterward, they adjourned to the sitting room, where Whit proceed to beat Fynn at chatraj. It was a respectable contest, and the boy's play suggested that, with practice, he'd be a formidable opponent.

Seated together by the hearth, Mistress Ella showed Grinner, who'd shyly asked, the rudiments of knitting. As she watched over his labored efforts, she told him the story of how she herself had learned. "My mother was not the most patient of teachers. Whenever I dropped a stitch, she'd give me a jab in the side. I was black and blue for weeks!" She smiled ruefully.

Grinner looked as appalled as Whit felt at the thought of someone poking the gentle lady with a knitting needle. The Lurker begged her for another story, as though he were a child, and Whit found himself wondering what sort of life the fellow had lived. He also itched to know what crime had landed him in a prison cell with Fynn.

The Lurker's presence complicated things. Whit had planned to leave Fynn under Mistress Ella's care while he rode to Cardenstowe to ensure that all was well there. After that, he had thought to go to Thraven in Langmerdor to see if he could unearth any record of Urlion's marriage to a young woman named Jana. He hadn't yet decided whether or not he'd take Fynn with him, though his gut told him it would be foolhardy to let the boy out of his sight for too long.

But now there was the Lurker to deal with as well. Grinner appeared harmless enough, sitting there with a skein of yarn in his narrow lap, but it would be foolish not to keep a close watch on him. Whit didn't relish the idea of taking the man with him to Cardenstowe, but he might have no choice.

When a bleary-eyed Quina came in to mend the fire for the third time, Whit realized how late it was. He sent the maid to her bed, and the party broke up.

Whit was about to follow the others upstairs when Mistress Ella asked for a private word.

"I hope you'll forgive me for not speaking sooner, my lord. I could see you were exhausted on your arrival, and so I decided to wait until you'd had a proper rest and a decent meal."

This could only mean bad news. Whit steeled himself to hear the worst—that something had befallen his mother—but the chatelaine alleviated this fear at once.

"Lady Rhea is well," she assured him, "but Taggart, her reeve, rode over last week to tell us there've been callers at Cardenstowe Castle in recent days. Royal army. The first time was to inquire why she'd failed to send a representative to the coronation of High King Roth."

"Yes, I know about this." Whit had heard about it from both Lord Ewig and King Roth.

The chatelaine's expression remained grave. "There's more, my lord. Earlier this week, the Nelvor king sent a personal letter to Cardenstowe to formally inquire why our lord had not yet taken an oath of fealty."

"How did my mother respond?"

"With the truth, my lord. She apologized for the omission and explained that you were still away. Sir Herst, the spokesperson for the king, then proposed Lady Rhea return with him immediately to Drinnkastel in your stead." A small smile curled her lips. "Unfortunately, her ladyship was taken with a sudden illness and found herself unable to travel. When Herst insisted she come nevertheless, Sir Nidden dissuaded him from forcing the issue by drawing steel against him."

Whit swore under his breath. Sir Nidden had always been a firebrand, and he'd long borne a grudge against the Nelvors. "Was anyone injured?"

"Fortunately not, but I'm afraid some unpleasant things were said on both sides."

Whit could imagine, particularly if Nidden's bristly feathers had been ruffled. He ran a hand over his face. "What was the outcome?"

"Sir Herst rode off in a rage, and your vassals proceeded to get roaring drunk. At least that's how the story was told to me."

This news was far from heartening. He was still mulling over what to do about it when he climbed into his bed, but the wine coupled with the warmth from his hearth quickly lulled him into a deep, dreamless sleep.

He woke to pale light streaming through the high windows. The lone caw of a crow transported him back to Cardenstowe Castle, where in winter, huge murders of the black birds festooned the bare trees. Halla had once complained about the racket they raised and threatened to take her bow to them. She'd likely been jesting, but he recalled how irate he'd been at the thought of her shooting down the sigil of his realm.

Halla often crossed his thoughts unbidden these days. *As soon as I'm able,* he thought, *I'll return to Mithralyn and scry for her again. I'll have to go to Lorendale as well, to set Aunt Inis's mind at ease.* Depending on what he saw in the stone, that was.

He'd made up his mind to ride for home that very day. He'd just have to figure out what to tell his own mother regarding his wayward cousin's whereabouts. He hoped Lady Rhea would be so happy to see him that Halla's failure to return with him wouldn't upset her too much.

Before descending for breakfast, he took up his staff and cracked open the door of Fynn's room. The youth was still curled in sleep, but the Lurker was up, perched on the foot of the bed. Whit noted that Grinner was wearing a green tunic that had once been his own. Then he noticed the blade the man was slipping into his boot.

Whit firmed his grip on his staff. Had he just interrupted some intended violence?

His face must have betrayed his thoughts, for the Lurker met his gaze defiantly, his pale eyes weirdly flat.

"I would ne'er hurt the lad," he said, keeping his voice low. "I ken ye don't trust me word, but I give it ye all the same. He's like me own flesh an' blood, Fynn is. Ne'er had anyone treat me so... like I were..." He frowned as he searched for the word that eluded him. "Like I were... *worthy*."

Whit blinked at the Lurker's odd eloquence. "He's... your friend. I see that." It seemed Fynn might have the right of it after all, with regard to Grinner's harmlessness. Still, Whit had heard too many tales about the unsavory habits of Lurkers to trust Grinner completely. Especially one with a hallowed chest—the telltale sign of a crennin user.

Fynn rolled over with a soft groan, then slept on. Whit inclined his head toward his own chamber, and after a moment's hesitation, Grinner rose to follow him.

Whit got straight to the point. "How did you find us? And for what purpose? I want the truth."

Grinner shrugged. "'Twere only by chance, my comin' here. Since I broke free, I been headin' for Glornadoor. I trekked through all o' Nelvorboth and thought I were on the road t' Karan-Rhad, but I musta took a wrong turn somewheres. I were just down the way a piece when I heard yer horses comin' and leapt inta the bracken. 'Twere then I spied Fynn ridin' wit' ye on yon fine white mare."

Whit gave a derisive laugh. "You expect me to believe you didn't follow us here?"

"How could I 'ave?" Grinner demanded, his voice rising. "Wit' no horse—only me two legs to carry me? D' ye suppose I *ran* after ye clear 'cross Drinnglennin?"

Put in that light, it made a chance meeting more plausible.

"As t' why I come here, 'twere t' make sure ye meant Fynn no harm."

Whit blinked. "I see. In that case, it seems I owe you an apology."

They stared at each other in an awkward silence that was interrupted by Fynn's appearance in the doorway, his hair sticking up around his head. He had on a frilly lace-cuffed ivory shirt Whit had been forced to wear to his cousin Pierce's name day ceremony. He'd hated the tunic, and when Lord Jaxe decided they'd spend a few days at the lodge on the way home, Whit stuffed the balled-up shirt up the chimney. Someone must have retrieved it after they'd left.

The shirt looked well enough on Fynn, though, who was tall and well-made for his years. Although he was bone-thin, the muscles in his arms and the curve of his calves were proof he'd worked hard at keeping fit while imprisoned.

"I'm glad you're up, Fynn," Whit said in greeting. "I'm leaving Trillyon for a few days, and while I'm away, I'll ask that you and Grinner keep close to the manor. It would be even better if you stay inside, but if you must go out—"

"We know," said Fynn. "We overheard Mistress Ella talking with the household yesterday before you got up. We're to have one of the men with us at all times. And she showed us the crawlspace off the library at the top of the house, in case anyone comes and we need to hide."

Thank the gods for Mistress Ella, Whit thought. Whoever she thought his guests might be, she'd worked out that they were in need of sanctuary. He should have given these instructions himself; that he hadn't done so showed how exhausted he'd been.

"Well then," he said, "I'll be off straightaway after breakfast. See that you mind whatever Mistress Ella says while I'm away." *I sound like my father,* he realized, and for some reason, it left him with a lingering melancholy.

But by the time he was on the road to Cardenstowe, his spirits had begun to rise. It had been well over a year since he'd been home, and in addition to his mother, he looked forward to seeing Wren, Olin, and other familiar faces. He wondered if they'd notice any changes in him now that he'd earned his rod of power.

As he galloped along the forest road with Rowlan in tow, he realized winter was over. All around him trees were in bud, and the scent of greening made the world feel made anew. The burden he'd assumed by defying the High King didn't seem as heavy as it had the day before.

Soon, he would be home.

CHAPTER 31
Borne

Borne stood at the prow as the *joltoras* entered the port of Rizo. Viewed from the water, the city appeared to be a hodgepodge of brick, plaster, and stone sprawling across the coastal plain. The Mausoleum of Zaena, Rizo's crowning jewel, perched above it, overlooking the narrow straits where the Mazarine River flowed to the Middle Sea.

Upon docking, Balfou and Borne left the captain to deal with the harbor officials, and went straight to their lodgings. They found a stack of correspondence awaiting them.

"Here's something that will interest you," Balfou said, looking up from a letter. "Drinnglennin's new sovereign is soon to be wed—to a princess who was raised in Gral. King Crenel is pleased to learn King Roth's bride-to-be has ties to our land, although he finds it strange the princess never came to court at Lugeneux. This connection bodes well for our future relations with the Isle."

Borne had no idea what he said in response. He excused himself on the pretext of seeing the men were settled, then retired to his room with several flagons of the fiery local *raki*, which he proceeded to determinedly consume.

He woke just after dawn with Magnus's wet nose in his ear, still wearing his rumpled clothes. The golden light promised a fair day, but Blearc's cudgel hammered in his head, and the brightness was a torture to his sensitive eyes.

He downed copious amounts of strong *chay*, a local concoction of water boiled with dark red leaves and mint, then decided to climb to the tomb overlooking the city. He wasn't likely to be missed for several hours; Balfou would be occupied most of the morning with Kurash, the *hazar* of the Basileus's army, who'd been sent to accompany the Gralian party to Tell-Uyuk.

So Borne set off with Magnus, and together they scaled the steeply ascending stairs to the mausoleum. He sweated off the worst of the rough alcohol on the climb, and by the time he reached the top, he was feeling almost human again. A pleasant breeze cooled his heated skin as he wandered through the lush gardens. He found a burbling fountain, from which he drank deeply before scooping cool water onto his face. Magnus lapped at the pool and found a shady spot to lie, his tongue lolling from his mouth.

From this high vantage point, Borne could see that the layout of Rizo was more orderly than it appeared from the harbor. The roads all spiraled into the great bazaar at its heart. On the outskirts of the city were the straits, edged with broad, green swaths, which were irrigated by the seasonal flooding. Beyond these, the land was sere and brown. To the northwest, the long line of a caravan snaked toward the city along the Great Khajalan Road.

Borne felt his heart leap, knowing there was so much to learn and explore in this land.

After the close quarters on the boat, it felt good to be on his own. As he breathed in the scent of aromatic herbs, the stone that had sat on his heart since receiving the news about Maura shifted ever so slightly.

He'd accepted this mission in part because it took him far from Drinnglennin and the pain of his past. In Gral, he'd managed to rise from a common mercenary to a knighted commander of his own corps. He'd learned over the past year that he was well suited to soldiering, and he'd proven that he could lead men; otherwise, Latour would not have recommended him for this position. Borne was determined to do his best to repay the marechal's faith in him, and this posting was a golden opportunity to put his old life behind him forever. Olquaria was a fresh beginning, and perhaps here he would find a place to call home.

He made his way into the cooling shadows of the mausoleum, a monument of shimmering columns and colonnades. Much of its beauty came from the simplicity of its design. The columns supporting the wide roof of the vault seemed to tilt slightly inward, drawing the eye to the magnificent statue of Zaena, the ancient Olquarian empress, at its heart. The legend went that, upon Zaena's death, people from all over the realm gathered here to wail and weep, and the evidence of this stood before his eyes. A glittering wall constructed of thousands of tiny glass jars, capped with silver, gold, and precious gems crescented the Basilea's statue. Each vial was said to hold the tears of those who had mourned this beloved ruler.

Confronted with this physical embodiment of sorrow, Borne felt a dampening of his newly lifted spirits. These days, he tended to avoid anything that evoked strong emotions; he read no poetry and eschewed music. His work and training as a soldier took up the lion's share of his attention and energy, and that was the way he wanted it.

The past was the past. Maura was to marry—indeed in the time it had taken for this news to reach Olquaria, she might already have wed. Knowing this made Borne strengthen his resolve to relegate her, along with Cole and Sir Heptorious, to the depths of his memory. If he was to go forward, none of them could be allowed to reside in his heart.

* * *

When Borne arrived back at the inn, he found the comte eagerly awaiting him with a much-decorated Olquarian officer. The stranger's face bore a jagged scar from his temple to his chin, and the off-kilter set of his axe-blade nose suggested it had known violence on a number of occasions. But it was the menace in the man's hooded eyes that put Borne immediately on his guard.

The comte's tone was deferential as he made introductions.

"*Hazar* Kurash, I have the pleasure of presenting Sir Borne Baxter, herald to his Royal Majesty, King Crenel. Sir Borne, this is Kurash Al-Ghir, *hazar* of the Khardeshe."

Borne had envisioned the supreme leader of the Basileus's famous armed forces as someone considerably less thuggish in appearance. To cover his surprise, he offered a low, respectful bow.

"I am honored, *sayien hazar*," he murmured, using the formal "esteemed" in his address.

Kurash frowned. "I was told you do not speak our language," he said, neglecting to return the same civility.

Borne inwardly cursed himself for this misstep. "Comte Balfou has been kind enough to instruct me in a few courtesies."

Kurash grunted, then turned back to the comte, reverting to his native tongue. "We will require you to be ready to depart at daybreak tomorrow. We shall be escorting the Tarazian caravan that has just arrived from the far east along with your party."

"We shall be ready at your call, *hazar*." Balfou's cooler tone indicated his displeasure with the *hazar*'s pointed rudeness to Gral's new herald.

If Kurash registered it, he gave no sign. He turned and stalked away.

Balfou's color was high. "I apologize, sir, for the *hazar*. I shall speak with the Basileus personally regarding this slight to you, and by reflection, to the sovereign we both serve."

"Please don't," Borne said. "I imagine the *hazar* is merely preoccupied with this newly arrived caravan."

In truth, he thought the man's snub had been deliberate, but earning the *hazar* a reprimand from his lord wouldn't enhance future relations between Kurash and himself. Mutual cooperation was imperative for the success of his mission.

He was relieved when Balfou, after making some further protest about respecting His Majesty's herald, agreed to make no mention of the incident to the Basileus. The two then went their separate ways—Borne to inform his men of their impending departure, and Balfou to pay visits to a few eminent Rizo nobles.

Borne followed the sound of D'Avencote's raised voice out to the paddocks behind the inn. He found his aide-de-camp gesticulating wildly as he argued with a *droma* drover in a mix of mangled Olquarish and Gralian. Two dozen of the humped beasts surrounded them, placidly chewing their cuds.

Upon seeing his superior, D'Avencote's relief was unmistakeable. "Thank the gods you've come, sir! This man says he's been sent by the *hazar*. He insists we're to travel on these ungainly creatures tomorrow. I'm trying to tell him that we need horses, not… whatever these are."

It was the young Gralian's first time to the East, and Borne had observed on the journey out that novelty made him nervous.

"*Dromas*," Borne said, "are the best-suited mounts for traveling in this heat." He reached up to scratch the small hairy ear of the beast nearest him. "This one's particularly fine, with that deep chest and those long legs. I imagine she runs like the wind."

The drover was still scowling at D'Avencote. "Son of a sow!" the Olquarian muttered. "Any one of my *dromas* is worth ten horses."

It was fortunate that D'Avencote's Olquarish was limited.

Pretending not to understand the insult either, Borne smiled broadly. "*Jemilar.*" *She's beautiful.*

Upon hearing this compliment, the drover's scowl relaxed slightly.

Encouraged, Borne pointed to himself and said his name. Then he pointed to the *droma* with a questioning expression.

The drover stroked the *droma*'s long nose. "*Kisa*," he murmured.

It meant windsong. "Ask him if it would be possible for me to take Kisa for a little run," Borne instructed his aide.

Poorly veiling his disapproval, D'Avencote passed on his commander's query in broken Olquarish.

The drover's eyes held a speculative gleam as he prodded the *droma* to a kneeling position. Borne suspected he was looking forward to watching the foreigner make a fool of himself. He didn't care; he welcomed the opportunity to test his seat. It wouldn't do for him to disgrace himself in front of the *hazar*'s party the following morning by pitching headlong off his mount.

Following the drover's signed instructions, he wrapped one of his legs around the saddle post and managed to remain in the saddle as the *droma* rocked to her feet.

The drover led them around the yard, Magnus padding alongside, while Borne adjusted to the swaying rhythm of the animal's gait. Then, grunting his satisfaction, the Olquarian released Kisa to Borne's control. At once, the *droma* broke into a trot and headed out of the yard toward the open country beyond. Magnus leapt after them, but at Borne's command, dropped back with reproach in his eyes.

Borne allowed Kisa to set the pace, and she lengthened her strange alternating stride until she was at a full gallop. She was fast—as fast as any horse he'd ever ridden—and once he'd succeeded in ignoring the feeling that he might fly out of the saddle at any moment, the speed was exhilarating.

By the time they returned to the courtyard, he felt confident he had Kisa's measure. The drover appeared to agree; his previously sullen face was split by a wide grin.

"*Jago*," he said. *Master.* The Olquarian touched his hand to his heart and bowed.

Dropping from the *droma*, Borne return the salute. He patted Kisa affectionately, then turned to his aide-de-camp. "Now you, D'Avencote."

The Gralian blanched. "Me, sir?"

Borne waggled the reins at him. "Up you go, man."

D'Avencote opened his mouth to protest, then closed it again and swung up onto Kisa's back.

Borne pretended not to notice him pitching forward onto the *droma*'s neck as she levered herself to a standing position. But he would have to be deaf not to hear D'Avencote's terrified whoops as they raced over the plains.

To save the man from indignity, Borne excused himself and headed back to the inn.

* * *

The following day, both Borne and D'Avencote mounted their *droma*s in front of the company without incident. The men gamely clambered onto their own mounts, exchanging good-natured banter and curses as they came to grips with the procedure. Borne and Balfou, who was an old hand at *droma* riding, left them to it and rode out to join their escort, Magnus trotting at Borne's side. Borne hoped his hound would be able to keep the pace in the heat. If not, he'd have to find him a place on one of the wagons.

Kurash and his Olquarians waited for them at the head of the caravan. Upon seeing them approach, the *hazar* signaled the advance.

Borne felt his pulse quicken as the caravan began to move. The air was ripe with the pungent stench of hundreds of *dromas* and rang with the jangle of their harness bells. The beasts were laden with clay vessels of oil, bales of silk, wool, and cotton, panniers bearing salt and precious spices, casks of *raki*, sacks of flour, and their own fodder. Many were hitched to wagons with undisclosed cargo concealed under heavy tarps.

"Any idea what's in those carts?" Borne asked Balfou.

"Cannonballs and powder, bows and bowstrings, arrows, crossbows." Balfou kept his voice low as he reeled off the list. "It appears the Basileus is stockpiling all the latest armaments."

"Well, that should come as no surprise. Why else would he request the services of an elite corps from Gral, unless he's preparing for some sort of military action?"

The crease in Balfou's brow deepened. "The Jagars have been unusually active along the border in recent months. Previously they were content to prey on solitary travelers who strayed into their tribal lands, but now the bastards have organized under a single banner and they've grown bold, running forays far into Olquaria's western territory." He glanced over at Borne. "Be forewarned: they're a cruel people, the Jagars. They have no interest in ransom and show no mercy, regardless of rank, to those who fall into their hands."

"Noted," Borne replied, "though I don't propose to get myself captured by anyone."

The caravan followed the shallow Paçay River south from Rizo. The hot breath of the land provoked a thirst, and Borne reached often for his flask of *chay*. The heavily sweetened drink made his teeth ache, but it was all that was on offer, except for *raki*, of which he'd had his fill.

He passed the time comparing his own men, adjusting to their unfamiliar mounts, to the practiced riders who made up the *hazar*'s famous Kardeshe, also known as "the Companions." This elite army's number—seven thousand—had been determined centuries ago so that each of Tell-Uyuk's seven hills had a thousand men to defend it. *Siap setan*—"ready to serve"— was the Kardeshe motto, and they had been the Basileus's steadfast protectors since the early days of the Before.

One of the companions caught Borne's eye and then kept turning in his saddle to stare directly at him, so that Borne was not surprised when the man eventually drifted back to ride beside him. Close up, Borne saw that while the Olquarian had the same tawny skin as his comrades-in-arms, his eyes were as green as a spring leaf and lacked the almond shape of his countrymen's.

"May I introduce myself?" the man inquired. "I am Mir Al-Zlatan."

Kisa's hoarse grunt brought Borne's attention to the fact he'd pulled back sharply on her reins. "Where in the world—?"

"Did I learn Drinn?" Mir flashed his strong white teeth. "My mother was a slave in the *zenana* of Zlatan Basileus."

"Your mother is from Drinnglennin?"

"She is," Mir affirmed, with another dazzling smile, "and no longer a slave. Once I was made a companion, I was able to buy her freedom."

Borne wasn't sure what to make of this sudden confidence. "Does your mother wish to return home?"

Mir blinked in surprise. "You mean to Drinnglennin?" He laughed, wagging his head from side to side, and Borne found himself smiling as well. "She was a child when she was taken by the Helgrins and traded in Olquaria. She barely remembers a life outside of the *zenana*, and still returns to the palace every day to gossip with her sister-slaves." He sighed. "Sometimes I wonder if she wouldn't have preferred I leave her there. But it would have done us both dishonor if I had."

Borne and Mir rode together for the rest of the day. The Olquarian proved to be an entertaining, loquacious fellow, and he shared a plethora of random information about himself. He had over a hundred half-sisters and half-brothers sired by Zlatan Basileus, intensely disliked kumquats, and was a master of the sling. He also desperately wanted to learn how to swim.

What was most interesting to Borne was that before Mir joined the Companions, he had been an *eniyara*, one of the premier athletes of Tell-Uyuk.

"Of course, it was hard to give up the thrill of *yaraket*," Mir confessed, "but when my skill at it brought me to the attention of my illustrious father, I could not refuse the advancement he offered me."

By the time they reached their stopping place for the night, Mir had appointed himself Borne's official translator and language instructor. The Olquarian had also made fast friends with Magnus by sharing tidbits of dried *droma* meat with the hound from the seemingly bottomless sack hanging from his saddle.

D'Avencote, who had remained within earshot of the two throughout the day, wasted no time in sharing his opinion of the man as he laid out a change of clothes for Borne in the lean-to they would share for the night. "I wouldn't be surprised if the fellow was instructed to befriend you by the *hazar* himself, sir," the aide sniffed. "He could well be a spy."

Borne pulled his soiled tunic over his head. "I suspect it's possible. But if so, he didn't invest much time in learning anything about me." He grinned reassuringly at D'Avencote. "I find him amusing, and it'll be useful to have another translator on hand."

D'Avencote looked stung. "I'm sure I can manage that role, sir."

"As am I, but I shall depend on you to perform more important services."

The Gralian brightened. "As you wish, sir."

They dined with the Olquarians beside a large pool of water, the lifeblood of these precious green enclaves in the desert. Platters of roasted goat, spiced rice, and flatbread stuffed with dates circulated among them, which they ate from common plates in the local style. Borne found the food delicious, but several of his men choked on the fiery peppers that accompanied it.

When D'Avencote suffered a bout of coughing, Mir thrust a flagon in the aide-de-camp's hands. "Drink this—it will help."

The Gralian managed to swallow a few gulps. Once he'd gotten his breath back, he asked, "What is this drink?"

Mir beamed. "Delicious, isn't it? *Droma* milk, mixed with their blood."

D'Avencote clapped his hand over his mouth and lurched away.

Mir attempted to follow him, but Borne gently laid a restraining hand on his arm. "I expect D'Avencote just remembered a duty he needs to perform." He lifted his chin toward a circular space beside the pool, which the slaves had been busy sweeping with bound twigs. "What's going on there?"

"A wrestling match, for our guests' amusement. Come!"

They joined the other spectators as two of Kurash's soldiers, garbed in baggy loincloths, stepped into the ring and faced off. One competitor stood a full head taller than Borne. His head was shaved, but he had a full black beard, and his bulging biceps glistened with oil. His opponent was a strikingly handsome man with deep-set dark eyes and long, flowing hair. He was easily a dozen years younger than the big man and half his weight, but from the way he danced on the balls of his feet, Borne suspected he would bring something of value to the contest.

"That's Halid Al-Zlatan, my half-brother," Mir said proudly, nodding toward the smaller man. "He's the current champion."

The match began without the usual pushing and grappling around head and shoulders that Borne associated with wrestling. Instead, the two men advanced immediately into a tight embrace and remained locked. Then they grasped the backs of each other's loincloths and began a slow circling.

Just as Borne was beginning to wonder if Halid had fallen asleep against the giant's chest, the fighters erupted in a blur of motion. The men bucked slightly apart and dropped to the ground, their arms and legs pinwheeling as each tried to gain the hold that would seal his advantage. The bald man grabbed Halid around the waist, hoisted him high above his head, then went into a spin. But before he could slam the lighter man down, Halid twisted like an eel in his grip, forcing the giant to topple to the ground with him. Immediately, Halid went into a roll, using his opponent's weight against him, and in the space of a heartbeat, the bald behemoth was pinned.

Borne whistled and cheered along with the approving crowd as Kurash himself entered the ring to raise the hand of the victor. The *hazar's* hooded eyes found Borne's, his look giving Borne a premonition of what was to come. He was not surprised when Kurash signaled Mir to his side.

Borne had already stripped off his tunic by the time the Olquarian returned.

Mir grinned. "You understand that my lord Kurash wishes the Gralian herald to try his luck against the local champion?"

Borne doubted the *hazar* had phrased his challenge so politely, but he nodded and smiled pleasantly back at Kurash before bending to pull off his boots.

Then he entered the ring and bowed to his long-haired opponent, who returned the courtesy.

When Halid came toward him, Borne spun away. After several repetitions of this defensive move, Kurash's men began to hiss with derision, but Borne continued to stay just out of his opponent's reach, waiting for Halid's patience to wear thin.

At last it did, and the Olquarian lunged low, grasping at Borne's right leg. Borne evaded the move, and Halid changed tactics, grabbing Borne's left arm in an attempt to drag him to the ground. Borne arched his back and scissored his long legs to wrap his powerful thighs around Halid's head, breaking the Olquarian's momentum while trapping him in a vise-like grip as they fell together to the ground. For a breath, Borne thought he had the man, but Halid somehow managed to pull his head back slightly and push against Borne's chest at the same time. Borne still had a lock on the man's head, but Halid executed a sinuous swivel and pressed his body tightly against Borne's, locking his arms around Borne's waist, which the Olquarian began to squeeze.

The air was slowly forced from Borne's lungs, and when he started to see stars, he was left with no choice but to relax his own pressure on Halid's head. As soon as he did, the Olquarian twisted, pulling Borne over on top of him. They somersaulted together, and Borne slammed face-down in the dust, with Halid triumphantly pressed against his back.

It was over.

Halid rolled off and offered Borne his hand. Still gasping for breath, Borne allowed himself to be pulled to his feet, and managed a gracious bow conceding his defeat.

To his surprise, the Olquarian pulled him into a bone-crushing embrace. "*Emas!*" Halid declared. The word meant both gold and brother. The victor lifted their joined hands to the shouts of both their hosts and the Gralians.

Mir ran forward and thumped first Halid, then Borne on the back. "I stand in awe, my friend!" he shouted as the crowd cheered on. "No one in memory has lasted so long against my brother! You've made a great impression with our people!"

Rubbing his aching shoulder, Borne searched the throng for Kurash, but the *hazar* was nowhere to be seen. Whatever the Olquarian commander had thought of the match would remain his own affair, but it seemed Mir was correct in his assessment of Borne's standing. The expressions of the Olquarians were decidedly friendlier, and more than a few of them gave him a thumbs-up.

A beaming Balfou came forward. "My dear sir! I'd no idea you could wrestle so well."

"As I recall, I lost," Borne replied, rubbing his sore neck.

"Well, yes," Balfou conceded. "That was a foregone conclusion against the great Halid Al-Zlatan. All the same, you
held up our side remarkably well."

Following the wrestling match, there was a definite easing
of tension between Borne's men and the *hazar*'s guard. As the
days passed, both camps began to mix more freely. On the last
night of their journey, once the *raki* got flowing, there was
even a friendly back-and-forth of songs.

Borne was almost sorry when the great dome of the
Golden Palace came into view. But riding through the gleaming gates of Tell-Uyuk to the rumble of drums and the clang-
ing of gongs, he recalled what the witch Hinata had foretold.
Your destiny lies to the east.

He raised his eyes to the gleaming colonnades capped by
spreading cupolas, the towers flying the white-and-gold banners of the Basileus. Catching sight of the emperor's sigil, a
snow leopard against the rising sun, a line of poetry ran unbidden through his mind.

> *"A jewel arrayed in niveous dress,*
> *rises above the azuline seas.*
> *Tell-Uyuk—where awaits what you seek to possess*
> *Go forth, and find your heart's ease."*

Borne spurred his *droma* on.

CHAPTER 32
Halla

Halla recalled little of the days following Nicu's death. Palan himself had beaten her violently for denying him the sadistic pleasure of prolonging her lover's agony, but that was the last she'd seen of the Albrenian commander. When she'd regained consciousness, she was lying on a hard, narrow pallet, her hands and feet roughly bound. From time to time, Nemia appeared to give her water and to apply poultices to her bruised body. On one occasion the woman tried to force a vile liquid down her throat, but Halla swallowed little of it.

She was surprised Palan had let her live, though she assumed it was for some grim purpose she would rather not imagine. Still, every day and night during her painful convalescence, she gave thanks that the bastard had spared her. More than ever, she prized her life, now that there was a chance she sheltered a part of Nicu in her womb. The idea that a child might be growing inside her occupied much of her waking hours—and the possibility that the beating Palan had so brutally administered might have killed the baby was never far from her thoughts, either. Halla suspected the potion Palan's whore had tried to make her drink was meant to kill the unborn child, but she had suffered no bleeding, which brought her comfort, although she was admittedly ignorant of these things.

Regardless of the presence of another life within her, she was determined to survive—if only to take her revenge on Seor

Palan de Grathiz. For Nicu, for Kainja, and for her daughter, Yenega, who was now an orphan, if the girl indeed still lived.

Which was why when Nemia informed Halla she was being moved from the Albrenian camp, Halla was not pleased. While traveling might offer an opportunity for escape, she couldn't kill Palan if miles were to soon separate them. When she demanded to see the commander, Nemia only laughed.

Halla pulled on the rough woolen shift and goatskin boots the woman brought her. Her own clothes had disappeared, along with her sword and knife. Someone had also cut off her hair, which felt oddly liberating. The loss would likely diminish her value at the slave market, where Halla assumed Palan was sending her to be auctioned off again. *I don't care,* she thought, as the tumbrel in which she sat rolled out of the camp onto the southward road. *I'll escape and find you, you whoreson, and cut off your balls to stuff down your throat.*

The journey was long and boring. When at last the wagon trundled to the outskirts of Altipa, the driver pulled up in front of a warehouse where other similar conveyances waited. He disappeared inside the low building, and Halla watched with a sinking heart as he emerged followed by a stream of women, bound wrist to wrist, who shambled past in eerie silence to be prodded into the wagons. Many of them bore disfigurements—burns, scars, or raw, weeping wounds. Some limped. More than a few had crude carvings on their left cheeks, marking them as failed escapees. All of them were broken, and pitiful to see. And every one was å Livåri.

The fat driver pushed several women in beside Halla. She whispered to the nearest, "Where are you all coming from, *sohra?*"

The woman turned to face her, and Halla drew a sharp breath at the livid bruises on her neck. She didn't seem surprised that Halla spoke Livårian.

"Many places," she replied in a hollow voice. "I was in Halbera, to the east. When my mistress found out that her husband was creeping into my bed at night, she tried to throttle me. She didn't care to hear that I had fought her man each time he came to me. I was sold the next day."

Halla didn't press the others to tell their stories. She'd already heard too many tales of what these women endured as Albrenian slaves from those she'd helped rescue.

The wagons got underway, headed due west. As they neared the coast, Halla wondered if they were to be thrown into the sea as punishment for their transgressions against their owners. Å Livåri as a rule were not swimmers. She was relieved when the ocean came into sight to see a ship anchored on the glittering water, and small boats waiting on the beach to carry them to it.

But the women around Halla began to keen and wail.

"What is it?" Halla looked from face to frightened face. "What do you know? Where are they taking us?"

The woman from Halbera huddled into a quivering ball, but a girl with burned hands answered. "The driver told us they are sending us over the water."

"To Drinnglennin?" Halla frowned. "That makes no sense. They'll gain no profit there. Slavery is forbidden by law."

The girl shook her head slowly from side to side. "No, not to the Isle."

"Then where?" When the girl didn't answer, Halla shook her. "*Where?*"

The girl's dark eyes brimmed with tears. "To a place from which no one ever returns."

Halla recalled then Palan's cruel promise. *I will send you somewhere that will make the Abyss seem like a paradise.*

The cart came to a halt, and the driver began hauling the women from it. When he reached for Halla, she twisted away from the man's outstretched hand and jumped down onto the sand.

The driver stepped back and made a mocking bow. "Ah, I forgot. Seor Palan told me that *you* were to receive special treatment." He gave her a sharp slap on the cheek.

Halla raised her hand to her stinging face, itching to return the favor. "Where are those ships going?" she demanded, and braced herself for another blow.

The fat man merely chewed thoughtfully on his blubbery lip. "I wonder if you *really* want to know."

"I do," Halla insisted, ignoring her drumming heart.

Beside her, the girl with the ruined hands swayed. Halla wrapped an arm around her waist to steady her.

"Help me get that one to the boat," the fat man growled, "and maybe I'll tell you."

All around them, women were stumbling over the sand. Halla half dragged, half carried the sobbing girl, who had started chanting an å Livåri charm to ward off evil, down to the shore. It reminded Halla of how frightened she'd felt when Bria's baba muttered such a charm after looking at her palm.

The first group of women was herded into the small boats. One girl with a twisted leg turned to hobble back up the beach, but a driver grabbed her and tossed her headlong into the water. She came up sputtering and didn't resist when the man pushed her toward the nearest boat.

Halla assessed the chance of an escape and found it to be extremely poor. *Better to try at the other end of our journey.* She could then carry back with her the whereabouts of all the missing å Livåri. This knowledge alone would be worth whatever lay ahead.

Provided she survived it.

She helped the burned girl into one of the boats, then turned to the fat man. "I did my part. Now tell me—where are we going?"

The man leered at her, revealing the stained teeth of a crennin user. "I usually charge for information, but seeing as it's *you*, I'm going to make an exception." He spat a stream of dark liquid onto the sand. "You sail south with the tide."

Halla frowned. "South? There's nothing in that direction, except miles of ocean, not until—"

The fat man's smile widened. "Until you reach the edge of the Known World." His multiple chins wobbled as he began to laugh. "You've earned yourself a one-way passage to the Lost Lands."

* * *

For the next three weeks, Halla was miserably, violently ill. From the moment they sailed into the converging waters of the Middle and Vast Seas, the ship was either plunging from under them or heaving toward the sky. Each time Halla vomited up her guts, she thought about the child in her womb, her feelings about its existence swinging like a pendulum between disbelief and anxiety. She had no idea what awaited her in the Lost Lands, but she guessed staying alive would be struggle enough for one, and she despaired at being responsible for two. In her worst moments, she even hoped Nemia had been wrong—but then thoughts of Nicu intruded, and she knew she wanted nothing more than to carry his line and spirit on.

Surprisingly, despite the punishing seas, conditions on board the nameless ship were slightly better than those on Halla's first voyage as a captive. The food was certainly an improvement—mostly salted fish or pork, served with occasional dried plums, or beer and beans, although few could keep anything of substance down. Halla mostly subsisted on tiny sips of water and the tasteless biscuits the sailors called jawbreakers. Nibbling these without appetite, she recalled with longing the superior taste of elven waybread.

Mithralyn seemed like a dream to her now. Had she really danced and wrestled with elves? In her weakened state, a faerie could have bested her. But at least she was alive. Several of the women, including Ralni, the burned girl, had not been so lucky. And as Halla soon realized, her spirit was still stronger than those of the other women, most of whom huddled together in silence, their empty eyes expressing their desolation.

"Perhaps you'll find your men in the Lost Lands," she said to Chooma, the woman with the cruel bruises ringing her neck, in an attempt to cheer her up. The bruises had faded to yellow, but Chooma's hands went often to her throat, as if she was constantly reliving the horror of strangulation.

"I pray they are not!" Chooma snapped back.

Halla took a shred of comfort from the woman's sudden vehemence. For much of the voyage Chooma had cowered under her tattered shawl and wept.

Patyah, a year or so older than Halla, was the only woman who'd offered any sort of companionship throughout the voyage. She'd been the bed slave of an Albrenian merchant, and the angry wound carved into her left cheek told the story of why she was on board. It was from Patyah that Halla learned what had been done to her hair.

"Why did you dye it?" the girl asked. "I can see from your roots what a pretty shade of red it really is."

"Dye my hair?" Halla tried to pull a strand of it into her line of sight, but it was still too short. "What color is it?"

"Black."

Black? Palan must have ordered this done while she lay unconscious. Perhaps he'd been afraid her flaming hair would be recognized on the way to the ship. More likely, he'd meant to humiliate her by making her appear å Livåri. If so, it had the opposite effect. In her heart, she was as proudly å Livåri as any of these women.

By the time she heard the call of land sighted, she was almost glad, so eager was she to find relief from the gut-wrenching pitch and roll of the hold. When the chains of the anchor rattled down, she breathed a silent prayer of thanks to the gods. She hadn't seen the sky for three weeks, and the thought of breathing fresh air was almost as intoxicating as the real thing.

There came no order up to the deck to bathe as they approached the harbor, and they were given no new garments to wear. Halla assumed that because there was no need to ameliorate their ragged appearance, it meant there was to be no auction once they were on land. This thought should have brought her relief, but instead she felt only trepidation.

She climbed out of the hold with the others into white, blinding light. It had been hot below, but the direct force of the sun felt like a physical blow. It took her eyes a few moments to adjust to the brightness, and once they did, she felt the breath leave her lungs.

They were surrounded by a forest of masts. Colossal ships—hundreds of them—creaked and rocked around their carrack. Halla's knowledge of seagoing vessels was limited, but from the size of these, they had to be dromons. Ships this big required one hundred men at oar, and were able to carry at least twice as many as passengers. Judging from their armaments—each was bedecked with towers and catapults—they were built for war.

Halla recalled Whit holding forth on the Jagars, the nomadic people of the Lost Lands. They were said to be fiercely private, shunning all contact with the outside world. Little was known of their ways, but the few outsiders who had managed to survive an encounter described them as primitive and brutal. The various tribes sometimes fought among themselves, but all supposedly gave their unquestioning allegiance to their leader, the *vaar*. She'd once heard Master Morgan say this man posed a grave threat—but she hadn't been listening closely enough to remember the *vaar*'s name, or why Morgan thought him a cause for concern.

If the size of the massive fleet left Halla feeling stunned, it was nothing compared to what she felt when she turned her gaze landward to the conglomeration of graceless, densely packed structures under the smoke-stained sky. A cacophony of grinding, pounding, hissing, and groaning reverberated over the murky water of the wide bay, fouled by black, oily liquid pumping from huge pipes into the sea. Beyond the long wharves jutting out from the dockyard, the port was a hive of activity. Workers swarmed back and forth, some manning treadwheel cranes to hoist timber onto wagons, others pushing wheelbarrows, still others driving ox and *droma* carts towering with barrels or piled high with sacks.

A ferry wended its way through the maze of tall ships to the carrack's starboard side. Rope ladders were tossed over the gunnels, and the crew began herding the women toward them. The first to reach the ladders gave a shriek and tried to scramble back away from the gunwales.

"Monster!" she screamed, as one of the crew made a grab for her. "There's a monster down there!"

Halla pushed her way to the railing to see for herself. The hairs on the back of her neck prickled as a hulking creature with deep-set blazing eyes raised its snout and sniffed at her, releasing a long hiss that ended in a growl. Small pointed horns sprouted above the holes that served as the creature's ears, and it was hairless from the top of its ridged skull to its taloned feet. It stood erect, like a human man, and it was naked except for a leather loinguard. Its scaly skin had a gray cast, and its powerfully broad chest and bulging arms signaled prodigious strength. Despite herself, Halla jerked back when it opened its mouth and revealed its dagger-like teeth.

To either side of her, the à Livàri women were being forced down the ladders. Those already in the ferry sobbed while jostling one another to stay as far as possible from the monstrous brute.

Halla swung onto the ropes, then lowered herself into the boat.

"Gods' grace!"

Halla tore her eyes away from the creature to follow Chooma's pointing finger. Toiling on the wharves were men with the blue-black hair and burnished skin of å Livåri. They had indeed found the lost men of the tribe, all of whom looked starved and frail.

Sudden shouts rang out on the docks, and the men left their tasks and scrambled to one side of the pier. A horde of monsters sprang past them down its length, hissing and growling, as the ferry approached. Something about the sounds they made was strangely familiar to Halla.

Before the boat even bumped against the pier, the creatures had descended on it, roaring horribly as they leapt aboard. Halla shielded her head from the flailing arms and legs as women all around her were snatched up and carried off.

As the screaming faded, Halla found herself alone in the boat.

"They've never done that before—refused one of you."

She looked up at the speaker. He was human, although barely more than sinew and bone. A vertical line with a triangle projecting from it like a thorn was branded on his left cheek.

He bent over and offered her a calloused hand. "I'd say you were lucky, but there's no luck to be had in this unholy place. You'll just be made to serve the *vaar* in another way."

Halla allowed herself to pulled onto the pier, trying to still the violent trembling of her limbs, for nothing she had ever faced in battle had been as terrifying as those few moments of manic assault. She attempted a wobbling step, but the ground swayed and rolled under her feet and she would have toppled over but for the man's steadying hand on her elbow.

"What are those... *things*?" She scanned the docks to be sure the marauders were really gone.

The man wiped large beads of sweat from his brow. His skin had darkened to copper under the unrelenting sun. "*Drakdaemons*," he said tonelessly.

"What manner of beast is *that*?"

"The *vaar's* creatures." He released his hold on her then bent to lift the handles of his laden wheelbarrow and began to trundle away.

"Wait!" Halla called after him, but he only quickened his step. She soon saw why—a lone *drakdaemon* was approaching from the end of the wharf.

This one looked shorter and less brawny than those who had taken the women. Its head was larger, but it had the same cavernous nostrils that exaggerated the brutal lines of its pointed snout.

Halla swung round, searching in vain for something with which to defend herself, but there was nothing at hand. Praying the beast wasn't familiar with the elven style of wrestling, she widened her stance, all the while fighting to keep her balance.

But the *drakdaemon* stopped several paces from her and growled, in perfect Drinn, "Come with me. I shall bring you to the *vaar*."

Halla felt her jaw drop. She was so surprised to hear the creature speak that when the *drakdaemon* turned on its horny heel, she found herself trotting after it like a stray dog.

None of the å Livåri men they passed paid them any heed; they remained bent to their labors, their ragged clothes drenched with sweat.

The din of industry grew louder as they left the port and entered a street lined with forges where smiths were hammering steel, tanneries stinking of piss, leadbeaters and lorimers, coopers and wheelwrights. In some, the *vaar's* creatures toiled alongside the men, particularly at work that made use of their brute strength. All the buildings appeared to have been recently erected. The street was wider than any she'd ever seen before, running straight and true without turns, and she guessed this was to accommodate all the traffic moving along it.

Leaving behind the clangor of the workshops, they entered a vast square with mud-brick buildings lining three of its sides. Hundreds of the *drakdaemons* were training here—slashing swords, thrusting pikes, and swinging maces at one another. Halla slowed to watch them, but her guide continued on, turning under an overhang skirting the square.

Reluctantly, Halla followed, but she felt instant relief as she stepped into the shade. Under the pounding sun, her shift had become stuck to her skin, and she was dripping with sweat.

Halfway around the square, they veered onto a street running toward a high, graceless tower. As they entered the building, Halla felt a surge of nausea, and had to lean against the cool bricks, willing it to pass.

Her *drakdaemon* guide, heedless to her physical distress, disappeared up the stairs. Left alone, Halla closed her eyes against flashing bright spots and slid down the wall, her energy spent.

When she came to again, she was over the *drakdaemon's* shoulder, being carried up the stairs like a carcass. She offered no resistance, for she had none left to give. The creature's scaled skin smelled of brimstone, reminding Halla of something her foggy brain couldn't grasp.

The *drakdaemon* swung her to her feet before an ornate wooden door, carved with the same rune she'd seen on the å Livari's cheek. He pushed it slightly open and made a short hissing sound.

"You may enter, Lash," said a voice from within.

Lash. The monster has a name.

The *drakdaemon* pulled Halla into a sparsely furnished solar.

A man sat at a table in its center, his head bent over a book. "What is it?" he said, without looking up. He too spoke in Drinn, and his accent was that of a cultured man.

"A cull, Lord," Lash growled.

The man's head jerked up, his surprise clear on his face.

"If I might speak, my lord?" Halla attempted to balance her tone between hauteur and respect. "I am Halla of Lorendale, and my brother, Lord Nolan, will pay a goodly sum to anyone who returns me unharmed to his care."

She was relieved to see the man smile, until she saw the chilling light in his dark eyes.

"You instructed me to bring any not taken to you, Lord," Lash said. "She is of the blood, and is already sown."

The man's eyes widened with amazement. "She's with child? An å Livåri child?"

Lash grunted, and Halla felt her heart flip in her breast. *How had he guessed this?*

The *vaar* rose from his chair and came around the table, his long white robes whispering over the tiles. The way he devoured her with his eyes made Halla lay a protective hand over her belly.

"You did well, Lash—very well. I shall send you a reward later. You may leave us now."

The creature bowed his misshapen head. As the door closed behind him, the *vaar* continued circling her.

"Lorendale, you say? So you are of the Konigur line?"

"Yes, my lord." Surely he would send her back to Drinnkastel, now he knew her worth in ransom. "King Urlion was my cousin, although removed by two generations."

The man moved to the cupboard and brought out two glasses and a decanter. "Sit at the table," he instructed.

Gratefully, Halla obeyed, for she was swaying on her feet. She drained the wine he placed before her, and was halfway through a second glass when a chilling thought made her set the goblet down hard.

Guessing the source of her fear, the *vaar* said, "There's nothing in the wine to hurt the child. You can rest assured that I will do everything in my power to see that you are safely delivered. Indeed, I will keep you under my own watchful

THE DRINNGLENNIN CHRONICLES

eye." He set a bowl of golden fruit and nuts before her. "First, you will eat, and then you will bathe and sleep. The long voyage must have been taxing."

The strong wine was already having its effect on her brain, and the force of will she'd been exerting ever since the *drakdaemon* had raced toward the ferry was beginning to waver. *This man may be acting the host,* she reminded herself, *but he is the cruel master of this unlovely world.* "You *do* plan to ransom me, don't you, my lord?"

The *vaar*'s rumble of laughter raised gooseflesh on her arms. "Halla of Lorendale, in whose veins runs the blood of kings." He filled the other glass and raised it to her in salute. "Through you, history will be made, and I am the one who will determine its course. I drink to you and your child, for the babe in your womb will give me the means to triumph over all who would oppose me."

Halla felt the blood drain from her face. "What do you mean?"

"Of course," he said, as if she hadn't spoken, "you'll just have to take my word regarding my forthcoming victory." He set his glass down with studied care, then offered her a look of mock regret. "Since you won't live to see it."

CHAPTER 33
Fynn

Fynn and Grinner locked eyes over the chatraj board at the sound of horses entering the yard. Whit had ridden for Cardenstowe less than an hour before, and he'd left strict instructions in the event of unexpected visitors.

Fynn sprang to his feet. "Quick! Up to the crawlspace!"

Grinner started to sweep up the game pieces.

"Leave those!" Fynn hissed, tugging on his friend's sleeve. "Come *on*!"

The à Livàri grunted and snatched up the board as well.

From the third floor landing, Grinner edged to the window facing the yard. "There be about forty-odd men down there," he said. "But it's all right—Lord Whit's with 'em, an' he looks t' be in charge."

Fynn gave a relieved laugh and joined him at the window. Whit and one of the men were approaching the manor. The stranger looked to be not much older than the wizard, and from the way Whit clapped him on the shoulder, Fynn decided they were well known to one another.

Still, Fynn and Grinner waited cautiously, and when the sound of voices drifted up from the sitting room, they crept back down the stairs to listen. Fynn gave Grinner a thumbs-up for taking the time to clear away any sign that they'd been in the cozy room.

"You were gone so long, we feared the worst, my lord."

"I've been… traveling," Whit replied. "Now, Wren. Tell me what's brought you and a company of Cardenstowe men to Trillyon at such breakneck speed? You nearly rode straight past me. And why did you insist we come back here before we could speak?"

"I followed the advice of your wise wizard friend. You must recall how Master Morgan always said secrets are best shared within four walls." Wren sobered. "I've news from Drinnkastel, my lord. Olin returned from the capital last night. He'd gone to seek an audience with King Roth to smooth over the damage done by Nidden."

"And did he meet with success?"

"He thought he did—at first. Roth accepted his apologies on your mother's behalf. But then after the meeting, Olin went to the stables to check on his horse—he's always been like a fool in love when it comes to that charger—and at any rate, he overheard two of Vetch's men talking about how the lord commander himself was preparing to lead an army on Cardenstowe to 'bring the insolent bastards in line.' So I came to Trillyon to leave men here as a safeguard on the off chance you came through on your return home."

"How fortuitous that you did, for that's where I'm heading today. If Vetch is advancing on Cardenstowe with an army, the household here may also soon be at risk."

Fynn and Whit exchanged a glance as they heard the sound of a chair scraping against the stone floor, but no one came into the hall.

"It's unlikely Lord Vetch would think to come to Trillyon, my lord," Wren said, "but with all respect, you should not consider returning home. Lord Nidden says if Vetch advances on Cardenstowe, the city is prepared to wait him out. And…" There was a small silence before the knight continued. "Your lady mother fears this royal army is being sent to arrest you. Olin says he heard something else while he was in Drinnkastel, my lord—a vile rumor."

From the pause that followed, Fynn guessed the man was reluctant to repeat it.

"Go on," Whit said.

"It's said that you're… you're wanted for treason, my lord."

"Yes, I imagine I am."

Because of me, Fynn realized, an all-too-familiar knot forming in his gut.

"You're not surprised?"

"No, although I assure you, I've committed no treasonous act."

"I never thought you had, my lord. That's why I'm here. Well, because of that, and the dragons."

Fynn wasn't sure he'd heard right, but Grinner's wide-eyed expression confirmed there was nothing wrong with his ears.

Whit gave an incredulous laugh. "Dragons? What nonsense is this?"

"No nonsense, my lord. There have been several confirmed sightings. It seems there's a drove of the beasts flying over the north."

"A *drove*?"

"Lord Grathin himself sent word out to all the realms. He's seen them in Fairendell with his own eyes, and his warnings have sparked wild speculation as to what the dragons' sudden reappearance in the world might portend."

"What sort of speculation?" Whit sounded more curious than alarmed.

"Those unhappy with the Nelvor succession, like Lord Grathin, say the dragons herald the coming of a dark age, foretold in the final prophecy of the lost *Chronicles*." Wren dropped his voice. "Which brings me to the last of my news, my lord. There was a council convened last week at Morlen Castle, the result of which is that the lords of Valeland, Morlendell, and Fairendell have sent a formal protest to King Roth over the diminished status now accorded their realms. The noble families of Nelvorboth and Tyrrencaster have been given priority of posts and honors under our new ruler, and there are an increasing number of Albrenians holding high positions in Roth's court, which the northern lords of the Isle deem utterly unacceptable."

Fynn had been so caught up in all he was hearing, he'd failed to notice that Grinner, peering round the door, was actually now in plain view of the occupants within. Before Fynn could pull him back, there was a sharp cry, followed by the sound of drawn steel.

"It's all right, Wren!" Whit cried. "Put away your sword. Come in, Grinner, and you too, Fynn."

Fynn joined his friend on the threshold.

Wren, sword still in hand, looked on them both with surprise before turning to Whit.

"Sir Wren," the wizard said, "as my sworn vassal, I am about to charge you with a confidence that you will honor with your life."

The knight returned his sword to its scabbard and straightened his shoulders. "My lord. You have my word."

Whit turned to Fynn. "This is Sir Wren, my liegeman. His family has served Cardenstowe for generations, and he has my unmitigated trust."

Wren's eyes narrowed slightly. Fynn assumed it was because, as in Helgrinia, proper etiquette demanded that a young person be introduced to a man his senior, not the other way around.

"Sir Wren," Whit continued, "you stand in the presence of Fynn Konigur, whose mother was joined in lawful matrimony to the late High King Urlion. Or so we believe."

Grinner made a choked sound, and Sir Wren's expression shifted from stunned disbelief to what appeared to be startled recognition.

"Can it be?" Wren whispered.

"I believe it can. You can see for yourself the resemblance."

Fynn felt his cheeks grow warm under the knight's scrutiny.

Sir Wren slowly bent his knee and lowered his gaze to the floor. "My prince."

Fynn flashed a helpless look at Whit. "There's… there's no need to bow! Please, sir, get up."

To make matters worse, Grinner was frowning at him. "Ye said ye was Helgrin," he growled.

"I am," Fynn protested. "That is… I was. When I told you that, I thought it was true." He felt a surge of resentment, but didn't know against whom to direct it. "I don't want to be anyone but me—just Fynn."

No one said anything as they continued to stare at him.

"What's this about seeing dragons?" he asked Wren, in an effort to make them stop. "Is it really true?"

To his surprise, it was Whit who confirmed it. "Yes, it's true. I've seen them as well." He turned to Wren. "I'm sorry I pretended not to believe you. I guess there's no longer any need to conceal their return to Drinnglennin. The two dragons I know of—indeed, I've met them—came to the Isle to make bindings. They spoke of discord between their kind over the decision to reveal their existence in the Known World. And then of course, there's the prophecy."

"A prophecy?" Grinner looked worried. "Somethin' t' do wit' Fynn?"

Whit walked to the window, as if expecting to see dragons descending, and recited:

"When dragons return to Drinnglennin's skies,
her darkest mage again shall rise
and thus unleash the wings of dread
'til all the Known World's tears are shed.
Blood of worm and blood of kings
shall fuel the fires around us ringed
by those unnatural enemies
before whom all are forced to flee.
The final outcome of the fray

not even dragons' might can sway.
The Einhorn Throne to him shall fall—
A bitter foe to rule us all."

"I s'pose ye'll be tellin' us there be elves as well," Grinner sniffed, but from the light in his eyes, Fynn could see he was hopeful.

Wren, who had been staring at Fynn as if he were seeing a ghost, finally turned his attention to Grinner. "May I ask who *you* might be?"

"He's my friend," Fynn said. "He was my cellmate in Toldarin."

"Cellmate?"

Whit waved for them all to sit. "I'll explain that later. At the moment, we need to decide on a course of action. If Vetch is coming after me, it's because he suspects Fynn is with me. We can't stay here. But if we can't go to Cardenstowe either, where *do* we go?"

Grinner resumed his place at the small table and started laying out the chatraj board. "Wha'?" he grumbled, when he saw Fynn's expression. "I were winnin' that last round!"

"I'll concede it to you," Fynn said. These men were discussing his future—it wasn't a time for play.

"If the lad is who you say he is," Sir Wren murmured quietly, "it could mean civil war."

Whit looked grim. "I know. But from what you've told me about the northern lords' protest, we're headed in this direction already. I've got to find somewhere to hide Fynn until I've found solid proof of his lineage. Somewhere no one would think to look for him."

"We could go to my grandmother's people," Wren suggested. "It's about as far as you can get from Cardenstowe and still be on the Isle."

Whit inclined his head. "I thought all your people came from these parts."

"On my father's side, yes. But my grandmother, Lady Helewysa, hailed from the far south. She was forever carping about the cold at Tamlow when my mother came north to marry. The entire household migrated every year to her family seat to spend the coldest months at Heversney."

"Heversney? Isn't that in Langmerdor?"

"It is. About twenty miles north of Thraven."

Fynn stiffened, and he felt Whit's eyes upon him.

"That's where we think we'll find the evidence we need," the wizard confessed, "but I can't risk taking Fynn there. Vetch will be watching all the roads, and it's too long a journey to expect we can avoid his men the entire way."

"Vetch will be watching for a wizard and a boy," Wren said. "But if the four of us were to make the journey together—and do so by water—as two knights traveling with their squires…"

Whit frowned. "You mean on the Kerl? The river's not navigable."

"It isn't usually, but with all the flooding this year, it might be." Wren sat forward. "It's worth trying, my lord. And I'll lay my last copper the king's men won't think to search the wetlands for us."

Whit pressed his lips together, clearly wrestling with a decision. "You do know what it means if you cast your lot with us, don't you, Wren? You'll be branded a traitor along with me, and sentenced to death if caught."

"I am your liegeman," Wren replied stoutly. "And I hope your friend as well."

Whit offered his hand for his vassal to clasp, then turned to Grinner. "What about you? Can you play the part of a squire?"

The å Livåri surprised them all by dropping to one knee and striking a humble pose. "At yer service, me lord." He looked over at Fynn with a sly smile. "I tol' ye, me people were mummers. Runs in me blood, it does."

Whit got to his feet. "Then we're agreed. We'll leave ten men here at Trillyon, and the rest can serve as our escort to Aredell before returning to Cardenstowe."

Fynn stood as well, his hands clenched at his sides. "You haven't asked me."

The wizard sobered. "You're right. I'm sorry, Fynn—I should have done so before asking the others. You, more than anyone, must have a say in the decision. Will you go along with this plan?"

Fynn didn't want to go to Thraven. He couldn't explain why, but the thought of it made the knot in his stomach tighten.

Grinner seemed to sense his reluctance, for he reached over and laid his thin hand on Fynn's arm, a rare gesture for him. "Do ye ken what ye said t' me back in that shitehole in Toldarin? That if we was t' ev'r get out, I should try an' find me people? And when I said 'twere no use—they'd have long fergotten me—ye said, 'Family ne'er fergets.' Well, I reckon there's sumbody who'll want t' know ye, and wha' become o' yer ma, down there in Thraven."

Fynn thought of Mamma, and how much she'd loved him. She'd kept a terrible secret from him, but she'd done it to protect him, to shelter him from harm. Perhaps her own mother still lived, and her father as well. His grandparents. Maybe they'd spent the last thirteen years in the anguish of not knowing what had become of their child, just as he had wondered about Aetheor and Jered since the day he left Restaria.

And there was Teca, too. She'd always cared for him, shown him such selfless love. Didn't he owe it to her to find *her* people, and tell them what a fine, brave woman she had become?

"All right," he said, releasing his fists. "We go to Thraven."

* * *

They left Trillyon that afternoon, along with the company of Cardenstowe men that Wren had brought with him. A fine mist fell from low clouds that hung over the spreading oaks and lindens lining the road as they set out.

They hadn't traveled far when Fynn heard the hoot of an owl, which was odd considering the time of day. He was just turning to Grinner to comment on this when a troop of men in silver cloaks burst out of the forest and plunged into their midst, swords drawn and steel glinting. Fynn and Grinner, riding in the center, were shielded from the initial onslaught, but at the fore, Whit and Sir Wren had barely time to draw their swords before they were engaged in a fight for their lives.

Fynn wrested his own blade out of its scabbard, his heart pounding at the prospect of his first battle. But he was hemmed in by the men of Cardenstowe, who seemed intent on keeping their horses between him and their assailants.

Over the clash of swords, he heard Whit shout his name. The wizard wheeled Sinead and began fighting his way toward him.

"With me, Grinner!" Fynn called, and the two of them pressed their mounts toward Whit.

All around them, men were falling. One of the attackers, hacking at Whit's vassals savagely with his axe, broke through their protective ranks and bore down on Fynn. The man came on so fast, all thought fled Fynn's mind, except the realization that he'd never trained for battle on horseback. Desperately he swung his sword.

It cut through empty air.

The man smiled, but instead of burying his axe in Fynn's skull, he reached for the bridle of Fynn's horse.

A knife whizzed past Fynn's ear to find its mark in the unprotected space between the axeman's helm and his mail. The bright spurt of blood from the death blow made Fynn's stomach flip, and hot bile surged into his mouth. Out of the corner of his eye, he saw Grinner leaping from his horse, presumably to retrieve the weapon from the axeman, who had fallen from his mount and slumped to the ground.

A big man surged up on Fynn's left, a full wiry beard and black hair springing from beneath his helm, the point of his flat blade directed at Fynn's throat. "Put up your sword, and I'll spare you," he growled. "It makes little difference to me if you don't—Lord Vetch's reward for a young fellow traveling with Lord Whit will be paid dead or alive."

Before Fynn could react, the man's horse reared with a terrible scream of pain. Fynn's would-be captor dropped his sword arm and fought to keep his seat. Fynn seized the opportunity to drive his own horse past him toward Grinner, who had clambered back into his saddle, the hilt of his bloody knife between his teeth.

The å Livåri jerked his head, signaling for Fynn to follow him, and they pressed in Whit's direction.

The wizard had made little progress toward them. Worse, it seemed he'd lost his sword and was now using his staff in an attempt to clear the enemy blocking his path. He swung it back and forth with lightning speed, sparks flew from the rod as Whit brought it crashing down against his opponent's sword, knocking it out of the man's hands. In the next breath, the wizard drove the butt of the staff hard into the man's chest, sending him backward off his horse.

Sir Wren fought beside his lord, slashing and parrying with practiced confidence. Still, when Fynn swept his eyes over the fray, he felt a wave of despair, for it was clear their opponents had the advantage. The silver cloaks outnumbered the Cardenstowe men at least two to one, and half of the escort from Trillyon had already been cut down. In the coming moments, Fynn's friends would die—because of him—and he had yet to strike a single blow in his own defense.

With a roar that was half anguish, half fury, Fynn spurred his horse past Grinner's, riding straight for one of the silver cloaks. At the point of impact, the man raised his shield and slammed it into Fynn's. The force of it jarred Fynn's arm, but he managed to keep hold of his shield and ram it forward, forcing his opponent's shield left and exposing the chink in the man's mail under the arm.

He stabbed his blade into his attacker's armpit, cutting through sinew and flesh, and the knight recoiled with a groan, a river of blood streaming from his wound. Fynn swallowed the vomit rising in his throat, pulled his sword back, and finished the man off with a slash to the neck.

Yet even as the knight went down, another took his place, wielding an axe and aiming a downward blow at Fynn's head. Fynn lifted his shield to parry it, then felt a powerful *wuff* of air rush past him. The man shot backward from his saddle, his axe flying from his grip, and collided with another horseman. The two men toppled to the ground.

Then Whit, with his staff upraised and a stricken expression on his face, surged up at Fynn's side

"This way!" the wizard cried, then spurred Sinead forward.

"Grinner?" Fynn called.

"Right behind ye! Follow Lord Whit!"

Fynn did as he was told. Just ahead of him, Whit stood in his stirrups, driving Sinead on with his knees as he thrust the butt of his stave into an oncoming attacker, fighting to clear a path out of the chaos. Grinner drew even with Fynn, raising his shield to ward off a descending blade aimed at Fynn's head. The fighting was at extremely close quarters now, and Fynn realized their opponents were deliberately pressing in from all sides. He couldn't see any of the Cardenstowe men; it seemed they had all perished.

A silver cloak lunged at Fynn, burying his axe in Fynn's shield. A tug of war ensued as the warrior strove to retain his weapon and Fynn his means of defense. When the axe head at last came free, its owner was momentarily thrown off balance.

Fynn seized the chance to thrust his sword hard against the man's chest, knocking him off his mount.

Fynn whipped his head around at a grunt from Grinner. A silver cloak, his smile mocking, was holding his sword point at the å Livåri's throat. "Throw down your weapon," he called to Fynn, "and the Lurker liv—"

A stave whirled past Fynn's head and slammed into the man's windpipe, killing him instantly, then spun back into Whit's hands.

The wizard reached over and dragged Fynn onto Sinead's broad back. When Wren came charging up, Whit seized the reins from his startled vassal's hands. "Take the å Livåri on your horse with you, Wren, and whatever you do, all of you stay quiet and close!"

As soon as Grinner leapt from his horse's back onto Wren's, the world went grey, and Fynn realized Whit had cast his shadow over both horses.

Without warning, the wizard pulled Sinead into a rear. Her lethal hooves flailed at the air, striking out at frightened horses and horsemen alike. They fell back from the invisible threat, and in doing so, opened a way out of the fray. Whit drove both horses through it, and in seconds, they were clear of their attackers.

As they raced down the road, Whit raised his staff, pointed it behind them, and shouted, "*Taear, trowch y do thoil é, os yw'n pocaslyn!*"

The sound of pursuing hooves was replaced by shouts of anger and fear. Through the haze of the shadow cloaking them, Fynn saw men pitching headlong off their mounts, their horses scrambling to find purchase on solid ground that had suddenly turned to a mire.

It was almost enough to stop the pursuit, but not quite. One rider had made it free of the muck and was pounding after them.

Color started to bleed back into Fynn's vision, and he realized that Whit's magic must be fading.

Whit spurred Sinead on, but she was carrying two riders and could not outrun their lone pursuer. Fynn turned to look back just as the silver-cloaked man behind them threw a war hammer, sending it spiraling toward Fynn. But in the second before it delivered his death, he heard a whisper pass from Whit's lips.

The hammer suddenly reversed direction and went spiraling back to bury itself in its owner's chest.

Fynn flashed a look at the wizard, who was paler than the moon.

They raced on.

* * *

Whit didn't slow their pace until they had put a few miles between them and the scene of the ambush. They turned onto the southern road, riding at a steady canter for Avedell, and they reached the river port just after dark. While Wren went to procure a boat, Whit hurried Fynn and Grinner past the watering holes favored by rivermen to a grubby pub called the Olde Rushes Inn.

Fynn consumed the lukewarm pasties of grizzled meat set before him, and washed them down with sour ale, but the victuals sat in his stomach like a stone. Flashes of the battle, and his woeful part in it, kept coming to mind. Grinner went at his food with his usual gusto, but the á Livári was quieter than Fynn ever recalled him being. As for Whit, it seemed as if the fight and ensuing flight had sapped his strength. He looked ill and shaken in the flickering firelight.

It was only when the wizard went to relieve himself that Fynn learned the true reason for his grave appearance.

"'E's in for it now, I'd say," Grinner muttered. "Though if 'e hadn't stopped that axe, ye'd be dinin' across the Abyss this night."

Fynn frowned. "What do you mean—in for it?"

"'E's gone an' broken the Code, Lord Whit has. It's an oath all wizards on the Isle's made to swear. I ken it from a play I seen once at a Gatherin' down in Glornadoor. Wizards in Drinnglennin been bound by it since King Owain's day. Whit used magic t' kill t'day. Only time a wizard's allowed t' do that is when it's in defense o' hisself or in the name o' the king. Different story, o' course, if it's duelin' another wizard."

"But he saved my life," Fynn protested.

"Aye, but they was king's guards what ambushed us. Now Whit's given the High King just th' glue 'e needs t' make the charge o' treason again' Lord Whit stick, and ye can bet yer ol' gran that once them wizards on the Tribus hear what happened…" Grinner shook his head. "I reckon 'e's done fer."

CHAPTER 34
Maura

Maura raced through the castle, her footsteps ringing on the marble floors. If she could find a way out of the city and into the open where Ilyria could easily see her, perhaps she would get to the dragon before Roth loosed his army.

She plunged down the wide steps leading to the main courtyard, then jolted to a halt.

A tall, veiled figure blocked her path. Her hand snaked out and grasped Maura's wrist.

Maura recognized Llwella's earthy green scent. "Let me go!" she cried, struggling to break free. But the woman's iron grip held her fast.

"Be still." The maid pulled Maura toward a shadowed alcove. Her voice was low but commanding. "I'm here to help you."

"If you wish to help me, you must release me," Maura protested. "I have to get out of the city at once!"

"And so you shall, as long as you do exactly as I say. Do you understand?"

From the courtyard came shouts and the blare of battle trumpets. Maura felt cold with dread; she would never reach Ilyria before the army rode out. Even if she made it to the gate, she would likely be challenged, then marched back to Roth. She had no choice but to accept whatever help Llwella had on offer.

"I understand. But please, hurry!"

Llwella opened her cloak and enclosed Maura within its folds. Maura felt the woman's slow, steady heartbeat against her cheek, then her breath was stolen from her lungs as they skimmed across the ground in a blur of speed.

When they came to an abrupt stop, Maura was suddenly alone under the cloak. She threw it off to discover she was outside the Havard Gate, a saddled palfrey standing beside her.

"How did you—?"

She turned to empty air. Llwella was nowhere to be seen.

There was no time to wonder where the maid had disappeared to, or by what means she'd brought Maura beyond the castle walls. The city gate was grinding open behind her. At any moment now, the High King's army would gallop through it, intent on killing Ilyria.

Maura snatched up the cloak from where it had fallen at her feet, fastened it on, then leapt onto the palfrey. As she galloped across the Tor, scanning the sky for the bronze dragon, the drumming of hoofbeats informed her the army was on her heels. She *had* to get to Ilyria before they did.

Ahead, the trail veered north off the main road. Whichever direction she rode, she would be in plain sight of the soldiers.

Raising her face to the sky, she called to Ilyria.

The rumble of the cannons was her only answer.

I can't lose her—not this way.

Maura dug her heels into the palfrey's flanks, and they pounded up the northward trail. "*Ilyria!*" she cried, and her heart leapt when, at last, a bronze blur shot over the turrets of Drinnkastel, a stream of swirling air in the dragon's wake.

Maura pulled hard on the reins, slipped from the palfrey's back, and waved her arms above her head. "Here I am! Here, Ilyria!"

The horse shied as the dragon's shadow fell over them, then with a frantic whinny it bolted away across the Tor.

Maura shielded her eyes to gaze up at the magnificent dragon, her scales glinting in the light. Despite her dread, Maura's heart leapt at the sight of her after so long.

Ilyria shot toward her like an arrow loosed from a bow. For a heart-stopping moment, the memory of the first time the dragon dropped from the sky above Maura came rushing back, and she felt a flicker of misgiving.

A cannon boomed, then another, sending up a billow of smoke. The dragoness burst through the brume, diving toward her.

"Hurry!" Maura cried. "Oh, please don't let them hurt you!"

A barrage of cannon fire burst behind her, as if the whole of Roth's arsenal had been ignited. Ilyria suddenly swerved, hung suspended on the air…

… and with a roar of pain and fury, she began to cartwheel earthward.

"*No!*"

Maura scrambled over the rough terrain, desperate to reach the place where her beloved Ilyria must come crashing down. The cannons fell silent, but the sulfuric stink of black powder still burned her throat. She stumbled and fell to her knees, half-blinded by her tears, her eyes fastened on the falling dragon. *You will not look away,* she commanded herself. *You will be with her until the end.*

Ilyria tumbled toward her, and Maura braced for the moment when her beautiful dragon would crash to the ground.

But just before she struck the earth, Ilyria swooped into flight, shooting toward Maura at terrifying speed. With a choked cry, Maura levered herself to her feet. As Ilyria dipped her right wing, Maura grasped hold and flung herself onto the dragon's back. Her breath was torn from her lungs by the speed of flight, but the familiar feel of the smooth, cool scales felt like home.

As Ilyria shot across the Tor, Maura felt a great weight fall away, a weight she'd born all these long months of separation. She was leaving Drinnkastel at last, and the greater the distance between her and the capital, the better. Her heart sang to be reunited with her dragon, and with each powerful beat of Ilyria's wings, an accompanying refrain echoed in Maura's thoughts: *Never again shall we be parted.*

Once they entered the clouds, she had no idea in which direction they were heading, and it didn't matter. She felt a bubble of laughter well up at the dragon's guile, which had enabled her to evade an entire army.

Never try to match wits with a dragon, she thought gleefully, as Ilyria soared onward across the sky.

* * *

They flew on for long hours, only emerging from the cold clouds after night fell. As they descended through the inky dark, Maura caught flashes of cresting waves and a dark isle rising from the sea.

Ilyria glided onto a stretch of beach bordered by the hulking shadows of bluffs. Maura slid from her back, but kept her hand on the dragon's neck, reluctant to lose physical contact with her. They had been parted so long—too long.

When the dragon turned her golden gaze on her, Maura searched for words to express how very sorry she was for their protracted separation. She prepared herself for recriminations, but instead Ilyria merely said, "We must conceal you, and then I will feed."

The dragon trundled up the beach, leaving Maura staring after her, until an impatient hiss spurred her to follow.

Running to the dragon's side, she said, "I want to tell you how—"

Ilyria's quelling look silenced her.

Maura swallowed hard and walked beside the dragon in contrite silence after that.

When Illyria disappeared into a hollow in the cliff face, Maura followed her into a large cavern illuminated by pale moonlight flooding through a gap high above. The cave's rough walls glistened with sparkling flecks of crystal, as if the earth had captured stars from the heavens.

Maura let out a slow breath at its beauty. "Where are we?"

"Dogg Island. It has been centuries since I was last here."

"You mean you've sheltered in this cavern before?"

Ilyria regarded her steadily. "Child, I am an ancient creature. We were not always confined to the cold, cruel north. Once, dragons ranged over every part of the Known World, and over the Vast Sea to the Beyond as well. There are few, if any, places I have not seen." Her golden eyes held a look of remembrance. "I bore my last clutch in this cavern."

Maura had never considered the possibility that her dragoness was a mother. "You have children, Ilyria?"

Ilyria turned her gaze away and looked out toward the hidden sea. "Had. They all perished in the Purge."

"I—I'm so sorry. I can't imagine how terrible that must have been for you."

"I mourn them still."

Maura understood, for her own sadness over Dal's death would remain with her always, and she had witnessed how Cormac's grief had shrouded him in a mantle of torment.

The dragon stretched like a great cat, exhaling a thin stream of smoke. "It comforts me to return here, and to remember happier days." Seeing Maura's expression, she asked, "Does this surprise you? Dragons experience all the same emotions as humans do; we just have a different way of expressing them."

"Yes, of course I know you have feelings!" Maura felt her face flush. "I expect you must have been so disappointed in me... when I didn't come back to Mithralyn with Leif. I didn't mean to hurt you, but I was confused at the time... about what was the right thing to do. I know now it was foolish to ignore Master Morgan's summons."

She looked down at her hands, fearing what she would see in the dragon's eyes. But when a low rumble rose in Ilyria's throat, Maura lifted her head sharply.

"Are you *laughing*?"

"A little. Did you expect me to chastise you?"

"A little," Maura confessed, although what she'd really expected was anger of dragon-sized proportions.

"I am reminded that you are newly dragonfast, and have much to learn of what this means."

"That's very true. But I want to assure you how precious our binding is to me. I haven't done a very good job of demonstrating this up until now, but I promise you I won't ever leave—"

The dragon snorted. "You mistake me, child. Being bound does not mean we must be literally yoked together for the term of your life. There have been bindlings who went years without an encounter with their dragons. Dragonfastness is not like a love affair that needs its flames stoked with pretty words or tokens of affection to keep it viable. It does not require vigilant attendance. It runs deeper than this. It's something we've become, something more—something greater—than you or me. A binding such as we share will always stand the test of time, even if we are long apart."

"But I missed you so!" Maura blurted out. "In Drinnkastel, for months after I left you, I longed to be with you so much it made me ill. Didn't you miss me at all?"

The rumbling this time was of a different nature. "Of course I did! But you were following your life's path, as we all must do. I could not hold your absence against you."

The stiffness of this last comment made Maura wonder if the dragon was telling her the whole truth. But she was so relieved not to have to face Ilyria's censure, she accepted her words at face value. "I wished I'd known that. And I'm glad you didn't suffer as I did. But then, what made you decide to come for me now? Was it because of Leif? Or because the other dragons have left Belestar? What has happened to—"

The dragon rose. "I must hunt and find you something to eat as well. After we rest, you shall learn all that I know."

Ilyria's abruptness worried Maura, but she knew there was no use in pressing her to speak until she was ready. "You needn't bother about food for me," she said. During the flight, she had discovered a folded cloth in the pocket of her cloak, containing a wedge of cheese, a crust of bread, and a small flask of cider. She produced it now. "That's odd. I broke off a hunk of the cheese earlier, but it looks perfectly whole now."

Ilyria sniffed at the cloak. "Where did you get this garment?"

Maura told her how Llwella had transported her out of the castle walls wrapped within the cloak, then left her with it. As she spoke, she idly returned her hand to her pocket, then gasped. "Look at this!" she cried, drawing forth a furred fruit. "I was just thinking how much I'd like a peach!"

Ilyria looked wary. "The dark faeries used to weave such garments. I advise you to exercise caution with this one. Its offerings do not usually come without a price."

Maura took a moment to digest this, recalling all the faerie stories she'd heard about the perils that befell foolish folk who dabbled in magic. It seemed incredible that Llwella would have relinquished such a precious thing to her.

She stared at the peach, wondering if it was safe to eat. The cheese she'd nibbled hadn't done her any harm. *You are dragonfast*, she reminded herself. *Be bold.*

She bit into the fruit, and its sweet juice filled her mouth.

* * *

Maura woke to the sound of barking. Bright sunlight streamed into the cave. She was alone, and she had no idea whether Ilyria had been gone all night, or had returned from her feed and left again.

The barking grew louder and more urgent. Maura wondered if there were actual wild dogs on Dogg Island, perhaps abandoned by sailors who'd come ashore to forage, or washed up from a shipwreck against the reef. Then it occurred to her that what she heard could be dogs with masters—hunting dogs, seeking a mixed-blood maiden wanted by the High King across the Erolin Sea.

It was possible. She wouldn't put it past Roth to put a price on her head for stealing away on the dragon he'd vowed to slay. But it was unlikely anyone would come all the way to Dogg Island to look for them—and certainly not so soon.

She ran her hands through her disheveled curls, then grinned when she felt in the pocket of her cloak and found a comb. She did her best to tame her hair and weave it into a loose braid before pulling her cloak close and stepping out into the crisp morning air.

Prior to becoming dragonfast, Maura had never seen the sea, but on her flights with Ilyria, she'd grown to love its capricious nature. This morning the tide was low, the beach littered with long spirals of wrack. Seabirds hopped across the sand between slick dark boulders or bobbed like miniature boats on the turning tide. Gulls hovered, diving into the waves in search of their breakfast. There was no sign of dogs, but she could still hear the strange single-note barking, occasionally punctuated by low belching sounds.

Her hand crept to her pocket to find the blade she'd envisioned. Feeling more confident with it in her grasp, she walked toward the shoreline, seeking the source of the clamor.

She sensed Ilyria was near, and looked up to see the dragon skimming over the bay toward her. The barking surged to a frenzy as the dark boulders at the water's edge heaved to life and lurched into the shallows on wide, wedged feet. Maura's startled cry turned to laughter when she realized they were sea lions.

Ilyria must have already fed well, for she ignored the fleeing creatures and glided to a landing, greeting Maura with a warm breath on her face.

"You look rested," the dragoness said approvingly.

"I slept better than I have in months. I'm ready for whatever the day may bring."

"More travel, I fear, and we must leave here shortly. But first, we will speak. I would feel better if we did so closer to the cave."

When they were settled at the mouth of the cavern, Ilyria proceeded. "I promised to tell you what I know and why I came for you. I'm not sure if you're aware that when Leif returned to Mithralyn, he and Rhiandra decided to go north to Belestar to urge my siblings to reveal their existence and bind again."

Maura nodded. "Master Morgan told me." Her pulse quickened at Ilyria's solemn expression.

"You should prepare yourself for the likelihood that something terrible occurred in Belestar after Leif and Rhiandra arrived." Her jeweled eyes glittered with pain, and Maura felt its echo in her heart. "Something so terrible that it has turned my siblings against me." The dragoness's breath darkened. "I am being hunted by them. And so are you."

"*Hunted?*" Maura gasped. "But... you always said the bonds between you and your siblings are unassailable—that this is what has kept your kind from dying out! What could Leif and Rhiandra possibly have done to change this? Master Morgan said they went to plead with the dragons to make bindings. Surely this can't have angered your sisters and brothers so!"

"I believed nothing could ever break these bonds until I saw a vision in the fire: my brothers, making their way south to

Mithralyn. If it had just been Aed and Gryffyn, I might have lingered there to learn their intentions, but once I saw Zal, there was no need. He had sworn that when he left Belestar it would be for one reason only: to settle old scores. And since none of my sisters were with the drakes, this can mean only one of three things: my brothers departed Belestar without the others' knowledge, or a rift beyond repair has occurred between these three and the rest."

"That is only two. Why else would they be coming for you, Ilyria?"

The bronze lifted her gaze to scour the clouds. "Perhaps because they are *all* in accord with Zal and his thirst for vengeance, and the drakes are merely the forerunners. The rest of my siblings may only be waiting for Syrene's clutch to hatch before they join in the search, which will not cease until they find us. After that, they will turn their fury on the rest of the Known World."

"But what of Rhiandra?"

"If the last scenario is the true one, Rhiandra no longer lives."

It was suddenly cold on this summer's day. Maura pressed close to her dragon. "It can't be. Oh, Ilyria, what has happened to my dear Leif?"

"I have sought them both in the fire, and can find no trace. I fear Leif too has departed this world."

Maura felt a wave of despair. Master Morgan had tried to prepare her, she knew, but the thought of Leif dead was too much to bear. He deserved far better—a long and fabled life among the elves, and to see his old gran once more.

Ilyria's tail curled around her. In silence, they watched the long white rill of surf roll away and return, echoing the sighing wind.

"I will not let them harm you." The dragoness's voice was both tender and gruff. "But there is no way back for us now.

We must travel far from Drinnglennin if we are to ensure your safety."

"*Our* safety, you mean."

"I have seen what I must do in the fire," the dragon replied darkly. "This time it is I who must leave you to follow *my* destiny."

Maura shook her head. "No. Oh, please, no, Ilyria! I cannot bear to be parted again from you so soon!"

"It is for the best, child, you must believe me."

"When must you leave me?"

"As soon as I've seen you safe from my wrathful brothers. I am taking you where they will not think to seek you."

"And where is this?"

"To Mandana." It sounded like a caress on the dragon's tongue.

"I've never heard of it."

"Not *it*. Her. Mandana was the bindling of Rust, my long-dead mate. If any of her family still lives, I know we can trust them to keep you safe."

Ilyria had told Maura about the drake Rust, who had been slain before the dragons could abandon the continent and flee to Belestar.

"His bindling? You mean there is someone else alive, besides Leif and me, who was once dragonfast?"

The dragon shook her great head. "Mandana died long ago. But after the Purge, she vowed that her children, and all the generations of her family to come, would pass down the promise to protect the dragonfast who had lost their dragons."

"Do Mandana's descendants possess some special magic? To make such a vow?"

"Magic of a most powerful sort."

"Then perhaps they can use it to protect you too!"

Ilyria remained silent, and Maura seized on the hope that Mandana's offspring might help them both. She rose to her